I0818259

Line of Communication

The Vincent Chen Compendium

Steve Rzasa

Lines of Communication by Steve Rzasa
www.steverzasa.com

Cover design: Fiona Jayde Media

International Standard Book Number: 9781733585194

Severed Signals © 2018, 9781986308359
Cryptic Commands © 2018, 9781719254199
Failed Frequencies © 2018, 9781724036421
Mixed Messages © 2019, 9781094670584

Books

Science Fiction

The Word Reclaimed: The Face of the Deep 1.0
The Word Unleashed: The Face of the Deep 2.0
Broken Sight: The Face of the Deep 2.5
The Word Endangered: The Face of the Deep 3.0
For Us Humans
Quantum Mortis: A Man Disrupted
Empire's Rift: A Takamo Universe Novel
Strife's Cost: A Takamo Universe Novel
Man Behind The Wheel
Multiverse
Severed Signals
Cryptic Commands
Failed Frequencies
Mixed Messages
The Echo Watch

Steampunk

Crosswind: The First Sark Brothers Tale
Sandstorm: The Second Sark Brothers Tale

Superhero

Airfoil: Origins

Fantasy

The Bloodheart
The Lightningfall
Just Dumb Enough (editor & contributor)

Urban Fantasy

Mercury On Guard
Mercury For Hire
Mercury At Risk

Timeline of Events
The Face of the Deep

2602
Baden Haczyk aboard *Natalia Zoja* discovers the last Bible in print

2604
Lt. Cdr. Brian Gaudette assumes command of *HMRC Weskeag*, Rescue Ops swift frigate

2605
Achille Duval and his family flee their colony aboard *Bienfaisance*

2612
Zarco Thread and surveyor crew of *Cazador* stumble upon missing Starkweather battle corvette

2613
Captain Vincent Chen commanding *RMS Marconi* investigates comms ferry malfunction in the Sylvanak Star System

2613
Captain Chen retrieves comms ferry 550 in the Tersane Star System

2614
Captain Chen returns home to Tiaozhan to face his family for the first time in a decade

2614
Captain Chen searches for a missing spy and a derelict starship

Book I

Severed Signals

The enemy of my enemy...

Vincent Chen keeps star systems in close communication with each other as he tends to the comms ferry satellites that connect the Realm of Five. When he responds to small colony's apparent malfunction, he instead stumbles onto an enslaved people.

The problem is, the enslaved used to be the oppressors.

They're all former agents of Kesek, the secret police that spent the last century suppressing religion by arresting, torturing, and killing believers—including Vincent's uncle. But it also includes the children and families of those agents.

Vincent is drawn deeper into the plot against them, until he's forced to choose the right side.

Whether he can forgive, however, is the most dangerous question...

The Realm of Five

circa 2613

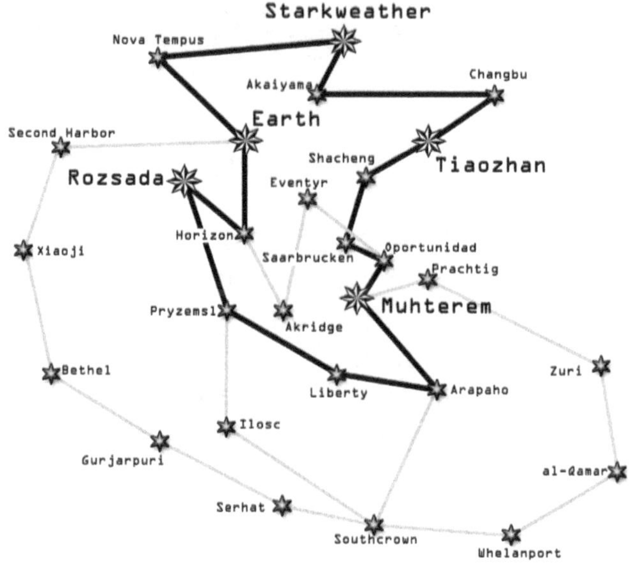

Chapter One

10 August 2613
Sylvanak Star System

No answer.

That's what I get when I prompt the main comms ferry for Sylvanak. Should send me a diagnostic summary of the past six months' operations, complete with glitches, component breakdowns, and tampering.

Twelve seconds go by. Six seconds for my signal sent by *RMS Marconi* to reach the ferry, and six for a response. Nothing,

Twenty-four seconds. Forty-eight. After a minute, I log the discrepancies. I hate those.

Even worse, the scanners can't find the comms ferry. Without it, the settlement in the star system has no way to send and receive communications across the light-years. Essentially, they're stuck talking to themselves, and limited to perusing only the data they have available on their local networks.

To be fair, it's the star system's fault. I may as well be using a stick to swish aside long grasses on the banks of the Xi Jiang River in search of a single frog. There's so much detritus clogging the nearby light-seconds I bet the navigation computer's chewing its figurative nails plotting a safe course.

I'm grateful. No matter how much MarkTel pays a guy like me, it isn't worth the risk of plastering my starship across a cometary debris field.

Captain Vincent Chen. That's what my Reach profile says. MarkTel classifies me as an Interstellar Communications Ferry Deployment & Maintenance Specialist. "Captain" sounds much fuller of bravado than "ICFDMS." As far as my family's concerned, that title might as well be "*Wàng'ēnfùyì* Ungrateful Child Who Never Visits Tiaozhan."

I use the ship's cluster of ion engines to pick my way through the sphere of shattered ice and rock. The central computer entry for Sylvanak tells me the first survey teams didn't pay much attention to the system when they made the nine-light-year hop through the sundoor. The star's a main sequence K, cooler than most that support human habitable worlds. Difference between me and them is money: they saw rocks chock full of rare metals. So, they passed word to prospectors and colonists looking for a star system easy to settle, if one had the wherewithal to extract basic supplies.

Unfortunately, like most interstellar equivalents of the old Gold Rush, it was a bust.

Colonists stayed, though, even as the prospectors lit out for more prosperous possibilities. Someone spotted an Earth-type planet hiding beyond the cloud.

It's an icy world, yet fit enough for hearty souls wanting to start new lives away from the busy space lanes of the Realm of Five. Even recluses need to stay in touch with someone, however, especially when said recluses have signed a royal charter for their settlement.

Studying Sylvanak's planet doesn't make the next hour more bearable. Nothing resembling the missing comms ferry appears. I twist about in my seat and expand the sensor radius out to their max range. Watching things at two light-minutes distance—almost 18 million kilometers away—means the results are delays, echoes of where things used to be a while ago, but since I've got no indication the ferry was bashed to pieces, it must have wandered off.

The sensors pick up residual ion tracks. Okay, that's good. Ferries have smaller ion engines. These tracks, though, are faint. Probably weeks old, far too dispersed to get a good read. I superimpose them over the ferry's pre-programmed course, a green arc floating on the inside of the bridge displays.

Nav rewards me with purple lines crisscrossing like webs, stretching beyond my peripheral vision. This isn't a freighter's command box. *Marconi* has a state-of-the art sphere that's essentially a giant screen surrounding an access port and my captain's chair. Sensors convert real-time data and extrapolated courses into those lines, splashing them over gorgeous photo-realistic imagery from the ship's optical scopes.

The picture's a tangled mess. *Zhēn shì luànqībāzāo.* There are dozens of possible trajectories the ferry could have followed if it indeed took a hike. I keep coming back to the ion traces. They're off, somehow. It occurs to me the ferry would have had to boost at a far greater rate than it's capable of.

Could be someone took it.

There's no shortage of valuable goods inside. It's a Raszewski sphere, the good old interstellar engine that makes leaping trillions of kilometers between star systems possible in the blink of an eye. Pirates have been known to go after them, even though they're tamper proof. If you try to reconfigure one to run a ship, you're out of luck. We're talking premium-grade self-destruct package.

That doesn't count the half-million worth of custom communications equipment aboard.

I need to send a signal to the locals. I spin up the Sylvanak colony at Alban Harbor. "This is *RMS Marconi*, MarkTel communications tender, to Alban Harbor Comms. I'm tracking the loss of Comms Ferry Nine Nine Zero. Can you confirm? Please send relevant sensor data."

I'm still 100 million kilometers from the planet, so it'll be nearly six minutes before they get the message. An immediate response is unlikely, so I figure I've got about 15 minutes before I hear back from the colonists.

Scans don't improve the umpteenth time I try them, so as soon as the ions push *Marconi* past the cometary cloud, I light the main engines. Anti-matter mains flare at the base of the ship's hologram, a model the length of my arm floating above my shoulder. She's awkward looking, what with four comms ferries docked along the forward spar, but the slender cooling vanes perched just forward of the main drives add a semblance of grace.

Marconi will keep up the acceleration pace of 25 gravities for an hour, then after a 10-hour break, she'll do it again. Don't want to put too much strain on the drive nozzles. Couple in the deceleration needed when I get near Alban harbor, I should get there in about a day.

Plenty of time to puzzle this out.

I reach for the Bible tucked into the seat cushion. Reassuring physical presence does wonders for staving off unease. The spiritual version carries more weight.

As soon as my fingers find the battered cover, my memories transport me to that dark basement eleven years ago. Uncle Ethan. Flashes from scrambler stun weapons. My mother wailing. Father cursing—and he never, ever cursed.

Sweat beads on my eyebrows. Our neighbors said we were lucky, that the secret police took only my uncle. They could have interned the entire family. Could have dumped us all on a forgotten moon, for having possession of a printed Bible.

We wouldn't be the first of Kesek's victims. Or the last.

The answer from Alban Harbor lifts me from my memories. It's equal parts irritating and reassuring. "*Marconi*, this is Alban Comms." The voice has a twang of an accent. "Glad to make your acquaintance. We were worried MarkTel would never get wind of the ferry's loss, and given our current lack of operational transports, we'd be up the proverbial creek. We'll have our comms techs send the last telemetry data we received from the comms ferry. It should get to you within the next half hour. Hope that'll provide some answers. Goodness knows we don't have any! Alban Comms out."

Okay. They know the comms ferry's gone, but they don't know to where. I unstrap from the command chair. No sense worrying further until I see the data.

Meantime, I'm hungry.

There's not a lot of space for human habitation aboard ship. My cabin is tucked behind the bridge. There's a greenhouse aft of that, stuffed full of greenery.

Confining as they are, it's nice to have constant exposure to living things. I'd never have survived being locked inside this rather large can for months at a time. Plus, I'll never go short of fresh eats before the next station port-of-call.

But meals are lonely affairs. The *Declaration*-Class comes equipped with a crew of 24 low-intelligence repair and maintenance bots, and one human being. It's the standard arrangement for dozens of the speedy, compact comms ferry tenders, and yet, MarkTel still installs a table with two chairs.

I don't get many hitchhikers, so the bureaucratic addition of a seat that always remains empty seems an oversight of the Extended Deep Space Travel Protocols. It reminds me, whenever I set down my tray, how I've retreated from civilization so I won't have to feel pain anymore.

A pair of lumpen bots, each one resembling a chrome beetle the size of my shoe, roll up to the table. One's adorned with blue lights, the other with red. They beep communications at me. My wrist comm translates: Upload complete. Data from Alban Harbor available.

Good timing. My salad's gone, as is half a Salami and Cheese Packet No. 6. "Thanks, Scarlet. Blue, go check on the brassjackets. See if they've completed fabrication of the new auxiliary cooling vane."

Blue trundles down the corridor toward the aft hatch. Scarlet waits patiently for orders. She and her companions would wait for days if I didn't have anything for them to do beyond their preprogrammed maintenance rounds.

"Lunch break, Scarlet." I tap the Standby command on my wrist comm. Scarlet flashes her lights in response, then disappears into an access vent.

So, the Alban Harbor report. It scrolls in tiny print along the face of the wrist comm. Doesn't matter what size the print, it's as baffling as my sensor results. Alban's long-range scanners shows the comms ferry doing what it's supposed to—staying in a spherical region of space just shy of the debris field, inside one of Sylvanak's touch tracts. The ferry is a simplified Raszewski sphere. Every 12 hours, the engine creates a compressed singularity at its core and leaps across the light-years to the neighboring system. Each of the three touch tracts around the sun leads to a different system.

Once arrived, the tiny comms department that holds reams of data and message dumps the lot into the Reach Information Network, and from there to individual and corporate accounts. Some communications relay to other ferries, and get bounced along from star system to star system until arriving, days later at their destination. A few hours later, Ferry 990 transits back to Sylvanak. Simple.

Three weeks, it all stopped.

Cut off. No record of attack, or explosions. There's no sign of the ferry moving off, either. One day, 990 is on station, readying to transit. The next, gone.

I chew a chunk of cheddar. "Not possible."

The navigation computer doesn't engage me in debate. Scarlet's wheels scratch deep inside the bulkheads as she follows the vent, running diagnoses as she goes.

Doesn't matter. I pull my delver out of my pants pocket, and let the wrist unit sync data. Without the ever-present handheld device, I'd be lost when it came to crucial information needed at a moment's notice. Stars, so would everyone else in the Realm of Five. There was a reason delvers were as common as shoes. They link to the Reach that's connected by the MarkTel comms ferries for interstellar information-sharing and, if you can't access that, you can still use it on local links with your shipboard computer. Holographic projections expand, spraying into the air over the table. Much better. I drag them out until they're a meter-wide swirl of light. Easier to read, this way, and lets me see what I suspected.

The data's corrupted.

By that, I mean there's errors in the construction of the sequence, plus a glitch in the time stamp. That's not terrible in itself. After getting bounced around a star system, through all manner of stellar radiation, some degradation is bound to occur.

It's when I get in behind the results—courtesy of my Specialist access codes unavailable to the average groundside comms jockey—that my stomach turns. Someone's fouled with the sensor records. Whoever did it removed a chunk of indeterminate length, then ramrodded the record back together to cover the missing time. It would appear okay to most individuals, but when you take it apart from backstage, you can see the sloppiness.

Why would Alban send me faulty data? Couple possibilities. One, they might think they could pull one over on a Specialist. Silly, but possible. Two, they didn't know the data was corrupted. Either one is a problem.

But it still begs the question of what happened to the ferry. Did someone else steal it? If so, why would Alban Harbor cover it up?

Maybe they stole it. Why swipe your own comms ferry?

Well, it wouldn't be the first time. I've found contraband narcotics, banned foodstuffs, even animals that were illegally genetically modified, all crammed inside the communications compartment and other spaces of a ferry. It's not unheard of. The regular transit schedules make ferries susceptible to smuggling.

Whatever the answer, it's clear I should talk to these people in person. It's within my authority. Can't arrest anyone—that'd be up to Crown Marshals. Speaking of which…

I compose a brief message, attach it to a copy of the data from Alban Harbor, and after bundling it with *Marconi*'s scans, compress it all into a message pod's memory banks. Two quick swipes on my wrist comm, and the tiny torpedo pops out the side of the ship. It'll scoot back to the sundoors, waiting there for either another ship or a backup comms ferry.

It gives me the chills. Standard protocol in a situation like this, yes, but it's done in case something happens to me, the ship, or both.

Not pleasant contemplation.

The planet Sylvanak is a gorgeous orb of blue, gray, and brown swathed in white clouds. Sensors mark a dusty yellow moon peeking over the far side from *Marconi*'s arcing approach. It could be a woven tapestry, like the rugs I have hanging in the ship's main corridor—handmade, one of a kind. Of course, everything I see is translated to my eyes by the scanning software. *Marconi* rushes back-first toward the planet, the main drives at full throttle to brake me into a wide orbit.

As soon as the velocity has subsided enough, I take over, flipping *Marconi* end over end yet again. She's lined up to leave for whenever this mess is solved. I tap my wrist comm, summoning Blue and Scarlet, plus four of their hamster cronies: Prep skipjack. They'll have the smaller orbit-to-surface craft readied for departure by the time I secure *Marconi*.

"Alban Harbor Comms, this is *RMS Marconi*, set for high orbit."

Their repeater detects my signal. I get automated acknowledgment before the first sentence is fully composed. "Captain Chen speaking. I'm requesting conference with your governor and whichever officials handle communications. I think we'll be best able to determine Comms Ferry 990's malfunction with an in-person talk. Please confirm."

The delay that follows has nothing to do with distance. I kept my request deliberately free of mentions of the corrupt sensor data. If there's someone mucking about, odds are good they'd also listen in on every transmission, especially if they've figured out how to make use of the comms ferry's high-end equipment.

I shake my head, glad for once I am alone. "Nobody needs to know how paranoid you get," I murmur aloud. "Bad enough you're talking to yourself."

"*Marconi*, this is Alban Comms." Twang was back. Must be the regular jockey. Shipboard clock told me it was midday in the colony's time zone. "Governor Nakano would be happy to meet with you following touchdown. I'm sending up the coordinates for a landing site. Please proceed to those at your earliest convenience. An escort will be there to greet you in two hours."

"Thanks, Alban Comms. I'll make the rendezvous."

"You're welcome. You guys must be bored up there."

"Just me coming down to the surface. No need for a banquet or anything wild."

Twang chuckles. "Roger that, *Marconi*. Alban Comms out."

The skipjack is a 10-meter shuttle tucked into *Marconi*'s hull. She's curved like a carp, as if she'd swim her way to the surface. Four wings tuck back as I drop through the atmosphere, winds buffeting us the whole way down. Even within the last 1,000 meters to the ground, winds remain steady.

The landing site is scorched earth nestled between spindly pines, each one shorter than me, clustered at the base of a crumbling cliff. Man-sized slabs of sandstone slump in a half-palisade.

Twang wasn't kidding. Three men await me as the skipjack's engines die off in a nasal whine. Two are tall, strapping guys in forest green coveralls stand to either side of a shorter, broad-shoulder man who must be the governor. He's got a smile as wide as *Marconi*'s drive nozzles.

"Captain Chen." He offers a hand. "Governor Ray Nakano. Pleased to have you as our guest."

The grip is as solid as the gaze he uses to inspect me. "Governor. Thanks. You have a place in mind we can review the data at our meeting?"

"Absolutely. The administration building." He sweeps a hand between the two men. "We'll ride back to the colony with my officers, if you don't mind."

Officers? They do have gray patches on their shoulders and chest. Local constabulary, I suppose. Armed, with small handguns and composite batons. Judging by the extended handle, they probably pack a mean stun.

We pile into a hovertruck with high clearance, a good thing because the road isn't finished. There's long gashes in it. Those gashes continue on either side, at odd intervals, as if something slashed not only across the dirt path but the forest itself.

My first view of the colony is a 3-meter-tall fence that appears as a silver grating hidden between the trees. We pass through a gap wide enough to accommodate several hovertrucks. Up ahead, the first buildings peek over low mounds planted with vegetable gardens. They're uniform gray polymer slabs, accentuated here and there with what I assume is local stone.

I glance back. The silver fence isn't nearly as weathered. Neither is the gate that two more green-clad men trundle shut.

"There's a lot of wildlife in this region we don't want to come in," Nakano says.

Handy for keeping people in, too.

Chapter Two

The administrative building is a dome set dead center of the colony, where eight streets radiate out at the points of the compass. Antennae and transmitter dishes stud the top. Sensor posts waver in the wind barreling across the top of the dome. We arrive from the southeast, waiting for a groundcar with six wheels to rumble past before Nakano's drivers pull us up a ramp that leads inside.

I don't see any other traffic besides the groundcar. Come to think of it, there aren't other vehicles parked nearby, either on the streets or in open berths. Perhaps they have a community lot where all vehicles are stored, a bunker reinforced against bad weather. Standard colonial design.

Nakano has us meet in the communications room itself. Nothing fancy. The structure is permacrete, like the rest of the dome, with metal grating as a floor. The comms array itself is a Mode Three colonial transmission setup. It isn't primitive, nor is it cosmopolitan. Simply functional.

Functional enough I recognize the main console, even if I don't know the young man seated there. He can't be older than 21—long, lanky, with Japanese script tattooed in fluctuating neon colors up both arms to his bare shoulders. He wears a thick blue vest and gray trousers, both of which are covered with pockets that could conceal every spare part he'd possibly need. His hair is shock white, with an orange fringe.

"Captain, this is my son Tatsuo, our communications director." Nakano sits at an oblong table of glass and metal.

"Comms jockey, Father." Tatsuo Nakano grins, a jovial, spindly version of his parent. There's that twang of an accent I'd first heard, one his father doesn't share. "Nice to meet you in person."

"Likewise. I appreciate the level of detail you included in the data you sent me about Comms Ferry 990's disappearance."

"Not a problem. We try to run a clean shop." He indicates the two women and two men scattered throughout the room, operating various scan and sensor computers.

We spend the next few seconds nodding at each other. Should I sit? Maybe I'm supposed to wait for an invitation. Social graces are worse to navigate than a planetary debris field, and I don't have my computer to guide me.

"Please, take a seat." Nakano gestures to his left.

Tatsuo takes the chair to his right. They both watch me, hands folded in perfect imitation.

I clear my throat. Okay. I shift my weight in the chair, fidgeting for the right spot. Definitely not the conforming contours of my bridge seat. "I'd prefer this information was kept amongst only us three."

"I understand. Sergeant?" Nakano flicks his fingers as if swatting an insect hovering over his shoulder. Both officers direct the communications staff out the communications room hatch, sealing it behind them.

"I guess this means bad news," Tatsuo says. "Since you kicked everyone out."

I set my delver in the center of the table. It syncs with the local computer, then projects the same data I viewed aboard *Marconi* except three times larger from holographic emitters embedded in the table. "Ferry 990. It's gone."

"We knew this," Nakano said. "I'd hoped you'd have new light to shed on the situation."

"Whatever happened to it, was deliberate."

Tatsuo frowned. "You mean sabotage?"

"I'm thinking theft." I bring up my analysis of the corrupt data, the forged time stamps, and approximate length of missing information bands. "There's a long gap in here. Longer than I first realized."

"How long?"

I hate delivering bad news. "Two days."

"Two *days*?" Tatsuo looks like he's swallowed anti-matter. "Blast. When we lost contact with the ferry weeks ago, I knew there must be a malfunction we couldn't register from groundside. But a gap in the data…"

"How bad is it?" Nakano asked.

"There's no sign of destruction, nor is there indication the ferry wandered off course." I don't mention the ion drive trail, because I have another theory. "It's possible someone stole it."

"Stole our comms ferry."

I nod.

"That's an awful lot of work to go through for something so common," Tatsuo says. "Why not grab one from a MarkTel deployment center?"

"Too secure. They don't let me resupply without an escort ship. A vessel can't wander around their restricted space." I widen the view of the scan data, but it only extends so far. "Did your groundside arrays detect any other ships in the region?"

"None that we are aware of," Nakano said. "We don't receive much traffic."

"I'd ask if you investigated in person, Governor, but from what Tatsuo said in one of your transmissions, Alban Harbor is short on space transports."

"We're not isolationists, and we're not trying to hide from the responsibilities of our charter. But you must understand, living this far off the main tract shift routes to the Five means we must fend for ourselves to a greater degree than the more populous, wealthier planets. When a starship breaks down, it can be weeks, even months before we can affect repairs."

"And with the ferry vanished, we couldn't get word out," Tatsuo murmurs. "We're lucky the parts we need—"

"That's all, son." Nakano raises an eyebrow, and gives Tatsuo a disdainful, sidelong glance.

Tatsuo cuts off his explanation. He gazes into the scan data hologram, jaw clenched. If I'd been verbally thrown off course like that, I'd sulk, too.

"Well, I need access to your raw data recordings," I say, hoping to draw attention away from their brief familial spat. "It's going to take a while to reconstruct what happened."

"And you'll want to exercise discretion, because you think someone among us is involved," Nakano says.

"What?" Tatsuo slaps his hands on the table. "Not possible. My staff wouldn't collude with some thief!"

"I'm not saying it was your comms people. Could have been anyone with a high enough skill level to falsify the right information, and gain access to the more sensitive records." I'm still puzzled by his comments about MarkTel. Any comms jockey worth his bandwidth knows—or should know—how tight-fisted the company is with their equipment. Grabbing a comms ferry from sundoor orbit is far simpler than attempting a raid on a resupply depot. He could be new to the job. After all, if he's Nakano's son, maybe the only reason he's director is because Daddy needed someone he could trust in the position.

Then again, Daddy doesn't seem all that pleased with the kid's work.

"You'll cooperate with Captain Chen in any way he needs," Nakano says. "That includes accompanying him on a search for the comms ferry if he has to take his ship back to the debris field. Do you understand?"

"Yes, sir," Tatsuo mutters.

"Captain, we will honor your request to keep this inquiry quiet. I don't want alarm spreading throughout our colony."

"I could see why you'd want it kept quiet." I shut down the data stream, leaving a copy available on their network as I reclaim my delver. "It's pretty peaceful out there. Didn't seem too busy."

"This time of day, most of our citizens are at work in the fields," Nakano explains. "We've taken years to perfect our crop of varmo root. Once we process this upcoming harvest, we'll be able to offer it for sale to the greater Realm, provided we can salvage this comms situation."

"Varmo root." I've heard it, somewhere among the myriad dispatches that flit to and from comms ferries. "Food additive? It's spicy, supposed to be magic on seafoods."

"We were negotiating a contract with wholesalers on Puerto Guijarro, for their restaurants. They're prepared to pay thirty thousand per ton."

"Per *ton*?" My brain goggles at the price. Most haulers would be lucky to get a hundred for the same amount of more common foodstuffs. "How much are you processing?"

"Enough to fill a six-brace, if we can get her running again," Tatsuo says.

Nakano silences him with nothing more than a stern look. Still, it's an interesting tidbit to file. These guys have a 150-meter cargo starship, a six-brace, sitting around somewhere in orbit. "Our royal charter will be fully settled within a few years," Nakano says. "Sylvanak will take its place as a prospering colonial freeholding aligned with Earth."

Smart move, sticking with the capital for protection and economic support. Nothing precludes Sylvanak from trading with the other Four major planets, but face it—Roszada wouldn't see much strategic value to this world, and it's too far away from Starkweather. Muhterem won't invest in a shipyard when the system lacks substantial mineral wealth. Now, Tiaozhan, they might string a trade route if it's valuable enough to hook onto the Path…

"Let me have my officers show you to temporary quarters." Nakano's offer jolts me from my internal memory review. "Tatsuo will link your comms network to ours, so you can access whatever you need with the greatest ease."

"Thanks." I stand up, figuring we're done here. "We can get started right now."

"Nonsense." Nakano smiles. "Allow us to demonstrate our hospitality."

Nakano summons the officers back in. The four of us leave, passing the returning communications staff. I'm not used to this kind of grand treatment, and after months alone with only my less than chatty bots for company, it feels nice to be—well, feted.

It hasn't escaped my notice, though, that they're leading me away from the one place on this chilly planet that I most need to visit.

The officers guide me to a short, single-story hut a few blocks from the administrative building. We pass a dozen people on the way—four more officers, plus scattered individuals and couples. They range in age from late 20s to mid-40s, by my guess. All are wearing variations on the green uniform, albeit casual versions. A few have jackets or vests thrown over top. Each person gives me an appraising look, followed by either a smile, a wave, or indifference. Nothing different from other colonies I've visited.

Yet, none of them seem to be either going to or coming from a day of manual labor, even though they're all physically fit. In fact, none of them bear sedentary bodies. Their clothes are clean. So are their hands. It could be the varmo root comes from fields tended solely by robots, but this colony doesn't seem large enough to afford a complete set of automated agro machinery. And as soon as they let me into the hut, I confirm another suspicion by digging into my delver—varmo root is not a huge crop. It's tended in small gardens.

Maybe that's what the gardens at the entrance to the settlement are used for. Could be more fields elsewhere. I shake my head. Focus. There's too much to consider that isn't relevant to my job. I've got to track down the missing comms ferry.

The hut is a simple pre-fab with a dining area, kitchen unit, and bunk tucked into a rear compartment. There's a tiny bathroom, too. I set my communications repair kit down on the dining table—which has two chairs, I notice. Not just MarkTel policy, then.

The hatch chimes. I pause in the middle of sorting a plasma torch from the wire cutters, threaders, and circuit patches. Visitors? This isn't the main corridor of the largest space station in the galaxy. No one knows I'm here.

Tatsuo's at the hatch. "Hey. Figured you might be ready to look over the system."

"Sure. I just got settled here, but…"

"Okay, not a problem. We can head back when you're ready."

I glance at him. He's smiling, which bothers me. I'm not around people enough to know how much smiling is due to genuine friendliness, or due to concealing uneasiness. If it's friendliness, then Tatsuo and I won't get along, because I'm solitary. If it's uneasiness, well, what's he worried about? I'm the repairman.

"Tell you what." I scoop up the kit, dumping the whole mess back into its case. Yes, I'm mildly annoyed I had my routine interrupted. "Let's head out."

I bypass him at the hatch. Those same two officers are positioned outside, ever present, seemingly uninterested in me. But Tatsuo stays locked to my trail like an asteroid dragged into a planet's gravitational pull. "Ah, the admin building's back this way."

"We'll get there. The only thing missing since my arrival is a tour of this lovely place."

"Okay, ah, I can get Father to arrange something …" He hazards a quick look at the officers, who haven't budged from by the hatch to the guest hut. "Are you sure you don't want to check out the comms array first?"

"I will. But you guys were in a big hurry to get me out of the building, so I figure if they're going to all the effort to cover their tracks, it won't make a difference if I take a ten-minute detour."

"Their…? Hold up a microsec! I told you, no one on my crew has done anything wrong!"

"I'd be more inclined to believe you if you weren't stalling me. At least, that's what it feels like. So, we take a stroll while I try to figure things out." I smile at him, and hope it's abundantly clear that this is not the friendly kind of smile.

I outpace him easily in this lighter than normal gravity, which after living aboard *Marconi* at near standard adds a nice long stride to my step. I follow the northeast road until the buildings end, which doesn't take long, considering the settlement is only a kilometer across.

There's the fields.

They're terraced up a gentle slope, seven levels, each one a broad arc larger than the one above. Twenty people are spread up and down, of varying ages, the youngest about 10 and the oldest, in her seventies. They aren't wearing green, but rather a hodgepodge of rumpled garb. Nothing matches. Every article is streaked with chalky dust or encrusted with pale orange mud. They're too busy picking at bunches of leafy dark red plants, the stems striped with yellow.

The officers on duty notice, though. There's six of them, the greatest single concentration I've seen since arriving. They're strolling along the edges and top of the terrace. Each one's got a scrambler, a security person's nonlethal weapon of choice. One hit and I'd be laid out flat, immobilized.

"Get him out of here, Tatsuo." The one who approaches us is tall, with an athletic build, and judging by the way his legs whir with each step, the recipient of prosthetics. He's a redhead with a thick beard and sharp hazel eyes. "Off limits."

"I know, Keegan, but he's new. He's the comms guy." Tatsuo points to the sky.

"Right. He doesn't need to be in the fields." Keegan glowers at me and stomps off.

Fields? There are six more terraces, spread out beyond this one, all the way to the shiny fence in the distance. More people work them—more people guarded by the same officers.

I'm not much for intimidating, but I summon my best glare that I reserve for Blue and Scarlet when they can't keep the other hamsters in line. "What kind of colony is this?"

Tatsuo chews his lip. "It's hard to explain…"

"You'd better start, because as soon as we get that ferry back up, I'm dropping the Crown Marshals down here faster than Lancers in an orbital combat jump, so help me God."

Tatsuo's worry evaporates. "Let's talk to Father. We can show you the comms data, and he'll make everything clear."

"That sounds like an excellent idea." Governor Nakano approaches with the two officers from my hut. If Nakano's perturbed by me uncovering his labor supply, the one guarded by armed security, he doesn't show it. "Tatsuo, I would have preferred to give our guest a personal tour."

"Sorry, Father. He insisted."

"I imagine so. Captain, please understand, this isn't what it seems."

"I was going to be generous and guess indentured servitude," I snap, "Except for the guns."

"It is, in a manner of speaking. You as a Christian man will see the benefit."

That kicks me out of my righteous indignation. "What does my faith have to do with anything?"

"Nothing. And everything. It's been a decade since anyone's had to worry about government approval to practice their preferred religion. You've commented on that yourself, haven't you? On the Reach, where anyone can read it."

He gestures at the workers. "These are the people who caused us all so much pain. They're Kesek."

Just like that, my anger changes course.

Chapter Three

Mother embraces me.

I'm screaming and crying, until my throat is raw. My brother whimpers next to me, like a pet who's been kicked one too many times.

The Kesek constables drag Uncle Ethan to his feet. "Ethan Chen, you are under arrest for violating the Charter of Religious Tolerance and willfully disseminating a text-in-violation, namely the Gospel of Luke."

"Leave him!" Father's in tears. "It is my document! He had nothing—"

"Sam, no!" Uncle Ethan twists around to stare in the faces of the Kesek constables. "It's mine, you understand? They had nothing to do with this. Leave them be. I bought the Gospel text. I was the one who introduced them to it. My brother and his family knew nothing of what I had planned."

The older of the two constables rolls his eyes. "I don't really care. Charter says we get ourselves a culprit, so we get a culprit. There's no room in the back of the groundcar for more than one, anyway."

They yank him to his feet, and jostle him through the door.

"Why are they taking him?" I ask Father. "You said it was the Good News."

"Good News to us." His hand rests trembling on my shoulder. "Folly to all others."

"But I didn't tell anyone we were reading today. How did they find us?"

"Our neighbors," Mother says. "It could have been anyone who saw Uncle Ethan coming and going."

"That's not right. They're our friends!"

"When people are afraid, Vincent, they follow the wrong path ..."

Governor Nakano's saying something about economic considerations but I'm only now tuning in. Swimming up out of the depths of that memory's harder than clawing through a compartment that's losing atmosphere.

"The colony was failing when we answered their call for assistance." Nakano's voice cuts through the haze. "The people had sought refuge from a galaxy that hated them. We knew they needed basic support—infrastructure, repairs, even rations. They agreed to a financial arrangement in which we would assume the responsibilities of their royal charter, in exchange for their labor."

"You keep saying 'we.' Who's that?"

"My people and I call ourselves Restoration. It's a movement founded with the goal of helping those who need it most."

"In exchange for imprisonment?" I point at the workers. "They're under armed guard."

"Non-lethal guard, yes." Nakano sighs. "An unfortunate necessity, once we ascertained their true identity. Each person from the initial colony was connected to the Royal Stability Police."

"To Kesek."

"Yes. Those who were not informants were constables, or higher-ranking officials. Somehow, they slipped through the cracks of the judicial system. With the Kesek's collapse in 2602, all former officers and informants were to be listed publicly. These people never were."

"Publicly listed, and pardoned."

"Of course, per the king's edict." Nakano stands in front of me. "But let's be honest, Captain: the pain their actions caused necessitates recompense, doesn't it? They not only caused great suffering to the likes of us, but they falsified their identities when we dealt with them in good faith."

"You could have contacted the Crown Marshals." My head aches. This is not something I want to confront. I never wanted to deal with it again, and having successfully tucked myself away into a solitary starship out repairing comms ferries in deep space, I thought it was over with. "Instead you've made them your slaves."

"No. This is a temporary measure, until the contract is fulfilled. They'd already agreed to the work, and we had agreed to the burdens of the royal charter." Nakano narrows his gaze. "The guards are an emergency provision, because Kesek has never shown itself to be trustworthy. Isn't that right, Captain?"

This is what I get for sharing my experiences on the Reach. "That information was private, to be shared in victim support groups only."

"I know." Nakano's smile is winsome. "I'm part of those groups, as well. Your story is one of hundreds, perhaps thousands, that I've read over the past decade, and when you arrived in orbit, memories welled up. For you, it was a beloved uncle. For me, it was my dear wife—Tatsuo's mother."

Tatsuo remains still as a sensor post, neither watching us nor the workers. He taps instead on his delver, scrolling through information I can't read, but it's related to navigation. The readouts are miniaturized versions of *Marconi*'s main displays. Tatsuo glances up. Maybe he felt me staring. Whatever caught his attention, he hurriedly stashes the delver and shoves his hands in his pockets.

"They took Nara from us, on a Sunday morning," Nakano continues. "We weren't even reading Scripture. It was breakfast. To this day I cannot abide the smell of *nori*, because it conjures the images again. She had a Pauline letter on her delver. I don't know who gave it to her. She hadn't let me read it. But Kesek found out. They always discover the truth, which is ironic, given their passion for stamping out what we call Truth with a capital T."

"Mother never came back." Tatsuo's tone is hollow. "Kesek contacted us and said she was in the hospital. Severe brain hemorrhage. We had to pay the entire cost, right up until she died."

Heat rises to my face. It isn't embarrassment. I clench my fists, as a fantasy of grabbing a scrambler from one of the guards runs its course. I'd knock down every one of the Kesek *hún dàn* on those terraces. Even the children. "I'm sorry."

"I appreciate your condolences, but you're in the same boat as us. We have all lost so much, but Restoration will make it right again." He indicates the comms antennae jutting from the administrative building in the distance. "Assuming you leave us to manage the situation of our own accord."

Their arrangement sounds strange, even downright extralegal, but until I see documents proving otherwise, I should take the man at his word. "You have proof."

"I can make the contract and the transfer of the royal charter available, but keep in mind, we've been without reliable communications with the nearest Charter Office for more than a month. They may not have processed the forms. They may not be aware of our—situation."

The thought of the men, women, and children working under guard still makes me uneasy, as if I'm diving into a planet's gravity well with malfunctioning sensors. But whatever worries I have get stomped on whenever I remind myself those people are Kesek. Sure, the king pardoned them. I understand. If he hadn't, he'd have been faced with mass incarceration, the wholesale ripping apart of a society trying to recover from Kesek's attempt to replace the king with their director. He'd made every single secret police file available to the public, and put names on a list. Most names. Some slipped through the cracks.

Some of the most militant kinds of Christians hunted them down and killed them—at least the Restoration wasn't doing that. These snakes were getting off easy.

I clear my throat, afraid I'll sound like a kid again. "Tatsuo was taking me back to the comms center. I've got a ferry to find, and you've got bigger concerns than not getting your messages."

The comms chamber is quiet, save for the murmurs of conversation among the staff. Can't be too much going on, what with their primary mode of communications missing. I catch snippets of signals between the comms staff and another source, perhaps with the ship they're trying to repair.

Tatsuo leads me to the primary access panels for the Mode Three module. It's a huge gray capsule, like a coffin for five people, tucked behind all the monitors and computers. The inside is a mishmash of circuits, lights, and bundled cables, strung together as impenetrable as the vine-webs of Fort Dean's jungles.

"Wow. That's … interesting." I lie on my back and scoot inside, brushing aside bundles as I go. "Hand me my kit, will you?"

Tatsuo passes the box. "We've had to get creative when things have broken. Some of the connectors are nonstandard."

I snort. "Nonstandard? If I had staff who jury-rigged communications networks like this, I'd fire them. Or reprogram them, in the case of my crew."

"Hey, they're not that bad," Tatsuo murmurs.

The handiwork dangling in front of my nose suggests otherwise. I straighten out bundles, replace worn-out connections, and re-route data from improper memory bank sites. It's a miracle they didn't have a cascading systems failure and lose every scrap of everything they've scanned or sent via comms signal. I yank out extraneous wiring. Why did they even need…?

One of the wires doesn't come loose. It isn't connected to the correct array. The wire leads clear out the backside of the module, where someone has cut a hole in the casing and patched it back up, only now with a hole poked through.

"Plasma torch." I waggle my fingers at Tatsuo.

He passes me the tool, and a transparent band. The band adheres over my eyes, so I can fire up the torch's dazzling purple-white flare without searing my retinas. A couple of quick cuts re-opens the hastily concealed compartment. There's a thin white box tucked to the backside, its edges twinkling with blue lights. The wire plugs into the center.

"Everything okay in there?"

"Yeah, sure is." I contort inside the module, arm twisting to the end of its reach so I can retrieve my delver. It balks when I try to sync with the white box. Okay. Hard wire connection it is.

That gets me in, and to my surprise, whatever's on the box isn't encrypted. The files are unlabeled, yes, but this thing being as hidden as it is, I'd expect a little more effort put into security. Whoever's messing around with the comms and the missing ferry seems amateurish.

The delver lights up when the search routine finishes. I get a close-up view of the same data packet Alban Comms sent to me other day, only this one doesn't have a foul-up time stamp. The comms ferry sits at the sundoor, waiting to make its transit, then abruptly fires up its ion thrusters. It drives off into the debris field, and as I speed through the recordings, it gets lost amidst the clutter.

Even more interesting is when the six-brace appears on the tracking information.

The cargo hauler fits the normal profile, though unlike what Tatsuo claimed earlier, it isn't in need of repair. It's completely missing its Raszewski sphere. Never seen that before. The only possible reason for a starship cruising about with a gap between the forward and aft hulls where a giant interstellar drive should be installed is if the sphere's singularity suffered a terminal collapse. Such a collapse would leave the ship intact, but render the mechanism that let the ship jump between star systems useless.

This isn't something a crate of parts is going to fix.

The worst of it, though, is the communications log. Clearly shows transmissions between Alban Comms and the ship. Those were definitely absent from the data Alban Harbor sent to me.

So, either someone cut it all without informing Nakano and Tatsuo, or they've been lying to me. Why lie about the missing ferry, though? The six-brace was running a search pattern, no question. Wouldn't they want me to know that? What was being hidden by messing with the data recording?

Answer: the ship. They didn't want me to know they had it. And I wouldn't have, if Tatsuo hadn't slipped.

"Captain? You stuck in there?" Tatsuo's efforts at light-hearted banter are painful.

"Nope. Finishing up." I slice the white box off the backside of the panel, and tuck it into a pocket. Then I secure the hidden access point, complete with its wayward wire, into the proper place on the module's wall. Someone planetside or elsewhere in the star system might be monitoring it. Tatsuo could know right now. All I know is, I've got to get this information to the Crown Marshals. This is going way outside my area of expertise.

I shimmy out of the module, and wipe off my hands. "Hey, I've got to get back to my skipjack for some additional equipment. Can you get me a ride there?"

Tatsuo glances around the comms room. No one's jumped up from their seats, though there are a few hushed conversations. "Okay. I'll get us a groundcar."

The ride out is far bumpier than my arrival, because, well, groundcar and not hovercraft. Tatsuo keeps his gaze fixed on the road, even when we ride over the gashes in the road. I check out the devastation to the forest, which stretches for a good kilometer or so in either direction. "That looks like quite the mess."

"Storm damage," he says.

Not likely.

There's no guards at the landing site, which is good news for me. Tatsuo waits for me inside the skipjack's hatch while I feign rummaging in a compartment just aft of the cockpit. "You need any help?"

"Nope. I'm good." I walk up to him. "But only after you get out."

"What? Why?"

I shove him. Tatsuo stumbles out the hatch, falling flat on his backside.

"Hey! You can't take off!"

"Watch me." The hatch is sealed, and the engines priming. I strap in. As soon as the happy green lights ripple across the control panels, I punch the thrusters.

The skipjack leaps into the air, making good use of the emergency liftoff boosters. They're meant for dangerous situations, such as a natural disaster, but I've coaxed the system into letting me use them at my discretion. I am the captain, after all.

No aircraft come after me, which is a bonus. Those communications I listened to indicated there's at least a few flitting around for surveillance purposes. Drones, possibly. Sensors pick up one a way off, but it isn't reaction.

I ping *Marconi* for an update. Blue and Scarlet don't respond. I put the whole robotic crew through contact protocols, but get nothing. The shipboard system just holds my messages in its queue, recycling them.

Great. They've fouled up my shipboard comms. Okay, relax. I can fix it on the way out of the system.

Proximity indicator blinks. There's an inbound ship.

The six-brace is angling for an intercept course, from behind Sylvanak's moon. It's accelerating way too fast for me to outrun it in the dinky skipjack. Even with a head start, this thing's engines are meant only for atmospheric flight and boosting into orbit to a waiting starship.

But *Marconi*, she's another matter entirely. She can outrun a six-brace. Not military fast, but she's got a narrow edge in acceleration over cargo vessels.

Meanwhile I'm pounding the comms booster every couple seconds, as I try frantically to wake the nav, to get through to the bots, anything. "Come on, guys, answer," I mutter.

Thankfully the skipjack's computer's still able to talk to the landing bay doors, so getting docked with *Marconi* is a breeze. From there it's a flat out run, and a climb up the ladder to the main deck. My boots slip on the rungs. I slam my shin against the metal bars.

"Blue! Scarlet! Where are you guys?" My shouts echo but go unanswered. I slip into the command chair, and Nav responds by bringing up that gorgeous view of space for thousands of kilometers around.

Special treat? A nice, 3-d rendering of the six-brace lighting up its main drives.

Blast. I command Nav to take the best arc through Sylvanak's gravitational field, calculating how to get the maximum boost from a slingshot maneuver. Once it's set, I override the automatic safety constraints and push *Marconi* to her unlisted 28 gravities top acceleration.

For many, many tense minutes, we race, the six-brace closing the gap as *Marconi* whips around the blue-white sphere of the planet between us. The six-brace wasn't set on a course to make the same maneuver as *Marconi*, and when they adjust to match my track, it takes more fuel and a harder burn to correct. It's enough of a mistake the gap holds steady.

"Come on, come on." I can't get out and push. The physics of the situation are what they are. All I can do is hold tight and pray for safety, for escape.

But why? These guys haven't done anything to me. So what if they catch up? I'm not breaking any laws.

So what's with my heart pounding?

Then, stuck there in the silence of the bridge with only the *shush* of the ventilation systems and the hum of the instruments, the numbers change in my favor.

Marconi's drive engines rumble the deck plates, and the whole bridge shell vibrates. Steady. Keep it up.

We're clear of the planet. The extra tug from Sylvanak's gravity tosses us away from our pursuers.

The gap opens.

"Yes!" I slap my hip pocket, where the Bible rides co-pilot.

Sensors flare red with warning. Laser strike? The computer sketches the slashing beam in bloody crimson on the displays. It joins *Marconi* and the six-brace by a thread, again and again. In real life, my ship shakes under each impact.

Damage reports spill in. The main fuel tank's burst. Water sprays in a massive fan, shimmering white crystals in jaw-dropping array. A rainbow even forms across the surface, where it catches light from the sun.

No fuel, no acceleration for the mains. I slap the control surface, shutting them down. Now we're hurtling along at several hundred kilometers per second. So is the six-brace, but it's still accelerating.

It's going to catch us.

I hear tiny tracks on the deck. Blue and Scarlet are behind me. Waiting. "About time you guys showed up. Get on damage control."

The rest of the hamsters appear, crawling on the wall. And speaking of crawl, that's what my skin starts to do. "Guys?"

All the brassjackets, my tiny aerial drones, swoop into the corridor. The whole crew is gathered in one place, like they're awaiting software updates. Except I don't have any scheduled. And this is a really bad time for—

Electrical pulses knock me to the floor. Dozens of them. Over and over. My senses flicker on and off. I can't see. My muscles won't respond. I reach for my wrist comm—emergency shutoff. Should reset all the bots.

Can't reach it.

My last sight before I black out is my mutinous robotic crew, gathered around me.

Chapter Four

I'm in the hut.

Have to be. The ceiling is not the one I wake up to day after day in my cabin aboard *Marconi*. It's a rough plastic, pitted and worn. The bunk beneath is far more comfortable. The entire room glows golden orange. A breeze flutters the curtains.

Curtains?

I sit up, way too fast. My head spins faster than *Marconi* on her axis in a high-gee turn. Nausea puts me on the floor, readying to heave. Steady. Focus on a single point.

It's more than imbalance that causes the sickness. It's disbelief.

My crew turned on me.

Not crew. The bots. They all came after me. Overloaded my nervous system. They're not equipped with scramblers, but have enough implements between them that they must have used them to similar effect. Risky. The attack could have stopped my heart, or my respiration.

Governor Nakano's sitting in a chair.

I advance on wobbly legs, ready to—do what? Punch him? Hold him hostage? I'm not armed. My pockets are disturbingly light. My repair kit's missing. Even the wrist comm is gone. All that stuff sits in a heap on the table.

Plus, he's got his two goons on either side of the room.

"I'm sorry things had to turn out this way." Nakano doesn't seem worried by the fact he's kidnapped a MarkTel starship captain. "But we couldn't have you spreading word of our operations. And before you start in about your beacon, Captain, we've already found and destroyed it."

"Doesn't make sense." Intense pounding on the sides of my head urges me to abandon my stupid charge. Instead I sink into the other chair, taking deep breaths, trying hard not to throw up. "If you'd left the comms ferry alone no one would have come looking. But you didn't get rid of it, did you? The sensor records. You were trying to figure out what happened to it, before I showed up."

"One would think it would be easier to find a manmade object in a star system over the weeks." Nakano sighs. "The debris cloud, though, is far better at concealing things than my people are. We'd had no luck at all. Then you arrived, and we barely had 24 hours in which to arrange things to your satisfaction."

"My satisfaction? You're running a slave camp!"

"No. If I am running anything, it is a rehabilitation center."

"There's no rehabilitation. You're using these people as your unpaid work force."

Nakano gestures to one of the guards. He hands the governor a delver. Nakano taps in commands, then lets me read. "I won't conceal any aspects of the arrangement from you. All the signatures are in order. We own this colony, not them."

He's right. The transfer of responsibility looks legitimate. I have no way of really knowing, not without researching it on the Reach or getting in touch with the nearest Charter Office. "But you have them under armed guard—"

"Really, Captain? We've been over this. They're Kesek. Don't pretend to suddenly care for them because the king has abdicated his duties. Pardon or no pardon, they carry their guilt, and so do their families. So do all who informed on believers during the decades of Kesek's oppression." Nakano opens my Bible. He treats the pages with reverence, turning them as gently as a mother rocking her child to sleep. "Do you know, this is only the third copy of the Word I've seen? The first was at Bethel."

My heart didn't stop when the bots shocked me, but it could have now. "You were at Bethel?"

"When the Word was reclaimed, yes. I saw Baden Haczyk. I heard him speak the Truth, a truth that had been suppressed for so long my fellow settlers and I didn't know we were missing the light it shed. As soon as the king dismantled Kesek and the ironically named Charter of Tolerance, the ban on printed materials—especially religious texts—came to a crashing halt. Then printing presses started up again. I bought one for myself. It didn't matter that he was foolish enough to allow all the other religions to regain their misguided books, too. The Word was in my hands, in possession of my family, for the first time in generations. Can you not see how wonderful that is?"

"I do. I wouldn't have survived without it."

"Then you understand why we could not tell you about this—arrangement. Let it run its course until we can transfer the charter back to the Kesek settlers, and when the time is right, we will announce it to the proper authorities."

"Time is right?" Fear makes my heart skip. "When I get back to my ship…"

"Your ship is being repaired, but you will not be at its helm. We have accepted your gracious donation to the Restoration cause."

"This is insane. You can't steal Crown property, and I can't donate what isn't mine!"

"Those details can be disputed later, however, since you won't be leaving our facility, you will not have the chance to bring it to anyone's attention." Nakano shakes his head. "It grieves me to do so, Captain, because you are a brother, but as the Scripture says, we must put on the full armor of Christ. This place is our armor. It is our bulwark against the forces of darkness that remain at play in the galaxy, even with the new freedoms we have been afforded. That is why Restoration is too vital to be left unprotected. And unfortunately, I do not think you can be trusted now."

He gathers up my personal effects, except the Bible, and starts for the door. I reach for his arm, fingers swiping cloth as I miss. One of the guards catches my wrist, slams it into the table. Pain lances through my forearm.

"Careful!" Nakano's stance is suddenly intimidating. The guard freezes, then releases my hand. "He's one of us. Or rather, he will be, once he realizes we are on the right side of history. Captain, my apologies. The foreman will be with you soon for your assignment and orientation. The work day is almost concluded; your first shift begins tomorrow morning."

"Wait!" I follow them out, cradling my arm. They don't lock the door; they don't even force me back inside. "My bots..."

"Reprogrammed. It was a simple software adjustment, Tatsuo tells me." Nakano smirks. "The boy is not as dense as he appears. As soon as you'd departed from *Marconi* when you first arrived, he relayed a set of instructions encoded within a local information update. Your ship's central computer helpfully applied that programming to your robotic crew. For all they knew, they were bringing to heel a dangerous intruder. You see, even if we let you outside the fence—which we certainly will *not*—you would have no means of escape."

I slump against the door frame. My ship. My crew. Both turned against me. That makes me alone. Really alone.

"You are free to visit throughout the colony. The fences will not allow you exit, and certain structures are off limits." Nakano smiles. "I pray you sleep well tonight."

He leaves with his bodyguards in tow. I'm left outside my new home in a prison colony, where I'm about to be sentenced to hard labor.

I stagger back inside, not bothering to seal the hatch. Waves of agony sweep through my body. MarkTel required all its comms jockeys get hit by a scrambler, so they knew how to deal with the aftereffects in the event of a pirate raid, but that was a device tuned to the voluntary nervous system. I'd been walloped with a cobbled-together version, that could have easily killed me. I'm not a drinker, but man, this must be what the galaxy's worst hangover felt like.

This whole plan of the Restoration is lunacy. If they're keeping me here, why bother showing me the stupid contract? Maybe it's to lull me to their side. I won't ever join them. Will I?

Can't deny I liked seeing all those Kesek people powerless. It galls me to realize I didn't mind the kids were put to work, too. It's penance. They're working off their parents' sins, I suppose, but I'd heard stories of Kesek youth informing on their classmates, on their neighbors. They couldn't all be innocent.

I keep seeing Uncle Ethan's face. That holds sympathy at bay.

But the idea of anyone held in bondage—whatever form it took—riled me all over again. Priority number one was getting out of here. In one piece. Let the Crown Marshals deal with this mess, arrest the whole lot, Kesek and Restoration. I didn't care.

Yet, I'd just argued with Nakano about his purposes. It was a half-hearted effort.

As I said, I like seeing them punished.

There's irony in my agonizing over my anger when the answers for it are sitting printed on pages right in front of me. But I've read all the admonitions. I know what I'm not supposed to do. Yet here I am, doing it anyway.

I bet the Apostle Paul could commiserate.

A shadow falls across the doorway. Someone knocks.

"Come in." I'm flopped in one of the chairs, barely able to hold my head up.

"You're Vincent Chen, I understand." The guy fills the hatchway. He's tall, broad-shouldered. Brown eyes sweep the room in a fashion that lets me know he's got training. He's looking for threats, I suspect. The guy has on gray trousers, black boots, and a cobalt blue shirt with the sleeves rolled up. It's smeared with mud. The blue stands in sharp contrast to dark brown skin. He's got a fringe of black hair that's gone gray at the temples and over his ears.

"Former captain Chen," I mutter.

"Nice to meet you. George Cotes." He extends a hand.

I glare at it, as if my eyes could turn into *Marconi*'s main drives and annihilate the digits with anti-matter. "That's great. What was your job? Officer? Or basic model informant?"

Cotes raises an eyebrow. "That's irrelevant. I'm the foreman of this work project, and you're my new laborer. Get up."

"Excuse me if I finish my afternoon break first." I wasn't about to leap through hoops, not when I had an escape to plan.

Cotes is motionless, then he sweeps with his foot so quickly I think I'm seeing double. The chair vanishes from beneath me. My backside slams on the concrete floor. The chair's tipped over, a couple meters away.

"Get up, and get moving," Cotes says. "I don't like doing things this way, but my previous supervisor had a tendency to—encourage others using methods I fully cataloged. Let's not make me use them."

I groan, and pick myself up. My legs are less wobbly. Bonus for me. "Okay. Time for the close-up tour."

Cotes shoves me hard, between the shoulder blades. "And for your information, I used to be known as Detective Inspector George Cotes, *Koninklijke Stabiliteitskracht*. That was my prior life. Now, you and me, we're the same. Shut up and move."

The words still give me chills. *Koninklijke Stabiliteitskracht*, translated as Royal Stability Force. No one called it that, except for its own staff. Everyone else whispered the name derived from the initials KSK.

Kesek.

Here I was, being prodded to the varmo root terraces by not just one of those officers, but a detective inspector, a man with the authority to conduct investigations throughout entire regions of the Realm of Five. Usually, they were assigned to a detective chief inspector as deputies.

The name Cotes rings a bell. It was whispered on Tiaozhan, though not as quietly as the other name with which it was always associated.

Ryke.

"I know who you are." The sun's low on the horizon, touching the tops of the trees. Everything's burnished by the aura. "I know what you've done."

"Son, there isn't a thing you know about me that matters, even if it were true back then. Get your tools." Cotes points to a grav-sled bobbing in the wind at the edge of the first terrace. "Gloves, gripper, and bucket."

The gripper is an instrument printed from resin that looks like a monster's claws hinged against a jagged, rectangular spade. The handle's shoddy, without good contour. Cotes gets a gripper of his own and demonstrates how to pull the roots free. The accompanying slurp of mud signals his success. "Get all the roots out. That's where the varmo is potent. You leave any behind, when the quitting mark hits, and you'll come back to take out the rest."

"The guards care that much?"

"No, I do, and you're under my watch. So, dig." Cotes moves to the upper terraces, where he converses with a woman roughly his age. She eyes me with resignation. A teenage girl digs beside them, singing a tune to herself.

I brush aside the nearest cluster of leaves, jam the gripper deep into the sopping soil, and pull. Half the thing comes out, speckled roots dangling. There's more tucked beneath, that disappear as the mud slithers back together.

"This would be a lot easier with bots," I mutter, and return to the attack.

"Except bots can't be punished for their wrongs." Cotes kneels beside me. He pulls varmo root free of the ground with an expert twist, leaving a gaping hole. There's not a chunk missing from his harvest. "People are better for that."

"The cost alone…"

"Isn't much different. You have to provide medical care, and food, and a little entertainment if you don't want a riot."

"Forget it. I wasn't looking for a debate." I'm scraping the bits of root out of a new hole. Pretty sure I only got the dregs, but I don't care. As I dig, I'm eyeballing each guard, keeping track of their movements, which ones are chatty, which ones are paying close attention to their work. It's a lot to organize. Makes me yearn for my delver, or the wrist comm. Some extra brainpower would be nice.

"If you think they'll go easy on you because you're not one of us, think again."

"I'm not Kesek," I snap. "I've got a lot in common with these Restoration guys."

"Have you? Willing to test that against everyone who's on their side? How many people have you spotted wearing green? I'm not just talking about the guards, mind you."

He has a point. Even from the terraces, I can see other colonists passing between streets. They're all wearing variations of the green jumpsuits. So far only Governor Nakano and Tatsuo are exempt—

besides the Kesek workers and their families.

"One of them," Cotes murmurs. "You've got a Bible on you."

"So?"

"It means you bear watching, like they do." Cotes shrugs. "Old training habits."

"I'll bet. Must have been a rough decade, without people to hound. Drove you crazy letting people read whatever they want, didn't it?" I fling the last bits of root into the bucket. Cotes, blast him, has six already. They're anemic, yes, but it's still six to my one.

"Let's get one thing straight, Mr. Chen…"

"Captain."

"Of your bucket, and nothing else." Cotes wipes mud from the gripper onto his bucket's rim. "You're not going to be rescued. Do you understand why? No one cares that we're here. The Charter Office was more than happy to contract us to settle the planet, then leave us unattended until we could pay them back. When those Restorationists showed up, we ended up paying, all right, just not to the people whom we actually owed."

"Whatever you two have going, I'm not interested. I've got a missing comms ferry I need to find for MarkTel. To do that, I have to get back to my ship, get fixed, and get out of here so I can come back with help. If the Restoration crazies have the ferry—"

"They don't. They won't find it either."

I scowl. "How do you know that?"

"On the latter point, because even though they overpowered us, they're not criminal masterminds. On the former, it's simple. I'm the one who stole your ferry."

Chapter Five

Dinner with the secret police. It's low on my priority list, but I'm starving. Breakfast was a while ago, aboard *Marconi*. Between running around this colony, and the time difference between my ship and the surface, it feels like I've fasted.

I'd rather be on my own at the table that mocks my loneliness.

Shift ends sharply, with the guards shouting commands to the scattered workers. We're lined up by a grav-sled, depositing our buckets. I get snickers from the assembled guards, plus a few settlers. There's eight roots in mine. Even the pre-teens have more than twice that.

"Better pull your weight tomorrow." It's Keegan, who by now I've figured is the overseer. He jabs a scrambler into the small of my spine. "We've got a quota to meet."

"Hey, in case you haven't noticed, I'm not one of these guys," I say.

He slaps me across the jaw. "Talk to me like a little brat, you get the back of my hand. You have a grievance? Come at me with your fists, like a man. Otherwise you'll just get spanked."

The guards guffaw as our line trudges away. The workers aren't herded to a communal building, like I'd assumed they would be. No prison cells. Instead, we get taken to a section of the colony I haven't seen yet, pressed up against the fence in a ragged triangle. Every building here is tinier than those nearer the entrance, and arranged in a different direction than the rest of the colony. They make up about a third of the total. Chunks of plastic and concrete are missing. Roofs slump.

There's scorched forest and ruined land for hundreds of meters outside the fence.

"You guys try digging there first and give up?" I ask Cotes.

"No. We tried planting a colony. The Restorationists took care of the rest."

He leads me inside a hut smaller than mine, though it does have a separate bedroom off to the left. The woman and teen girl are already there. The girl stretches out on a lounger, feet propped on one end and a stained pillow bunched up on the other. She looks up from a battered delver. "Who's that, Dad?"

"Vincent Chen, MarkTel communications." Cotes pecks the cheek of the woman. "Hey."

"Hey, you." She's scrubbing at a mud-spattered shirt over a sink in the compact kitchen. "This stuff never comes out."

"Ready for dinner?" Cotes pulls thick packets from a tall crate leaned against the far wall. "I'm cooking."

"My hero." She sets the shirt aside, and faces me. Blue eyes narrow. She wipes her hands on her coveralls, and for the first time, I notice the mending done to not only her clothing, but Cotes' and his daughter's. "This is the captain, I take it?"

"Yes, ma'am. Chen, this is my wife, Azalea."

I nod, but I'm in no mood to shake hands. Even with a lady. After all, she married this guy, the one who traipsed around the galaxy locking up Christians. "Good evening."

"They caught you, too." She shakes her head. "Well, there goes that hope."

"I wasn't here for any rescue mission, ma'am. I've got an assignment."

"Yes, but I'd say the job description's changed."

No point arguing. I wait against the wall, arms folded. Cotes opens the packets and distributes them on the table. "Supper's served."

"My favorite! Protein bars and nutrient bags." The girl rolls her eyes.

She snatches two and curls back up on the lounger.

"Larissa, join us at the table."

I could have heard her sigh from *Marconi* if I'd cracked open an airlock, but she obeys. She tears a bite off a brown protein bar the size of a delver, glaring at me while she chews. "This guy's one of the people you used to chase all the time, Dad? He doesn't look dangerous."

"You know things were different then." Cotes gestures me to the table. "Sit."

"Yes sir, Mister Foreman." I'm hungry enough even something as flavorless as the nutrient bag is appealing. I drain half of it in one gulp. Gah. Like licking a deck plate, though honestly, I don't have an actual point of comparison.

"Chen, this colony was never meant to be this way. I know you hate Kesek. It's easy enough to sense without you saying a word. When I was pardoned, I took my family from Earth and set out for somewhere we could settle in peace."

Azalea nods. "We met many good people along the way."

"Good people?" I frown. "Yeah, ex-informants make great neighbors."

"You think they had it easy? These families turned people in to Kesek custody because they knew they could be next, if they said the wrong thing or read the wrong book. They did what they did out of fear," Cotes says.

"Fear you propagated."

"You're right. We did. *I* did. But that was a different man. I saw the results of my service to the Realm. I was hurting people when I thought I was helping them. That much was evident long before the coup and the Kesek collapse. What started out as a way to keep terrorists from ripping the Realm apart centuries ago became an insidious creature subsisting on it like a gigantic parasite."

"So, you all ran away from what you'd done and wound up here."

Larissa snorts. "Hey, I didn't do anything. I was a kid. Then I got to spend secondary education moving from habitat to habitat. Growing up with other teens spraying 'K' next to obscene threats on your console gets old, okay?"

I could identify with that, sort of. Someone carved a cross onto the flanks of our family groundcar when I was seven.

"Sylvanak was perfect," Cotes says. "No one around for light-years, abandoned by miners, and the planet itself was untouched. We set up a quiet settlement, found the varmo root growing nearby, and came up with an agreement among ourselves to sell the crop to help pay off the royal charter."

"That was when the trouble started," Azalea interrupts. "My word, the Restorationists… they came within a few months of us setting up the charter."

"It would have showed up in the registry," I say. "They saw it and came around to … what, make a deal? Did they get wind of the varmo root?"

"No, that was icing on the proverbial cake." Cotes' expression is sour, and my guess is it has nothing to do with our meal of rations. "They found out our connection to Kesek. Ironically someone in the Charter Office informed on us, even though we'd done our best to stay low key."

"Low key? All they'd have to do is search the registry of people pardoned for either Kesek service or pay. It's easy."

"Well, however they did it, they showed up and destroyed our ship." Cotes tosses aside a food wrapper. "Together we'd saved everything we could manage to get that ship, and our supplies, all to make a new home. In one afternoon, the Restorationists scuttled her, and bombarded most of our colony."

The gouges in the forest. The blackened land. Orbital weapons fire? I shivered. That means they have a pulsed particle cannon aboard their six-brace. Those cargo ships come standard with laser turrets for clearing away floating debris. It shouldn't be equipped with a military-grade weapons system.

"You can imagine how much of an impression they made on us. We weren't unarmed, but with a ship in orbit, weapons trained on what was left of our new home, what were we going to do? We surrendered. And they stayed. The Restorationists keep us as their labor force. In return, we get to live here."

"What about the charter?"

"The charter's a sham. Oh, we all agreed to transfer ownership. At gunpoint. The guilt they laid on us..." Cotes shakes his head. "It isn't misplaced. There's a lot we did wrong. All of us."

"Not all of us," Larissa murmurs.

I feel she's being too quick and defensive, so I blurt out, "Never informed on any kids your age?"

"How dare you," Azalea says.

"Easy, everyone," Cotes interrupts. "Captain, I didn't bring you in here to let you insult my family. I wanted to tell you the truth. These people are here illegally. They've imprisoned us as outright as if we were dumped in Jagged Rock on Mercury."

"You *should* be in prison," I continue, feeling they deserve the insults. "The king never should have let you out."

I realize I'm being the worst dinner guest in the history of shared meals, but I can't delete the image of Uncle Ethan, of the maroon-jacketed Kesek officers hauling him away, of our neighbors watching on their delvers as their home security sensors record the arrest. My heart's pounding worse than if I were trapped in an asteroid storm.

I shove back from my chair and say, "I'm not hungry."

"You leaving?"

I pause at the door. "Yeah. As soon as I get my ship back."

"They'll have it locked down."

"I think I can solve that problem. Pretty handy with shipboard systems."

"It isn't at the landing field where you came down. They've moved it."

"Are you going to tell me where or do I have to guess?"

Cotes frowns. "Southwest corner, half a klick beyond the fence. I'd stay clear of it."

"Lucky for us all, I'm not you."

There's few guards inside the settlement once night falls. No glow paths to light the way, or even rudimentary streetlamps. Guess that's enough to encourage people to stay indoors.

Better cover for me.

I slink along the buildings, winding up four blocks from my hut before pausing by the edge of a storage unit. Boots crunch on dirt and gravel. Low voices murmur. I key in on them, straining for the words, while filtering out extraneous sounds—the rustle of pine branches, high-pitched keening of some avians that flap by. Worse than a corrupted signal trying to cut through background radiation.

The guards walk by. Their conversation's over, apparently, because I don't hear another word from them.

I finally exhale, lungs burning. Okay. Only another half kilometer of this.

Going out the front gate is a bad idea. By the time I make it toward the entrance, I can see the only lights visible on this nighttime excursion. Floodlamps hovering over the gate illuminate a golden circle in which four guards stand ready. Two inside the fence, two outside, all armed with scramblers—and pistols. Can't tell what model, but they're not stun weapons.

"Wonderful," I mutter.

I backtrack along the fence, searching for a weak spot. The thing's threaded with enough sensor fiber that I know I'll set off every alarm in the blasted place if I so much as bend a thumb's worth out of place.

The bottom, well, that's another story. It's not been maintained with as great care. In some places, the fence juts into the soil. In others, there's a few centimeters' worth of clearance.

My convoluted track dumps me back at the tumbledown part of the settlement not far from Cotes' house. The ground outside looks even more nightmarish in the pale glow from the moon, shadows pooling in craters.

Some of those craters are nice and close to the fence.

I brace myself against one particularly lopsided residence and plant my boots against the mud-encrusted lip of a crater. Quick prayer for, I don't know, invisibility? Stealth? Poor observation by the guards? Any of those will do.

Swift kicks break through the dirt. To my ears, each blow seems as loud as a cargo hatch slamming shut. But no one comes running, thank God.

Soon as I'm satisfied by the size of the gap I've created, I flatten out like I've got to worm around *Marconi*'s access shafts in pursuit of a broken bot. It happens. It also gives me an appreciation for the techs who spend their lives maintaining a starship's innards. Not for the claustrophobic.

I squeeze under the fence, heart thumping against the ground. Rock tears at the front of my shirt. Come on. A meter more.

Three-quarters of the way out, fencing snags my pants.

A flare of light ripples out from the point where it caught, ghostly blue, like someone threw a rock into *Marconi*'s water tank and watched the splash spread.

That someone's me. I've tripped the sensors. My escape attempt's been registered.

I yank myself through, caution irrelevant now, and scramble into a run. Shouts echo from the front of the settlement. I catch tiny silhouettes flitting through the lights. I curve a course away and around, leaping over downed trunks, scraping my sides on branches, weaving around boulders.

Where's that landing field?

Cotes said all the shuttles would be there, including the skipjack. It can't be far, not if the Restorationists use it in a regular basis. Half a klick.

Lights. Pale blue ones. Black outlines of trees block the view, but not all of it. There's enough I can make out the sharp lines of landing craft wings, the aerodynamic fuselages.

One's shorter than the rest, with two pairs of stubby wings folded into diamonds. That's my ride.

There's no guards. Not surprising, given they expect everyone to be locked up snug inside the fences, enjoying their family dinners before they wake up the next morning for another day of forced labor.

I grimace as I sprint onto the paved tarmac. What do I care? They're all criminals, and people married to criminals, or with criminals as parents.

Can't help remembering Father's anguish when Kesek took his brother.

My skipjack's illuminated by a blue beacon. She shines like a work of art. Minute and a half. That's how long it'll take her to go from cold start to airborne.

Except someone's changed the access codes.

I pound my fist against fuselage. None of my backup access numbers work, not even the owner's dead key, a code that's supposed to reset the entire system. If I had access to the Reach network on my delver, I could piggyback the local network and signal MarkTel for a complete reboot.

One that would take me at least three days, assuming there was even a comms ferry around.

The shouts are getting nearer. The alarm remains strident.

There's no time to argue with my suddenly stubborn aircraft. I choose one of the other ships, a gig twice as large, flat and curved, like a stone perfect for skipping. This one's access panel's a simple civilian model. Easy enough to bypass—once I remove the panel and cross circuits underneath.

"He's there! Stop him!"

That's Nakano. The high-pitched screech of scramblers rings in my ears. Blue-white energy bursts slap the fuselage, and the tarmac. I duck inside, frantic for the cockpit. Light trickles in through the canopy.

I throw myself into the pilot's seat and start the ignition sequence. Well-tuned ion engines thrum to life.

The thrill of success makes me grin, until two pairs of rough hands grab my arms.

They drag me from the cockpit and toss me through the hatch. I hit the tarmac hard, breath knocked out. This must be how Tatsuo felt when I ditched him.

Speaking of Tatsuo, he's there, hair all disheveled and surrounded by guards. Nakano stands in front of them, hands clasped behind his back, dressed in rumpled shirt and trousers. They're stain-free, spotless. Somehow, in the middle of local night, every hair's slicked with precision.

"This is unfortunate, Captain." My holography instructor sounded less patient, even on a good day. "I'd had hope a brief incarceration would reveal the benefits of staying in our good graces, but you've failed to be redeemed. I'll have to reinforce the lesson."

He gestures. The guards advance on me, scramblers turned stock first.

I kick the first one in the knee, gaining both a scream and a satisfying *crunch*. Blows rain down, one at a time, then a handful. I get to my knees, lashing out as best I can, but even though I connect a few hits, there's too many against me. I bring my hands over my head and hunker down, absorbing strike after strike. Pain rolls over me in an unending wave.

I never should have come here.

Chapter Six

The third day of work.

I'm still one massive bruise. There's ugly black and blue marks on my arms, legs, and torso. Cotes assures me I didn't sustain internal bleeding. The medical sensor had that figured out in a microsec. Doesn't mean I don't feel awful.

Also doesn't mean I get time off to recover.

It's back-breaking. Scooping roots, racing the mud to make sure it doesn't fill the holes back in. I'd give anything to be back aboard *Marconi*, dealing with software headaches or plowing through hours of repairs to a glitchy comms ferry. At this point, with my sides hurting and my arms burning, I'd even sit at that stupid table with its two chairs for endless meals, lack of companionship aside.

Once again, I'm done with people.

There's a break at midday for water and rations. Guards inspect our loads. They kick over several that aren't up to their standards.

I get Keegan.

"What is this? You pulling roots out one at a time with your fingernails?" He picks up the bucket. "Speak up."

"I'm a little sore," I say. "Think it's slowing me down."

"Push through it." He slaps the bucket down on my shoulder. Roots fly into the mud. "Looks like you'd better catch up."

There's somebody I wouldn't mind catching with the business end of a scrambler. Yeah, I know, not supposed to kill, but that doesn't keep my brain from churning out elaborate fantasies. Such is the result of too much free time on a starship.

"I'll get him back on course, Keegan." Cotes hands me a water tube. "He's had a rough go."

"Yeah, you'd know about rough go, Kesek." Keegan spits on Cotes' boots. "You know the deal. The governor wants production doubled for this last load. Three more days, 'til the ship leaves orbit."

As soon as he's gone, I wave Cotes closer. "They're leaving?"

"Don't I wish. No, it's a shipment of varmo root headed for Puerto Guijarro. Long way off from here, even at top acceleration. Eight tract shifts to that system, maybe ten. But worth every light-year's distance."

"Let me guess: they keep all the profit."

Cotes nods. "They're not handing out shares, that's for certain."

What a crew. Ex-secret police on one hand, crazed kidnappers on the other. Not sure if it counts as kidnapping when the victims are almost a hundred people of a small settlement. Piracy? Slavery?

I'd wish for *my* crew's help, but I recall they got reprogrammed against me. Great.

A woman drops her water tube. The contents spill out, soaking into the mud. She's short, and thin, with close-cropped blond hair. Her lips are chapped. No one makes a move in her direction.

I've only drank a third of mine. "Here."

She's got lovely green eyes, but there's a hard set to her expression. She takes the tube, eyeing it as if I'd given her a drink of anti-matter. There's an ugly scar on her right hand, jagged lines that have reduced her hand to a twisted mess. Takes me a moment to realize those lines form a capital letter I. "Appreciate it."

Then she's back at her task, swigging the water and tearing open a ration pack. I sink on my heels, waiting for her to get out of earshot. "Friendly."

"Tanya? She's a bit rougher than most."

"What's the data on that scar?"

"She was an informant, one with close ties to Kesek on her home planet. Everyone knew it. Wealthy, popular with the ruling set. Then everything flipped over, and she spent a year on probation while the Realm sorted through all the files. She walked out of the local Crown Marshal office, and got a dozen meters down the street before a gang of Hindi decided she needed a permanent reminder she'd had people imprisoned."

The mere sight of the scar makes me ill.

"Not enough punishment for you?" Cotes points at a balding, brown haired man off by himself. There's a robotic rhythm to his digging, as if he's perfectly programmed for the task of excavating roots. "Yancey. He was a constable at Nova Tempus. When the coup happened, a riot broke out in his city. His bosses wanted to open fire with railers on the crowds. Yancey talked them down. Should've gotten a commendation. Instead, he gets locked up by the military, and those same rioters murdered his wife and children. Yancey never complains about it. He feels like he deserved it."

Railers? I can't imagine someone wanting to obliterate unarmed civilians with those guns. They're reserved by the military for fighting combat robots and armored vehicles. An electromagnetically-accelerated projectile would shred a person like a wet leaf.

"You've had it rough, Chen, I don't deny it, but consider for a microsec that maybe, with the tables turned, these people have suffered enough before the Restorationists got their hands on us," Cotes mutters.

"Suffered enough?" His lecturing doesn't combine well with my pain. "I lost friends. Whole families were spirited off to re-education camps, or penal colonies worse than this. And my uncle—I never saw him again. More than ten years, and we still have no idea where he died. The records you talk about, the ones the Realm opened for everyone to read? Ethan Chen's in there. We got a 'Confirmed Deceased.' I could spend the rest of my life cruising the galaxy and not come within a hundred parsecs of wherever he's buried—if there's even a body. Don't tell me about suffering."

"Hey!" Keegan's back, and I realize I've gone over our break time. Everyone else is back to digging. "Ex-captain. Pick up your gripper and start scooping."

"Aren't you a ray of sunshine? *Wáng bā dàn.*" I stand up, legs resistant. "Relax, Mister Boss. I'm on it."

Keegan grins. I have a half second to realize that's a bad thing before he buries the stock of his scrambler deep in my gut. I want to curl up and not die, but he holds onto my shirt, keeping me dangling. "Got to admit, I didn't think you'd fit in with these Kesek worms, and guess what? I was right. You've got too much fire. They're better at following orders. What, you didn't get enough of a beating last night? You want a taste of some—"

Too bad he's not eavesdropped communications coming through *Marconi*'s array. Then I could shut him off with the tap of a screen. Oh, well. This will have to do.

I slash the gripper across his arm.

Keegan's diatribe cuts off in a howl. He lets go, and the scrambler splats in the mud.

I smack him across the jaw with the flat side of the gripper, leaving a red mark blooming on his cheekbone. "How's that for backtalk?"

Before I can grab the weapon, though, Keegan plants another punch in my side, then brings up his knee. This time I've got no energy left for a counterattack, let alone resistance. My body goes limp, sliding through mud.

Puts me closer to the scrambler, though.

Times like these, I wonder if divine intervention is at play. Does the Lord really provide a weapon, even a nonlethal one, in answer to prayer? It's an interesting thought, one I'd normally hash out to myself, or maybe Blue, if he's in a listening mood while recharging.

Out here, with angry guards converging and an irate Keegan about to stomp me, I skip past theological debate and grab the scrambler. I roll onto my back and swipe the back of Keegan's knee. He drops.

A blur of green appears in front of me. I don't bother clearing away the muck on my face to see who it is, and fire. The heat from the energy discharge sears my face, and the static makes the hair on my arms stand on end. The guard slips and lands on his back. Legs and arms tremble. He's immobilized. Lungs and heart working, yeah, but that's it.

Keegan kicks the gun out of my hand. He gets back to his feet, face red behind splotchy white mud. He drags a stubby cylinder from his belt, and presses a button. The cylinder extends and expands until he's holding a half-meter baton of adjustable polymer. A power source glows red inside.

Funny. I always figured I'd die floating in space, not lying in mud.

"Keegan!" Cotes grabs his arm. "Let the young man be. He's under a lot of strain."

"You telling me how to do my job?" Keegan swipes mud from his mouth.

"Wouldn't have to, if you were doing it right."

Keegan breaks free. "Back off, or you're up next!"

The first strike comes down with a *whirr*. The pressure on me is intense, but there's no pain. That's because someone's laying across me.

Cotes.

Keegan pummels him, again and again. Cotes doesn't cry out, but groans fight through clenched teeth. After a dozen hits, Keegan's panting. Guards ring us, but no one shoots.

"Rather it was the brat, but you were a nice substitute, Cotes," he growls. "It's about time. That was for mind-sifting my sister."

He spits again, this time on the back of Cotes' head. Guards lead him off, with Keegan muttering something about "infirmary." The remainder shout orders at us. Cotes and I take a couple sharp kicks before everyone disperses for work.

"Hand." Pale fingers move Cotes, and help me up. It's Yancey. He considers me as if meeting an exotic species of bug from an unexplored planet.

"Yeah, I'm okay." Not really. Even though Cotes was the one getting pounded, being sandwiched between him and the ground wasn't pleasant. Pretty sure I'd be scrubbing mud out of every pore.

Cotes leans against Yancey. His face is streaked with mud. But he's standing.

"We should get you to a medic," I say.

Of all things, Cotes chuckles. "Medic? As in, the medic we took you to see when the guards dumped your heap outside my door? Don't get all damage control on me. There is no medic, Chen. There's med-kits, so if you want to run a sensor over me to pinpoint bruises, I'm happy to sit still."

"You could have something broken."

"No, not with Keegan. He knows I'm the foreman, and one of his best producers. The man has a quota. He's not going to incapacitate either of us. He's far too skilled at inflicting pain that lasts the entire day without inhibiting a worker's output."

"Thoughtful guy," I mutter.

What about him?"

Cotes pats Yancey on the shoulder. "Thanks." He limps back to his bucket, to his spot on the terraces. Azalea and Larissa aren't around—I assume they're working a different site today. But the rest of the workers notice.

"Hey. Hey!" I stagger to him. "What was that?"

"What was what?"

"You know. You—threw yourself on top of me."

Cotes wrenches varmo root from the mud. He nods.

"Okay, but…" I can't bring myself to say it.

"Why?" Cotes shrugs. "Easy enough, Chen. You've seen Keegan in action. I've seen enough of that in my lifetime I'll never erase the nightmares."

"Sticking between me and Keegan, that's your penance?"

"It's what I owe. Plus, we need to keep you alive."

"I'm touched." Guards walk by, scramblers at the ready. I keep my head down, my hands in the dirt. Neither man offers me a drink, or bandages. Either would be nice.

"You do have our only method of rescue."

"What, my ship?" I shake my head. Every ounce of frustration gets channeled into my next excavation. The roots come out in tattered clumps, but blast it, I get every bit out of the mud. I slap the mangled mess into the bucket. "Sorry, I'm fresh out of optimism. They reprogrammed my loyal robot crew into a mobile scrambler horde, and locked me out of *Marconi*. I can't even take the skipjack out of the atmosphere—little good it would do us. You can't fly a shuttle or a lander far enough to escape a star system, even if you could miraculously take it through a sundoor. Oh, and yeah, we're fresh out of ways to call for help! Even these vac-heads can't call for backup or pass along their fake story about the charter, because they went and lost their comms ferry!"

Cotes glowers at me. The guards glance back. Whether they've heard my tirade nor not, delivered in an angry whisper through clenched teeth, is up for debate, at least until they walk off sniggering. That's when I figure I'm not getting beaten again.

"Unless you have any genius ideas, or maybe a spare Raszewski sphere in your root bucket, I'm going back to digging varmo and recovering from my wounds. Maybe in a week I'll be better suited to planning an escape."

"Might go better if you could call for help."

I snort. "Right." I've tried that, in the form of uplifted prayer. No answers yet. That's okay. I don't usually get lightning bolts from the heavens or a whispered word from God. His answers tend to be subtler."

"How about we bring the comms ferry back online?"

"That'd be something I could do, Cotes, except I can't find it. No one can."

"Except me."

I squint at him in the harsh sunlight. "How hard did Keegan hit you on the head?"

"Think about it. The Restorationists don't know where it is." Cotes scrapes his gripper on the bucket. "That's because I drove it off."

"Not possible. You can't override a comms ferry's station-keeping by remote. You have to hardwire it."

"I can and did with a special access code."

"What? There's no such code! Why would MarkTel put something like that in? No one would..." The rest of my thoughts evaporate, like water in vacuum. Oh. Of course. "Kesek."

Cotes nods. "It's the first thing you memorize when you make detective inspector. It lets any Kesek officer override a comms ferry for whatever use he or she deems vital. It was my last-ditch gamble, when our other options failed. I thought MarkTel had stripped the codes from all the ferries, or at least put in safeguards against it."

"Newer models wouldn't have it," I murmur. "But MarkTel's still upgrading its fleets with newer models. Sylvanak's got one of the 20-year-old ferries."

"I realized that after I got access."

"Where is it?"

"Stuck inside a cometary fragment, and shut down."

I whistled. The Kesek access code must be more than a simple remote control for navigational purposes, then. No one but comms jockeys like me—not even groundside operators—were supposed to be able to shut off a comms ferry.

"I knew getting a message out would be difficult. If the Restorationists intercepted it, who knows what they'd do to our people, including my family? I needed another way. This was perfect to cast as a malfunction. That kept our hosts busy, and triggered alerts with MarkTel that something was going on."

"Then what? You expected a lone comms jockey on a single ship to mount a rescue effort?"

Cotes smirked. "I assumed you'd replace the ferry and find the old one, then work backwards from there. Never expected you to storm down in person."

"Well, you got the stubborn one."

"Apparently."

I look around. No guards nearby. Plus, we're still working as we conspire, so staying busy helps. "Okay. This can work. I need a way to gain access to their systems, and use that code of yours. Any suggestions?"

"Possibly. I didn't dare sneak into their comms again. They locked things up tight after the first breach, but they think it's one of their staff who got drunk and messed around. I did manage to snag spare parts. Larissa's got most of them for her brassjacket—"

"Wait. Brassjacket?"

"She's refitting one. Not for general knowledge, Chen. Why?"

I grin. "You should have told me sooner. I've got an idea."

Chapter Seven

I've never seen a more beautiful robot.

Okay, let me clarify. Every day for the past few years has been spent in the company of either hamsters scooting around the deck of *Marconi*, or ducking as brassjackets flit by overhead. After trusting them with my life on more than one occasion, they turn traitor.

Gazing upon the gleaming automaton hidden under the sofa in Cotes' house is something of a revelation after four days of digging roots without artificial assistance.

It's the size of my fist, shiny with chrome and bronze lines. The disc-shaped body fits easily in Larissa's palm when she holds it up. Tiny hoverjets are mounted at eight intervals. This thing would be incredibly maneuverable and nimble in zero gravity.

"He's a lot better looking outside than in." Larissa manages to sound like a proud parent, even as she pops the top lid.

Wow. Yeah, the innards are cobbled together from three different sources I can identify, plus two others I can't place—until I pick out circuits from a delver, and possibly a power cell from a scrambler. "Still, it's impressive. Where did you find all this stuff?"

"In the refuse. And the storage units the Restorationists keep their tech in. You know, the stuff they're going to replace the worn-out equipment with."

"No one's noticed them missing, I take it, or else you wouldn't have this bot."

Larissa grins at her dad. "I had some help with finding the stuff."

"I don't condone theft." Cotes inspects the ceiling. His cheeks go dark. "Not usually."

"I'd say you're forgiven in this instance. Send the Lord a signal about it." I actually don't know how theft while enslaved counts in terms of the Commandments, but repentance is a tricky thing. "So, this bot…"

"He's ready. Except… I can't operate him. No one had a full AI available to, um, borrow, so he's just limited intelligence. Needs a remote operator."

"What about your delver?"

"They're dumb." Larissa hands it to me.

I wince. So much for that plan. Dumb delvers are preloaded, without access to information networks—or, say, remote operation systems for bots. The only way to alter the contents are to link via hard wire. Talk about prehistoric.

"It's all right." Cotes puts his hands on Larissa's shoulders. "We can find a way around this. Maybe there's something we can find aboard the landing craft at the field."

"I wouldn't recommend sneaking out there, even at night." I work out a kink in my back muscles. The bruises there throb. "But if we could get ahold of one of the Restorationists' delvers—wait. We don't need theirs."

"You just said we do," Larissa points out.

"Thanks, yes, but I was being a moron. We just need mine." I smile. "You've already got the receiver implanted in this bot…"

"Josh." Larissa's cheeks go curiously dark.

"The bot's name is Josh?"

"Yeah."

Cotes' expression makes me glad he's no longer a Kesek detective inspector. "Your bot's not named for the Josh living on Block Eight, the one whom I always find you working near when you're on the west terrace, is it?"

Larissa rolls her eyes. “Dad, please, let’s stay on course.”

Cotes turns to me, but there’s still suspicion in his tones as he says, “All right, Chen. We need to get your delver. If they followed protocol, they’ll store it with the rest of confiscated items. They’ve kept all our personal electronics since the day they arrived.”

“And replaced them with this junk.” I toss the dumb delver on the bed. “Larissa, we’ll need your help getting in.”

“That’s the easy part,” she scoffs. “It’s getting your top-model MarkTel tech to speak with my transceiver that’s gonna be like decrypting a comms ferry’s nav computer.”

I pull up a chair at their table, and spread out the pieces of Josh in front of me. “Thankfully for you guys, I didn’t fall asleep during that training holo.”

Grandfather told me a story about why our traditional New Year’s celebrations are full of noise-makers and firecrackers. A monster called Nian would savage a village, scaring the people into submission. It was a wise old man who rallied them by using drums and making an incredible racket that the creature ran itself to the brink of exhaustion. Only then could the villagers kill it.

I can’t help thinking of Nian lurking around this settlement, except there’s more than one monster.

Rain sweeps in during the last shift. It buries us in sheets of water, turning the already muddy ground to an impassable morass. Doesn’t mean we get to quit early, though. Keegan seems to take delight in having us pull roots—or attempt to pull roots—a half hour beyond usual. Why should he be bothered? He and his guards all wear ponchos that cover them down to their boots. Judging by the red lines glowing on the sides and sleeves, they’re laced with heating threads, so none of them shiver like we do.

I grit my teeth and keep the mounting frustration reined. Focus on the plan.

Hours later, when I’m full of dry, crumbly rations and am relatively dry, Larissa and I sneak off into the dark.

The rain hasn’t let up. Clouds are thick. No stars, no moon. It’s a good thing Cotes' daughter has run this path before, to the storage shed, or I'd be lost. Tough enough to keep track of her, as my eyes adjust to the dark, even though she's a couple meters ahead.

The storage shed is stuck off to the side of the terraces, a simple cube in a formation of more prefab cubes, four rows of three columns. Tiny red lights glow on access panels. They look simple enough to crack open.

Until I realize they're bio-locked.

"That's just great," I mutter. "You wouldn't happen to have Restorationist skin cells under your belt, would you?"

"I don't need them. We're not going in the door." She leads me in the narrow lane between storage cubes. It's even darker here, swimming in their shadows. Larissa stands on tiptoes, reaching to the top.

There's grates, one on either side, above average person height. They're covered with cantilevered awnings, presumably to keep rain out, but they must serve to ventilate the interior.

I grab Larissa's arm. "Hold on. They're probably lined with sensors. You pop one open…"

"Relax. I've taken care of that."

I roll my eyes. "If this is such a breeze, what do you need me for?"

Boots squelch in mud. The murmur of voices drifts through the steady hiss and splatter of the rain.

"To take care of them if they get too close!" she whispers.

I peer around the edge of the cube. One guard. Talking to himself? Nope, he's got a wrist comm. Light pulses from the open top of one of his pockets. Delver, probably. He's carrying a scrambler. Got a hand beacon fixed under the weapon's barrel. It brightens every shadow it sweeps across.

"Hurry up," I mutter to Larissa.

"Give me a boost." She's got the grating open, without any sound, mercifully. No indication of alarms, and the guard sure isn't sprinting in our direction.

I help her stand atop my knee. She pulls herself up the wall and shimmies through the vent, squeezing through the narrow opening with such agility I'm going to recommend she's on MarkTel's scans for a shipboard tech if she's interested. Cotes might object.

The guard's boots are near. He stops. More murmuring, with a crackling, static-filled response. He slaps his hand. The static clears. “Lousy comm on the fritz.”

I restrain the urge to take it apart for him. Easy enough fix. Probably a loose component.

I shake my head. Are you spaced? This is a theft, not a repair signal!

There’s a noise from inside the cube. Tapping. Larissa’s ready to get out. All she’s got to do is climb up the shelves, and slide back out the ventilation opening. Simple.

Except that guard’s almost on us.

I slap the wall, a heavy, wet sound. Doubles as a warning to her and a distraction to the guard. He turns toward our aisle. The light cuts down the darkness.

I’m already gone, around the front of the cubes.

“Singh here. Checking a disturbance in storage block.”

Static. “Probably the sensors glitching,” a scratchy voice says. “Storms always foul them up. Finish your rounds, Singh.”

“Gimme a microsec.” Singh shuts off the wrist comm. I can hear his steps clearly, even though I’m on the opposite side of the building. No sounds from Larissa, though. Please, don’t try to get out now. Stay quiet.

I ease along the cube’s wall, until I’m poking my head around the corner into the very lane the guard left. I’ve made almost a complete circuit. Suddenly, his light switches angles.

Good he’s headed out.

I head back the way I came, quickly, but taking care not to make noise. It’s a rough task, considering how thick the mud is. Fortunately, the rain picks up, which means, yes, I get more soaked. Plus side, it covers my footsteps. Perfect.

Perfect until I run smack into Singh.

What’s that vac-head doing here? He’s backward! Must have crept that way around the corner, keeping his light shined down the other alley. Well, it doesn’t really matter, because a second later he swivels, and the two of us stare like a pair of Faraday’s Planet goggle-fish. At least the dummy has his beacon pointing at our waist.

Singh lifts his wrist comm.

I grab his arm with one hand, and swing a wild punch with the other. He ducks. My fist careens off the cube wall. Blast! Nothing’s broken, I think.

The scrambler muzzle pokes under my chin. Heat sizzles deep in the barrel.

I let go of Singh's arm and shove it aside, simultaneously wrenching my neck out of the line of fire. The burst is near enough the screech sets my ears ringing.

I plant a punch in his gut, then hook his leg with my ankle. A good shoulder to the ribs slams him into the mud. His scrambler's mine.

One blast renders him insensate.

Something scrapes down the side of the cube. "Chen? What happened?"

"Shhh!" I step over Singh. Larissa's tucking a bundle into her pocket, staring at me wide-eyed. "Come on!"

"What about him?"

"Don't have time."

"Someone's going to find him!"

Leave it to the Kesek inspector's daughter to remind me about hiding a body. "Okay, hold on." Only place available is the cube. I grimace. "Help me get him up."

It takes a lot of grunting, a fair amount of contorting, but we get him stuffed through the same vent Larissa exited. Singh's body lands with a meaty thump inside. Here's hoping he stays out cold. "Let's move!"

We bolt.

Cotes keeps hot tea coming as I work on our top-secret project through the night. By the time morning dawns pink and orange, bathing his home in the neon lights, I'm exhausted, but mostly dry, so there's that.

"Looks good." Cotes sips from his mug. "No loose parts."

"Not for Josh the bot." I have a bundle of cables, hair-thin and shorter than my hand, taped to the side of my delver. Its screen flickers, yes. That's to be expected, given how I've altered its programming. I rub my face with the back of my hand. "One way to be sure."

I tap a few commands.

Hoverjets puff and hiss. Josh rises, wobbly at first, then steadying mid-air over the table.

"Aced." I grin. "Okay, buddy, how's your maneuvering?"

I input the links between Josh's nav software and the map of the settlement Cotes provided me. He swoops over to the open hatch, and out into the air.

"Look at him go!" Larissa squints into the sky. "He's responding so well."

"Cue the awards ceremony for you, kid," I say. "He's your handiwork."

She grins. "Better let you drive him, though, since you know what we're looking for."

"That was my idea." And I know precisely where to take him.

A klaxon blares. Cotes slams his mug down.

"What is that?" It sounds bad. I ignore it, best I can, and guide Josh to the administrative center.

"General summons," Cotes says. "Keegan's calling the settlement leaders in for a discussion."

"The guard." Larissa puts her hands to her mouth.

"Someone found him, I'd imagine. Relax. He likely didn't see you. It was Singh?"

I nod, too nervous to formulate a polite reply. Almost to the admin building.

"Man's got a bad habit of chewing raw varmo leaves. Not nutritious, but serves as a narcotic. We'll get this sorted out." Cotes and Azalea leave. "Stay here. Come find us if there's any trouble."

"Be careful," I say.

"You too."

Larissa waits by the door, my sentry. She's got her dumb delver, providing her an excuse to pretend her attention's elsewhere. Meanwhile I nudge Josh along his trajectory. Larissa's right: he's not much smarter, AI-wise, than a playful puppy. Discretion isn't preprogrammed, so I watch the sensor feed for approaching people.

Keegan's impromptu meeting provides great cover, though. After an initial flood of workers from their homes, kept separate from Restorationist settlers by the ever-present guards, traffic trickles to nothing. I keep Josh tucked between houses. Finally, the way is clear. I speed him ahead to the administrative building.

The same two guards stand on either side of the hatch, which is propped open. Someone else approaches—Tatsuo, pushing a small grav-sled laden with electronics and medical supplies. He's about to leave a side street to center the main thoroughfare.

"Tatsuo." Governor Nakano comes up the road, behind him. He's alone.

Tatsuo grimaces, the expression clear enough on Josh's visual scanners, then faces him. "What now, Father?"

In that moment, I send Josh the command: Conceal.

The bot zips down, around a bend, and secures itself among the supplies on Tatsuo's grav-sled.

I exhale. Wait for it.

"Why aren't you at the terraces? Keegan has his hands full determining who disabled one of his guards," Nakano said.

Tatsuo rolls his eyes. "I've got better things to do. We still haven't located that blasted comms ferry. And since you've decided—without consulting me, your comms director—that Captain Chen should join our labor pool, there's a lot of work to be done. Excuse me."

He pushes the sled into the building, right into the comms center. The staff are all gone. Drawn off for Keegan's interrogation session, no doubt. On the plus side, there don't appear to any sensors capable of detecting an unauthorized robot in the building. Good thing, because I'm not sure Josh could outrun them.

"What'd you find?" Larissa flips through screens on her delver, flicking her gaze up every so often to watch for guards.

"Potential." I turn up the volume on Josh's speakers, to the conversation Nakano seems intent on continuing with his son, no matter the latter's indifference.

"This is an important matter. We need to present a unified front to our comrades."

"I think you can be unified enough for the both of us. Go give your speeches to our devoted followers and keep justifying how we're stealing from the people who were here before us." Tatsuo yanks circuits from the comms console as if he's planning to throw them.

"No one is stealing anything."

"It's bad enough when you lie to everyone else. Don't do it to me."

"What lie? The people here needed our assistance to make this colony self-sufficient and profitable. They have the blood of thousands, if not millions, on their hands. The king was a fool to pardon them, we both know this. Our purpose is to restore their innocence through the lessons we apply."

"We can't make them our subjects!" Tatsuo snaps. "Keegan's out there berating the people we conquered. His guards beat anyone who talks back. Stars, Father, they're our slaves! You have no plans to turn over ownership to them. This charter's a sham, and you know it!"

Nakano steps closer. For being taller by a half meter, Tatsuo cowers considerably under the steely gaze of his father. "If you cannot bring yourself to support our cause, then recuse yourself from it. I won't have you mucking about. Find the comms ferry and notify me immediately. Do not concern yourself with anything else, unless you want to try your hand at laboring alongside these people whom you hold in such high esteem."

Tatsuo glares at him, wordless, as he leaves.

"Very interesting," I murmur.

"Call Josh back," Larissa hisses. "We'd better get to the meeting."

"On it."

"What was the governor saying? Was that his son he was threatening?"

I smile. "It sure was."

Chapter Eight

We're late, but no one notices. It took me a bit to fly Josh back to the Cotes house, then find a place to stash him that would hold up to cursory inspection, if the situation arose. By the time Larissa and I reach the meeting, the two crowds are focused on Keegan and his guards. Fortunately, Singh's not among them.

"This won't go unanswered!" Keegan doesn't need an amplifier to harangue us. He's red-faced and bellowing like a garrosk, and at this point I'd rather take my chances with that six-legged, ursine predator than this guy. At least the garrosk didn't smack me around.

"Our man's injuries are bad enough he's off shift, but don't you think for one microsec the rest of the guards will slack because of a man down." Keegan points at the crowd of workers, in their dusty, muddy clothes. "Quota still applies. If anyone among you knows who attacked Singh last night and shoved him inside a storage cube, speak up now."

There's not even a ripple of acknowledgment from the workers. I slip between them, Larissa beside me, until we reach Cotes and Azalea at the front. Yancey's with them, somber, eyes trained on the ground.

Cotes lifts his chin, eyes locked on Keegan like pulse cannons ready to strike.

Keegan notices, apparently. Next thing I know, he's in Cotes' face. "If none of you people can make up your minds who the perpetrator is, we'll make it up for you. I'm not picky."

"True, but you need us to work," Cotes says. "Unless Restorationists suddenly want to get their hands dirty, instead of profiting off our hard labor." He steps toward the Restorationists, their green uniforms reminding me of a human forest. "How about it, folks? Care to try your strength at pulling roots? It keeps you fit."

"Get off it, Kesek!" a woman hisses. "This is your punishment."

"We've been punished enough, and pardoned by the king himself."

"Not nearly enough! No amount will bring back my sister's mind." Keegan shoves Cotes back into the crowd.

Azalea slaps him. "Don't touch my husband again."

Keegan snarls, then hauls back his scrambler.

I slide between them. "Hey, now, we don't need this to get crazy. This gets crazy, too many people get beat up, and next thing you know, we miss quota. No one wants that, right? This is all about what's best for the colony, and the bottom line."

Larissa comforts her mother. I keep myself positioned between their family, and Keegan's guards. Not the safest place, mind you.

Keegan lowers his gun, and smiles. It's one of those, I'll-eat-you-first kind of smiles. Again, I wish for the garrosk. "Fair point, Captain." He says the last word like it's a joke and a slur wrapped into one. "Let's keep things civil. I'm a reasonable guy. You all get 48 hours to produce the person who took out Singh. Miss the deadline, and I'll pick a dozen at random to whip into shape—after the quota's filled."

Murmurs build in both crowds. Governor Nakano's here. It's all I can do to nod cordially instead of spitting. "There's the head man himself," I say. "Let's see what he thinks."

"I've already approved of Keegan's proposal, Captain," Nakano says. "We, of course, cannot miss our deadline and thus our economic opportunity. But discipline must be maintained." He raises his hands. "All of you return to your assignments. The appropriate punishments will be levied unless the perpetrator is brought before us."

Since I'm the perpetrator, I keep my mouth shut. Getting

"punished"—whatever that meant—and possibly locked up—would not help my escape, nor would it do these people any good.

Tatsuo, I realize, isn't among the crowds.

Guards disperse us to work, apparently satisfied we've been chastised. Cotes intercepts Nakano. There's a moment when I see guards close in. My fists clench, wary of an attempt to brutalize Cotes, but he merely engages Nakano in hushed conversation. Nakano seems unimpressed; he waves off Cotes and leaves with a pair of guards in tow.

"What'd you say to him?" I ask Cotes.

"I was presenting the case for a review of the charter. The governor said he'd consider it." Cotes sighs. "Like he's said he'll consider it a dozen times before. One of these days it may bear fruit."

"You're patient, I'll give you that."

"Not infinitely." He edges closer, and lowers his voice. "How did your walkabout go?"

"Josh was great. He found something we can use."

"Access to the communications?"

"No." I frown. "But possibly better. Hang on a microsec. You already hid the comms ferry. Can't you call it back?"

"I can. There's tremendous risk."

"Look, I already zapped a guard into the mud and committed espionage—not really, though, since this isn't a government, I suppose. Anyway, risk is the norm. When we're ready, you have to call the ferry back so I can bounce a message to it and force it to make a tract shift."

"All right. I have the setup hidden in the camp."

"Hidden where?"

Cotes shakes his head. A pair of workers walk by. "I'll keep that to myself. What about the thing you can use?"

"Not a thing. A person." I clap Cotes on the shoulder. He raises an eyebrow, regarding my hand as an alien creature, then smirks. I withdraw it immediately. Between this strange gesture of camaraderie and my earlier concern about him possibly getting beaten to a pulp, I can't unscramble the signal. Meaning, these are the guys I hate. Doesn't matter if they stay behind while I get out of here.

Then again, maybe it does.

Guilt buries me. The way they're treated, it's wrong. Doesn't matter what they've done in the past—and yet, I can't dismiss their sins, either. Uncle Ethan won't leave.

Yancey passes by, head down. So how does that balance out? Uncle Ethan's disappearance, weighed against the deaths of the Kesek guy's families at the hands of the people whom he oppressed? It's no wonder God keeps warning against us pursuing vengeance. Makes a mess of everything.

"Chen?" Cotes folds his arms.

"Sorry. I was elsewhere." I rub my forehead. Got a blossoming headache dragging me down as hard as a planet's gravity well. "Right. Tatsuo. He's the weak link. Let me talk to him."

"It would be nice to have the comms director in our corner, to make sure any messages we send aren't detected," Cotes says. "That still leaves the problem of the six-brace in orbit."

"Oh, I've got more in mind for good old Tatsuo than looking the other way while we call for help. He's the governor's right hand, even if he argues with dear-old dad." I smile. "All part of the risk."

"What do you need from me?"

I glance at Larissa, who's talking with Azalea and another family. "Get your daughter to send up Josh on a flyover of the settlement. I need updated positions of the guards. If you guys can ID the important buildings for me—like storage, and wherever they keep weapons—that'd be a big help."

"There is an armory, where extra scramblers are kept locked up."

Keegan's watching us. I can feel it before I look in his direction, and offer a cheery wave. "That's the best news I've heard all morning."

We get a brief break for the meals. During it, I start moaning about a sharp pain in my side. Some hyperventilating goes a long way toward making me woozy. Cotes loops my arm over his shoulders. "Keegan, I'm taking him to the med bay. The new guy's still not used to these work conditions."

"No one's leaving the terraces while we got a quota to fill." Keegan blocks our path.

"Well, that's fine. I'll let him pass out in the mud, right in the middle of the steps, and you can explain to the governor why we missed the harvest he wants, because you were so scared of one weak spacer getting medical treatment."

Keegan sneers at us, but he doesn't force us back onto the terraces. Instead, he steps aside.

"Thanks much."

Once we're a couple blocks away, hidden from view by the buildings, I straighten up and quit limping. My head's still spinning. "Surprised he didn't send a guard."

"He doesn't have many to spare. You've seen how they're watching us likes hawks this morning. He's looking for a guilty party." Cotes winks. "Good thing you could play a mean hand of kanat without giving anything away."

"Life among robots must give me an edge." There's a pang of sorrow. Funny how much I miss those traitorous lumps of plastic and circuits.

The med bay is in a long, round-edged building. It's a single story, with an office of transparent walls and a windowless section lined in red. Exam rooms, probably.

Cotes lets the entry scanner read his retinas. The hatch hisses open. "I'll root around for a med-kit."

"I'll make certain I lose my way."

There's a maintenance port on the backside of the administration building. The hovercraft in which I rode from the skipjack's landing site to here is parked inside, with cowlings removed from the hoverjet manifolds. A young woman in green uniform lays underneath. She glances at me sideways. "Can I help you?"

"Yeah, you seen Tatsuo around? He asked me to meet him here."

"Should be up in comms." She frowns. "Where's your guard?"

"In the medbay. Foreman needed a kit."

"Oh. I'll send Tatsuo a commnote, let him know you're here."

Before I can summon a clever retort, she's tapping a message with greasy fingers on her delver. There's a hatch on the other side of the maintenance room. I point. "I'll head inside. Thanks."

"Hey, wait! You're not authorized to enter."

"Oh." I place my hand on the access panel. It pulses red. I smile at her. "Would you mind? I don't want to be late after being summoned by the governor's son."

She's unmoved by my charms, no matter how broad my smile. She holds up her delver. "I'll wait for his confirmation, thanks."

Which leaves me with nothing to do but sweat it out. I spot Cotes over the woman's shoulder, half-out the medbay hatch. He gestures as if to say, "Problem?"

I keep smiling, because I'm not going to tip this mechanic off to my partner in potential crime. Her delver chirps, and she looks puzzled by the response. "That my cue?"

"Um, yes. Tatsuo says he's waiting for you." She palms the panel. It responds with a green light, and the hatch slides open. "I'll take you up."

He said that? Could be a trap. Fine. I'm out of options. And I get an escort. How nice.

The comms center is deserted still. No telling where Tatsuo's staff went, but I'm not going to argue. He has equipment from the grav-sled piled in a corner. When the mechanic and I first enter, he's hunched over the primary consoles, inputting commands. I bet the mechanic has no idea, but it's obvious to me Tatsuo's typing nonsense. He's waiting.

"He's here, sir," the mechanic says.

"Thanks, Angie." Tatsuo keeps his back to us.

Soon as she's gone, I lean against the console, arms folded. "You can stop faking now."

"Yeah, I can." Tatsuo swivels in his chair. He looks haggard, way too worn out for a groundside comms jockey. "You had me curious with that stunt you pulled downstairs, so I let you up here. What do you want?"

Kinda forgot to pray up to this point, so I take a microsec to shoot off a plea for the right words and protection in case I've made a terrible mistake. "A fellow comms specialist's help. I want out of here, and I want to bring the authorities down on this place."

"You're crazy. I could call up Father, or Keegan, and you'll be digging roots for the rest of your life, just like the rest of the Kesek colonists."

"Yeah, you could, but you're not. I understand why."

"I don't think you do. These people have a place, and we have a goal. We're going to keep things as they are until the economic conditions are ripe."

"Don't blow plasma in my face." I dig into my memory for his words, as recorded by my new favorite bot Josh. "Too bad your dad has no plans to turn over ownership to them. This charter's a sham, and you know it."

Tatsuo's mouth drops open wider than a hangar bay's hatch. "How did you…? No one heard that. We weren't… How?"

"Not important. What is important, is your doubt. This isn't the way to punish Kesek, Tatsuo. I don't care how self-righteous you Restorationists are. The king pardoned them. Whatever they've done, that'll sit on their consciences. We don't get to play judge."

"How can you not get it?" Tatsuo pushes out of his chair, a rocket ready to launch. "I won't apologize for them. Someone has to make them pay."

"And you think the Restorationists are it? Your dad's using the ex-Kesek settlers to enrich himself, and the rest of your cronies. Sorry, Tatsuo, you don't get to fake your way out of this. God didn't put it on us to continue the misery of the last century by doling out punishment. They should get the chance to live their lives in peace. It's the only way for us to show them how wrong Kesek was, about everyone who believes."

Tatsuo grasps the back of the chair. "I know. I've been trying to deny it, but you're right, it's fake. That's why I've had it with father. But I'm a coward. I could have called up the Crown Marshals any time before the comms ferry disappeared, told them everything that's happened, and ended it."

"You've got the chance to make it right."

He nods. For the first time since Tatsuo showed me the workers on the terraces, he seems … happy. "Thanks. So. What do you need from me?"

"Access to the scrambler arsenal."

Tatsuo winces. I can't blame him. He's progressed quickly from arguing with the governor to joining me in full-fledged insurrection. But hey, desperate times … "Okay. The access isn't a problem, it's the timing. The guards aren't real soldiers, anyway. They're more the bullies amongst Father's people."

"Good to know. Leave the timing to us."

"What about calling for help? The comms ferry…" Tatsuo's eyes narrow. "Wait. You wouldn't be asking for my help if you didn't already have a solution."

I give him a thumbs-up. "Your job is to make sure the six-brace riding over our heads doesn't see what we're up to when we call it back—and preferably, doesn't see much of anything. I'm slightly concerned about that pulsed particle cannon."

"Don't be. The governor would never endanger his precious crops." Tatsuo scowls.

"Well, then, I know the perfect place for our little uprising."

We shake hands.

That night, the workers gather outside Cotes' house. Everyone's there, or so I'm assured. Larissa counts them. Eighty-eight, including the Cotes family, and me.

"I've picked people to help with our action," Cotes says. "Yancey will take the group to the armory, as soon as Tatsuo unlocks it. Tanya has twenty women and men who've agreed to cut holes in the fences at scattered intervals. The idea is to set off as many breach alarms as possible while Yancey's group is unloading the armory."

"Cause maximum confusion for the Restorationist guards. I like it." Speaking of guards … "We don't seem to be attracting their attention."

"Mess hall. It's dinner for most of the colony. Last I heard the menu included beef imported from Liberty. They keep it locked up with the rest of their supplies."

"No stale rations for the bosses, I guess." I look out over the crowd. Everyone's gathered in tight knots, engaged in overlapping conversation, but as soon as I walk forward with Cotes, the din dies down. Soon all I can hear is the chirps from insects overhead. All eyes are watching me—even the bugs', or at least, that's what my paranoia indicates.

"Thanks, everybody, for showing up." What else am I supposed to say? Everyone knows the plans. They don't need encouragement. They've been ready to kick the Restorationists off Sylvanak long before I got here.

But Cotes whispers, "You got this ball rolling, Chen. Be there when it goes over the edge."

Right. I clear my throat. I wonder how many of the faces in front of me have locked up friends, fellow believers, or how many have called Kesek to make the faithful disappear. I start a couple sentences, then delete them. They're generic uplifting stuff. It takes me forever to settle on what I don't want to say, yet really should.

"I forgive you."

Chapter Nine

There's no applause. I wasn't expecting any. Most of the gathered colonists look perplexed.

"Look, I know you're depending on me for this plan," I go on. "But I shouldn't be here. I didn't want to stay and help you out. Each of you is held here by the Restorationists because of what you've done, or your families have done, a lot of years ago. Stuff that hurt my family. When Kesek took my uncle away, it left a gaping wound among my relatives. As much distance as I've put between Tiaozhan and those memories, as many months as I spend alone in deep space, I've never escaped it. So, I hated you."

I suck in a breath. Not inspiring words, but now that they're released, they won't be locked up again. Better try to prove I can change. "I was wrong. I'm not supposed to hate anyone, not even my enemies—and believe me, that's what you were. But it's the whole point of the book I carry with me, the same book Kesek worked for decades to eradicate. Scripture is clear about what we Christians are to do. We don't always want to acknowledge the truth. For that, I am sorry. Never giving you the chance to get away from the past—just like myself and fellow believers wanted to do ourselves—keeps you prisoner to it.

"I won't be party to the Restorationists' plans. They've made themselves oppressors, the very thing they hated, and they let their need for revenge eat them up. No more. This ends tonight. Me learning to forgive you is a miracle, and if that's the case, we can hope for a second miracle when we get this thing started. So, anyway, Godspeed and good luck."

The vacuum of deep space makes more sound that this crew when I'm finished. Cotes greets me with a handshake. "Not bad."

I roll my eyes. "Yeah, right. Come on, we've got work to do."

Several people, including Yancey, come up to us. He doesn't speak but gives me a handshake as warm as any I've gotten from a satisfied customer. Tanya stays distant. She nods, either in recognition or agreement.

Okay, then. I've got my army of ex-Kesek officers and informants. Weird.

Tatsuo meets our group at the armory. It's one of the storage buildings just beyond the block of twelve Larissa overflew, a squat, windowless structure with sloped sides. He palms the access panel, then allows a retinal scan. The hatch opens.

"Wait." Tatsuo blocks the entrance. "Are you sure about this?"

"Absolutely. Are you?"

"No." He shrugs. "I've picked a side, though, so I'll see it through."

"Good enough for me."

"Here." He hands me my wrist comm, plus an identical unit with white markings. "I never locked it down, so your access should be intact. The other one's a spare. I figure you'd need it to stay in touch with this—group."

"Nicely done." I affix the comm to my arm, and toss the spare to Larissa. "Take Josh…"

"Yeah, I know, I've already got him in the air." Sure enough, the tiny brassjacket hovers over her shoulder. She's got my delver tucked in her jacket pocket. "I'll keep you up to date on where the guards are."

I glance at Cotes. "You sure she never got your training?"

"Never anything formal." Cotes emerges from the bunker with a pair of scramblers. He gives me one, then primes the charge on his.

The weapon hums. "She picked up plenty from paying attention to me, though. Always wanted my little girl to be prepared."

"If you say so."

As soon as the scramblers are dispersed, Tatsuo hurries off for the comms center. Cotes and I lead the bulk of the group to the mess hall.

Meanwhile, alarms pierce the evening sky. Flashes of light flicker at the corners of my vision, all around the camp. Whatever Tanya's group is doing to the fences is working. I count eight, then ten, ripples that can only be produced by someone trying to cut holes. Bootsteps beat dirt throughout the settlement. Here and there, guards shout.

Not everyone's been distracted, however. Keegan and a large contingent of his guards have gotten word about the roving band of workers, who are all obviously not in their houses eating dinner like good, submissive laborers. He's got twenty-four men lined up across the main avenue. Scramblers are aimed our way. "That's enough. Lay down your weapons and get back inside."

"Not happening, Keegan." I shoulder my scrambler. The workers on either side of me, Cotes and his wife Azalea included, are aiming at the guards. "You get rid of yours, unless you can't count higher than twenty-four—because we've got more than that."

"I can count. But we're not playing games." Keegan draws a pistol from its holster, a sleek AkTek model. Pretty sure it's the make favored by Kesek in their day, which layers on a whole new slab of irony to the situation. He's also not the only guard packing a real gun. There's at least ten more.

I can hear the murmurs, feel the people shifting their stance. If they break now, we're done. Question is, how willing are any of us to die for this?

Cotes doesn't flinch. His aim's steady. "One last warning. Put down the weapons, and you won't get hurt."

Keegan sneers at him, but he's got the gun aimed at my head. Fear and second thoughts compete as I get this personal look down the muzzle of something that's going to punch an armored bullet through my skull. "We should have vaporized everyone before we bothered setting up shop on this rock. I don't care how much varmo root would have been toasted in the process. It would have been worth it. In fact…"

He lifts a comm unit to his mouth. "Alban Harbor Security to *Thorn*, acknowledge."

The static screech is enough to make him drop the device.

"They're in position." Larissa's voice is startling through my wrist comm, but enough of a prod to action.

"Now!"

Our group opens fire, scattering among the buildings and side streets as we go. Cotes drops to a knee and lets fly burst after burst from his scrambler, white-hot pulses shrieking across the distance. Guards flop like discarded toy figures. Yancey is right with him, taking them out in single-handed grip.

Keegan's aim goes wide, for which I'm thankful, because the bullets punch dirt rather than my face. I flop to the ground—instantly regretting it, as pain shoots through my ribs—and send pulses into his chest with my scrambler.

Before the guards can regroup, more scrambler shots light up alleyways on either side of their contingent. Two groups of six, moving silently along the buildings while Cotes and I confronted Keegan—that was Cotes' plan. I was sure they'd be noticed.

I'm okay with being wrong.

Within minutes, the chaos subsides. What few actual gunshots were let loose caused little injury. We have a handful of colonists with scrapes, but no direct hits. Doesn't look like many of Keegan's guards had their guns drawn. The whole herd is flat in the dirt, twitches fading,

"Get them into the mess hall," Cotes orders. "Make sure they're all bound. Strap them to the furniture and the support beams. Post four people at each access hatch, armed with scramblers."

"We'd better get to the comms center," I say. "Sounds like from Keegan's failed call Tatsuo has the system locked up tight, but he'll probably need help."

"I figured." Cotes kisses Azalea. "You've got this?"

"I'm taking our group out to the airfield," Azalea says. "We'll get one of the groundcars. Yancey's coming with us. We'll make sure the landers stay on the ground. Is Larissa all right?"

I check my wrist comm. A tiny map outlines the settlement, with a blinking light for my position. "She's got Josh monitoring us."

"I'll go check on her first." Azalea and Yancey leave with their group, which frees up Cotes and me to head for the comms center, with six colonists in tow.

Taking backup is a smart move, because we encounter three guards on the way. Dusk lights up with scrambler bursts. A short, stocky colonist flops down. Cotes and I stun the guards.

"Everett, stay with Vick." Cotes kneels beside the stunned man, holding his shoulder as the tremors subside. "Get him inside."

"Sir." Another colonist helps Everett move the stunned man out of the road.

"You've got these guys well-trained," I tell Cotes as we hustle for the administrative building.

"They already had it." Cotes smiles. "They needed a refresher course. Granted, in our day we were on the other side of this uprising, which is why I recommend we take care when we reach our target. If I were Nakano I'd have people posted at the entrance to the administrative building."

He's right, and my finger's ready on the firing stud, except the people Nakano has left are comms center techs armed with scramblers, instead of guards. Also, they're all lying in a heap.

A figure ducks out of the door.

"Got him!" I squeeze off a shot. The pulse slaps and hisses against the hatch frame.

"Hey! Cease fire, Captain!"

Cotes pushes my scrambler down. "Tatsuo?"

Tatsuo steps over the limp techs. "Sorry about that. I didn't know if it was you."

"Yeah, well, it seems you took care of business here well enough. Where's dear old dad?"

"I don't know. Last I saw, he had eight guards with him. Keegan?"

"Drooling in the mud." Sad I didn't have more time to enjoy it.

"We're all set up inside whenever you want to call that comms ferry back." Tatsuo glances between Cotes and me.

Cotes frowns. "I've already got my access point elsewhere in camp. If I can get back to the house…"

"Never mind that," I say. "Tatsuo's got way better equipment. He'll get you ready."

Tatsuo narrows his gaze at Cotes. "You sent the comms ferry away?"

"Yes indeed."

"Unbelievable."

I push them inside. "Let's get cracking, gentlemen."

Cotes gives me the coordinates for the ferry. Wasn't kidding about it being lodged against a cometary fragment. I shake my head, ruing the fact that a Kesek guy trained in the bare basics of comms override managed to take control of something that wasn't supposed to be vulnerable. Of course, if I had the same secret codes he did, my job would be a lot easier.

"It's on the move," he says. "We've got a delay of six minutes."

"Works for me." I take over the navigation controls, and set the ferry on an intercept with the buoy I released when I first arrived. Here's hoping it's still floating around out there. Could be the six-brace *Thorn* already blasted it out of space. "Tatsuo, you got all the data we need?"

"Pulling the last of it from Father's files." He grimaces as he taps a panel with the finality of a man ejecting a damaged drive nozzle. "His private files."

"Relax. I'll make sure it gets to the right people." Setting a course for the ferry to take back to the Sylvanak star's sundoor is easy enough, as is reintroducing the original programming for the tract shift timing. Problem? Making the route circuitous enough to avoid not only the debris surrounding the star, but also disguise the ferry's movements. It should be random enough to give it the appearance of another set of debris. "But I'm not sending anything until I'm sure it won't get intercepted. No sense tipping the governor off."

"Don't worry. They're still locked out. None of the Restorationist comm frequencies are operational, including aboard *Thorn*—though *Marconi* can still send and receive."

"That won't matter if everyone else is blind and deaf." I urge the ferry on its way. Finally, I sink back into the chair. Big mistake. I'm so exhausted I could melt into the cushions, sinking in deep sleep.

"Hey." Cotes kicks the chair, sending a jolt up my spine. "Your wrist."

I'd missed the unit's insistent flashing. Larissa, with an update from the Josh bot? "Go ahead."

"Captain Chen? Where's George?" Tinny shouts nearly swamp the voice. Takes me a microsec to realize who it is.

Cotes grabs my wrist, wrenches it nearer his face. "Azalea? What's wrong?"

"Governor Nakano left in Chen's skipjack. We tried to stop them. Yancey kept the guards from the rest of the craft and… they shot him. He's bleeding badly. I don't have a med-kit. George, they got away! They took her!"

"Took who?"

"Our daughter! The governor took Larissa!"

I've never run so fast in my life. My lungs agree, burning by the end of our headlong rush to the landing fields.

I'm the one with the presence of mind to snatch a med-kit, which puts me a few seconds behind Cotes and Tatsuo. The settlers at the landing field are in disarray, shouting at each other, with a handful clustered around Azalea. She crouches by Yancey, who's sprawled on his back. His head's propped up by a bundled jacket. He looks much paler than usual.

A broad, dark stain covers his torso.

"Sir." He wheezes, gasping for breath.

Cotes grabs his hand. "Steady, Constable."

"We… kept the birds on the ground. Governor escaped. We apprehended ten guards and Restorationists. Your daughter…" Yancey clutches his side, and moans.

"Back up, back up." I wave the scanner over Yancey. That's not good. The bullet went through, but tore apart his insides. "He needs major regen. Tatsuo, keep pressure on the wound. We got nanites in this box?"

There are, thankfully. I inject them above the wound, then find the delver tucked in the med-kit that's programmed to operate them. One set of commands directs them to heal as much damage as they can, prioritizing the critical parts.

"Is that enough?" Azalea says.

"We can stabilize him, but if he doesn't get to a habitat or a starship…" I shake my head.

"Chen, we can't let him get away with this, or with my daughter." Cotes' hand grabs a fistful of my shirt.

"I got that." I rub my temples. Think. Nakano's up, flying my skipjack—my ship! "Can we track him?"

Tatsuo slips a delver from his pocket. "I'm still patched into orbital sensors. Ah… he's headed for *Marconi*."

"Not *Thorn*? What's he up to?"

"*Thorn* might think it's you flying, and with surface-to-orbit comms scrambled now, they have no way to determine who's piloting. Heading to *Marconi* is a safer bet. Father has the new codes that overrode your shipboard systems, including the programming that altered your bots."

"Plus *Marconi*'s the only one that has an operational Raszewski sphere, so he can bail to another star system. And we're stuck here…" I stare at the gig, the same ship I tried to steal when I was locked out of mine. "Perfect. Cotes, Tatsuo, you've got scramblers?"

They look at each other, puzzled. "Of course," Tatsuo said. "We kept them strapped on."

"Good. Load up." I wave at Tanya, who's just arrived with her gang of fence breakers. She hurries to our knot gathered around the wounded settler. I try not to think about Yancey facing armed gunmen with only a stun weapon. "Make sure Yancey doesn't die. We've got a starship to hijack and a girl to save."

We take the gig into orbit without any problems. Smooth flying. However, second thoughts about this plan strike again when *Thorn* appears on our sensors. They amplify as the six-brace fills our forward windows.

No evidence *Thorn* has powered up its pulsed particle cannon. We're blessed in that regard. But there's a laser turret on the dorsal hull. It's powerful enough to cut open this tiny craft's fuselage, as evidenced by how quickly it cut open the much thicker skin of *Marconi*'s fuel tanks.

"If they shoot at us," Tatsuo murmurs, "Is there any possibility they'll miss?"

I shake my head.

"So, when the hull fractures—"

"Don't think about it," Cotes says. "That's an order."

Couldn't have put it better.

That turret tracks us the entire way, until *Thorn*'s hull finally blocks its aim. Even when Tatsuo blows out a breath louder than the life support vents, I don't unclench my hands from the controls. They could still have point-defense missiles, or another laser turret tucked under the bow. Six-braces are built for customization. We're edging around the ship to avoid its own weapons.

Only when *Thorn's* hangar bay hatch yawns open, spilling warm light into space, do I relax. There's plenty of room to fit the gig, plus another small craft. Empty racks fill the back half of the bay. Awaiting varmo root cargo, perhaps?

As soon as the hatch shuts and the bay pressurizes, Tatsuo patches into the intercom. "Thanks, guys. Thought for a moment you wouldn't let us in."

"Tatsuo, what's going on?"

"Easy, Reggie. Father's gone to take control of *Marconi,* so we can get out of this star system. Bring everyone down. I've got a message to deliver, about our next steps."

"Right. Bridge out."

Tatsuo and I stand in front of the gig, with him pointing his scrambler at my back, as four men come stomping down the stairs from the upper decks, Reggie must be the bald guy with the beard in the lead. "You got him?" He asks.

"Not quite." I step aside.

Tatsuo's bolt strikes Reggie in the chest. Another man goes for his gun, but I tackle him to the deck.

Cotes emerges from behind the gig, and stuns two more. "Chen!"

I slam the guy's wrist to the ground. His gun flops from his grasp. I slap it across the deck, and roll against the bulkhead, hitting my back in the process Not pretty.

The final stun burst leaves him helpless.

Tatsuo wipes his brow. "That's it."

"*Zhēn da ma*? Really?" The gun's bio-locked, so I toss it in the gig and seal the hatch. "Four people?"

"Our standard watch aboard *Thorn*. That means we're the crew now."

I nod. "How about that, gentlemen. We're pirates."

Chapter Ten

Marconi drifts along in high orbit. She shows no signs of boosting out of Sylvanak's gravity, and sure isn't firing up the main drives. *Thorn*'s sensors show them cold as a cargo hold open to the vacuum of space.

Good news is, the fuel tank has been repaired where they attacked me, so when the time comes I'll be able to put this blasted star system behind me.

"She's not moving." Cotes leans over the Nav panels, knuckles resting on the map of nearby space.

"I noticed. Slide over." There's four seats up here—helm, nav, comms, and auxiliary systems. Whoever designed a six-brace's bridge did not have aesthetics in mind. It's a box with rounded edges, flat deck, ugly metal stanchions. Certainly not the curved sanctum I'm used to.

Makes me anxious to get *Marconi* back.

Cotes does as he's told, and plunks down in the Nav seat. Tatsuo accesses the comms panel. I run through the pre-flight system at helm, but hold my finger above the control that primes the anti-matter drives. As soon as I give it a go, Nakano will know we've started our engines.

"What's his program, Tatsuo?"

He shakes his head. "I don't know. He could be planning his next move. Father's deliberate. He won't take rash action. Then again..."

"Then again, what?"

"Let me speak to him."

Cotes frowns. "Unless you're negotiating for my daughter's release, that's out of the question."

"Hold up." I spin my chair around. "What if it's simpler than we think? You and your father partnered on this project, right?"

"Yes."

"What if he's just waiting for you? To make sure you're safe."

Tatsuo scratches the back of his head. "Father wouldn't abandon everything the Restorationists have worked for."

"He would, if he kept you safe. Everything he's done has been because of what happened to your mother, Tatsuo. There's no way he'll leave you behind when things fall apart—which they have. But you're right. We'll only know for sure if you talk to him."

"Okay." Tatsuo glances at Cotes.

I sigh. This is another reason working with an all-robotic crew has advantages. "Cotes, this is an order."

"I don't think we're in the same chain of command."

"Sure we are. I'm the captain, you guys are my crew, and this is my ship. For now. Until we get *Marconi* back. Then I'm still the captain. So, Tatsuo's calling the governor."

Cotes folds his arms. "Then the two of you had better not foul this up, because if anything happens to Larissa—"

"I'm not gonna let anything happen to her, Cotes. Trust me." I fire up the main drives. A ragged rumble builds through the deck plates, smoothing into a vibration that stays in my bones. Not so finely tuned, this ship. "Tatsuo, route secondary comms access to me while you're talking."

"Got it." He taps several panels, then clears his throat. "*Marconi*, this is *Thorn*. Father, is that you?"

It's a long five seconds with only the engines' tremor to keep us company. Cotes narrows the nav scope until the blip for *Marconi* and the white circle for us fill his screen. I make sure *Thorn* stays on course, assembling a program from memory in the meantime. Once Tatsuo gets the governor on the signal, I've got a limited window.

"Tatsuo! You're unhurt?" The governor's relief can't be hidden, even in a voice-only comms relay.

"Not a scratch." Tatsuo's cheeriness, though, is a little thick. "We're coming to meet up with you."

"Good. Once you connect, we'll disable *Thorn* and leave. We can start over elsewhere. I'm afraid the traitors in our midst have led to our ruin."

Tatsuo squirms. "Can you be certain it was traitors? Maybe the Kesek settlers had greater skill than we anticipated."

"Their only skill is in oppressing true believers and inflicting pain on those who oppose them. It's best for us to wipe the dust from our boots and start anew."

The program I'm building for seizing control of my ship comes together well, considering I'm missing one critical piece. I snap my fingers. Tatsuo turns, mouthing *"What?"*

I point to his console, then mine, then back and forth between the two. *Permissions code!* I exaggerate the words, so he can read my lips.

Tatsuo's expression lights up. His hands fly across the controls.

"I can't believe we can just up and walk away, Father," he says. "We've invested so much into this venture—our time, our energy, our money."

"Money is not a worry. I have the first load of varmo root aboard. It's been stockpiled for quite some time, as a hedge against such an emergency. While it will not establish any fortunes, it will be enough for us to regain followers and materiel."

"To what end?" Tatsuo nods at me.

Sure enough, the permissions code appears in the data stream from his console to mine. I grin. That's what I needed. Time to wake up, Blue. He and Scarlet are going to do me a big favor that'll go a long way to their redemption. I package the code inside the program I've built, and watch the communications signal between *Marconi* and *Thorn*. The key is timing, and bandwidth. When they're talking, the most data get exchanged.

"Of course, I'm ready to follow you, Father, but I worry we're leaving too much on the planet," Tatsuo says. "What if they follow us? Or send the Crown Marshals?"

"You needn't worry. No one will follow us, not with the girl as insurance. George Cotes is a cunning man. Keegan should never have made him foreman, no matter his supervisory experience. I suspect the two colluded in my downfall. That no longer matters. If anyone attempts to apprehend us, we simply jettison her."

There's no trace of anger or fear when he says it. The words come across as plainly as if he's reading a navigational forecast clear of asteroids. Cotes starts to rise from his chair, but I shove him down, shaking my head vigorously at the same time. We're gaining on *Marconi*, and I've sent my program along masked behind the ongoing father-and-son chat. Patience.

"We shouldn't do anything hasty," Tatsuo says. "I'm almost to you. Let's talk options."

"I would certainly like to hear them, son, but my mind is made up. We will find financing and support, then use the king's list of former Kesek officers and informants to locate another colony. Restoration cannot be achieved unless those who have sinned undergo true penitence.

And no matter the outcome, the girl will have to pay." He switches off.

"Father? Wait!" Tatsuo tries to re-establish the link. No dice. He stares at me. "Did you get in?"

"The program made it. Now comes the hard part." We're closing fast on *Marconi*. I spin *Thorn* bow over aft end, and set off the mains again, this time decelerating. It's overkill, yeah, for this kind of close-quarters maneuvering. Protocols dictate ion drives for precision. But I figure Cotes is getting antsy.

"We board and take them out," Cotes says. "I've scanned their ship. Eight life signs. Split ourselves up. Chen, you know the ship so—"

"So, I'm in charge." I tap my chest. "Captain."

Cotes grinds his teeth. Really glad he's no longer Kesek. He's probably remembering the old days, when he could lock me away for simply being a Christian—and having too much snark in my arsenal. "Fine. What's our strategy, Captain?"

"Tatsuo, you head for the bridge. Stall Nakano. I'll take out the intercom. Then Cotes and I will clean out the six guards."

"That's not good odds," Tatsuo frets.

"No worries. Cotes is Kesek." I smile. "Besides, I bet we can swim better than they can."

Docking goes smoothly. *Thorn* slides up alongside *Marconi*. Whoever's at the controls of my ship has figured out enough to get the collapsible gangplank airway to match airlocks. The vessels hurtle along, velocities identical, with a 20-meter transparent tube of reinforced polymers linking it. I slip through microgravity like a carp dodging rocks in a stream. Cotes drags Tatsuo along, who's completely bewildered.

You spend enough time in deep space, you experience gravity outages. People like Tatsuo—and the bulk of his Restorationists—live on stations and planets, where those shortages are either rare or nonexistent. Consequently, their zero-gee maneuvering skills are nonexistent.

That'll come in handy.

We line up in the airlock. Artificial gravity exerts its reassuring grip. The outer hatch closes. The inner one opens.

A thickset, balding man with a thick moustache glares at us. "Who are they?"

Tatsuo zaps him with the scrambler. One down.

We drag the guard's limp form into the airlock and secure the hatch. Cotes takes his comm and his weapon.

"Get up to the bridge, Tatsuo." I pop open an access panel. Even the smell of the stale spaces between the bulkheads is comforting. Every odor, every texture is familiar. After almost a week planetside, and outdoors, it's good to have the reassuring feel of *Marconi*'s deck plate under my boots. "I'll get the intercom offline. Keep your dad busy until we get up there."

"On my way." He disappears down the corridor, toward the stairs.

More boots sound on the deck, coming from the hangar bay. Cotes kneels at my side. "Whatever you've got planned, do it quick."

"Working on it." Got to bypass the linkage between the central computer and shipboard comms, which means I need a back door into said computer. That's the whole point of the codes I sent. My wrist comm lights up with a holographic projection of the data I need.

Meantime, I get indicators from Blue and Scarlet. They've

acknowledged my presence aboard ship. Standing by.

The approaching boots hit the loose deck plate in Section Three.

"Activate Fire Suppression in Section Three," I order Scarlet.

There's a sharp hiss. Wisps of white trickle around the corner. A man and a woman in green jumpsuits stagger our, coughing.

Cotes sights them and puts them down, two presses of the firing stud. He doesn't flinch.

Blue trundles out of a vent. Cotes pivots, aiming for the new intruder, but I shove the barrel aside. "Easy. That's my, ah, first officer."

Cotes eyes him. "Are we set?"

"In a sec … yes." The holo shows me the repeater arrays for the shipboard intercom. They're all gray, instead of green. Red would be a malfunction. I switch my wrist comm over, as if to communicate with the bots, and get nothing. Perfect. That means anybody else aboard the ship can't use the repeaters, either, no matter what kind of personal devices they've got. "Okay."

Cotes checks the charge on his scrambler. "That's three. Should be three more guards, plus Nakano and Larissa."

I nod. "Scans showed them at the bridge."

"Show me the layout again."

Without gently reminding him I'm the captain, and thus in charge of this foray, I flick up a tiny map of *Marconi*'s decks. We're on the lower level, behind the hangar bay and sensor arrays. I load the scan data we recorded from *Thorn*. "We can see where everyone was prior to our boarding, but I killed the internal sensors when I shut down the intercom. Didn't want them sneaking a peek at us as we close in."

"Good idea."

We tread carefully to the upper deck. I don't see anyone. Cotes and I crouch beside the greenhouse. Cotes puts his finger to his lips. What's his problem?

Metal clinks. Murmured voices. The sounds seep out of my cabin.

I motion into the greenhouse.

We slip between the vegetation racks just as two guards emerge into the corridor. "Where's Al?"

"No idea. Jackie was on the lower level with him. Said something about meeting Tatsuo."

"That whiny brat. He's too soft for this."

"Whatever. He's talented with the comms. Who else was gonna hide us?"

Their voices cut off as they halt by the hatch to the greenhouse, which I've left open. "Hey. Did you…?"

"No. I closed it when we boarded." I hear a squeak of static. "Blasted intercom's still fried."

"We should go check downstairs."

"Wait." I see a dark-skinned man's head poke into the room. He's two meters away. If he turns 90 degrees right, he'll see…

Eyes widen. "Hey!"

A scrambler's screeching bolt zips overhead, striking him across the shoulder and neck. He flops into his companion, a tall blond guy. The blond yelps and fires—with a gun, a Hunsaker loaded with heavy ordnance. Tomatoes explode in red pulpy mess. Green leaves shred.

He's shooting at Cotes' position. I throw myself into his stomach, grappling for the gun. This is ill-advised, I get it, but my gut reaction is to get the gun away. Occurs to me midway through the wrestling match there's an easier solution.

Don't realize it until the next gunshot rips into my side.

It's excruciating, like holding my body way too close to a plasma torch—which I've done, only this lasts long beyond the point I would have jerked my arm back. Searing, burning.

The guy's strong, but I strain for my wrist-comm. Should have done this earlier.

I enter the command.

Lights go orange. A tinny klaxon moans. And we both float off the floor.

Blondie lets go of his gun, surprised I assume, and grapples for a handhold. Unfortunately for him, I'm the only nearby large object. I swing my feet up, and kick off. We drift apart, him flailing, me somersaulting.

Soon as I complete a spin I zap him with the scrambler.

"You're hurt." Cotes soars to me with the grace of a diver. He rips part of his sleeve and inspects my wound. "It went through, so that's good. Clipped your ribs. Should be an easy fix."

"Fantastic." My teeth grit so hard I think I'll shatter them.

He shoves the cloth against the wound. I could punch him. "Tuck your shirt in. The bleeding should stop soon."

"I think Scarlet has a better bedside manner than you." The blood on my shirt I can ignore. The globules undulating in zero gravity, merging with one another, are harder to overlook.

We leave the stunned guards drifting in the corridor. I spiral toward the bridge hatch. When it opens, and the last guard comes through, Cotes and I take no chances. He gets three scrambler flashes to his torso and arms. He twists in slow counterclockwise circles, eyes lazy, arms akimbo.

"Father! Don't!" Tatsuo's voice is reedy. There's the sound of scuffling.

Cotes and I slip through the hatch like a pair of missiles loaded for firing. It's not good. Larissa writhes in Nakano's grip, aiming a pistol at—Tatsuo. Neither father nor son are having good luck swimming in zero-gee.

"Him?" Nakano glares at me. "You trade your place at my side for an alliance with this interloper? Tatsuo, I've given you everything!"

"Father, let her go!" Tatsuo flails for the back of my command chair.

"Listen to your son, Governor." Cotes lets his momentum carry him into the bridge. He swings his legs up.

I don't know whether the scrambler can immobilize Nakano before he pulls the trigger, At least the gun's pointed at me and not Larissa.

Nakano presses it to her head. Great. I don't believe in jinxing things but… "You will all leave. This ship is mine. It's my recompense for all you've taken."

"Hurt my daughter and I'll take a lot more," Cotes grumbles.

"Easy," I murmur. I swipe a command into my wrist comm. Nakano's writhing too much in the zero gravity for me to get a clean shot. Don't know if Cotes can manage it. Either way Larissa could be killed.

"Nakano, listen: let the girl go, and turn yourself in," I say. "I'll switch the gravity back on. It'll be okay."

"You're worse than Tatsuo," he snarls. "A traitor to your people, to your kin. You help Kesek revolt against us."

"There isn't an us. I'm no Restorationist. If I'm going to have peace in this life, I must take the first steps, otherwise I'm letting the old hate eat me from the inside." I rest my finger on the firing stud. "Let her go."

"No." Nakano fidgets. His grip tightens on the gun.

Larissa remains silent, but she exchanges a look with Cotes. He nods, subtly.

No idea what it means. Time to trust them.

A buzzing builds around us. Ventilation shafts pop open. My brassjackets spill into the bridge, hoverjets hissing, their tiny frames whirling around us like leaves caught in an autumn storm.

Nakano slaps at them, then fires.

The instant his gun is away from Larissa, she breaks free.

I brace myself against Cotes' legs and push. He soars backward, and I race ahead. Tatsuo throws himself across the space, gliding under my chest, shoving Larissa away.

Bullets embed in the bulkheads. My console sparks, spraying crystalline fragments. Nakano's underneath me. He struggles to right his wayward course, and bring the gun to bear.

Good luck with that.

I toggle the gravity back on, and bypass the safety protocols—which means there's no gradual restoration. We all drop like stones. Someone's bones crunch. Tatsuo yells. Larissa slides down the sloped edge of the bridge.

I land on Nakano's back. He cries out, and tries to grab me, or maybe shoot, but since he's lost his gun it does him no good.

"Well, Detective Inspector," I say to Cotes. "Too bad you can't arrest anyone."

Cotes helps Larissa up. They embrace. "This one's your collar, Captain."

Brassjackets flock around the perimeter of the bridge. Blue and Scarlet roll up to the entrance hatch. [Intruders bound,] they message to my wrist comm.

"Welcome back." I give them a salute.

Chapter Eleven

Yancey's stable.

Tanya took me seriously. She and her cohorts raided every medical supply kit until they'd not only extracted the bullet but managed a field transfusion. Med-scanners kept an eye on the nanites.

We got the comms ferry to send its emergency call, complete with my data report. Five days later, a Rescue Operations frigate shifts into the Sylvanak system. Beautiful big ship, white with blue trim, carrying a huge sickbay and top-level staff.

A pair of shiny barges are at the landing field to take the Restorationists away, as well as get Yancey up to that sickbay. The captain shakes my hand. He's in his forties, tall, broad-shouldered, with red hair that's got a few streaks of silver.

"I'm impressed, Captain Chen. These aren't the kind of people I would have bent over backwards to help."

"Had to be done, sir." I straighten up, trying to match his posture. Not easy. "The rain falls on the good and the bad all the same, as it's said."

"Outstanding." He smiles. "I'll get Lucinda to patch up your friend."

"Their friend."

"And we'll escort you out of the system when you're ready. The Charter Office has reps coming this way to investigate the colony. Between our ships we should get them back on their feet."

"Thanks for that."

"Thank you for standing up when you didn't have to." He claps me on the shoulder and heads back to the barge.

"Who was that?" Cotes approaches.

I shrug. "Nametag was something old French."

"Think I might have seen him on old Kesek bulletins." Cotes faces me. "Chen—Vincent, I can't say it enough..."

"Then don't. One thank-you was plenty. You guys have a lot of work to do to recover. No sense wasting time on me. Besides, I've got to get back to hopping between stars."

"If you're ever this way again, stop by. We owe you our families' lives."

"*Nǎ lǐ nǎ lǐ*. Not at all. I owe you my life, so that makes us even."

We shake hands. "Godspeed, Cotes," I add.

There's no apologies to be had. Not anymore. We've come to grips with our pasts.

I watch as Tatsuo is herded aboard a barge, with other green-uniformed Restorationists. I hope he does, too.

Three days later, *Marconi* shifts out of the Sylvanak star system. By then, thoughts of Uncle Ethan subside, leaving me with fonder memories of family. The pain's still there, but it's manageable.

I unstrap from the bridge, and head out to the spine where the comms ferries are docked. Four spheres, like eggs, awaiting deployment. My job to get them in place, so people separated by impossible distances can speak together.

I think about Cotes' family, and Governor Nakano's.

Sometimes those impossible distances can be bridged.

Book 2

Cryptic Commands

Watch your back...

Vincent Chen makes sure his comms ferry satellites don't harbor malfunctions.

He'd prefer they didn't hide people inside, too.

The woman left comatose aboard one he recovers is on a vital mission. She must stop criminals from stealing classified secrets and selling them to the highest bidder.

But those criminals know she's on the run, and Vincent is caught up in the chase.

Determined they stay silent, she's left him only one choice: to seek help from his fellow comms jockeys, in hopes theycan fend off a raid and keep the data safe.

When their plans fall apart, Vincent must rely on others when he'd rather be on his own.

And trusting anyone is dangerous...

The Realm of Five
circa 2614
Starkweather
Nova Tempus
Akaiyama
Changbu
Earth
Second Harbor
Shacheng
Tiaozhan
Rozsada
Eventyr
Horizon
Xiaoji
Saarbrucken
Oportunidad
Prachtig
Muhterem
Pryzemsl
Akridge
Zuri
Bethel
Liberty
Arapaho
Ilosc
Gurjarpuri
al-Qamar
Serhat
Southcrown
Whelanport
Primary trade routes (the Tiaozhan path)
Secondary trade routes

Kapteyn
The Realm of Five
Saarbrucken Region
circa 2613
To Tiaozhan
1 Tract Shift
Shacheng
Tersane
Oportunidad
Saarbrucken
Muhterem
Altair
To Arapaho
1 Tract Shift
Primary trade routes (the Tiaozhan path)
Secondary trade routes

Chapter One

01 November 2613
Tersane Star System

Unauthorized biological presence.

That is the last thing I want my ship's sensors to warn me about.

Maybe not the absolute last thing. Singularity destabilization would be worse, especially in those fleeting seconds before the Raszewski drive bends space-time so that *RMS Marconi* can blink across light-years. Getting myself stuck between two points in space simultaneously rates low on the list.

But *Declaration*-Class comms ferry tenders are well-maintained machines, what with a couple dozen hamster robots roving their autonomous selves into every niche, into every access tunnel, into every storage space. The backups have backups. If things became especially dire, the ship's navigation computer could park my command around the nearest comms ferry and send a distress signal.

So, I'm understandably relieved when *Marconi* clarifies the original warning. The biological presence is aboard Comms Ferry 550, the one I'm close to intercepting.

Tersane is a dull orange star, not worth much to its surrounding system in terms of heat or other radiation. What it does offer is not one but three touch tracts leading to three different star systems, each of which harbor anything from scattered settlements to major manufacturing centers.

I queue up the visual feed from *Marconi*'s sensors, so I can get a good look at 550's exterior even as I parse the data from the scans. There's not much to see at the moment, except for the glare from the anti-matter mains. I've got the engines firing opposite my direction of travel, decelerating toward the ferry's position. I'll have to cut thrust soon, so as not to damage the ferry with the super-accelerated particles streaming from the drive nozzles.

There's enough data unimpeded by the radiation blasting out of *Marconi*'s backside to confirm the initial scans: a bio sign. With all the interference, though, I can't get more specific.

"Perfect," I mutter. "Guess I'm going for a spacewalk."

550 is due for replacement after a decade on station. It's one of three comms ferries orbiting Tersane, and MarkTel likes to stagger these tasks so multiples in one system never go offline at the same time.

As soon as *Marconi*'s velocity drops below a few dozen kilometers per second, I kill the main drives and kick on the ion drives. Mains are good for brute force acceleration; it's the ions you want if you need to fine-tune your course and make precision maneuvers.

Nothing appears amiss with 550. Nav reconstructs a holographic image derived from the sensors. It's a silvery sphere, burnished bronze in swatches facing the star. I instruct the sensors to run a more detailed analysis while I query the ferry for an update. *Marconi* is only 40,000 kilometers away, so I get the response in less than a second.

Hmm. The readout spills down the spherical surface of the bridge, which has my command seat plunked in the middle. Numbers and words skitter, filling a good quarter of the starry field *Marconi*'s sensors paint across the surface. No major glitches. Limited malfunctions. A record of every tract shift 550 made during its service, complete with transmissions sent and received…

Hang on.

There's one filed under Code 77A. Hatch Access.

"You've got to be kidding." I'm well aware that, as captain and sole Interstellar Communications Ferry Deployment & Maintenance Specialist aboard, no one is listening. Except maybe the bots, and their audio pickup isn't the best. "That's my job."

I double check. No other comms ferry tender has made a scheduled stop. Nor should they. MarkTel doesn't accidentally book two tenders to check on the same ferry.

So, either the Code 77A is an error, or the hatch suffered a malfunction…

Or someone opened it.

It takes a good ten minutes more to close the remaining distance, until *Marconi* slides alongside 550, a handful of kilometers away. Sensors are certain—there's a bio sign inside. And it's weak, without discernable form.

Marconi is in station-keeping mode, using thrusters to keep it steady. I'm on my way to the airlock on the lower deck, not far from where the skipjack shuttlecraft is docked. I pass a pair of hamster autonomous robots hard at work replacing a buckled deck plate. They're silver bugs, albeit the size of my boot, with stubby antennae and pincers, the latter of which are handy for repairs. One of the two has a blue stripe along his side. He stops what he's doing and wheels after me, like a loyal pup.

My wrist comm blinks a message at the same time lights flicker across his silver shell. [Destination?]

"Heading outside to see what kind of critter snuck its way onto 550," I say as I clamber into the spacesuit.

Blue doesn't respond, waiting as I make certain the seals of the orange suit are secure, and the white ceramic plating is in place. Finally, he repeats his inquiry. I swipe the response, [Extravehicular inspection.] Then I add, [Standard protocol.]

Blue wheels away, flashing instructions at his partner, who's still busy at repairs. He'll relay the message to the other 14 hamsters aboard, plus the eight brassjackets that hover about the maintenance spaces. Anything goes wrong, they'll work in conjunction with *Marconi*'s computer to make sure I'm safe and the mission continues.

It'd be a lot easier if there was another person aboard. But people are expensive.

As soon as the airlock lights cycle from red to white-blue, and gravity dissipates, I trigger the outer hatch and drift into space. The first few seconds are always disorienting. I pick one star—any star will do—and focus on it and it alone. Running a section from Luke's gospel helps narrow that focus. I've been reading the whole chapter, so it's the easiest bit to recall.

550 spins in front of the Tersane star, a gleaming pearl against a ruddy disc. My suit's HUD gets an update from *Marconi*'s sensors, while the visor darkens against the harsh glow from the sun. Tiny thrusters on the suit's back and shoulders propel me toward the comms ferry, as I pinpoint the hatch's location.

Quick bursts from the shoulder jets slow my approach enough I can get a grip on the handles inset in the ferry's hull, just outside the hatch. It doesn't appear anyone's physically tampered with its locking mechanism; that leaves software intrusion.

The compartment inside is spare, with a few sealed lockers on one side and a diagnostics screen on the other. It's lit up pale blue.

Makes the spacesuited figure a teal statue.

My heart rate rockets so bad sensors warn me it's elevated. No kidding! There's a person floating *inside* 550!

I pull the scrambler attached to my midsection. It's a stubby gray weapon, vibrating with an energy charge that, when fired, will shut down the voluntary nervous system. Makes the average person as limp as a piece of unpowered memory fabric.

But the person—body—whatever doesn't move. The sensor rod affixed to my suit's right wrist informs me that her vital signs are far too low for a person in good health, yet simple scans can't find a cause.

Her. Yeah, it's a woman. That much is evident from the shape of her suit. Probably my height, which is to say, not tall.

I spool a signal across the general citizens' communication band. "Miss?" Or is it, ma'am? What's the protocol for polite public speech to an unidentified woman hiding inside a piece of MarkTel communications equipment with a value well over a half million? "Miss, are you hurt? I have to inform you you're trespassing on MarkTel property."

That's me, Vincent Chen, consummate gentleman.

I pull myself inside the compartment. The visor's interior rim glows with soft orange lights. Her face is serene, as if she's enjoying the most peaceful nap in the galaxy, but there's a waxy quality to her skin that doesn't look healthy.

The sensors bring back more results: blood pressure low; heart rate low too, but steady; body temp below normal; brain activity minimal.

She reads like she's in stasis, yet I've never heard of anyone this deep in hibernation just hanging around in a suit. It's the kind of state you'd need a full-fledged chamber to achieve.

Whatever her state, I can't leave her here. First, though, I interrogate the onboard screen. There's no sign of malfunction, but it confirms the Code 77A I received during the initial query.

Wait a microsec. This is new: a command sent from *outside*, triggering the hatch release. It's the same MarkTel code I used to gain access. Except the logs also confirm there was no MarkTel ship in the vicinity.

So, this lady got dropped off on 550 without her vessel being seen?

I shake my head. There will be time to dig deeper beneath the records after I'm back aboard *Marconi*. For the moment, I have a patient who needs recovery.

A clarification: I am not a medic.

MarkTel makes sure all its comms ferry jockeys have basic med training, so they can render aid in situations such as this. It also helps when a jockey is injured or ill by cutting down on time needed at a station-borne recovery center.

Why interrupt the comms ferry deployment schedule if you can keep going, right?

There's no sickbay aboard *Marconi*, so I do what my bots have done with me when I was in dire medical need—lay her on my bed. I'm thankful I recently changed the sheets and cleaned the mattress; who knows how bad my body odor had made it? When you're the only human aboard a ship otherwise crewed by two dozen robots, personal hygiene doesn't come up often in conversation.

Which is good, because if I had all two-dozen nagging me, I'd be dismantling a lot of CPUs.

Blue and his partner, Scarlet—the hamster with the red stripe on its flanks—wheel into my cabin with a bundle of medical sensors from storage. I've already got a scanner out, from the med-kit that resides under my bunk. There's no foreign chemicals or gases in the woman's suit, so I unlatch her helmet. There's a faint *click*, followed by a *hiss* as air pressures equalize.

First thing I notice is cinnamon. It's barely there and gone so fast I figure I imagined it. I mean, she should smell pretty bad being locked inside that suit, even if it was for a couple days. Because that's what the med-scanner tells me—her condition is at least 72 hours old.

She's got a mix of Indian and Southeast Asian features. Malaysian, perhaps? But no delver, no wrist comm, no ID holo, nothing to verify who she is. Her hair is jet black, shining with violets and greens under my cabin's overhead lights, and tied up behind her neck. Short nose, soft lips barely parted…

I blink a couple times. *Jiāodiǎn*. Focus, Vincent. It's not like you've never seen a woman before.

Well, no, but the last time I'd been this close to one was when a supervisor yelled at me for unauthorized modifications to *Marconi*'s bulkheads. I'd painted them. Who wants to stare at monochrome surfaces for weeks on end?

She didn't like the handwoven rugs that replaced them either.

Scarlet nudges my boots. She's got an intravenous solution and monitor ready.

"Right. Thanks." I let Scarlet hook the IV to the woman's veins—on her wrist, after I've removed a glove—while I fasten the monitor to the bulkhead shelves behind the bed. It unfolds like a mechanical flower, spreading sensor petals over my patient. A hologram of her internal and external workings, rendered in multi-color wireframe, floats nearby, in one-tenth scale.

That's odd. She's showing signs of her vitals coming around. Without outside influence?

The monitor beeps. Nanites. More specifically, nano-surgeons, microscopic robots flitting around in her bloodstream and elsewhere in her body.

"Not cheap," I murmur. She must have one nova of a health ranking. Even on my Rank Four, courtesy of MarkTel, I'd have trouble scraping together the finances for a continuous nano-surgeon presence. Granted, those were only allowed for hazardous situations.

Her eyes flutter open.

I was expecting them to be dark, not a dusty blue flecked with green.

They're unfocused, the eyelids fluttering.

Her heart rate spikes.

The monitor deploys a slender, spidery arm toward her shoulder. A subspray glistens.

"Hold on." I tap a command into the wrist comm, and the arm freezes. "Let's not introduce anything into her system while the nanos are at work."

It takes a couple seconds, but her pulse slows to a level that doesn't make the monitor panic. The woman's arms twitches. Reaches out for—the sides of the bed? Or a hand to hold?

"Miss?" I keep my voice low, and calm. "Miss, I'm Captain Vincent Chen. You're aboard my ship. Can you hear me?"

She isn't looking at me, or even the ceiling. I have a feeling she can't see much of anything. Words spill from her lips, but they're jumbled, nonsensical phrases made up of at least three languages.

Suddenly, she goes slack as a bot with a failed charge.

"Miss? Miss!" I grab her arm.

She's off the bed in an instant, spacesuit and all, with my forearm caught in a grip that makes a hamster's pincers seem as tough as the rehydrated noodles I had for supper. My brain registers the change in horizon—specifically, when the bulkhead becomes the ceiling.

I slam onto the deck plates, air *whooshing* from my lungs.

She comes down at me, arm drawn back for a punch. I roll out of the path. Her fist smashes where my face should have been, making her scream.

I tackle her against the bed, shoulder and forearm shoved up under her neck. Where's my scrambler? Having the stun weapon would make subduing this maniac a lot easier, but it's attached to my spacesuit's belt, and the spacesuit is down in the airlock on the deck below. Because I'm clever like that.

Can't blame the absent-mindedness. Why would I think I'd need a stun weapon available for use on a comatose woman?

Except she was now far from comatose. She brings a leg up at an angle I'd have figured was impossible, except it cracks across my upper back. The blow loosens my grip enough she wriggles free, but it also gives me room to get the blazes out of there. I scoot backward and stagger upright.

"Hey. Hey! Calm down! I don't want to injure you! You need medical attention—"

She dives for me.

I slip aside and grab her spacesuit as she hurtles past. I throw her onto the bed, face first, and slap at the [Resume] command tab still flashing on my wrist comm.

The monitor's inspection arm jabs down with the subspray. It sputters against her neck, below the hairline.

She groans. The fight leaves her body as quickly as a skipjack ejecting from its docking cradle. She tries to get up, but she only possesses enough strength to roll onto her side.

I hold her shoulders. "Take it easy. I'm not going to hurt you. You're safe."

"Safe." It's the first thing she says that I understand. Her eyes roll up, exposing the bright white sclera.

Great. I didn't want her to pass out. "Hey." I gently rock her shoulders. "Who are you?"

"Izzy." She locks her gaze with mine, and seems—puzzled? Disoriented? "You're… a captain?"

You bet I am. "Captain Vincent Chen, *RMS Marconi*." I have a feeling my posture improves by a couple centimeters. Which says something about my bravado, considering this patient just tried to assault me. Correction, *assaulted* me.

"Then… I got out?"

"Out of the comms ferry I'm supposed to replace? Yes. So, you'll have to tell me what you were doing inside one. That's illegal."

"I know. It was … the best way I could think to escape."

"Escape. From space?" That close to a sun, hiding inside a comms ferry's armored shell would be a decent idea. It would not keep all the hazardous radiation out, but it was better than floating in the void in a spacesuit for days on end.

"From the people trying to kill me."

Her head lolls against the pillow. She looks so peaceful, serene, even angelic.

Until she starts to snore. And drool.

I chuckle. Man, Vincent. A few weeks in space without human

contact and you go all weak-kneed at the sight of the first lady to cross your path. Albeit, beautiful lady.

Who showed up inside a restricted satellite in the middle of nowhere.

I instruct Blue and Scarlet to remove her spacesuit—after I've checked the med scans and they've confirmed she's got clothing underneath. They also restrain her, so she doesn't go wandering about the ship. It'll be another few hours before she wakes up,

Meanwhile, I'd better dig out the cot from storage, the one meant for long-term planetside trips.

I'm bunking in the greenhouse for the foreseeable future.

Chapter Two

Replacing Comms Ferry 550 is a lot simpler than dealing with my passenger-slash-patient.

It's a matter of instructing 550 to jet out of its programmed location, using thrusters to boost toward *Marconi*, while I detach ferry 810 from the central spar.

I'm leaned back in my command chair, at the heart of *Marconi*'s spherical bridge. Nav gives me all the course projections I'd ever need, and then some, with purple and green lines slicing across breathtaking views of the surrounding space. Tersane fills a huge circle in one corner, framed by sensor readouts that warn of possible flare and sunspot activity. This star's fairly stable, so I'm not too concerned.

As soon as 810 clears the clamps adhering it to *Marconi*'s spar, ion thrusters embedded across its hull push it toward its destination. Space being space, it's not as if it just parks there and sits still. No, gravity and its own momentum will remain forces it has to constantly dance around. The thrusters will keep 810 in approximately the region it needs to inhabit. Fortunately, the touch tract in which we're parked is large enough—several hundreds of kilometers across—that it doesn't have to be precise.

There's been recorded incidents of comms ferries colliding with incoming starships. The results are—unpleasant. Two objects merging when space-time connects their coordinates? You don't want to think too hard about what it looks like.

But there's only been a handful of incidents over more than four centuries of interstellar travel. So, even if an occasional tramp six-brace or cargo navastel comes blinking through the so-called "sundoor," it'll know whereabouts 810 lives.

The comms ferries pass each other en route to their respective destinations, sending electronic pings to confirm distance, velocity, and trajectory. My palms are slick with sweat. I've got commands input into the control console, waiting for 550 to arrow for its docking cradle. I'd be happier if 809 weren't sitting there on the starboard side of *Marconi*'s hull. Last thing I'd need is a collision.

But 550 slows with a last-minute burst from its ion thrusters, reducing its forward velocity to only a few meters per second. That'll work. I send out the grapples, which show up as one, two, three, four white lines linking the ship to the comms ferry. They flash green, in rapid succession.

A few seconds later, there's a tremor through the deck plates, right up into the sides of my chair. Contact. Ferry secured.

I blow out a breath and toss off a prayer of thanks. You'd think I'd get used to recovery and deployment. Nope. Something could always go wrong. Something usually does, so I'm especially happy with this outcome.

Blue and Scarlet roll through the open bridge hatch. [Cleaning and maintenance?] Blue asks.

I hit [Standby] on my wrist comm. Standard protocol is to send the hamsters aboard the recovered ferry, to check for problems, but for one thing, I've already been aboard.

For another, I want to be there in person to figure out how this Izzy lady got into my comms ferry.

[Patient is awake,] Scarlet sends.

"Thanks." I unstrap from my chair and head through the hatch.

The living quarters aboard *Marconi* aren't anything to signal base about. A short corridor leads down the port side, with compartments to the left, and a hatch to the Raszewski sphere ahead. Engineering and Fuel Reserves lay beyond that. My cabin, where I've got the patient secured and recovering, is right behind the bridge. There's a greenhouse next, where verdant shades lend startling color to what's otherwise a very gray affair.

Well, except for my rugs. Brilliant oranges of a sunset, the earthy tones of an eagle in flight. They add needed variety of texture to the bulkheads, right next to a single table with two chairs. I brush my knuckles across the handwoven wool as I pass.

The woman—Izzy, I remind myself—stares at the ceiling. She's wearing the clothing that she had on under her spacesuit—dark blue leggings, matching tank top. As soon as my boots cross the threshold into the cabin, she turns her head. "Captain."

"Sorry about the restraints." I stand nearby, arms folded. "You weren't in the calmest of moods."

"And for that I apologize." Her voice is matter-of-fact, with little inflection, but there's a hit of musicality behind the tones. I wonder how well she can sing… "I was disoriented when I came out of sleep."

"Let's talk about that." I undo the straps and help her sit up.

Her arms tremble. "Water?"

"Of course." I pull a bottle from the shelf and hand over a packet of dried fruit.

"Thanks. I didn't think I'd be so hungry." She swallows water and rips open the bag. Half the contents disappear.

"You're welcome." I keep my stance easy, nonchalant, but you'd better believe the scrambler's in place at my right hip. It's a comforting weight; I'm not in the mood to get banged around the deck plates of my own cabin again. "Maybe you'd better start at the top."

"Unfortunately, there's not a lot I can tell you, because of its classified nature."

"Classified. Your hitchhiking qualifies as a Crown offense, Miss… Izzy."

She smiles. "Operative Isabella Sayro."

Operative. "Employed by—?"

"An intelligence gathering organization. That's all I'm at liberty to divulge."

That certainly explains how she went from unconscious to kicking me like an empty food pack in a couple of seconds. "I'm sorry, you're a spy?"

"The preferred term is field operative."

"I don't suppose field operatives carry credentials."

"Not when they're infiltrating enemy organizations. You must understand, Captain, that I can't say anything more about the details of the operations. Not until I contact my superiors."

"Okay." Have to say, this is *not* covered in the MarkTel regs. Picking up stranded travelers? Yes. Spies hidden inside a comms ferry? No. "Let's restart the data download. How did you wind up inside my comms ferry?"

"Much as you did when you came across and found me," she says. "I drifted."

"And opened a hatch that's secured by MarkTel access codes."

"Which I possess."

My eyes widen. So much for trying to play it cool. "Are you serious? They don't hand those out. Blast, they don't even give them to the station-side techs unless there's permission from higher up!"

"I understand this is perplexing for you, Captain, but the free-ranging nature of my work necessitates I have access to things most people don't."

Heat floods my face. Well, she has a point. I wish I thought of it before sounding like a first-trip rookie. "I guess that's possible but listen: I can't just let you wander about my ship when I don't have a clue who you really are. I'm requesting you stay put in my cabin until we reach port."

If that's a problem, she doesn't show it. A slight shrug is all I get. "If I were you, that's what I'd do to maintain security aboard ship."

"Good. So, there's food in the shelves, and the bathroom's in the corner. If you want fresh eats, I'll be harvesting from the greenhouse later today."

She glances to the left. A long, broad window opens from my cabin into the greenhouse. Better than having a display screen of scenery or even, if I had the money, a physical painting. "Is that standard for *Declaration*-Class?"

"Yeah, but I've expanded it considerably in my spare—" Her statement fully registers. "Wait a microsec. You know what kind of ship this is?"

"I'm passingly familiar with stories about them." She points to the ceiling. "This cabin seems the right dimensions, if I remember the schematics. There's a galley, too?"

"If by galley, you mean a closet-sized room with a food processor and a sink, yes."

"I forgot about that." She smiles. "Two chairs for a one-man crew, correct?"

Right. My least favorite design feature. For a guy who wanted to so badly to get away from home and the memories associated with it, I'd sure gotten mopey about being on my own. Seriously going to have to send a commnote in to the techs about that one. "It'll be nice to share a meal for once."

Did I just say that aloud? Izzy's smile broadens. Yes, yes, I did. Can't help but grin, even if I'm as sheepish about it as a student hoping for a dance. "Something from the greenhouse will be nice, thank you."

"Sure." I jerk a thumb over my shoulder. "I've got to go check on ferry 810, make sure it's ready for its test transit and transmissions."

"Of course. I'll leave you to it, Captain. But first—when do you expect us to make the nearest port?"

"All goes well, we'll transit in an hour to Saarbrucken, then it's part of a day to my repair rendezvous. Quick trip."

"I see." She stands up. Her right leg wobbles, then buckles.

I swoop in, arm instinctively around her waist. I slip my shoulder under her right arm. "Get your bearings first, Operative."

"I forget being brought back up by the nano-surgeons isn't something my body responds to well." The color's drained from her cheeks.

"Have to say, I was surprised to see them in your system. Monitor shows they're all disintegrated now."

"Yes, they're effective when we need to go to ground—so to speak." She straightens. Her leg isn't shaking anymore. "I think I'm okay."

"Sure. Perfect." I let her go, trying to ignore the fact that she doesn't smell like the solvents, plastics, and body odor that usually make up *Marconi*'s aromatic mix. She's more like the greenhouse, with a hint of perfume.

Vincent, focus, please.

I palm the latch on a closet and rummage for an extra black jumpsuit. "This is one of mine, but it should, ah, fit okay. If you want something more utilitarian."

"I appreciate that. Oh, and Captain? If you haven't already, please keep my presence secret. I'm afraid the people looking for me would not take kindly to my continued survival."

Oh. Right. She did say someone was trying to kill her. I'd marked it up to her being addled from her sleep state. Apparently not. "You're really being hunted?"

She shrugs into the jumpsuit. "Hazard of the occupation, as you can imagine."

"Yeah, I can. Protocol dictates a signal to the Rescue Ops frequency, and another to MarkTel, so emergency services are available but—" I scratch the back of my neck. "You must be worried about someone intercepting the call."

She nods. For all her fighting prowess earlier, she looks far more vulnerable wearing a somewhat baggy version of my jumpsuit. "Please. Let me sort this out. As soon as we reach your port of call, you can contact whomever you must."

It feels like a bad idea, except—she was hiding inside that comms ferry from someone. And she's got military training. It was dumb luck and her own bewilderment that let me best her. That, of course, and a paused monitor waiting to inject somebody with a sedative.

I've already recorded a report of what happen so far. If anything happens, I can dump that. But she's got no weapons. And no access to her suit, which is stowed in the same locker where I keep mine by the lower deck's airlock. "Okay, I'll hold off. But you're going to have to trust me to keep you safe. I'm used to working solo."

"Except for your stalwart crew." She lifts her chin.

What? Blue and Scarlet wait patiently outside the hatch. And they're joined by a couple more hamsters, plus three brassjackets, the latter of which bob on tiny hoverjets like diaphanous, spindly insects. "Really, guys?" I swipe the command, [Return to next tasks.] They scatter like children caught eavesdropping on a grown-up conversation. Which, to a degree, they are.

Izzy chuckles. There's that musical sound I'd wondered about. "I'll wait here, Captain. Feel free to lock the hatch if you need to."

Oh, I will. Not that there's anything in the room she can use besides food and clothing. I've got my delver tucked by my command chair on the bridge. My Bible, though, rests on the shelf above the bed.

She catches me staring at it. She looks as surprised as I must have when she said she's an intelligence operative. "Oh, my. Is it—real?"

"Sure is."

"I don't have anything printed." Her fingers caress the beat-up cover. "Let alone a Text-in-Violation."

"It's not anymore."

"Of course. Old habit. I was only finishing secondary school when the ban was lifted, and the Charter of Tolerance dissolved."

"Yeah, me, too."

"Tiaozhan? Your accent suggests it. Plus, the way you walk."

I had no idea there was a Tiaozhanese walk. "That's right. You?"

"Here and there."

Come on, Vincent. She's a spy. You're not going to get data from her like you would sniffing for her square on the Reach. Speaking of which… "Right, so, I'd better take care of the ferry."

"Yes. Certainly." She picks up the Bible. "If you don't mind—"

"Not at all." I close the hatch and head for the bridge. Stop. I turn back, and lock the hatch, before retracing my steps.

Comms Ferry 810 performs admirably.

With five seconds counting until it shifts, I make the sign of the cross. Can't hurt.

The image of 810 flashes blue-white and disappears. Nothing but stars on a black background, hanging like my rugs in the corridor.

A timer starts up, red numbers flickering on the screen next to 810's coordinates. Fifteen minutes until it returns.

This is a blank trip, as we jockeys call it—a test run to make sure the Raszewski drive works in the wild. Bonus? 810 didn't explode. I've only seen it three times in my entire four-year career. Those cost money. Not my money, but the more malfunctions you experience, the worse your reputation.

Since I've got the time, I head downstairs to the lower deck and open the spacesuit locker. Izzy's—Operative Sayro's—suit hangs next to mine. The sensor sweep came up clean, but I figure a second inspection can't hurt.

There's nothing to be found, not a weapon, or a delver with encrypted information. Not even an ID readout. The suit's label has been ripped free. There was a nametag at some point.

Something's stuck in the sleeve lining, on the inside layer. A ring. It's slender, only a millimeter, red with silver slashes. A pale yellow light pulses on it.

I drag the arm of my suit out, with its sensor rod attached, and let the device scan the ring.

That gets me an instant flood of data. Transferred to my delver on the bridge, according to the wrist comm. I request the data be displayed here rather than trekking upstairs again.

Operative Sayro's face fills the tiny screen. Isabella Sayro, age 27, Intelligence Service of the Realm.

Sweet nova. She's ISR? I didn't even know they still ran. There were rumors they'd been disbanded long ago, when the Realm of Five's secret police controlled everything. Thinking about Kesek makes my stomach clench. When the Royal Stability Force or *Koninklijke stabiliteitskracht* as they were officially branded made it their business to outlaw all religion—and the written materials thereof—Christians like my family had no choice but to worship underground. Kesek had insinuated itself into all levels of power in the Realm, pushing everyone aside until they'd tried to overthrow King Andrew II himself and arrest Congress.

That had failed. And organizations like the Crown Marshals and Rescue Operations became the public face of a new, freer Realm.

But apparently, ISR got its marching papers back, too.

Why carry around this ring? It'd be dangerous if she were, in fact, running undercover. Of course, she'd have to have some way to prove her identity if she needed help.

She said no credentials, however. Maybe this was something she wanted kept secret.

A warning indicator flashed on my wrist comm. Four minutes until

810's scheduled return. Good. The sooner I got this job over and us gone, the better.

I'm up the stairs and into the corridor outside my cabin in a flash. Nav sends me a second alert—tract shift.

Must be an error in the notifications. The red timer digits are clear: three minutes, thirty seconds remaining, and the space where 810 should be is blank.

But that's what the sensors are concerned about. A pale yellow indicator appears on the great, curving screen at the sundoor to Kapteyn, where comms ferry 551 sits. Unidentified vessel. Sensors can't pin down a hull registry, and it isn't broadcasting a transponder. That's bad. Only kind of starships running unmarked like that are pirates, and the odd smuggler.

It accelerates away from the tract shift at blistering gravities—44, according to the sensors. There's no mistaking the trajectory. Nav draws a purple arc heading straight for us.

I spool up a signal on the citizen's band and copy it onto the channel reserved for MarkTel communications. No way they can ignore it. "This is *RMS Marconi*, on MarkTel comms ferry repair and replacement, Vincent Chen commanding. State your intentions."

Sounds pretty authoritative. Wish I had my Bible stuffed into the side of my seat, instead of—

"They found me?"

Izzy's voice sounds so clear and so undistorted by the intercom that she could be over my shoulder. That's what I think, until her breath brushes my scalp.

Blast. She *is* over my shoulder!

I spin the chair. "How'd you get out of my cabin?"

She's staring at the approaching ship. "You have to get us out of here, before they blast this ship to pieces."

"Lady, spy or not, I'm not taking orders from—"

That's when a red diamond flashes out from the yellow marker for the unnamed vessel.

Missile inbound.

Chapter Three

Twenty-one minutes.

I have that long to figure out what we're going to do before the missile gets here.

It would have been nice if the intruder had at least sent a response to my message before trying to blow up my ship. When you're talking tens of million kilometers away, it takes nearly two minutes for a signal to travel the distance.

"Maximum thrust," Izzy says.

I've almost forgotten she's here, preoccupied as I am with flashing red lights and a grating klaxon. Once I've killed all the obnoxious reminders, I glare behind me. "Get off the bridge and back to my cabin! You're gonna want to strap in, too. This is bound to get rough, compensators or no compensators."

"You can't outrun them." She reaches for a graphic, expands it so she can better read the data cascading beside the intruder ship's marker—which Nav has helpfully relabeled with a red triangle, now that's shown itself to be decidedly unfriendly. "Your maximum acceleration barely tops 25 gravities."

"Stop touching." I brush her arm aside. She isn't wrong, though. With the intruder doing 44 and me able to nurse *maybe* 27 out of *Marconi* if I'm willing to rough up the main drive nozzles, we're still in a vulnerable position.

Of course, even if I stay put and don't light the mains, it'll take our new best friend several hours to reach our position. Which begs the question—why bother? Why would they destroy us and chase us down? All that'd be left is an expanding cloud of free-floating particles and our constituent atoms. Maybe a big hull fragment or two.

I stare at the approaching red diamond that is the missile. One assumes that missile is the destroying kind…

"Stop sitting there and do something, or I will!" Izzy snaps.

"Relax," I say, my palms sweating and my heart pounding. I trigger *Marconi*'s ion drives, so we can move clear of the region in which 810 is supposed to return. There's no need to foul up its station when we get out of here. At the same time, I call up a miniature hologram of *Marconi*. Not the most graceful-looking of vessels, with two comms ferries dangling from the bow spar and bulging engines situated behind its own Raszewski sphere, but the long, slender cooling vanes do lend it a semblance of artistry.

"What sort of countermeasures do you carry?"

"The basics—sandcaster canisters, point defense laser turret."

Izzy sighs. "Might as well be a luxury yacht."

"I'd have to improve the menu first and add another bed." Time check: eighteen minutes. I eject a quartet of sandcasters, sending them hurtling along the missile's trajectory. Each one's only moving a few dozen kilometers per second, but then they explode, showering purple sparks in broadening clouds. "Besides, I don't think we have to worry about our imminent destruction. That missile isn't putting our nearly enough radiation to be anti-matter or even x-ray boosted."

"Then it's—?"

"Disabler warhead. Not comforting."

Izzy nods. "They want us alive."

"Well, I'm going to take a wild guess and assume they want *you* alive, not me," I mutter. "Speaking of which, I thought you said these people wanted to kill you?"

"They do. But they need information first. I imagine my death will be slow and delayed."

Seeing her standing beside me, face bathed in the rainbow glow of the tracking and sensor displays, I feel the urge to put myself between her and whatever danger's coming my way. Pretty heroic, as far as gut responses go.

Of course, my guts will get equally fried along with every bit of matter aboard my ship if we don't get out of here.

There's a burst of light from the displays, and for a single, startling moment I assume the missile's exploded. But it's too far out, still burning through space for us, and the cloud of sand that will hopefully shred it to pieces. *Marconi* registers the arrival of 810 on its return trip with zero fanfare, and dutifully shows me the distance between us as the ions push us away from the comms ferry.

"Standby." I gesture behind me. "I'd strap yourself into the galley chair. Safest place when we make the tract shift."

"What are you doing?"

"Sending a distress signal." I spool it up and reach for the panel that will activate the recording. "My bosses and especially the Crown Marshals are going to want to know about this."

"No." Izzy catches my wrist. Her nails dig into the skin. It's been a very long time since a girl held my hand, and if memory serves, it was a nicer sensation. "You can't tell anyone I'm here. Any contact will jeopardize my mission."

"I'm more worried about jeopardizing our lives." I pull my wrist free, but it takes more doing that I'd planned for. She'd got a good grip. "How else am I going to explain your presence when we make station? Besides, I'm more concerned about the armed vessel trying to blow us up than your mission."

"Captain, please." She drops the Bible into my lap. "Some things are worth pursuing with the utmost diligence. Like the truth."

Was she seriously trying to guilt me into keeping my mouth shut about recovering her? Granted, I'd already agreed to do so, but us being under attack altered the equation. I tap the panel to start the distress call—

And get an earful of howling, grating interference as a reward.

"What is it?" Izzy claps her hands to her ears.

"Jamming! Prevents us from getting any signals out!" I holler over the din. Where's the cutoff? There. The obnoxious sound dies. My head's still buzzing.

"I should have anticipated such a tactic. It keeps us from calling for help."

"Handy for them." And for Izzy, too. She doesn't have to wring her hands about me accidentally letting her identity slip. Which I wouldn't. But I can't fault her for being paranoid.

I pivot the chair. A control board containing four orange switches dangles from an actuator arm. I flip them with a side swipe. In return, *Marconi*'s miniature hologram sprouts four sets of hair-thin lines. Each one is a spar made of ExForm molecules, loose and wriggly to start with but solidifying as soon as I run power from the Raszewski sphere through them. Another timer starts up—because apparently, I can't have enough of those—right next to a lever pulsing with blue light. "Again, strap in."

She hesitates, then touches my shoulder. The sensation flees as she jogs down the corridor.

I shake my head. What I wouldn't give for a Rescue Ops swift frigate to drop into the system. Something with a lot more firepower to send these guys running.

Everything's bathed in blue. The final alarm before the shift.

With ten seconds left on the timer, and energies from the Raszewski sphere humming through the hull, I position my hand over the lever. There's a tiny percentage, a fraction of a chance really, that when I pull it, nothing will happen. I don't recall the tech behind it, but let's just say that even something as powerful and complex as an interstellar jump drive will fail.

If it does, I'll have to reset and try again.

And that means I'll lose time. Time in which the missile could end up my coordinates.

Like I do before every tract shift, I pray for safety and success. Then I throw the lever.

Lights swirl. Sounds muddy and stretch into a moan, as if *Marconi* is straining to leap from one star to the next. Somewhere in the back of my brain, I know the artificial singularity in the sphere is connecting two points in space. Does that mean there's two of the ship? Two of Izzy? Two of me? And why does it feel like I'm stuck here—or there—forever?

Memories rush into the void. I'm a child again, on a hillside overlooking my settlement, tucked between the stunted aspens of Tiaozhan's West Province. Pale pink leaves flutter to the ground. A gray delver balances on my knees. Not gray as in color; a handheld device not linked to any networks, especially not the Reach. That's how my younger self can read the Gospel of Luke without the secret police tracking me down and arresting my family.

The sun's brilliant overhead, making the sky a gauzy blue…

Blue lights.

Marconi bucks like she's hit turbulence, except that doesn't happen in space. Sounds accelerate, and lights sharpen. I blink rapid-fire, trying to get rid of the double image. Looks like I have ten fingers on each hand.

Nav comes to life, swapping out all the star positions and scans from our departure point for those of our destination. We're in the Saarbrucken System, about fourteen light-years away. Scanners start feeding me data on everything they can see within a few light-seconds, which makes for a rippling cascade of coordinates for ships and objects—first the stuff within 300,000 kilometers which shows up in a second, then two light-seconds, three, four, until the display's crawling with pricks of light and their attendant labels.

Four ships already, moving about within the immediate vicinity. No comms ferry, of course, because 810 is still sitting back at Tersane.

Footsteps come up the corridor. Izzy's at the hatch, looking nauseated, hand pressed to her stomach.

"Are you okay?" I ask.

"I always end up wishing I'd either eaten more or not touched any food," she says. "One second I'm fine, the next I feel as bad as someone recovering from a viral infection."

"Fluids help. There's cider in the galley."

"The brown liquid? I saw the apple tree in your greenhouse. Is it your own?"

"Yeah, it takes a while to make, but it's worth it." I instruct Nav to give me a new timer, based on the last known velocity and acceleration of our pursuer. "Here's the deal, Operative Sayro—"

"You can call me Izzy, please." She smiles.

"Sure thing. Izzy." I don't mention that's how I've thought of her from the moment I've found out her name. "We've got about eight hours until that ship can tract shift from Tersane to here. So…"

I activate the main drives and ease *Marconi* up to the maximum acceleration. The steady rumble that permeates my body fades after a couple seconds, to a reassuring vibration in the deck plates. I unstrap from the command chair and stretch my arms. "We get started."

"I assume you have a plan for how to evade them once they arrive," Izzy says. "We'll have a good start, yes, but with their superior acceleration they'll catch us. All they have to do is look for our drive flare and back trace our course from the sundoor."

"Right, I figured that. But I also figured that if I accelerate for as long as possible and then cut the drives a good chunk of time before they're due to tract shift, there'll be nothing to see. We zip along at our final velocity and I can use the ions to slow us when we get nearer our destination—which I'll have to do from the get-go, anyway, because of the ions' limited power."

"And this station to which we're headed. It's safe?"

"Safe and trustworthy." I pull up the schematics. The ship dwarfs *Marconi*. You could easily park six *Declaration*-class comms ferry tenders along her forward hull. In fact, there's already two of *Marconi*'s twins berthed. "*RMS von Arco*. She's a comms repair and resupply galleon. Think of it as a mobile space habitat for MarkTel's communications operations. Mobile, but slow. We'll stop there and get help."

"I'm surprised you're not making for the nearest Crown Marshal's office."

I shake my head. "None in this system. But we're back on the Tiaozhan Path, so a Rescue Ops vessel with marshals aboard should be passing through, if there's not one here already. I don't suppose you'd like me to give one a call now."

"It's still risky to blow cover. Get us aboard your refuge, Vincent, and we'll go from there." She rubs her hand over her face, and for the first time since she came aboard, I notice the dark circles under her eyes. She looks weary.

"As much as I want to help you out, I think it's about time you told me exactly what's going on."

"There's little I can say."

"Your ring's already said quite a bit." I fish it from my jumpsuit pocket. "Clever way to keep your ID hidden."

"Yes, well, I still need a method of proving my true identity when I check in with my superiors and report on my mission. Though, do be careful with it."

"Oh, yeah? Rough edges?" I finger the ring, noticing an indentation…

Sparks jolt my hand. "Yikes!"

Izzy laughs. "It has a nice feature. There's enough of a charge stored to act as a miniature scrambler, though given its small size, it's good for a single shot. In case of emergencies. I already had to use it to slip past my more observant criminal colleagues. May I?"

I hand it back. What little data there was on her is stored on my delver.

"I'll have to make certain you've cleared this information from your records." She slips the ring on her finger.

Ah. So much for me playing spy, too. "My systems are open, Izzy. Do what you need to."

She regards me with a curious look. "You've proven trustworthy enough. You asked about my mission. I was sent to infiltrate a criminal enterprise that has been operating in this region of space for a couple of years. They've been amassing resources for something big, and for the longest time, ISR had no inkling of what that something was—until I spent the past three months gaining their trust."

Criminal enterprise? It could be worse. It could be a band of my so-called fellow believers taking an entire planet hostage. "I take it whatever they want is bad news for the Realm of Five."

"Yes, and for MarkTel, in particular."

"What do my employers have to do with it?"

"Comms ferries carry every byte of data transmitted from planets, stations, and ships in a given star system. They are the only way to surpass the light-years separating the stars, and being more economical to run than a starship, less costly than a messenger service."

"You could be quoting the MarkTel operations manual," I mutter.

"Come on, Izzy, this is primary education stuff."

"Bear with me. This criminal organization, like most, has found it impossible to tap into the comms ferries because of the sheer sturdiness of MarkTel's encryption software and hardware. It's near impossible to break into a ferry's systems and steal the data."

I nod, slowly. "If you wanted to steal something, it's easier to attempt it at the source."

"Correct. In this case, at a place where comms ferries are opened up and the people with relevant security clearance can access all the secrets of the galaxy." She points at Nav.

It makes sense. If I were to abandon this job for a life of piracy, it'd be what I'd try. *Von Arco* isn't just a moving depot for repair. It's also where every comms ferry that shows up gets cracked open and its guts examined, CPU by CPU. For a short span, records of every single data transmission made for months on end are vulnerable.

Trade receipts. System traffic reports. Even secured military communications and sensor data. Sure, a lot of it is encrypted to varying degrees, but if you could steal the data itself, you could take all the time you wanted to break into it.

"This gang," I say. "You're telling me they're coming after *von Arco* itself?"

"Yes, but they're also coming for me. *Von Arco* is a target of convenience—Saarbrucken System is on the Tiaozhan Path, yes, but is primarily a transit point, with little commercial or military significance. It's the least likely to have regular patrols."

"Right." I scratch the back of my neck. Those are concentrated at Tiaozhan itself, and further down the line toward Oportunidad and Muhterem. "To do that, you'd have to know *von Arco*'s schedule—unless you'd been tracking it. Wait a microsec. You said they've been up to something for *years*."

"Biding their time. Choosing the best target. They had it well planned, indeed, until they discovered who I was."

"They found out you're a spy?"

"They think I'm from a rival faction." Izzy smirks. "My connection to ISR remains secret. But I had to flee, because they knew I was leaking word of their plans to someone. Hence my unauthorized ride on your comms ferry, for which I apologize."

"Hey, don't worry about it. I'd rather a protocol got broken than someone killed you."

Whatever she takes that to mean, it makes for an awkward silence that feels like it stretches as long as the weird eternity in a tract shift. I clear my throat. "Ahem. Right, so, we'd better get to *von Arco* fast so we can warn them—without getting ourselves shot by your crime buddies when they show up in-system."

"It's more than that, Vincent. You have to get me aboard that ship." Izzy leans against the hatch frame. "I'm the only one who can stop the worst security breach of the past century."

Chapter Four

We're six hours underway when *Marconi*'s internal lights fade.

"Night" time. The ship's programming to mimic the approximate 24-hour night and day cycle that humankind hasn't managed to break free of for half a millennium. Can't blame the designers, really. No matter what's been tried, every bit of research shows humans are way happier, well-adjusted, and healthier if they don't disrupt their circadian rhythms.

It also means I've gone way too long without a good snooze.

Izzy sacks out immediately. I've made sure I have a stash of clothing tucked into the greenhouse, in a duffel bag wedged under a shelf of lettuces. The cot is deployed beside the apple tree. Love that smell. Quite a bit different than aspens, I'll grant, but when you're stuck aboard a starship that's an enclosed environment, you take what scents of Nature you can get.

It should be the perfect place to sleep, with the constant breeze from the air circulation vents making the leaves sway, and the gurgle of water in the vegetable beds providing gentle white noise. I say should because my brain is like a hamster's CPU stuck in reboot—the same information recycles. There's no reset panel, either, and I sure can't shut it down at will.

I try running every verse I know about resting in the Lord, to clear my thoughts, or better yet, shove them out an airlock and replace them with something calming. No luck. Apparently, God wants me as awake as I feel.

On the seventh attempt, I push off the cot and rub my face in a vain attempt to do what the memory verses couldn't. The deck's warm under bare feet. As much heat as the ship's cooling vanes bleed off so the mains don't burn out, there's plenty residual to keep the cabin temperature comfy.

I've got on a T-shirt and a pair of drawstring pants, both bearing the MarkTel logo. Most of the corridor lights are extinguished, with just a handful of dim orange ones providing enough illumination so I don't stub a toe. No boots for this walk—I'd rather Izzy stay asleep. A glance through the cabin hatch porthole shows her snoozing away in my bunk.

It's one thing having a stowaway to bring to *von Arco*, but that she has to be a beautiful woman… well, it makes my decisions all the more complex. Any guesses as to when I shared a kiss with someone who wasn't a relative? Too long ago, again. The best thing to do is treat her like another one of the bots, albeit with increased politeness. Intelligence operative or not, she's to be protected. Father would never forgive me if something happened to her on my watch, and grandfather? Well, let's say his reaction would make Father's seem saintly.

My shadow, long and exaggerated, clambers up the bridge hatch. I'd locked it when we turned in for the night. Could she still get in? Who knows what kind of access ISR operatives have? I'm assuming since she popped the lock on a comms ferry, she might be able to break into the bridge whenever she wants, but I'd rather err on the side of cautious optimism.

I trigger the lock with a DNA swipe. The lightning inside responds to my presence, and when I power up the main displays, even the sprawling starfield that fills my view is subdued.

First thing's first. I need the complete scans of ferry 550, the one I replaced with 810. It's still docked on *Marconi*'s bow spar, but the scans conducted both by Nav and by 550 itself will be more useful.

A giant image of the ferry fills the screen, two meters across. Data for our current course gets squashed underneath, resting at the feet of my command chair. A new set of data brackets both sides of the huge picture—internal sensor readouts, systems analyses, and the trajectory of any nearby starships that passed 550 within the past week.

There's nothing of interest for the first few days. 550's sensors have limited range; they'd only pick up what was going on in the vicinity of the touch tract leading from Tersane to Saarbrucken. Four days ago, a navastel cargo ship transited through the sundoor, then lit for deep in-system with a delivery of foodstuffs to a developing settlement. Nine hours later, a six-brace skipped through on its way to Saarbrucken with a load of hand-produced paintings and furniture bound for the Tiaozhan Path.

I accelerate the playback, instructing the computer to search for anomalies. You know—strange thruster patterns, fluctuating velocities, mass readings out of sync with heat signatures, weird drive flares.

One such anomaly appears three days ago.

A small ship, only 90 meters from stem to stern, sails past 550, at three light-seconds' distance. Velocity was only 200 kps, but as soon as it passed, it rolled and accelerated with its main drives to the next sundoor around the star.

Strange. It didn't make any query of 550's public message storage and wasn't close enough for an attempt to board or capture 550. I'd assumed someone had grappled the ferry and dragged it near, so Izzy could get aboard.

The ships' ID comes back as *August Rain*; however, it's got a very short itinerary. Cargo ships are supposed to run with a complete history of where they've been and where they're going, accessible by MarkTel communications systems, for public safety considerations. It's a protocol meant to cut down on piracy, and make sure no one goes ramming their starship into a space habitat, either accidentally or intentionally. In practice, though, many shippers—especially those of the Expatriate Cooperative crews operating outside the regulation of the Realm of Five's major commerce houses—alter not just their transponders to reflect a false ID but also fudge their records. It serves a dual purpose, by preserving lucrative trade routes from competitors and, ironically, keeping pirates off their tails.

So that can explain what *August Rain* was up to. Except when I run a back trace on its course, the purple line reverses out of 550's scan radius. It's a simple enough matter for Nav to extrapolate, and even I can eyeball it—runs from the first sundoor where 551 lives.

It appears *August Rain* transited through that sundoor, took a long swing past 550, and then left again. Not at all unusual for a cargo ship skipping the intermediate star system en route to a trade deal. The oddity is the ship's deceleration, followed by its acceleration. Traders valued time. They wanted to get their goods from Port A to Port B, *hěn kuài*. Slowing down makes no sense.

Unless they dropped something mid-trip.

If I were letting a person off so he—make that *she*—could board a comms ferry, I wouldn't want her to take a leap out an airlock at a blistering velocity. For one thing, she might not slow down enough to make the rendezvous without dying.

I filter 550's sensor records through *Marconi*'s more sophisticated scanners. There it is. I highlight what looks like chemical rocket's flare, running an extended boost, almost obliterated by the sun's glare in the background. I drop that interference back several notches, focusing the scanner evaluation on the new target. It builds me the picture I've been searching for.

A tiny rocket.

It's got room for a person to ride in, and judging by the gravitational distortion twisting the scans, it comes equipped with its own compensator. I whistle. "Not cheap. Not cheap at all. I could buy another skipjack for that price."

Sure, shuttles have their own modest compensators, but they're weak by virtue of their smaller size, limiting acceleration to less than a dozen gravities.

This thing, though, subjects itself to a punishing 20 gees, not too far off from *Marconi*'s power.

I suspect the fuel burned out pretty fast, and there's no way it held up for long under that strain. The sensors records reveal its disintegration a few minutes after it slows down not far from 550. More than that, it breaks down molecularly. There's nothing left for inspection save a smattering of particles that swiftly fade into the background of space.

And there's that life sign the comps squawked about when this whole mess started.

"*Jīngrén*," I murmur. "Amazing. She drifted in after her ride vaporized."

No doubt about it: Izzy has access to all the tech toys. Clearly befitting an ISR operative.

Of course, that doesn't answer how she got that thing smuggled under the nose of her criminal buddies—pretend buddies, I mean. Or why she didn't simply stay aboard *August Rain* until she reached her destination.

I set up a search on the Reach information network for any activity by a ship calling itself *August Rain*, or one matching its drive flare profile. Could be useful, but I could also get thousands of results of similar craft. It's hard to tell one cargo ship apart from the other if you don't have military-grade scanners, which are a step up from even what *Marconi* sports.

The search takes another ninety minutes, during which time I page through my Bible. Can't focus on a single section, so I wind up skipping from verse to verse in disconnected books. That's not conducive to good study, but sometimes I can't help it. This long in the command chair, fueled by paranoia and hobbled by lack of sleep, my brain can only absorb what my rear end can put up with.

Instead I pace a tight circle around the bridge's confines. Thankfully Nav doesn't fuss about me walking on the sloped bulkheads, because it means I'm stepping on what's essentially a giant display screen. Who knows how the computer feels about bare feet on its tech.

I lean on my faith to guide me through this. What am I supposed to do? Protocol dictates I contact *someone*, but twice now Izzy's convinced me not to. Which, again, I don't mind, because the possibility someone's listening for our transmissions is real. I'm not going to let slip that I found her hiding inside comms ferry 550 if it'll get her killed.

It comes back to life, and the sanctity of it. Never killed someone, and I don't intend to start. There's been situations in which I've had to harm others. Whether they deserved it or not isn't up to me. But I made those choices to safeguard the lives of the innocent, the oppressed, and if someday I feel convicted to ask for forgiveness, I'll get on my knees and do it.

Speaking of knees…

I get down on the flat patch of deck plates around the command chair and hold the Bible to my chin, eyes closed, like Father taught me. The prayer queues as easily as the routine for a tract shift: fingers touch to my forehead, then chest, then left shoulder, and right, as I murmur, "*Yīn fù, jí zǐ, jí shèng shén zhī míng,* amen." A deep breath. "I thank You, my heavenly Father, through Jesus Christ, Your dear Son, that You have graciously kept me this day; and I pray that You would forgive me all my sins where I have done wrong—"

The hatch creaks.

"Hey!" I swipe the scrambler up from under my chair, its business end crackling with pent-up energies, aiming for the shadow in the gap.

There's pain in my wrist, and the weapon's gone. Izzy has it in her hand, aimed at the deck. She's wide-eyed, hair askew, but right before I figure she's going to zap me into unconsciousness, she thumbs the power off. "Vincent! Is this the greeting you reserve for guests? Shooting them?"

"You got the jump on me!" I snapped. "Like a pirate ship hopping from behind an asteroid. Blast. What are you doing? I had the hatch shut."

She shakes her head, looking more bemused than insulted that I was going to shoot *her*. "It was left ajar. I couldn't sleep. When I saw the lights on the bridge, I came to see if you were all right. Then I heard you talking—sorry, I was worried you were making a transmission. We'd agreed not to."

"You're right, we did, and I wasn't making a transmission." A funny though twists my mouth into a smile. "Well, not in the sense most think of one."

Her eyes flick to the Bible still gripped in my left hand. "I didn't read much of it, you know, but what I did I found … fascinating."

I gesture for her to sit, while I fold my legs beneath me on the deck. She curls up in the command chair. Consummate gentleman, remember? "How so?"

"Well… especially toward the end, it seems to be about the dead man."

"Dead? He's probably the most alive of anyone you'll ever know."

"But this was in an era that lacks the cutting-edge medicine we have, correct? Long before nano-surgeons in sickbays. So, when he died, he should have remained dead. It's impossible."

"Not with God."

Izzy watches me, and I imagine I can see questions streaming through her mind in an unending flood of data, like the sensor readouts I've spent hours perusing. "And then it says we have to believe this is true, because we're evil?"

I shake my head. "Because no one is good. And you don't have to believe. He wants all of us, every last human, to come back to him. We've been estranged for a really long time. Give Luke 15 a read. The prodigal son."

"You believe you're at odds with him, then."

"I was, like everyone else."

"So, when did you decide to believe?"

"I wouldn't say I decided. Never pushed a button on my soul labeled, 'Load Faith,' or, 'Activate Christianity,' and then the program started running without glitches. He came after me. Chased me down. I heard and believed, courtesy the Holy Spirit."

Izzy frowns. "That makes even less sense than the man who's been dead three days but can suddenly walk through walls. Are we talking quantum superposition?"

That gets me to chuckle, but I cut it off fast, because I know she's being earnest. "Sorry about that. I'm not making fun of you. It's just, this is the thing—we try so hard to explain it. You said it yourself. It doesn't make sense. Faith doesn't make sense. One of the early guys, Paul, he went on about how insane it was. Other people think we're chumps, basically. We're running around getting ourselves ridiculed, beaten, even killed, over the claim a carpenter's kid in the Ancient Middle East was executed and came back to life."

"That is something that amazed me when I read reports about Kesek's activities."

That name again. I wish I had the scrambler in my hand, even though Kesek's been disbanded for more than a decade and we're nowhere near their ex-operatives. But the feeling passes, when the reminder comes that even they can repent—and many have. "You mean, why some didn't just give up?"

"It'd be easier," she says, "But I can understand loyalty to a cause. Even to a person."

"He was—is—more than a person. If He hadn't died, we'd never be reconciled to God, and then this galaxy would be a lot darker place than it is." I brace my knees with my arms. "Keep reading, if you like. I'm no expert, but I grew up in this faith. I watched family members disappear because they wouldn't back down."

She smiles. "I knew there was something special about you."

As much as that comment makes the heat rise in my face until I'm sure my hair must be about to activate the fire suppression systems, I scramble for humility. "Hey, the only thing special is what He puts there. The new man, and all that."

She cocks an eyebrow.

"Believer lingo." I rub my face. "And now I'm babbling."

"Don't worry about it. It's nice to have someone to talk to who isn't all about criminal activities or intelligence briefings."

"My intelligence is limited to the workings of comms ferries and this ship."

Izzy leans against the chair's headrest. "You're the same one I heard about, aren't you?"

"The same … what?"

"Vincent Chen. I knew the name was familiar." She closes her eyes a moment. "Three months ago. Somewhere off in the Twenty Territories. A report came through from Rescue Ops, the frigate *Weskeag*, I think. Captain Brian Gaudette commanding. It said a MarkTel employee discovered a tiny settlement on a remote planet, full of people being held against their will."

I scratch the back of my neck. "I may have noticed."

"Come now. It was *you*. The man who single-handedly freed them and regained his ship."

"Not single-handedly." I grin, and waggle both sets of fingers.

She laughs. At my dumb joke! I wish the sound would go on forever, and we could just sit here in the warm cocoon of *Marconi*'s bridge, trading stories and chuckles while the Reach search runs its course.

My delver beeps. I forgot I'd set the computer to display the results there, so I could carry them back to my bunk. Back when I cared about sleeping.

"Something promising?" Izzy's watching me as sharply as a scryhawk targeting its prey at the end of a long dive. I saw one rip a Rozsade lemur out of a tree so fast you'd think the lemur had sprouted wings.

"I was looking for info on the ship that dropped you off." No sense in obfuscating. After all, I'd left the massive image of 550 bright and bold on the screen, with all the readouts merrily glowing alongside. Suffice it to say I would make a terrible spy. "Nothing personal, Izzy. You have to admit, it's the strangest situation I've encountered."

"Stranger than Sylvanak?"

I shrug. "Much more pleasant, then."

Now it's her turn for color to bloom in her cheeks.

The search turns up zero. What a vac-head I am. If she'd been riding a spy ship, was a simple network peek going to give me the answers? "You must be either crazy or brave."

"One has to have both in spades to work for ISR," Izzy says. "I won't kid you, Vincent: this is dangerous. Even now, you're putting your life on the line simply by talking to me. I can't thank you enough for helping me, but once we arrive at the *van Arco*, if you want to leave, I won't blame you. The crew aboard ship can help me make contact, and you can get back to your job. Your real job, that is, not the one where you transport spies instead of communications gear."

She makes a good point. Of course, the more she talks, the more determined I become to not let her down.

"If I abandon you to whoever's hunting us, that makes me a coward, and that's *not* going to happen." I hold out my hand. "I promise."

She shakes it, and we hold the grasp longer than is prudent. Prudence is not on my mind right then, even as the alarm bells in my heart ring out. "I'd better get some sleep." Izzy shifts in the chair.

"Me, too."

Neither of us moves.

"Or…" I drag out the pause. "We could talk some more. For a while."

Izzy smiles again. I could watch her do that through every tract shift coming up. "I'd like that."

Yeah. So would I.

Chapter Five

By the time the next timer nears its end, I'm ready.

Granted, I'm slouched in the command chair, sipping on a cup of warm cider. There's enough sugar in there to get my body powered up. Food can wait. With ten minutes left on the timer, I'm not willing to indulge in any distractions.

Even made sure I used the bathroom before I sat down.

Izzy's right there with me, holding onto the chair. I glance up at her, and nod, as if to say, "It's okay. We've got this."

She reaches down and squeezes my hand.

Any moment now, our pursuers should be popping through the sundoor from Tersane into Saarbrucken. Within a few minutes of that, we'll know whether or not they can track us.

Marconi's ions are running, albeit they're being used to slow us rather than speed us up. If our plan works, the pursuers shouldn't be able to see us. But I rest the heel of my hand on the control panel for the ions. I'm shutting them down soon, just in case.

Now.

The soft tremor dies out. The ship's hurtling along, its stern facing our destination, sensors passive and scanners offline. With the mains cooling, we're not emitting nearly as much heat from the vanes, either. For all intents and purposes, we should appear as a hunk of metal.

Izzy adds another bonus to the equation. She digs underneath the main control panel, working without words, until a tinny klaxon erupts. "Kill it."

I do so, even as I realize it was warning me she'd messed with something vital. A moment later, she straightens, and brushes hair from her face. "There. Your transponder won't give us away, either."

"Really?" I query the system. How about that. We're officially the navastel cargo vessel *Golden Orchid.* Kinda rings a bell. "Nice work. Do you always travel with fake transponders in your pocket?"

"They're useful in emergencies."

Blast. I was kidding.

The timer reaches zero.

Nothing.

Okay, so my calculations could have been off. Theoretically, so could the computer's, though its chances of making a mistake are infinitesimal. "Give it a bit. We'll see."

The next five minutes are torturous. So are the next five, and the next, and so on, until we're at half an hour past the time.

"They're late," Izzy says.

"By a while." I peer at the scans. This far out from the sundoor, there's a delay of a few minutes for light to reach our coordinates. Even so, there's no reason a ship that was shooting missiles at us half a day ago should be taking its sweet time finishing the job. "They seemed intent on catching you, so this waiting around is… odd."

"I noticed." She pokes my shoulder. It's a playful gesture—at least, it's what I imagine such a gesture from a close lady friend should be. Makes it difficult to focus on the readouts. Or anything but her proximity. "There's always a possibility of their having suffered a malfunction."

"How likely?"

"Not very. From what I saw, they possessed well-maintained ships."

"That isn't reassuring."

"The truth rarely is."

I grin. "You said it, not me."

A light flashes. Incoming from the Tersane sundoor. Sure enough, a vessel appears in the tract shift, right where I'd expect one. Small enough to be our adversary's. I grip the armrests. This time, they've got a transponder up. Says they're the *Boxelder*, an Expatriate-flagged six-brace.

"If we burn now, they'll spot us," Izzy murmurs.

"I know. I'm not anxious to do it anyway." It's been nearly nine hours since we lit the main drives. Close to the safety-mandated 10, but not quite there, so if we accelerate at full thrust now, we'd run the risk of fracturing the drive nozzles. Meaning, we'd be stuck without our most powerful engines. Not a happy thought. "Let's see if they notice us. Then we can try the ions again."

Of course, the light delay means that when the ship finally accelerates away from the sundoor at a modest 30 gravities, it actually started to do so a few minutes ago. Nav adjusts for the lag, giving me a projected course, estimating where the vessel is, based on where it was and where it's going. It also throws out a few possible trajectories if it were to alter course or speed. A lot of variables to juggle, but I'm fine with—

A second ship transits.

"Blast," Izzy snaps.

The new arrival has the same approximate mass and is also IDed as Expatriate. The name's *Wamsutter*.

"Both headed this way," I mutter. "Course is separated by a few light-seconds and widening. In-system destinations."

"And neither is our friend?"

"We've got no way to know. Even if your buddies are heavily armed, they're not putting out a wacky energy surge. As far as Nav's concerned, we've got two cargo ships traipsing their way into Saarbrucken."

"One has to be them. Think of it. They wait at the sundoor for another vessel to arrive, then time their transit at approximately the same time after observing the vessel. It gives them time to rig up a false transponder, and adjust their drive systems accordingly, to mimic a cargo vessel."

She's got a point. It's not that difficult to fake; I imagine it's downright easy for whatever criminal enterprise. "Okay, then. What's our plan?"

"Continue to *von Arco*. Even if they can't find us, they'll proceed with their raid."

"No argument there. Okay, this is the tricky part." I close my eyes.

"Prayer?"

I don't give her response, except for a finger raised to the ceiling.

Well, no sense in making a long speech. I activate the ions.

Our velocity trickles downward. *Von Arco* is on the sensors, but it's still hours away, toward the first planet of the Saarbrucken System.

Neither of us breathes as we watch the two ships. If they're going to react, it will be about eight minutes before we see it—four for the light from us to reach them, and vice versa.

I don't exhale until 15 minutes have passed. Nothing. Not a budge from their courses.

Izzy hugs me. "Thank God."

Amen is right.

Both ships disappear from the scanners later, after their initial burns subside. Nav can't tell if they've changed course using ion drives; as far as we know, they're on the same route. Won't be until they fire the mains again that we know for sure. Meanwhile the sensors give me a dizzying array of crisscrossing lines indicating possible courses. That helps me plan our next move.

Which, it turns out, is to spend hours under constant deceleration until we reach the one thing on the displays I'm interested in: *RMS von Arco.*

The comms repair and resupply galleon spreads across the screen, filling our vantage point as I guide *Marconi* into a near approach with thrusters. The automated beacons balk at our fake transponder. There's no *Golden Orchid* on MarkTel's registry. But once I transmit the proper comms jockey code and let Izzy finesse the transponder, the beacons are satisfied. They issue a recorded greeting and guide me with a constant stream of coordinates to the ventral hull, with the other two ships of our size docked above us. It's ironic that a huge ship like this, geared for the sustaining of interstellar communications, doesn't have a human on the other end of the signal to say, "Hello."

But then, that's Carl for you.

He greets us at the airlock as soon as the indicator lights confirm a solid seal. "Vinnie! How're you doing?"

Captain Carl Passarella is a veteran comms jockey and the guy in charge aboard *von Arco*. Unlike me, he's been at this for thirty years. Also, unlike me, his crew includes 16 humans, so he's never lacking for conversation. Carl's head only reaches my chin, but he's built like a hefter robot that spends his days shoving cargo around. It's really not fair that he's as old as Father and yet has more hair than I do—a thick, black mop of curls that, like his moustache, is losing ground to an onslaught of gray. When he grins, flinty blue eyes come close to disappearing.

"I'm good, Carl. Tired, but good." His grip is as overpowering as a hefter's, though to be fair, I've never shaken hands with one. Probably for the best. I don't want a cybernetic replacement for a perfectly good right arm.

He peers around my shoulders. "And… you brought a guest." The way his moustache twitches, seemingly of its own accord, is a big blazing beacon that I'm in trouble with Carl. And since his seniority is way up there, whatever he puts in his reports carries weight. Admittedly, not as much weight as Carl's torso carries, but close.

"Yeah. Isabella Sayro. She was—a person in distress I picked up."

Carl offers his hand and gives a brief bow. "Miss."

"Thank you for taking us in, Captain Passarella, though I must inform you my visit here is more official than a rescue."

I gawk at her. Weren't we supposed to be keeping her persona a secret? "I'm pretty sure there was rescuing involved."

She smiles—at Carl, not me. "Of course, Captain Chen was instrumental in saving my life."

"That's more like it."

Izzy elbows me, but the smile remains.

Carl, however, glances back and forth between us like he's watching a satellite oscillating between orbits. "'Kay. You two are going to have to fill old Carl in on this—whatever this is. 'Cause unless Vinnie here stopped off at an invisible space station…" He consults his delver. "Your itinerary doesn't mention picking up hitchhikers. Which is against protocol, I'll remind you."

"Look, Carl, I kinda had to bend the protocols." I shrug. "Well, it was more like snap them in half, put them aside for a day, then start gluing them back together in hopes no one would notice. And since we're apparently heading in that direction—" I gesture for Izzy to continue.

She's got her ring on, the one I dug out of her spacesuit. She holds it in front of Carl's delver.

"You married a hitchhiker?" Carl's eyes bug out so hard I'm afraid they'll ricochet off the bulkheads.

This couldn't possibly get any more awkward.

"No, Captain, but if a man like Vincent asked a woman like me, she'd happily accept," Izzy says coolly.

I stand corrected.

Carl blinks a dozen times before remembering he is, in fact, the captain of this ship and the Man In Charge. He instructs his delver to query Izzy's ring, at which point the same holographic rendering of her credentials expands into view. "ISR," he murmurs. "I thought you guys were still frozen."

"Kesek's absence over the past decade has demanded a radical restructuring on the part of the Service," Izzy says, "but rest assured, we have been keeping watch on threats to the Realm's security even while everyone was scrambling to get out from under the secret police's collective boots."

I'm simultaneously impressed and disturbed by the swift change in her persona. Warm comments to me aside, she's all authority. Even Carl manages to improve his posture by a few centimeters. "Izzy's on an important mission, Carl."

"Aren't we all." He's still staring at the credentials. "All right, Operative Sayro. What is it MarkTel can do for you?"

"I need access to your coding center," she says. "The criminal enterprise I've recently infiltrated is on its way here to steal the data, both civilian and military, stored on the comms ferries docked aboard your ship."

"Truth? That rusts." Carl shakes his head. "I've got nine ferries under my care, including the ones Vinnie brought with him. I'm gonna need confirmation from your superiors and mine."

"That's not possible. If you leak word of my presence, through any channel, the people looking for that data will kill everyone aboard this ship." Izzy steps closer, so she's glaring into Carl's face. He's leaning back but hasn't brought himself to step away. "They have already jammed our transmissions once; their ability to intercept is known."

Carl looks at me. "She's not crazy, right?"

"They shot at us. And they're here in Saarbrucken, somewhere. We just don't know where. They pulled a clever swap at the sundoors and we lost track."

"All right. Lemme think." Carl tugs on the end of his moustache.

"If it's the security of your data that bothers you, Captain, let me set your fears at ease." Izzy smiles. "I have no desire for any transmissions to leave this ship. Nothing's going to leak out. But if you don't let me do my job, *everything* will."

"Hard to argue that," he mutters. "Fine. I'll get one of the techs to take you down there. Vinnie, you stick with your ship for the time being. Get whatever repairs and replacements you need to the quartermaster. 550's the one you swapped out, right? Good. All right. We'll take it off your hands and swap you…" He pulls up a schedule blazing in purple letters on his delver. "877. She's undergone a full refit. Good? All right."

He heads into the corridor, slate gray jumpsuit an ungainly lump in an otherwise immaculate corridor of eggshell white bulkheads and a glossy black deck. Yellow lights line the edges of the floor and ceiling.

"You'd better catch up with him," I say to Izzy. "Carl's getting flustered."

Izzy rolls her eyes. "How can you tell?"

"Sensors detecting sarcasm. Seriously, though, he starts to jabber, like a corrupted commnote left on a loop. Just use small words and soothing sounds."

"Is that how you manage him, 'Vinnie'?"

I make a face I'm certain looks like I've swallowed a bot. "He likes his nicknames. Be thankful you're 'Operative Sayro' to him."

"I'm used to Izzy, too."

"That you are." Ahem. "I'll check over the ship and make sure we're good to go. What else do we need to get done before our friends show up?"

"Ideally I'd like Captain Passarella to get this vessel underway."

"Well, it's not going to be much of a chase, but if we can get her into the Holt Rings, there's a better chance for concealment. Saarbrucken, the planet, is the next orbital body in-system, and there's a lot of traffic we'll pick up between there and the Holt Rings. Ice miners, metal haulers, and such."

"Enough traffic to hide a ship as big as this?"

"Some of those haulers are easily twice the tonnage won't be a problem." I put my hand on her shoulder. "I'll talk to Carl about it while you start working on the code center. Just don't, ah, break anything."

She laughs. "You have little faith in my abilities."

"Besides being a decent tactical advisor and conversationalist, you haven't demonstrated you can safeguard a comms system."

She punches my shoulder. "Rude."

"Hey, my observation is what it is. But I trust you to get it done."

"Thanks. I'll check in with you when I'm done."

"Hold on." I hold up my wrist comm. "Exchange signals."

Izzy links her device to mine. "I'll see you in a while."

She leaves me in the corridor. I watch her, and her reflection walk to the end, where she intercepts Carl. There's a grace to her movements, like a dancer or an athlete shows off. Then I remember how swift she was when she was trying to break my face. And that was when she was shaking off the aftereffects of hibernation. Yikes.

Something nudges my boot. Blue and Scarlet. "Hey, guys. You bored or what?"

[Inspection of Comms Ferry 550,] scrolls across my wrist comm.

I wince. Perfect. I'm so busy giving Bible studies and pining over the pretty girl I completely spaced on doing an in-person look-see around the insides of Izzy's temporary living quarters. "Thanks for the reminder. Lead the way."

If course, that doesn't register in their primitive processors, but a simple [Proceed] message gets them scooting through the airlock. I follow them into the bow spar, and from there to the hatch that accesses ferry 550. The air aboard *Marconi* already smells different, courtesy of the recirculators aboard *von Arco* interchanging the somewhat stale air on my ship with a fresh set. If memory serves, *von Arco*'s got its own, much larger greenhouse that supplements the breathable air supply. It'll be nice to have some of that to savor when I'm off on the next trip.

Funny. Hadn't thought until now that the next trip will be without Izzy. It'll be back to the same old silence, except for the shipboard sounds to which I've grown accustomed.

Contemplating that makes my chest tighten. Kinda wish I'd never found her.

With the way 550 is oriented to *Marconi*, I have to open the hatch and clamber up into its cramped compartment. There's air now, and with orange lighting, it feels less stark than when it was lit only by the stars.

I query the diagnostics screen inside the compartment. There's that Code 77A, the one Izzy used to get inside the comms ferry. Nothing odd about that. ISR has communications access codes, like she said, but…

Hold on. That code's been recycled.

When I dig deeper, the diagnostics screen tells me there's a discrepancy between the current MarkTel iteration and the one she used. Not enough of a difference to reject access, but the computer dutifully recorded it to show me it was possibly corrupted. In need of repair.

Maybe Izzy was undercover so long the code she had didn't receive an update. MarkTel likes to do those every month or so, and there's often a lag when the updates make their trips down the trade routes.

It's still weird she wouldn't have something that was top of the line, considering the unique rocket she rode to hitch this ride.

Blue and Scarlet, meanwhile, are trundling all around the inside of 550, their treads sticking to any surface available. Scarlet halts overhead, a pincer extended. [Foreign object.]

It's a while oval, a couple fingers across. Reminds me of a seashell I saw on Tiaozhan's Endless Beach, an unbroken shoreline stretching 2,000 kilometers on the east of the main continent. This thing, though, pulses slowly with internal illumination. Makes me wonder if it's going to hatch. [Radiation emissions?]

[Tachyon pulse.]

No wonder the ship's sensors and even 550's internal scanners didn't catch it. Scarlet's data, shared through my wrist comm's readouts, show it's barely putting out enough of the particles to—well, I have no idea what it's doing.

But I bet I know who does.

Chapter Six

If Izzy's surprised by the object nestled in my outstretched hand, she doesn't show it.

Carl's got her set up deep in the code center at the heart of *von Arco*, four compartments aft of the bridge. It's a spherical room, like my bridge and Carl's, except the top and bottom concavities are crammed full of hardware. There's more computing power tucked in these hexagonal columns than a fleet of *Declaration*-Class ships carry. Miniscule lights ebb and flow like ocean waves, making me wish again I was back on the Endless Beach. There's even the accompanying noise of their operation, the *shush* of coolant, the *hum* of the processors. I imagine myriad brains talking to each other, like a subdued crowd waiting for a concert to begin.

"I apologize for not telling you about its presence." Izzy sits on a ladder, her hands deep in an open panel on one side of a computer column. "It's a Precision Tachyon Beacon. Not standard for ISR operatives by any means, however, a recent addition to undercover assignments. I planted it inside your comms ferry, so I could leave my superiors a way to track me down if … well, the mission was compromised."

Translate that as, if she were killed. "You could have told me after

I'd picked you up. My bots are unhappy about finding odd objects stuck inside our equipment. It throws their diagnostics routine into snarl."

"I imagine it doesn't do yours any good, either."

"Why'd you stash it inside the ferry instead of keeping it on you?"

"Our information as to when the next tender such as yours would be along wasn't precise. If I'd been in hibernation a few days longer, the signal would have gone out via the nearest comms ferry and been bounced down the line to my superiors."

I shiver at the thought of being in an induced state of suspension for weeks. "That's a long time to be asleep."

"No worse than a medically-induced coma, though the risk of synaptic functions in the brain deteriorating does increase for every day a subject is left under." Izzy shrugs. "And then I didn't have the chance to go back into 550 to reclaim the PTB."

"I'd have looked for it, if you'd asked."

"Well, I actually assumed you'd already found it and were keeping its discovery a secret."

I chuckle at that. "Look, we've been hanging around each other for less than a day. Your spy training hasn't rubbed off on me. Come to think of it, you haven't given me any lessons."

"I'd have to clear that with my superiors," she quips.

"I'll bet. Still, Izzy…"

She glances down at me. "I'm sorry."

"Don't be. I'm just happy it's not an explosive."

"Vincent! Give me some credit. I'd have detonated it by now." She winks.

"Not funny." Except, I'm grinning.

Carl, meanwhile, is standing at the hatch leading into the code center. "Operative Sayro? How complex a procedure is this? Are my techs gonna be able to undo your handiwork?"

"I'm programming a subroutine to prevent the comms ferry databanks from being accessed by an unauthorized source," she says. "Naturally, it won't prevent anyone from stealing a physical component—that's where you boys come in."

"Oh, I've got us underway to the Holt Rings." Carl stamps a boot on the deck plates. He's right; I could tell when the ion drives fired up a couple minutes ago. "It's a start, but when you think we're not under surveillance, I'd like to light the mains, so we can get their quicker."

"Might as well run out a big bold sign saying, 'Here we are,'" I point out. "Though chances are, they already know where to find us. At least, a general whereabouts."

"I'm not going to give them anything more specific, Vinnie," Carl mutters. "Whatever you and this gal are mixed up in, my crew doesn't need to get hurt over it. We clear?"

I nod.

"'Kay then. I'll be on the bridge." He clomps away with all the subtle sound of a garrosk. And they have six legs. Though Carl might be hairier.

"I doubt that will keep our pursuers off the scent, so to speak," Izzy says.

"It's worth a try." I pat the PTB against my leg. "I'll hang on to this, okay? Leave it back on *Marconi* for you."

"I appreciate that, but why don't you keep it on your person? If things get worse, we'll need it close by to trigger our call for help. And with all this encoding equipment—" She taps a column. "I'd rather you not go to far."

I grin. "Practical. Keeping me as close as possible."

"Careful, Captain. I have work to do."

I toss her a sloppy salute, and head off into the corridor. Soon after, I realize there's an out of tune song playing. Someone's piping it through his or her delver, perhaps? Then I realize, it's me. Whistling.

Perfect. I shake my head but can't banish the sense of being in microgravity even though my boots are firmly adhered to the deck. You're hopeless, Vincent.

I'm okay with that.

A klaxon sounds from the bridge. "Vinnie!" That's Carl's soprano tones, not nearly as invigorating as my love-sick notes. Neither of those sounds can be good. I jog the corridor, dodging a pair of hamster bots trundling out of a maintenance shaft, and duck through the hatch.

Von Arco's bridge is three times as big as mine, with the command chair set on a raised platform at the end of a catwalk. Carl's there, flipping his way through holographic data like me paging through the crinkled paper sheets of my Bible. He's got two more crew in here—a blond guy seated at Helm, and a dark-skinned woman at Navigation/Tactical. The "Tactical" aspect of that console makes me want to laugh. The ship has one, possibly two pulsed particle culverin aboard, which is better than nothing, but odds are whoever was chasing us would have a set of full-fledged particle *cannon*. Not to mention missiles. Which *von Arco* lacked.

"We've got a drive flare," Carl says. "They're in a hurry, too. Pushing 45 gravities. That cuts out merchants and pirates."

I nod. "I don't think I've ever clocked a pirate at anything more than 30."

"Truth."

"How far out are these guys?"

"Too far." Carl manipulates his displays, which consist of a holographic tank that looks like an old bathtub and three curving screens. Nothing like the wrap-around, immersive sphere that's *Marconi*'s bridge. If I get any more conceited about it, there won't be room on the bridge for my ego. The holo tank coughs up a purple line shooting from a red marker right smack into *von Arco*'s blue pip. I wince at the number that appears between the two. "Twenty light-seconds. They'll be on us in a few hours."

"And the Holt Rings?"

"We'll get there about the same time. Traffic's looking good, too." Carl swipes his hand across a panel, and thirteen more indicators light up. "Got that many ships between here and there, most accumulated around the rings. Rock haulers and the like, either coming back from Saarbrucken or heading back to the planet. Once we get in their mix—"

"We can pull the same trick our buddies back there did when they came through the sundoor." I clap Carl on the shoulder. "Sounds like a plan."

"That's what I said."

"Sounds like *my* plan."

Carl snorts. "You sit a spell, young spacer, and watch someone with more klicks on the main drive."

"Captain?" The young woman taps a monitor. "Got a problem, sir. The target ship's throwing out enough interference to foul up all communications within half a light minute of their coordinates."

"And they're bringing it along with them." Carl sighs. "See if you can punch through it. Get word to any navy or Rescue Ops vessels in the vicinity."

"Working on it, Skipper, but be advised, it's more sophisticated than anything I've trained against."

"Run Protocol Eight Nine, then."

The woman's hands are a blur against her controls, but I know Protocol 89. If it were going to have some kind of effect, the myriad red and orange squiggles undulating across her monitors would have turned green by now, bright yellow at the least. Instead, the ominous colors darken. "Blast it. No good, sir. Recommend we drop a buoy."

"It'd take too long to boost out of the affected region," Carl says. "Standby on the buoys. We may be able to kick one loose in the Holt Rings, see if we can slingshot it around one of the major asteroids."

"Aye, Skipper."

Wish my crew were that respectful. I suppose, in their own silent robot way, they are. "What can I do?"

"Check in on the other captains. Let them know the score and tell them if they've got anything stashed aboard their ships that could prove useful in a fight, I want a tally."

"You think it's going to come down to that? I assumed they'd disable us—" I cut myself off as the realization sets in.

Carl pantomimes shooting me. "Right on target, Vinnie. If they want the data aboard those ferries, what's protected by *von Arco*'s computers, they're gonna have to board us. I've got plenty of scramblers aboard. But these guys… a criminal organization?"

I nod.

"Better hope the rest of the gang has something with more stopping power."

I'd completely forgotten it wasn't just myself, Izzy, and *von Arco*'s crew aboard. The two other comms ferry tenders docked along the forward hull are *RMS Baviera* and *RMS Fessenden*. They're familiar names in this region of the Realm of Five; my repair and replacement routes have overlapped theirs plenty of times the past couple of years.

On the starboard side, Captain Rebecca Dale is upside down in a ventilation duct aboard *Baviera*. When I knock on the rim, it sends a metallic *boom* echoing down its length. Rebecca tilts her head, and grins. "Hey, Vincent."

"Captain Dale."

"Oh, don't go formal." She shimmies out and lands in a crouch. Rebecca's got dark brown hair braided in a long ponytail. She brushes smudges from her jumpsuit. The sleeves are rolled up and her forearms are, well, a mess. "What's the download? I heard you and Carl were conferencing. And that you brought a stowaway."

Man. I know rumors travel fast, but on a ship full of comms specialists, the speed of light has nothing on the speed of gossip. "Short version? That lady's a spy, and there's a starship run by some angry individuals following us with the intent to disable, board, and steal."

Her eyes, a dusty hazel, go wider than I thought possible. "Really? Wow, that's great! Nothing ever happens on my run. Nothing! You know, the most exciting incident I had in the past six months was two comms ferries bouncing off each other when the docking grapplers failed? That's boring. You? You get a planet-wide revolution and stowaway spy!"

I hold up my hands, warding off the plasma torch she's brandishing. I don't really think she'd accidentally zap me in the side of the head but I'm cautious like that. "It wasn't planet-wide. And two ferries colliding is a big deal."

She tucks the torch into a holster on her belt. "You're nice. So, what can I do? Set some traps?"

"Traps? What traps?"

She rolls her eyes. "The kind you set for raiders!"

I scratch the back of my neck. I really hadn't intended to recruit this enthusiastic of a participant in our defense, but hey, I'm not gonna argue. "Forget traps. Unless you can figure a way to flood corridors with something noxious when the time comes."

"On it," Rebecca says. "Oh, and weapons."

"That's more of what I had in mind."

She leads me to an equipment locker and palms it open. "Top secret, okay?"

I cross my heart.

"Cute." Rebecca brushes a spacesuit aside and pushes on a corner of the locker wall behind it. Half the wall pops open. Two Hunsaker Black

Bull pistols, big bore handguns, matte black with glossy gray stocks and grips.

I whistle.

"That's an affirmative, Captain." Rebecca checks the charge for the magnetic assist and loads a magazine. She hands me the gun and a spare magazine. The second one goes on her belt. Three more magazines go into pockets. "There. Ready to repel boarders."

"Perfect." I give her a salute. "Thanks, Captain."

"Thank my mom." She salutes back, her smile blazing enough to ignite a star. "Starkweather Navy."

My next interaction is as dark as the inside of a nascent nebula and lasts all of thirty seconds.

Captain Mason Calhoun is stern as a primary school teaching bot. Delete that—as stern as the person who has to maintain the bot. He doesn't let me aboard *Fessenden.* He doesn't even let me in the airlock. The tantalizing scent of barbecue drifts out when he answers my intercom buzz. He's tall, with spiky black hair and a bristling goatee. Tattoos cover his arms, up to his shoulders—no sleeves on that jumpsuit, definitely not regulation—and there's a pair of silver control bands on his wrists flashing with indicator lights. "Captain Chen."

"Captain Calhoun." Way too many captains aboard. I was starting to recall why I steered clear of resupply ships like *von Arco* and why living on my own in deep space was preferable. "We've got a situation."

"Captain Passarella sent a commnote. Pirates?"

"More like organized criminals."

He nods. One nod, a simple jerk of the chin. "Armaments?"

"Ah, that's what I was going to ask you."

"Only scramblers. That's all I'll need. And this." He holds up a knife. Better specify. He holds up a cutting implement with a blade as long as my forearm. Nimonic alloy, easy to compress down into the handle, 50 centimeters long with a chemically-treated edge that could cut through most anything except, maybe, a bulkhead.

"Okay then. So… keep in contact. Carl will have more instructions."

"We're running?"

"Trying to. But it's probably gonna come down to a boarding."

He nods again. "Sounds good."

"Okay." I stand there for another second, before I ask the question that's been nagging me since the hatch opened. "Is that—?"

"Brisket." He closes the hatch centimeters from my nose.

I sigh and shake my head. Oh, yeah. We're doomed.

My last stop brings me back to Izzy. She doesn't show any signs of slowing on her work. In fact, she's got two more columns opened up, with their guts hanging out and glowing cables strung between them. "Carl's going to go apoplectic when he sees this mess."

"This mess is what's going to keep our friends out there from stealing whatever data they want." Izzy blows hair from her face.

I wag a water tube her direction. "Thirsty?"

"Thanks." She snatches it midair and takes a slug. She wipes her mouth with her sleeve. "How are we looking? Carl told me."

"Not good. It's a race to the Holt Rings. Once we quit burning, and they do too, we can use ions to alter our course. So can they, and that makes it complicated to figure out from which vector they'll come, but maybe we can confuse them."

"Don't worry. We'll be okay." She frowns. "This is the part where your kind pray for safety, isn't it?"

"That's kind of a reflex for me. Already done." And doing it again, right now, while we spoke.

"Are you… can you add me in there, too?"

"Izzy, when I pray for safety in a situation like this, I don't hog the request. It's for all of us. I don't want innocent life taken and I don't want anyone hurt. Not even our pursuers. But especially not you."

She hands the tube back, and for a moment, our hands overlap. "I'm beginning to understand."

Chapter Seven

It's a race.

Albeit, a slow race. I shouldn't say slow, when the velocities of the ships involved are measured in hundreds of kilometers per second. And it's a race with a foregone conclusion: the pursuers *will* catch up to us. *Von Arco*'s acceleration is measly compared to theirs, and with their speed already above 1,500 kps and climbing—thanks to their initial burn away from the sundoor—there's no way we can outrun them.

Out-maneuvering, though, is another matter entirely.

I'm standing next to Carl on the bridge, with Izzy by my side. She mutters something about "lapse in cross-connection" but since I'm obsessing over the Nav display I'm not paying it any mind. So far, our gambit has merit. The count of ships within a light-minute of our position is up to twenty. Carl wasn't kidding about their size. An ore hauler goes cruising by, a light-second away, and even though it would take us a few minutes to intercept it, *von Arco*'s sensors zoom in for a closer look. She's a bulk freighter, with huge anti-matter main drives plowing a hull shaped like a pine cone through this section of space. That much radiation spewing from the drives means we steer clear.

Carl's killed our thrust. We're hurtling along at 900 kps, which is decent, even though our pursuers are rapidly gaining. In a few minutes it won't matter.

"There we go," Carl says. "Time to make like an in-system rust bucket."

The Holt Rings fill the center monitor like an exquisite necklace. Make that a septet of them. Seven rings of rocky and icy debris drift around a common center of gravity. Each one's of varying size, with the narrowest only 10,000 klicks across and the biggest, a collection of hundreds of asteroids strung out in a two light-second ellipse. Some rings rotate at such a speed you don't want to get anywhere near them with a large craft like ours, while others are full of huge ice chunks that leisurely tumble end over end.

I reach over Carl's arm and expand one section of the Holt Rings using his controls. "Perfect. There's four ships in the mix right now, and more heading in. Nothing left to do but pick a drive signature to mimic and play along."

"That's what I said, Vinnie." Carl angles the control board out of my reach and straightens his posture. Doesn't reduce his girth any but gives him more the appearance of a stately—if short—oak, instead of a shrub. "Helm! Change our course to heading 310, mark 35, thrusters only."

"Aye, Skipper." The kid at Helm has a such a deep voice he reminds me of my uncle's baritone. That was my favorite part of singing hymns before Kesek took him away.

"I'd better let the captain do his captaining," I mutter to Izzy.

She hides a smile behind her mouth. "What about the others?"

"Rebecca and Mason? They're ready." I waggle my wrist comm. "I sent them commnotes reminding them to lock down their respective ships and stick to *von Arco*'s main corridors. Rebecca's, ah, enthusiastic about repelling boarders. I think Mason wants me to leave him alone as much as I wish these guys out there would leave us alone."

"Sounds like you have quite the crew ready to fight."

"Not crew. Colleagues. For a bunch of people who spend our time in deep space sans human interaction, I'm actually surprised we've coordinated as well as we did."

Carl clears his throat. "Not all of us are loners."

"And I'm glad it's working out, so far."

"Captain Passarella, do you have a schematic of your ship I could access?" Izzy asks.

"Of course. Bailey will bring it up for you."

Bailey must be the dark-skinned Nav/Tactical crewman, because she's got the three-dimensional deck plan for *von Arco* floating beside her console before Izzy manages to turn around. Airlocks pulse red, as do twin cargo bay doors and the fuel loading ports. There's also a central hatch leading to the cradles where two barges are secured.

"That gives them a lot of options," Izzy murmurs. "These are all sealed?"

"Sealed and magnetically reinforced," Bailey says. "I've got loading hefters rearranging cargo in the holds to physically block entrance. Airlocks are another matter."

She brushes her hand through the forward section of the hologram. Sure enough, tiny replicas of hulking hefter robots, each taller and broader than a human by a couple meters, are pushing containers around as easily as I'd pick an apple.

"These conduits." Izzy flicks one of the airlocks. It enlarges, as do three pulsing orange lines. "Coolant?"

"Self-sealant supply. Feeds into the capillary network." At Bailey's command, a honeycomb design in pale gold ripples along the entirety of *von Arco*'s hull. It's standard equipment aboard any space-going vessel—a webbing of thin tubes filled with a foamy mixture that, when the tubes shattered under impact, rapidly expand and congeal to plug any gap. They were the main line of defense against high velocity debris that penetrated not only a ship's electrostatic shielding but the thick armor plating.

Izzy smiles. "Redirect hamsters to those airlocks. Have them standing by with plasma torches when the time comes."

Bailey arches an eyebrow at Izzy and swivels in her chair. "Skipper?"

"You heard the lady, Nav. Get ready."

"Aye, sir."

"That'll make quite the mess," I say.

"We can hope so," Izzy replies.

"Hang on," Carl mutters. "Coming up on the Rings."

Most travelers to and from Saarbrucken give the Holt Rings a wide berth. Not us. *Von Arco* dives right into the spinning array of debris, and at our velocity, I understand why Carl wants a degree of decorum on his bridge. The helmsman's rigid at his console, as both he and the ship's computers work in sync to keep *von Arco* from being mashed by the largest chunks. Several rocks the size of skipjacks barrel by—or maybe, we barrel by them, less than 5,000 klicks away. Izzy grabs my arm when an ice spear whips across our path at half that distance. I run through every formal prayer I can think of, resorting to quick bursts when I'm distracted by the readings.

On the other side of the Holt Rings, the ore hauler is joining a second ship on its course change in-system, toward Saarbrucken itself. Carl sees it, too. "Velocity on those vessels?"

"A thousand kps," Bailey says, her voice as tense as her expression. There's sweat on her brow. The helmsman doesn't speak, and barely seems to be breathing. "But they're dropping speed as they redirect. Using ions."

"Lance, sweep us through those clouds at bearing 27, mark 285. Engage our ion drives, enough get us to match their trajectory."

"Aye, sir," Lance booms.

The kid's good. Very good. Good enough I can tell our pursuers are having issues tracking us. Bailey's been unable to break through the jamming, sure, but the ship is hanging back on the edges of the cloud, taking a more cautious approach through the fringes rather than plowing through the middle. I can't tell if they're still targeting us. Their course seems like it's veered off ours.

"Cloud's coming up," Lance says.

"El-stat shielding charged and ready, sir," Bailey says.

Carl favors me with a smirk. "You owe me for every scratch on my hull."

I bow. "Absolutely. I've got a decent crop aboard. Want apples?"

"Do main drives burn?"

We sweep through the edge of the debris cloud. The holographic model of *von Arco* flashes with purple as speedy projectiles enter the electrically charged field surrounding the ship. Bolts of lightning leap from the hull to each one, immolating the fragments. The discharges increase in frequency until it's a bizarre, space-bound thunderstorm, complete with thumps and rumbles where larger pieces make it through the el-stat shield. They gouge the hull.

I picture an apple disappearing from my greenhouse trees with each successful strike.

Some punch a couple meters in but are stopped by the sheer thickness of the ship's hull. Broken capillary sheathing expels self-sealing fluid, plugging the holes. But none of the compartments suffer damage.

Thirty seconds of this armrest-gripping, teeth-clenching, eye-watering rough ride, and we're through. The ore haulers await, as if patiently expecting us to join their procession.

"Whew!" Carl swipes moisture off his face. "We keep this up, I'm gonna need to vent *all* our heat and suck in vacuum to cool us off."

"Nice work shaking them." I point at the red pip indicating our pursuers. "They're taking the long way around."

"Yeah, it'll buy us some time." Carl grins. "Plus, now they've got to figure out which one of us is the right ship."

I blink. "Blast. Your transponder. I completely spaced that they..."

Only takes me a moment to realize Izzy's joined in the grinning. Apparently, she and Carl are in on the same joke. "What?"

"I lent Captain Passarella one of my false transponders," Izzy says. "We've been running under an assumed name as soon as we entered the Holt Rings."

"Yeah, one that matches up with the IDs the rest of these haulers are using." Carl chuckles. "Boy, I gotta say, Vinnie, if you get tired of having this gal on your ship, she'd be welcome on mine."

"That's assuming ISR doesn't need her back." I wink at Izzy.

Alert klaxons resound throughout the bridge. All our warm and fuzzy feelings get stripped away by the harsh red lighting.

And my stomach sinks at the sight of six red triangles hurtling around the Rings.

"Missiles out! Six incoming!" Bailey snaps. "Time to impact, three minutes forty seconds!"

"What in the starry skies are they doing?" Carl's going pale. "They shoot those off into a crowded navigation lane, they could hit bystanders!"

I glance at Izzy and she knows what I do. I can see it. "They don't care. They're risking the damage they'll do to others if it knocks all of us out at once. Check your scans, Carl. I'm willing to bet they're carrying disabler warheads."

Carl confirms it and follows up with a streak of harsh words that really shouldn't be uttered in mixed company. "Even if they don't blow the haulers up, they might as well! Those disablers will shut down every major system aboard and they'll be left to drift into an ice shard or an asteroid!"

"Yeah, well, they're not interested in playing nice. New plan: forget subtlety."

"Roger that," Carl growls. "Helm! Full burn and get us out of here. Evasive maneuvers!"

"Sir, I do that, we're going to crack a drive nozzle or two," Lance says. "They're still cooling from the last burn."

"Worry about repairs later, when we're not dead!"

Von Arco leaps ahead, and as much as I second Carl's decision to pour on some speed, I know Lance's right. This isn't a warship. Even if it was, we're nowhere near the nine to ten-hour safety window demanded before the next burn. The tremor that builds in the hull cuts through the reassuring rumble of the main drives. Translation? The ship's drive nozzles are displeased, and the longer we run at full thrust, the greater risk of a major break.

But it doesn't matter.

Those missiles race into our midst, splitting off in pairs to go after *von Arco* and the ore haulers. Bailey targets them with laser turrets, and launches sandcasters, but those missiles buck and weave on their paths unlike any strike I've seen. Whoever these criminals are, they must have a gigantic budget, because I'm not even kidding—a laser *hits* one missile and the thing just scatters the beam into incoherent light.

Then they explode.

Electromagnetic pulses ripple across all three ships, frying drive controls, shutting down the command lines for the ions and chemical rockets and even the thruster banks. Main power dies. Raszewski spheres go offline. Forget weapons or defenses.

Von Arco hurtles along, a dead metal box filled with air and gravity. That's it.

Bailey slaps her consoles, which are reduced to glassy panels. Lance pushes away from his controls, which are dark and unresponsive.

"Where are we? What's our heading?" Carl's punching commands into his delver. Soon dim yellow emergency lighting flares up, giving everything on the bridge a sickly hue.

"I can't tell, Skipper," Bailey says. "Let me run an extrapolation on my delver based on our last trajectory. That will give us an idea."

"No guarantees we won't hit anything," Lance grumbles. "I'll go check through the telescopes."

"Do that." Carl gives Lance a push between the shoulder blades. "Then you and Bailey get down to Auxiliary Power, and tell the chief engineer to give me whatever he can. As soon as we can get something back to the ions, we need to slow down."

They're gone in an instant, leaving Izzy and me following Carl out of the bridge. "What do you think?" I ask. "Where are they boarding?"

"I would aim for the starboard airlock," Izzy says. "They won't have to concern themselves with the comms ferry tenders, and it's one of the bigger airlocks."

"Then we'd better send those hamsters to get their work done."

"Here." Carl holds up his delver. It transfers command codes to mine. "Get the hamsters to do whatever you want. I'm rounding up the crew in the main corridor to the starboard airlock. Move it!"

I hurry with Izzy, but even as we do, there's a *clang* through the hull.

She skids. "That's not possible. How did they board so fast? They were still closing on our position."

I listen. The noises that follow are quieter, more distant. "That's not a ship docking. The clamps deployment is all wrong. It's something smaller—a barge, maybe a skipjack."

Izzy stares at me.

"During the chase and the fight," I continue, "They must have launched a shuttle. It would have been moving at the same speed as their ship. All it had to do was decelerate enough to match our velocity. If they did it with ions and thrusters, while we were watching the missiles and the debris, they could have slipped through."

"That means they're boarding us *right now*," Izzy snarls. "Come on!"

I was already sprinting down the corridor, so I don't know why she was yelling at me, but I figure, it's an emergency.

Let it slide.

Rebecca and Mason meet us at a junction. The starboard airlock is 10 meters down.

"Hey, guys." I draw the Hunsaker and make certain it's loaded. "Ready?"

Mason nods. He's got the knife in one hand and the scrambler in the other. Rebecca has her gun in a two-handed grip. She grins. "Tell me where to aim."

I point at the airlock.

"Wait. There's a chance we can still block their way." Izzy touches my arm. "The hamsters."

"Yeah, I know." As if there aren't a thousand things bashing into each other inside my head. I swipe through the delver, find the commands Carl gave me, and prod the hamsters into action. The first one hits the port side airlock. I tap into the security imager's feed, and sure enough, there's the little guy scooting across the airlock ceiling. In seconds his plasma torch severs the correct conduit. Nasty, thick gray goo spews into the compartment, expanding so quickly the hamster barely slips out the hatch and seals it upon retreat. "Wow. Okay, that'll gum things up quickly."

Mason twirls his knife. "Do I still get to use this?"

"Ah, probably?"

He nods.

"Right." I issue commands to the remainder of the hamsters and let them do their thing. "We should probably still take up defensive positions."

Rebecca frowns. "Do you know how to do that?"

I shrug. "Crouch behind something. Shoot. Repeat?"

Banging echoes from the airlock. I check the delver. That's not good. The imager feed is blank. "I think our line of defense just faltered."

"Then let's not stand around here yakking." Rebecca palms open the hatch to the nearest cabin.

Mason mimics her move. I do likewise. So does Izzy, tucking in behind me. She plucks the scrambler from my belt.

Emergency lights blank out in our corridor. The only illumination's from my delver, and the sparks issuing from around the edge of the hatch. Sparks? Perfect. Speaking of torches.

"Are you up to this?" Izzy murmurs under the hiss of the cutting.

"I have to be. They're not going to walk in here and steal what belongs to a bunch of other people. Military and business aside, there's a bunch of personal data stored in those comms ferries. Data that belongs to families. I'm not going to let them take it and, what, force people to pay to get it back? That's not right."

She smiles, and right then I could take on an entire pirate ship full of bad guys. Which, apparently, I'm about to do.

Right up until the smoke tinged with purple comes streaming out of the vents. Whatever it is, it sets us all to coughing. Dizzy. Scenes swim.

The hatch comes crashing down.

The next minute is a whirl of confusion—screams of scrambler bursts and people, Rebecca's gun booming in the confines, Mason stabbing someone in the gut but nothing coming out of the guy except sparks, dark shapes with no faces and armed with their own scramblers…

"Get to the code center!" I shove Izzy behind me and fire at one of the oncoming raiders. The face explodes in sparks and greasy liquid. "Protect it!"

"Not without you!"

Rebecca's already backing down the hall with her, tugging her arm. "Come on!" She fires again, one-handed, and a second raider hits the deck.

Mason's on the floor, groaning. He's not bleeding but he's not okay, either.

"Vincent!" Izzy grabs my hand.

"I don't like the idea of dying," I say. "But I'm not afraid."

And I'm not. Really. If this is how it goes, I'm ready. Yet I want to stay, to see the people I care about, to help others…

Izzy kisses me.

It's a brief, fiery contact, like a plasma torch's burn, and then she's gone, hurrying away with Rebecca.

They can barricade themselves in there. Carl can block off passage. Buy time for us to get help.

I turn back around—

And am struck down.

It doesn't hurt as much as I think it should. More of a lightning strike than a sharp pain. My body goes numb, buzzing, tingling, and there's a jab to my ribcage.

Everything's sideways, because I'm sideways. And my vision's gone completely glitchy—seeing double like a bad tract shift, sounds smearing, and thoughts jumbling.

I'm ready to go home. Sorry, Father, Mother. It's my time. He's calling.

Boots obscure my vision. A woman's voice, muffled behind a mask, says, "Secure them. Find her."

No! Izzy.

I failed her.

Chapter Eight

I really have to stop getting stunned. It can't be good for me. Time for a med-scanner checkup when I get back aboard *Marconi*.

If I ever get out of here.

Where *here* is remains unclear. It's a cabin, that much is for sure, but whether it's aboard *von Arco* or the enemy ship, I have no idea.

I shake away the last haziness. Getting hit with a scrambler isn't terrible. You lose control of your voluntary nervous system, but the bonus is, your heart keeps pumping blood and your lungs keep pushing air, so—in theory—you don't die or lose consciousness.

That means it was the gas that knocked me out. It doesn't seem to have any lasting aftereffects, except a bitter, metallic aftertaste that won't flee my mouth no matter how much I swallow.

The cabin is dark, except for a single, brilliant white light overhead. I might as well be in direct sunlight, it's so warm. Which is good because I've been stripped down to my undershirt and a pair of pants like the kind I wear when I'm sleeping.

The downside? They're not my pants.

I've got no boots either, which explains why my feet are cold. I frown.

Deck plates aren't usually this chilly. Like aboard *Marconi,* there should be plenty of residual heat from any number of systems—especially the main reactor—to warm a starship pleasantly.

Only reason I can think of why they're cold is because someone wants them to be cold. And, since my ankles are shackled to the chair with a tight-fitting binder, I can't lift them.

Straps restrain me all over. There's a pair atop my legs, another wide one around my waist and again across my chest. My arms are locked in place on the arms of the chair. About all I can move is my head and neck.

That's when I notice the chair itself is bolted to the floor.

I squint past the light. This is bad. The bulkheads are devoid of lockers, or hatches. Wait. I crane my neck until it aches. There's one behind me.

Pain seeps into my body. I've got some remarkable bruises on my arms, probably from when I took a tumble, and there's a spot on my side that promises to be obnoxious. Whether it's muscle or bone that's damaged, I can't tell. But I've got bigger problems right now.

Our pursuers captured me.

And they apparently employed androids as shock troops. They weren't intelligent, it seems. That level of AI is banned. But they were sentient enough to plod forward, dealing out scrambler bursts and taking hits from conventional weapons. It's much easier, if you're a pirate, to use your lackeys, but these guys must have a budget that…

Money. It comes back to that again, doesn't it? Money and resources. Izzy has them in spades, obviously, because who knows what kind of gravity well ISR possesses for that kind of stuff.

The criminal enterprise she was talking about, though, must have backing that comes close to rivaling what she can marshal. Their ship can blend in, carries precision disabler missiles that are harder to kill than a comms jockey rumor factory, and androids for its dirty work.

Whoever they are, they're no one to be trifled with. Makes me regret, yet again, that Izzy chose my comms ferry to hide in.

Yes, that's selfish of me. Once the woe-is-me feeling passes, I know it doesn't matter who was inside 550. I would have helped the person nonetheless. No matter the situation. And MarkTel regs could go to blazes.

Some things are so ingrained you can't stop yourself. Which makes me wonder, in my still semi-addled state, why I keep stepping into the messes when I know I don't have to?

The answer's simple: Father taught me better. Even when Kesek was rounding up our friends, he didn't despair. He didn't cast blame about. When things got bad, he showed us where to turn.

Man was full of darkness, but the Light of the World would always triumph, even if we didn't see it in our lives, or even in this universe.

Sounds pretty good to me.

At least, it does until the hatch squeals open. The sound makes me jump, because up until then, the only noise in the room was a soft buzz from the light, and the whisper of the ventilation.

Everything goes dark.

All that talk about Light of the World, the feeling of peace and bravery it instills, shrivels into a cramped corner of my brain. Fear roars.

I'm not lying. The idea of death doesn't scare me. Torture? Pain? Those are another story.

"You're gonna have a hard time getting me to say anything, because I'm not helping you get what you want. That data is privileged information, and you've got no claim to it. The people aboard our ships will do whatever it takes to stop you. So, you can gravity-wrack me, or do whatever it is you do to tear helpful things out of people's brains, but you'd be better off kicking me out an airlock for all the good it will do you."

There. That sounds bold. Stupid, probably, but bold.

It's so long until the reply comes that, for a while, I wonder if I imagined the hatch opening and I just spouted a challenge to myself. Then soft laughter fills the room. "For someone who doesn't have anything to tell me, you certainly said a mouthful."

The light flares, twice as bright, and I jerk my head away, eyes pinched shut. Once the blobs clear from my vision, I can see the woman standing a few meters in front of me. She's on the edge of shadows, hands behind her back. She's young, maybe my age and Izzy's, or younger. Her face is so youthful it's hard to tell. She's got reddish-brown hair cut short, curling to the nape of her neck. Her eyes sparkle, cloudy gray and blue, and there's a sternness to her expression that rivals Mason's.

Speaking of ... "Where's Captain Calhoun?"

"Being cared for in our sickbay."

"Cared for like this?" I yank on the bindings. Bad idea. They tighten until I grimace.

"Use caution." Her voice is the same melodic one I heard before I blacked out. "Those bindings are responsive. The more force you exercise in an attempt to free yourself, the worse they confine. Relax and you'll be more comfortable."

I'm not sure how she expects me to relax at the launch of what's likely to be a terrible interrogation, but to humor her—and cut off the increasing pain—I will my arms to go limp. Turns out she's telling the truth; the bindings slack, though not enough for me to get free.

She takes a step to the right, coming further into the circle of light. She wears a white jacket over a dark blue shirt and a set of matching trousers. No insignia, no nametag, nothing that could be used for identification. "Captain Vincent Lupine Chen."

Did she have my MarkTel file? Nobody says my middle name. Nobody save for Mother, who gave it to me. Father grudgingly accepted the name because it was her favorite flower but let me take a moment to exhort all parents everywhere in the galaxy to never name a child in such a way. I'd rather have the restraints tighten up again. Or get shot with a scrambler. Maybe both.

She holds up a delver, a tiny thing no bigger than my wrist comm. She separates the halves and draws apart a transparent sheet. The sheet fills with, well, me—my face, my ID, my MarkTel employment records, my last full med scan, recent evaluations, Reach news posts that bring up my name, even things I wrote in response to discussions and debates. She chooses one in particular and uses two fingers to lift a tiny blue planet from the surface. "Sylvanak. That's when you showed up on our scans. But there's other instances of taking measures beyond what's required of a comms jockey. You've had some close calls."

"Pun intended?"

"Very much so." She smirks. "Tell me about your stowaway."

"Why bother?" I jerk my chin. "If you raided my data you already know everything. I filed a report. Didn't get to transmit it, thanks to your jamming."

"Which wasn't constant. You didn't send any messages to your supervisors or to Rescue Ops. No one knew that woman was aboard your ship until you showed up in Saarbrucken. Why?"

I close my mouth. Izzy asked me to keep her mission secret. The less I say, the better.

The woman nods. "You're loyal to her. I understand. She's got that effect on people. That's why we're in this situation."

"Where's Captain Calhoun?" I ask.

"I told you, sickbay. Yes, he will be questioned." She tips her head sideways. "What did she promise you? Money? A cut of the profit from the data?"

I snort.

"I'll file that under 'no.' Captain Chen, I think we can help each other. Izzy has a plan. We want to know the specifics. We have a general idea, of course; we wouldn't have pursued her this far if we didn't."

"You won't get the data," I snap. "She's taken steps to ensure it's kept safe. And Carl—Captain Passarella—he'll destroy it first."

"No, he won't. We've already come to an agreement with him."

They had Carl, too? "No way. He'd never make any deals with your kind."

"He has. He's quite safe, and unharmed. It's Izzy and one other we need to worry about."

Rebecca. She took Izzy to protect her and keep the data safe. But if this lady was having the conversation—which so far was way less deadly than I'd expected—then they didn't have either of them. "I don't get it. What do you want from me?"

"Two things." She stows the mini delver in her jacket and ticks off points on her fingers. "One: assurance you're not involved in any criminal activity. Two: your cooperation."

I burst out laughing. Sorry, but at this point, after all the mounting strain that led to a brief gunfight with androids and my subsequent incapacitation, it just felt fantastic to let off some steam in the form of a good chuckle. "Lady, you're as much a vac-head as I anticipated. You read all those files and still don't know a thing about me."

"I know you love Izzy."

So much for the laughter. I couldn't have been as struck as if she'd hauled off and slapped me.

"Don't play like you don't know, Captain Chen," she says. "Izzy has that way with people. She'll confide and seek. Whatever a person holds dear, Izzy will latch onto and exploit until she makes that person feel like he is the gravitational center of her orbit. I've seen it too many times and had to clean up major messes because of it."

"It's—that's not true." All the interest she showed in my faith, in *me*... it was real. She wouldn't bother reading if she were faking. She wouldn't waste time being as kind as she was. Would she?

"Tough to consider, isn't it?" She paces left. "So, I'll ask you: what is her plan?"

There's no energy left to be bold or clever or even mildly annoying. The idea that Izzy's played me this whole time... "I don't know."

"She told you she's ISR."

They know. I can't bring myself to nod.

"And that we've hounded you to steal the data? That she'd infiltrated our ranks and found out our devious plan? That she'll be the hero of the Realm—and you along with her—when you foil us?"

This time, I do nod. It's over anyway.

"I'm sorry this had to happen to you, but as I said, you're not the first." She holds up her hand. There's a ring on it, just like Izzy's. A quick squeeze, and I'm looking at credentials—the same kind Izzy had.

"My name is Julianna Ward-Verge," she says. "Operative, Intelligence Service of the Realm."

Thoughts collide with the impact of meteorites on the outer hull. "You're—with Izzy?"

Even as I say it, I realize that can't be true. They wouldn't have chased her down if they were on her side.

"She told you her name is Isabella Sayro, an operative with the same rank, I take it."

"Yeah, she did."

"Her name is false. It's an identity she'd never used before, but given the magnitude of her deception, I'm not surprised she came up with a new cover." Julianna douses her ring ID. "Her real name is Izzara Neoh. She *was* an ISR operative, one of our best. ISR recruited her while she was still in secondary school. Age sixteen and they inducted her into a spy's education. You have to understand; our agency was a mess back then. Kesek had all the power. Through their control of the king and Congress, they'd stripped away resources and imprisoned people until we were left with a shell. It wasn't until Izzy and others were recruited we had a fighting chance to destroy Kesek."

Julianna smiles. "Then, of course, our work was done for us. When the incidents of 2602 devastated the Home Fleet and led to the near coup that could have unraveled the Realm, a combination of Starkweather military forces and Expatriate volunteers—concerned private citizens, let's say—gave us a chance to act. ISR operatives helped capture Kesek's leadership. Our agency gained a second chance."

"You're—you're talking about when the Word was reclaimed. When religious freedom was reborn."

"That's right. I'd forgotten from your file. You're a Mosbyan believer from Tiaozhan." A flicker of something crosses her face. Mourning? "My brother—he's all right now. Our family had a terrible schism because of the things you believe."

"I'm sorry," I say, not knowing how to deal with her statements. "It's in the book, though. He brought a sword."

"So I've heard." Julianna sighs. "That's not like me to deviate from script."

"Wait. Izzy was ISR. What happened?"

"She became disillusioned by our rebirth this past decade. Thinks we're going to be Kesek, Version 2.0. But that's as far from the truth as we are from the other side of the galaxy." Julianna jabs a finger my direction, and I'm glad it's a digit and not a Hunsaker. "Kesek came close to making me an orphan. How could she think I'd let that happen again? No, if you ask me, she was looking for an excuse to pursue financial gain. Simply put, she got bored."

"And now, what, she's…" My brain finally compiles all the data. I stare at Juliana, jaw slack. "Blast. She's not here to protect the data. That was never her idea. She wants to *steal* it. This whole thing with me rescuing her from ferry 550, the story about the criminal enterprise wanting to make money off the swiped data—that was all a lie spun so I'd help her out."

"Unfortunately, yes." Julianna smirks. "And you've proven far more resourceful than we've given you credit. There's not many who can outmaneuver us."

A spike of anger drives through my confusion. "You disabled three ships moving at high velocity! You could have killed a bunch of people!"

"It was a calculated risk, but we ran the course extrapolations before we fired. The odds were good we could secure *von Arco* without civilian casualties."

"How good of odds?"

"Let's not discuss that. Izzy's plan—"

"I told you, I don't know. Really. She was in the code center forever, rewiring the computer columns and saying she was preventing *you* from stealing the data. Sounded like a way to stall until we could get help or, worse came to worse, destroy the whole mess."

"Blast." Julianna frowns. "That means she must have been trying to access it. We have to stop Izzy. You have to convince her you're still ignorant of her true identity and a willing ally."

"What? Why me? Can't you guys blaze in and pull her out of the code center?" I scowl. "You've probably got a cargo hold full of androids. Rebecca would be happy to turn her gun on Izzy instead." In that moment, so would I. Keeping the anger from bubbling over is harder than recalibrating a comms ferry's security system from scratch. Trust me, I've tried.

"No. It has to be you." Someone knocks on the hatch. Julianna strides past me. "Because Izzy's got a hostage."

Chapter Nine

The restraints snap free. I rub at my wrists, and make sure I've got circulation in my legs again, before I stand up. Shaky, but mobile. Also, I don't vomit all over the deck plates, which I consider a bonus.

There's another person in the room now. I'd never have picked him out of a crowd if I'd been asked to describe a suspicious individual. Medium height, medium build, sandy hair, brown eyes, a complexion that wasn't tanned yet wasn't pale—completely nondescript. The only thing about him that screamed, "Intelligence Service of the Realm" was the identical jacket and clothing underneath.

"There's a ship en route," he says. "Boosting at 35 gravities. It has to be her ride."

"I'd wondered when they'd show up." Julianna gestures to me, almost as an afterthought, as if she hadn't had me tied up in a creepy interrogation cabin. "Captain Chen, this is Operative Raymond Ward, my partner and our helmsman."

Ray nods at me. "Captain. You're aware of your role in this operation, I take it."

"I wouldn't say aware. More like, reeling over the sudden change." I shake my head. "Still not sure how you two sending me in there to talk to Izzy is better than whatever raid plan you had in mind."

"We tried that," Ray says. "The androids worked well, but we hadn't expected your people would put up the fight they did. You bogged us down in the primary corridor's junction and that gave Izzy the chance she needed to escape. Of course, your sending one of your fellow captains with her gave the perfect cover. Congratulations."

This guy does sarcasm as well as I do. "If you'd told me ahead time who I was dealing with, there wouldn't have been a need for any of it. We could have, I don't know, made a citizen's arrest or something."

Ray snorts. "Please. You'd have all been killed. Izzy knows when she's cornered. A woman who's spent her entire adult life first pursuing Kesek, then going after pirates and organized criminals, is not going to quail at the sight of a handful of comms jockeys."

"Boys, this is a debate we can have later." Julianna puts a hand between us. "Right now, we need Captain Chen's assistance, so we can resolve this matter with minimal casualties. First, we assess the situation and make our decisions appropriately."

"We'd better do it quickly." Ray folds his arms. "ETA on the new arrival is six hours. I want to get *Havoc* moved off from *von Arco* so we have a better angle of attack should it come down to an armed conflict. Anywhere else is better than being docked to her hull."

"Then do that." She touches his arm, and he flashes her a tight smile, before he departs. It's eerily reminiscent of the interplay between Izzy and me. Of course, too late, I put the names together—Ward-Verge and Ward…

"Let's check on your colleagues." Julianna is gone through the hatch before I can ask about my hunch.

I follow her down a narrow corridor that's just as sterile as *Marconi*'s before I added personal touches in the form of my rugs. Everything's a shade of slate. Black and yellow hatch patterns demarcate the outlines of several hatches, and I don't see an access panel for code entry or even for palm scan.

I catch up with Julianna. "That guy, Operative Ward, he said there's a ship coming toward us. I take it that's bad."

"Most likely Izzy's compatriots. It's a six-brace, though by the way it's maneuvering, we suspect it's been heavily modified." She raises an eyebrow. "You did your research on this, didn't you?"

I rewind back through the last day or so, coming up against my late-night Reach queries. "*August Rain*," I murmur.

"One of their aliases."

"She jumped ship onto my comms ferry back at Tersane."

Julianna nods. "Don't be alarmed. We know their capabilities. While they do carry disabler warheads like we do, that's where the similarities end. *HMS Havoc* is designed for stealth and overwhelming power fitted in a deceptively small frame. She'll handle herself quite well with Ray the helm."

"Ray being your husband."

She stops outside a hatch on our left. This one is white, with red double lines painted around the edges. "He is. Perhaps more importantly, he's my partner. We preserve each other's lives and watch over the safety of the Realm."

"Except when you're shooting missiles at its citizens."

"Sometimes the safety of a civilization and the well-being of a few individuals are not compatible." She holds up her hand to the hatch. A red light flashes on her ring.

The hatch slides open.

Carl's seated by a bed, on which Mason's laid out. It takes me a moment to realize this is a cramped version of a sickbay, with the single diagnostic bed, rows of cabinets squeezed into the bulkheads, and med-scanners dangling from an overhead apparatus similar to—but looking way more advanced than—the rig my cabin has.

"Vinnie!" Carl's up and ripping my arm off in a two-handed shake. "Thank the stars. I thought you were dead! Mason, too!"

"What, that he was dead or that he thought I was dead?"

"Either. Both." Carl grins. "Good to see you up and around, Captain."

"Likewise, Captain." I check on Mason's vitals. They seem steady, but he's fast asleep. "What happened?"

"He reacted badly to the sedative gas," Julianna says. "We have him stabilized. I introduced a swarm of nano-surgeons to repair damage to his lungs. Don't worry, he'll recover, and with improved breathing function."

"That's a lot of risk you're taking to prevent data theft," I mutter.

"You're underestimating the importance of what those comms ferries contain."

"No, trust me, I get it. We're only just out from under Kesek's shadow, right? Decades spent where they could walk into a public place, or into a house, or even right into this sickbay, and drag out everything and anything from our delvers. No such thing as freedom of information." I point in what I figure is the general direction of *von Arco* and the docked ships, but I could be aiming at a tumbling rock for all I know. "Our job is to deliver the information. All those worlds out there, the billions and billions of people with disparate ideologies and conflicting desires, they're held together by the comms ferry network. Without us, you've got no Realm."

"I absolutely agree. That's why it's vital we don't let anything in those ferries fall into the wrong hands."

"Then why don't you just purge the data, and delete…" I lose the rest of my thought as new ones intrude. ISR doesn't care one whit about privacy. They're a spy organization. What do they care about? The "safety of the Realm." Which, to my mind, means secrets. Secrets that benefit the Realm of Five, its king, and the powers behind our governments.

Secrets about our enemies.

"There's something in there you want," I murmur. "Some data stream that went into the ferries and you're worried Izzy's criminal faction will get ahold of it. They'd make it public or sell it."

Julianna considers me with that steely gaze, before finally nodding. "More likely, sell. ISR has listening posts established throughout the Realm. We use them for observation of radical Tiu Martian elements—and sometimes Hamarkhis, where they overlap. Tiu groups have been agitating for a renewed Martian reclamation. The want the planet back."

"No one's allowed to set foot on Mars," Carl scoffs. "Come on, it hasn't been settled in centuries, and the last time Congress was stupid enough to let the Marties attempt a pilgrimage, the Tiu hijacked it and wiped out the Home Fleet at Earth!"

"Exactly so. That's why ISR has kept close tabs on Tiu maneuverings during the turmoil of 2602 and in the ensuing eleven years. We've taken this long to get reliable sources inside their movement—no easy feat, given their fanaticism. But our reports from those agents are routed through normal comms ferry networks to hide them in plain sight, as it were."

"So, what, there's classified reports in the data Izzy's trying to steal?"

"Classified reports, and frequencies that could identify those agents. We'd lose years of intelligence, not to mention the lives of our agents." Julianna crosses her arms. "You're a good man, Captain. You have to be, from what I understand of your faith. Can't you see why we're taking the steps we have?"

What I can see is ISR scrambling to clean up a mess caused by one of their own ex-operatives. "I suppose."

Carl clears his throat. "This is all very deep and what, but when are we going to take my ship back?"

I make a face. "Since when did we lose it?"

"Since Izzy assumed control of its primary functions," Julianna says. "Here."

She pulls out her micro delver and activates a hologram. It's *von Arco*, half a meter long, with *Marconi* and the other ships firmly moored in place. There's a new addition, and it's not the shuttle I expect. Not the shuttle we heard. It's a short, sleek starship, hull as black as a singularity, with strange angles and a hull that looks as if it were randomly generated by a drunken program. There's six cooling vanes, and even partially stowed, they stretch on for much farther than any ship that size should have. I'd be surprised if 45 gravities were her maximum.

"There's no entrance to or egress from the ship, except for the airlock we forced. Izzy knows this. She's sealed herself inside the code center, with your Captain Dale. We've had no communications in or out."

"The rest of the crew's safe?" Carl asks.

"They are either in *von Arco*'s Engineering spaces or aboard here." Julianna enlarged the aft portion of the ship. "We're in contact with one Bailey on Captain Passarella's crew. She's agreed to provide reports to Izzy saying she's working on restoring power, albeit only after Captain Passarella's explicit order to do so."

"That way Izzy thinks we're still helping her." I rub my forehead. Headaches aren't usually a problem for me. Seems like my brain is making an exception. "And I get to waltz in and tell her I've got some grand plan to get us out of here."

"You will indeed. We'll stage your escape, and you maintain the pretense that you think you're dealing with a criminal enterprise. But tell her we've told *you* that we're ISR. And that you don't believe it."

"This is crazy. You think she's going to believe me when I lie about knowing you guys are really spies? While she's lying to me about you guys being criminals? I play along with her lie while I'm lying?"

Carl rolls his eyes. "I'm confused just listening to it."

"Don't strain the old processors, Carl." That was unnecessary, I know, but the idea that this operation hinges on my performance as a proficient liar is insane. Sure, I've told lies before, especially when they've helped right a wrong. Does lying to the bad guys make me a bad person? A sin's a sin.

Point is, I'd rather not have to think about it. "Okay. Pretend I'm still on her side. Then what? Get her to surrender herself? She's going to operate on the scheme that she's running for her life. She'll be pretending to be desperate—or in all likelihood, actually be desperate, because she *knows* who you guys really are even if she's faking that fact to me."

"It's no more complex than a dozen operations I've run." Julianna's tone betrays increasing exasperation. I remember similar strain in Mother's voice when I questioned every single detail of the jobs she gave me around the house. "Tell a story. Everyone's done that as a child. It's make believe, Vincent. Only the stakes are much higher, which makes it a moral imperative you sort out your confusion and disdain, so this gets done."

"Don't tell me about moral imperatives," I mutter. "I'm familiar with the best of them."

"Fair point."

Carl claps my shoulder, hard enough the impact stings. Payback for my smarmy comment, no doubt. "Hey, Vinnie, I'm just glad it's you not me having to pull this off. I'm ready to back you up, whatever you need."

"Thanks." I focus on the fact that one of my fellow captains is potentially in danger. "Okay. Make believe. I'm escaping from criminals, who told me they're ISR, but I don't believe them. I still say it's a stretch."

"On the contrary," Julianna says, her smile expanding, "How do you know we're actually ISR? Trust is based on available facts, Captain Chen. Give a person enough facts, you can win his trust. As Izzy did with you."

My guts churn. It's an uncomfortable thing to digest, my complete and utter gullibility. "Now you're insinuating I shouldn't trust you."

"I'm asking you to contemplate your role in this. Rely on your faith, if you have to, but never forget, there are consequences for inaction and action, alike."

Carl's not offering further advice, but I can guess what he's thinking. Rebecca's one of us—a comms jockey and a captain. Our people are aboard *von Arco*, possibly soon to be in harm's way.

It's my fault.

Not entirely. I'm not a complete fool. Izzy's the one who's steered us on this course, as surely as if she were the nav computer. My actions are my own, though, and the sooner I own up to it and ask forgiveness for my mistakes, the sooner I can move ahead.

I can't believe I fell for it. For her.

But when I take a second to examine the situation from a cold, rational perspective, it was genius on Izzy's part. Who better than a lonely comms jockey with a soft spot for people in danger—a fact she picked up from news about my prior exploit—to rope into a dangerous scheme? Civilization's expanded deep into the cosmos over the past five centuries, but some instincts are hard to change.

The one about helping a person in distress, for example. Especially a kind-hearted woman.

Father would say it was worth it, male or female. Mother would remind me to guard my thoughts as I acted with compassion.

I'm going to go with, I can be a vac-head sometimes.

"Fine." I run a hand through my hair. "Let's plan this escape of mine."

"Good. First, you'll need this." Julianna hands me a white oval.

"Izzy's tachyon emitter." I make a face. "She said it was to send word to ISR if she needed."

"She gave you a half-truth. It is a Precision Tachyon Beacon, meant to summon assistance. What she left out is, it's been continuously pulsing for a long time."

"How long?"

"By our calculations, since before you picked her up."

If this keeps up, I'm going to have a hard time lying to Izzy's face.

"However, we've got another use for it." She hands it to me.

Perfect. I'm bait.

I rub my forehead. "First off, how about you get me my jumpsuit back? I'm not putting myself in harm's way in my pajamas."

I sprint down the corridor, panting until my lungs burn. Scrambler bursts slap against the bulkhead. Halfway down I hit the deck, scraping my knees and shoot wildly over my shoulder. Bullets carom off the bulkheads. Thankfully shipbuilders know this kind of thing happens, not just in a military setting, and makes the hulls thick enough that high-velocity projectiles shot from magnetic-assist pistols don't open us up to catastrophic decompression.

An android stomps toward me. It proves an easy target, taking several hits before it staggers against a stanchion. Sparks sputter. A pall of smoke drifts up to the ceiling, drawn into the ventilators.

Shouts follow up. That's my cue.

I hit my wrist comm. "Izzy! Izzy, I'm out, but they're coming after me! Headed your way!"

The footsteps and yelling behind me are certainly convincing. I find myself accelerating to get away from the ruse, and I'm in on it.

White fumes tinged with blue come spraying into the corridors. A clunking sound echoes behind the bulkheads. Izzy rerouted the coolant from Engineering. I smother a grin, in case Izzy can see me on the ship's internal security sensors. Nice to see evidence Bailey was playing her part from the aft section of the ship.

Footsteps falter. I'm in front of the code center hatch. I pound on it. "Izzy! Let me in before the coolant builds up!" I throw in some ragged coughs for effect.

The hatch pops open. Izzy's face greets me.

I do my best to look relieved, rather than hauling off and slapping her.

Until I see she's pointing a gun in my face.

Chapter Ten

It's not just any gun. It's Rebecca's. Which means she doesn't have it. And I seriously doubt she would have shared the spare with someone who wasn't one of her people.

"Hey, relax! It's me." I grin, and it doesn't take much to fake it, because I really am happy to see her.

Her face could be a sheet of hull plating.

"Come on! The coolant!" I push forward. "We don't have time!"

She backs off, and thankfully, a smile blossoms. "You never cease to amaze me."

We get the hatch shut. I can still hear the coolant hissing outside. Nice that I didn't have to breathe any of it in to keep up appearances. But now I've got bigger problems than choking toxic fumes.

Rebecca's curled up in a corner. She could be asleep, except it hasn't been that long since I saw her race down the corridor with Izzy in tow.

"Don't worry, she's okay." Izzy kneels beside her. She presses a hand to her neck. There's such a look of concern etched on her features, it rewinds me to hours ago when she was my—friend? Companion? Hitchhiker? Whatever the title, she was Isabella Sayro, ISR operative.

Not Izzara Neoh, former ISR and current wanted criminal.

I'd better get used to the rewound version.

"We should get her to sickbay." I put an arm under Rebecca's shoulders, as if I'm planning to pick her up.

"Don't move her," Izzy says. "She caught a scrambler hit, but she's likely still unconscious because of the gas they pumped into the air."

"Yeah. I caught some of that myself."

"I saw that. I thought you were gone." She's still got the gun, but at least it isn't pointed at me. "What happened?"

"Passed out. When I came to, your buddies out there had me locked up in an interrogation room. Bright lights, straps on the chairs, the works." This wasn't so hard. The tricky part was taking the true story and altering its course, so it wound up at a different destination.

"And yet, you're here."

"They slipped up." I roll my eyes. "Didn't think that a comms ferry jockey would know how to access an airlock's bypass mechanism, just because it's not my ship. I stunned a guy but then they let more of those androids out of their pen."

"Fortunately, you retrieved your gun."

"Fortunate nothing. They had it sitting right there. These criminal masterminds you're so worried about got sloppy." I frown. "But they were claiming some strange stuff."

Izzy's put her gun away—Rebecca's gun—finally, and she folds her arms. "Such as?"

"Such as that they're ISR and you're the dangerous one."

She laughs. "That's a good one, coming from people who've tried to kill me. I suppose they paraded some false identification?"

"The whole works. Look, all I know about these people is that they're dangerous." That part didn't require any embellishment. I'd rather be stuck too close to a blue-white giant star in full-on solar flare mode than between Izzy and the ISR. "They opened fire on civilians and boarded a MarkTel vessel, without a single worry for the outcome. They're obsessed with getting their fingers on this data."

"Then we'd better act quickly to prevent that possibility."

I join her at the nearest computer column. "I thought you took care of it."

"I did. But there's a chance they could break through my encryption."

"I wondered. Too bad Carl's captured. He'd be able to give the commands to delete everything in the comms ferries and anywhere else on the ship their data's been transmitted."

"Let's not use the annihilation option." Izzy swipes a raft of commands across her delver's screen. Whatever she's done, it causes the swirl of lights on the computer columns to follow a new, regimented sequence. "I have a way to store whatever vital information is on there."

"Wait, we can't take it off the servers."

"Why not?"

"Because the thing's got a security measure in place. It'll auto-wipe if someone attempts an unauthorized transfer, and we'll be right back where we started." Which, frankly, I wouldn't mind, but thousands of people in multiple star systems will be awfully disappointed, up to and including a pair of very pushy ISR operatives awaiting the outcome.

"The good news is, Vincent, it already thinks there is a malfunction." She smiles. "Now, give me the PTB."

"The PTB?"

"Yes. It was a good thing you were able to get it back from our adversaries. I'm surprised they didn't take it off you."

My heart ramps up. This isn't supposed to happen. The PTB has a very specific role to play, according to Julianna. But I can't bring myself to admit I've got the device tucked in a jumpsuit pocket.

The hesitation lasts only a second because Izzy continues with, "My delver's programmed to pick up the tachyons and confirm its presence."

"Hey, give me some credit. They either didn't notice it in my jumpsuit or they had no clue what it was. I mean, up until we met, I didn't, either." I present the oval device with a flourish. "And the proper response is, 'Thanks, Vincent,' to which I reply, 'You're welcome, Izzy.' Then we can get on with saving the day."

She shakes her head, but there's a smile there, which I'll take as a sign of victory. She lifts the PTB from my hand. "You'd think those people would have paid closer attention to you."

"They probably weren't worried about a single comms jockey who spends all his time alone, talking to robots. I mean, you escaped, right?"

That gets a chuckle. "I'm likely more qualified to make a stealthy escape, Vincent."

"No doubt. So, how's the PTB gonna help us? You said it acted as an emergency beacon to your ISR pals. The real ones."

"It does. But it can be modified, by qualified personnel, to send and receive compressed streams of information. With this, we can get the classified data stored in the comms ferries to safekeeping if security here is breached." She opens the PTB like an egg. There's a half dozen ports for wired connects, and the blinking lights associated with the transceiver. The delver gets propped into an open hatch on the side of the column. Izzy drags wires from deep inside, connecting them first to the beacon and then to the delver.

Stall. Stall! "Wait, you're just going to broadcast? Where, back to another comms ferry?"

"ISR is on its way to pick me up." The delver lights up with a miniature navigational display. It's nearly identical to the one Julianna showed me, except *August Rain* is seen from a different angle. "They'll intercept the transmission and be sure the classified intelligence reaches its proper source."

Lies and more lies. "Oh. That's good. So, what's the plan for getting out of here? That ship's still docked to us. And I doubt we can take a stroll down the corridor to the hangar. A skipjack or a barge isn't going to get very far before they stop us again."

"Of course they won't. That's why we're taking *Marconi*."

Ah. She's thinking ahead. "Okay, but we'll have to make it quick."

Izzy enters commands. Here's hoping Julianna's preparations paid off. And that Izzy doesn't catch on to them. "I trust you're familiar with *von Arco*'s layout."

"Sure. We can drop into either one of the access tunnels, overhead or under the deck. From there it's a tight crawl to the docking airlocks, but not impossible."

"Good. But I'd rather use the door." She reaches my belt with such speed, I have trouble believing my gun's gone until it's in her hand. The muzzle's a meter from my chest. "You'll make an excellent hostage."

I keep my hands loose at my side. Faking nonchalance at this point seems overrated. "What are you doing?"

"Making it look like I'm willing to negotiate." She jiggles the PTB, without altering her aim. "This? It isn't working. It was programmed just fine when I got into the comms ferry. And I've been receiving tachyon readings. But the uplink that will allow me to transmit the data from the computer columns won't function."

"They must have done something to the beacon while I was knocked out." My hands are sweating. A muffled noise rises from the deck. Rebecca. She's coming to. Perfect. Like we need two hostages.

"You said they didn't find it."

"Maybe they did, and put it back, as a trick."

Izzy's expression is cold. "Vincent, you're a kind man and a caring soul. That makes you a terrible liar. Remove the magazine from your gun and set it on the deck."

I follow her instructions, moving slowly, in case she gets spooked and puts a bullet through me. "Let's make sure we're firing on all rockets here, okay?"

"Gladly. Kick the gun away."

I send it spinning across the deck.

"Good. Now, switch places with me."

We pivot around an invisible center, eyes wary, and I know then the deception has failed. Who was I kidding? It's in my nature to help people, not lie to them. Not long-term. At least Julianna and her people were able to sabotage the beacon. "Izzy, look—nobody has to get hurt."

"Are you their negotiator now?" she says. "Sent to guarantee my safety? What are they offering?"

"I don't know. I just need you to give yourself up."

She chuckles. "That's right. You of the strict moral code. No sense of gray in that black and white mind. You've been such a gentleman this trip, I almost felt bad getting you to do whatever I wanted. And it was so *easy*."

If her plan is to get me riled so I'll do something stupid, it's working. "I can't believe this. I rescued you because I thought you were in trouble. Do you think anyone else would have done that? Some pirates would've dumped you out an airlock. Carl himself would have probably kept you locked up."

"Well, you did lock the cabin hatch."

"Not that it worked!"

Izzy shakes her head. "I won't deny my fondness for you, Vincent. It wasn't all an act. You're a handsome man, after all. But it was far too simple to let you prattle on about the things you love, those fantasies of a life after you die."

"Is this the plan, then?" I mutter. "Insult me and then shoot me?"

"No. The plan is for you to disable the countermeasures and transmit the classified data to my waiting friends aboard *August Rain*."

I gawk, as dumbfounded as if she'd grown drive nozzles and cooling vanes. "Are you insane? *Bái chī*! I don't have the codes needed to—"

"Don't lie to me." It's a sharp, sullen command, issued with all the firmness of a trigger being pulled. And believe me, with the soft hum from the Hunsaker pistol filling the air between us, I'd rather not think about anything trigger-related. "This is the part where I've done my research, Vincent. All comms jockeys carry those codes. It has nothing to do with the starships and everything to do with their ferries. Enter the code and transmit the information."

I may have exaggerated when I told her I wasn't afraid to die. There's always fear, to an extent. But I'm not worried about what happens next. "No."

"There's consequences for this refusal."

"Hurt me all you want, Izzy. You've already lied to me and betrayed my friends. Nothing's worse."

"There's that stubbornness again. That blind reliance on old, musty words. I'd wondered if the threat of your death would be enough." She shifts her stance.

Points the muzzle square at Rebecca.

"Hey. Hey!" I start forward, unsure of what I'm doing but convinced I have to do *something*.

"Get. Back." She fires.

The shot punches into the bulkhead, a few centimeters over Rebecca's head. She's awake, eyes bleary through half-open lids. But aware. "Chen? What's…?"

"Stay put, Captain." I glare at Izzy. "Leave her be."

"Enter the code and she'll live."

"You know what? I don't trust you. Excuse me if I don't believe a single syllable of that sentence."

"You really don't have a choice."

"Oh, I really do." I pull the delver close and start tapping in a series of commands.

"Well done." Izzy smiles, and for microsecond, she's the same woman I let myself fall for. "Once you've cleared the security, transmit to the signal that's input. I've set it all up."

"Fine. Just don't shoot." I swipe in a few more lines, then hover my finger over the "send" interface. If I've fouled up even one thing, this is going to end badly.

"Do it." Izzy leans nearer to Rebecca.

I press "send."

Red warning lights erupt throughout the code center. A klaxon follows suit, threatening to give me a splitting headache. Rebecca grinds her teeth, and I let loose a string of Mandarin that Father would slap the back of my head for uttering.

"Turn that off!" Izzy's got her free hand clasped to the side of her head, as if one palm can block out the sound assaulting both eardrums. "What did you do?"

"Sent and received, Izzy!" I shout. "Only, you know, I may have mistyped the end signal. Sorry about that. *August Rain* missed its chance."

She swings the gun around and fires at my face.

I'm already slamming into her torso, head first. I wrench her gun hand around, praying I'm not aiming at anything vital, and pull the trigger as many times as I can. Got to empty the magazine.

The shots embed in the ceiling. Rebecca scrambles from us, staggering across the deck for my discarded weapon.

Izzy's fast. She brings her elbow onto the base of my neck, then her knee into my chest. Pain and lack of air drive my grand strategy of my head.

She shoves me against the wall and fires again.

This time I get an intense poke in the side, like someone's shoved a sensor rod against my ribcage. That sensation's rapidly followed by a terrible burning, a sharp, searing agony. My hand comes away soaked with blood.

Izzy kneels beside me. "I'm sorry it had to be this way." She leans closer and puts her hand against my face. Our lips touch. Funny thing is,

I know I'm going to miss this, even though she just shot me.

"I'm sorry, too." I grab her hand and slap it against her own cheek. Then I give her ID ring a twist.

The blue-yellow pulse ripples across her like waves on a lake. She trembles, shudders, convulses, before collapsing on her side.

"Down but not out." I drag myself up the wall. Really hope Julianna and Ray have been paying attention.

Despite all the disruption she's experiencing, Izzy's trying for the gun again. I'm not sure I can hit a woman, especially one I've just kissed.

A pistol's stock slams across her forehead. She's knocked out cold.

Rebecca straightens from her attack. She rubs her matching bruise. "Ladies first."

Chapter Eleven

August Rain didn't have a chance.

Maybe they were expecting Izzy to have somehow incapacitated the ISR ship, or maybe they were rushing in for a rescue attempt, having realized she'd failed.

Either way, *Havoc* made short work of them.

The ISR ship lay in wait, drifting free of *von Arco*, until *August Rain* was a scant light-second away. A flurry of blasts from twin pulsed particle cannons stripped the cooling vanes clean off *August Rain*'s hull, leaving it unable to accelerate, and then demolished its engines.

Most of the ship remained intact. Guess Julianna wanted prisoners.

Also, seems like *Havoc* is a pair of huge guns and some missile tubes with a Raszewski sphere and main drives strapped to the tail end. It's a strange envy that teases the back of my mind as the ISR crew bids their fond farewell.

"This incident is unofficial. It never happened." We're all lined up in the corridor near the airlock, holding our delvers. Ray walks the line, sweeping his ring across the devices as he passes. They beep and flash red lights in response. "Any mention of anything other than a pirate attack is punishable by imprisonment and fines."

"That mean you're going to snoop in our delvers like Kesek?" I scowl at him. "You guys are all warm hugs and handshakes, aren't you?"

Ray glares at me and returns to the ship.

Julianna shakes her head, that sly smile having returned. "He likes you."

"He's got a socially unacceptable way of showing it."

"Don't worry about that. Ray's… not always a people person. But rest assured, we have no interest in your personal data. What he did was set up a notification process in case you violate the agreement. This was, after all, a classified incident. It's more for your safety. No one wants the lowlifes of the galaxy finding out that you were involved with ISR."

She raises her voice, so everyone can hear her next statement. "The Realm is indebted to you for your service. You didn't have to risk your lives; we thank you for that. ISR will compensate you directly."

That engenders excited whispers as *von Arco*'s crew disperses to their stations. Soon, it's just me, Rebecca, and Carl standing there with Julianna.

"This mean I'm cleared for departure?" Rebecca asks Carl.

"Any time, Captain." He hugs her around the shoulders. "You all right to travel solo?"

She shrugs. That's a planet-sized goose egg on her forehead, but it doesn't seem to have diminished her spirit. "I've got a schedule to keep. I'm already behind, and since I can't use, 'Held up because of spy caper' as an excuse, I'd better get burning."

"Truth. Check in with Bailey. She'll loosen the clamps when you're ready to boost."

"Thanks." She nudges me. Right in the injured ribs. "See you around, Captain Chen."

Ow. I rub at the sore spot. Nothing some nerve blockers won't cure. Having a swarm of nano-surgeons knitting the bone back together sure helped expedite me from laying in a bed to walking around in no time. It was just a graze, after all. "Likewise, Captain Dale."

The levity flees her for a moment. "Say hey to Mason for me, when he wakes."

Right. Captain Calhoun's still groggy, sequestered in *von Arco*'s sickbay. I give Julianna a sour expression that, hopefully, lets me know I'm not happy that ISR's risky play left one of my colleagues sick. "I'm praying for his speedy recovery. Did you get your gun back?"

"Keep it." Rebecca shakes her head. "At the rate you're going, you're gonna need it."

She's gone to her ship. Carl slaps me across the back, letting loose a guffaw that would have scared a garrosk. "Vinnie, you're a piece of work, you know that? No rush for shoving off. I got my techs on *Marconi*'s fuel supply and your comms ferry. It's getting designated 171. You're heading off to Tiaozhan, my boy."

Perfect. Whether or not I'll be obliged to put in a family visit remains to be seen. Given the lack of commnotes between us, my showing up unannounced could be a sore spot. Sorer than my rib cage wound. "Appreciate that, Carl. I suppose I've got a spell to sit while you get everything done?"

"Tomorrow afternoon, at the latest." Carl nods at Julianna. "Ma'am, I'll thank you not to make a mess on your way out."

I can't suppress a snicker as he leaves for the bridge. "You guys at ISR sure know how to make friends."

"That's not my problem," Julianna says. "We accomplished our mission. There was minimal impact. Whatever you may think of our methods, Captain Chen, they pale in comparison to Kesek's."

"You can keep comparing yourself to them if you like," I say. "It won't help Mason get out of sickbay any faster."

"Point taken."

She still hasn't left, which is odd, because I thought theirs was a simple arrest mission. "Something else you need?"

"Our prisoner has requested to speak with you before we depart." Julianna shrugs, an almost childlike gesture. "I couldn't think of a way to broach the subject with your colleagues present. I imagine it's an uncomfortable prospect."

That's putting it mildly. "Her request? I don't believe it. Sounds like your chance to get more intel from her. Am I the bait again?" If it sounds bitter, that's because I am. There's a gaping hole in my chest like a micrometeorite through a ship's armored hull.

"Not at all. You won't be monitored. I wouldn't trivialize something like that. If you accept her request, I'll have her brought to the airlock. I'll wait on one side, and Ray on the other. No intercom."

She seems sincere, but there's been so many lies passed around I can't keep track of the truth. But a final chance to speak with Izzy… "Fine. If she wants to."

Julianna nods. She offers her hand. "Thank you again, Captain. We'll be in touch."

"Really?" We shake. "I'm hoping I never see you two again."

"The needs of the Realm override our hopes, from time to time."

Everything happens exactly as she promised.

I'm in the *Havoc* airlock with Izzy, face to face since she shot me and I stunned her. Julianna's inside *von Arco*, behind the hatch. Ray's outside the other hatch, in *Havoc*'s cramped corridor.

Izzy and I spend a good thirty seconds staring at each other, with only the creak of metal in vacuum to interrupt the silence. "Is this an apology?" I finally blurt.

"For shooting you? Yes. There could have been another way. There usually is. But you forced me to act. I was desperate."

"That's a terrible apology, just so you know."

She nods. "I trust you mean for more than your injury."

"I won't lie. Not like you. I thought—something happened between us. Something real."

"It was real." She touches my hand.

I yank it away, but she grasps it back, and I seriously think she's going to try and take me hostage—like she's got a weapon stowed somewhere, ready to deploy. There's a flicker of movement from the airlock porthole. Ray? He's watching us, ready to intervene. I shake my head.

Izzy's grip on my hand is firm, but not aggressive. "Vincent, I did what I had to do. This is the life I chose. ISR was too confining. They took steps I wasn't willing to take any more."

"Yet you're willing to break the law. To steal. To endanger others."

"It's no worse than what they had me do. I have far worse deeds to atone for."

"How're you going to atone by committing crimes?"

"Stop looking at everything so black and white, Vincent. You're so very much stuck on right and wrong."

"Because someone has to. I can't let others step on the innocent. Doesn't matter if it's difficult or not."

She smiles. I wish she'd stop that. "You have such heart. It's what I found the most appealing about you, from the very first. I hope you never lose that."

"This is nice and all, and I mean that loosely because you shot me, but what do you really want?"

Her expression becomes one of bewilderment. "I…I wanted to say good-bye."

"Okay. Good-bye." I turn for the hatch and beckon for Julianna. I'm done.

"Wait." Izzy's at my side, again. "Do you…? I mean, can you…?"

"I can't do anything if you don't come out and say what's on your mind, Izzy." There's a distant hope she'll say what I've been daydreaming, even though she's bound for incarceration.

Whatever it is, my response doesn't elicit a declaration of any kind. It's like watching a flower freeze in deep space. I've seen it happen, in the wreckage of a doomed ship. "Nothing. Never mind. I wish you well."

She raps on the opposite airlock. Ray opens it. He's got binders waiting for he wrists. A few minutes, and *Havoc* will leave, with the ISR operatives and Izzy aboard. Last chance.

"Hang on." My turn. Ray gives me a sour look, but as far as I'm concerned, the guy's just part of the bulkhead. Not worth registering.

Izzy folds her arms.

I didn't want it to end this way. How did I picture us instead? In *Marconi*'s gallery, sharing a meal, the lights dimmed, the glow from a candle making Izzy's face golden, her smile dazzling.

The heart's a tricky thing. What it wants isn't always right.

"I hope I can see you again sometime," I say. "Maybe then, whenever it is, we can be different. Better."

"Are you sure?"

"No. But it's as close as I'm going to get."

And then I kiss her. Not my best idea, but at least there was no gun involved. And I really was going to miss her, as bad as it seems. At the same time, I wish ISR would take her far away.

Ray pulls her from the airlock and it slips shut.

I stand there until Julianna opens the other hatch. "Good-bye, Captain."

"Yeah." I scratch the back of my head. "Don't keep in touch."

The next afternoon, I ease *Marconi* away from *von Arco*'s docking clamps and initiate a full burn on a course for the Shacheng sundoor. Next stop after that, Tiaozhan.

I miss Rebecca and Carl already. Even Mason.

Blue and Scarlet putter around the corridor, not coming onto the bridge but sticking close. They can't sense my mood. Then again, maybe their sensors are delicate enough they judge the change in my heart rate, my breathing, my movements.

I let them do their thing and I do mine.

It's nice to be by myself, for now.

Book 3

Failed Frequencies

There's no place like homeworld...

Vincent Chen would rather stay far away from his birthplace. But when he's called back to Tiaozhan, it's his job that's on the line.

His superiors at MarkTel don't like the publicity his adventures have brought the company, which holds the monopoly on galactic communications. Vincent dutifully promises to keep quiet for the duration of his stay.

Except his younger brother has other ideas.

Martin Chen is mixed up with dangerous smugglers, who're furious he's encroaching on their business, and they won't let him simply walk away.

It'll take all Vincent's savvy and a partnership with a legendary law enforcement officer to keep his brother—and himself—alive.

And his family intact...

The Realm of Five

circa 2614

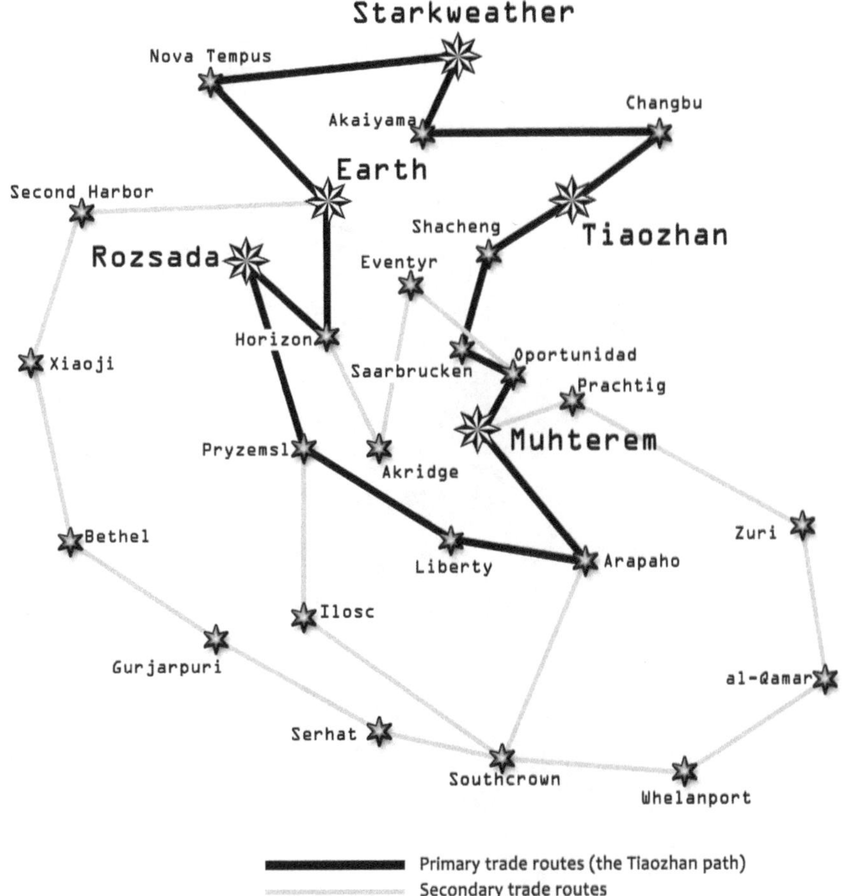

Tiaozhan

Eastern Hemisphere

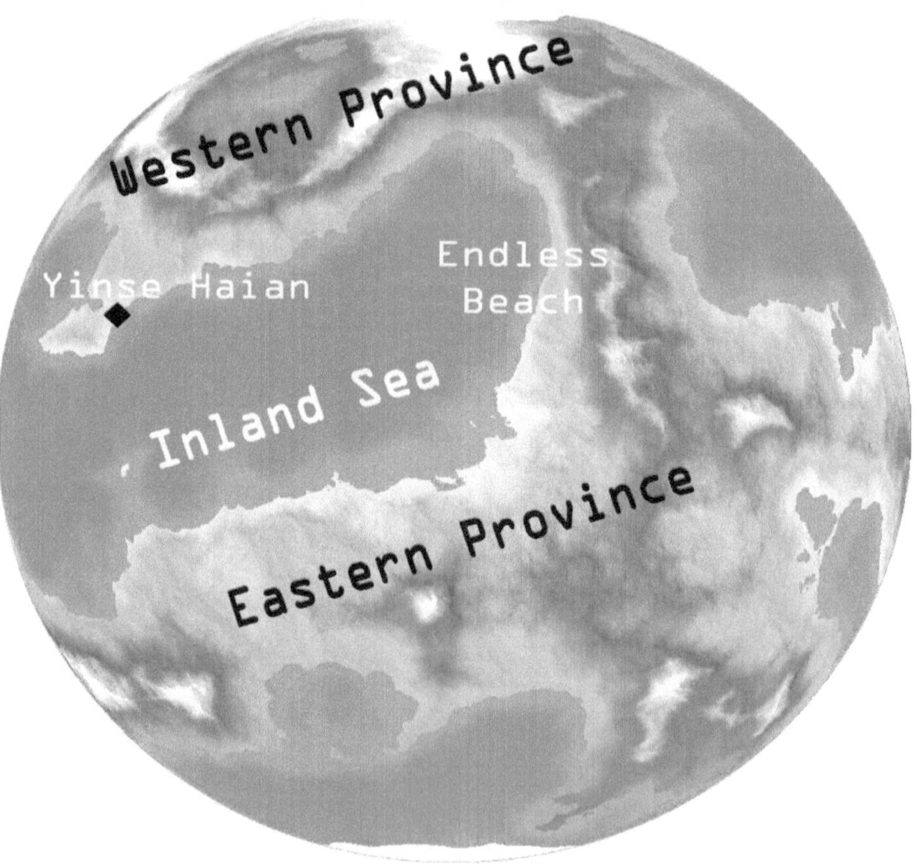

Chapter One

05 January 2614
Tiaozhan Star System
Tiaozhan, Western Province

I didn't want to come back here.

Yet, here I stand, facing the permacrete and sandstone walls that failed to keep me safe from all the galaxy's evils. The walls of the Chen family compound.

There's still time to boost my skipjack shuttle craft into orbit. It sits on the glazed soil tarmac, a 10-meter man-made bird of prey ready to leap from the ground. Steam rises from the ion engines as they cool in the crisp morning air. Tiaozhan's rising sun splashes ruddy hues across the landscape, turning the skipjack's white fuselage and the pale green grass a stubborn pink.

It's too early. I lose track of time when I'm aboard my comms ferry tender, *RMS Marconi*. She runs on Galactic Standard like every interstellar craft out there, so when I made the tract shift into the Tiaozhan System a few days ago, it didn't occur to me I'd be at the Chen household close to dawn when I made planetfall.

Finches tweet madly among the stunted aspens clustered in the hills overlooking the compound and its adjacent tarmacs. Other than the unseen avians, my only companion is Copper. He's one of the twenty-four robots who crew *Marconi*, and the one who drew the short straw, as it were, to accompany me to the surface. I can disconnect, but only so much.

Copper's a tiny brassjacket who can fit into the palm of my hand. He reminds me of a dragonfly, albeit a pudgy, metallic version with four miniature turbofans in place of wings. A black stripe encircles his frame.

He beeps twice. Three yellow lights blink. The question [Proceed?] appears on my wrist communicator's screen.

Copper's a bit of a pest. I can't tell if he's asking for orders or trying to prod me out of my reticence. If it were any of my other bots, I'd guess the former, but Copper is the oldest unit aboard *Marconi*, and the one whose operating system resists updates these days. I tap the key for [Stand by and follow] in hopes it will keep him docilely hovering over my left shoulder.

I hoist my duffel bag over the other shoulder. Yeah, I could make it to the skipjack's cockpit and ignite the fusion-ion drive before anyone makes it to the gate. But who am I kidding? Perimeter sensors embedded in the walls have already alerted Father. If his habits remain the same—and why would they change?—he's been up since the first finch opened its trap.

This is ridiculous. I'm an Interstellar Communications Ferry Deployment & Maintenance Specialist. If that doesn't sound impressive enough, people call me "Cap-tain." Or people would, if I had human crew. Bots aren't much for titles. I've withstood months of solitude in distant star systems, managed the malfunctions of ex-pensive communications gear that's vital to all worlds of the Realm of Five, and I've endured way more than any MarkTel employee should in the name of a paycheck.

To be fair, this job doesn't *require* getting myself captured and subsequently freeing captive settlers, nor does it *require* helping spies foil data theft, but any way you look at it, they were my duty.

Instead of letting those accomplishments and trials buoy me, I stand here like a vac-head, forcing myself to choose between buzzing in at the vehicle gate for visitors, or DNA swiping the family door to the right of that gate.

This would be a lot easier if childhood were full of happy memories. Don't get me wrong. I can smell Father's baking and hear Mother's singing as surely as if they happened an hour ago instead of ten years.

But this is also the place from which Uncle Ethan was dragged off in binders almost twelve years ago for the crime of possessing the wrong document. And the wrong faith…

Mother embraces me.

I'm screaming and crying, until my throat is raw. My brother whimpers next to me, like a pet who's been kicked one too many times.

The Kesek constables drag Uncle Ethan to his feet. "Ethan Chen, you are under arrest for violating the Charter of Religious Tolerance and willfully disseminating a text-in-violation, namely the Gospel of Luke."

"Leave him!" Father's in tears. "It is my document! He had nothing—"

"Sam, no!" Uncle Ethan twists around to stare in the faces of the Kesek constables. "It's mine, you understand? They had nothing to do with this. Leave them be. I bought the Gospel text. I was the one who introduced them to it. My brother and his family knew nothing of what I had planned."

The older of the two constables rolls his eyes. "I don't really care. Charter says we get ourselves a culprit, so we get a culprit. There's no room in the back of the groundcar for more than one, anyway."

They yank him to his feet and jostle him through the door.

"Why are they taking him?" I ask Father. "You said it was the Good News."

"Good News to us." His hand rests trembling on my shoulder. "Folly to all others."

"But I didn't tell anyone we were reading today. How did they find us?"

"Our neighbors," Mother says. "It could have been anyone who saw Uncle Ethan coming and going."

"That's not right. They're our friends!"

"When people are afraid, Vincent, they follow the wrong path…"

The sounds of people shouting and scrambler stun weapons shrieking fades into the insistent tweeting. Finches flit overhead. I'm back, feeling the morning sun warming the back of my MarkTel-issue black jacket, not raising my fists against officers of the king's secret police in our compound's basement.

I glance downslope. There's fifty compounds along the plain these days, several more than when I left. Ten-story agro-towers poke up from their midst, gleaming sides revealing myriad crops inside. Should be a homecoming sight.

Instead I wonder how many turned on each other to escape Kesek's wrath.

Even as I'm catching my breath from the unbidden return of those memories, the family door slides open.

Father smiles at me.

Some people daydream about what they'll look like when they're older or, if they gave access to the tech, run a med-scanner analysis to produce a hypothetical rendering. I have no need. The aged version of Vincent Chen walks toward me, hair jet black, too, but fading through gray to white the closer it gets to his ears. His expression is a lined, bemused version of the one I see in the mirror, but skin tanned by the outdoors, and eyes the color of emerald-streaked storm clouds. He's wearing the plum colored shirt he favors with the sleeves rolled up. How can it be anything but threadbare after all these years? It isn't, so he must have finally gotten a new one. Mustard-brown clay smears his forearms and his brown trousers; his fingernails are caked with the stuff.

"All this way," he says, his voice the smooth, steady tenor I have to admit I've missed. "And you've forgotten which door to use? Deep space must have terrible effects on one's memory."

I chuckle. Such is the humor of Walter Samuel Chen, Assistant Chief of Hydrology, Western Province. "Hey, Father."

"Hey, indeed." Father grasps my shoulders. "It is good to see you home. *Hong quan.*"

"*Hong quan.*" I've never had a better embrace.

Hong quan isn't our traditional greeting. Tiaozhanese add it to their vocabulary once every 54 months. It roughly translates as "Magnificent Return." It's a time when all Tiaozhanese citizens, no matter where they live, celebrate our planet's founding.

Why 54 months? That's the time elapsed between the first colony ship's departure from Earth and the day our first child—a girl—was born on this planet.

So it is that during the Magnificent Return, which lasts 54 days, millions of Tiaozhanese from across the galaxy come home, streaming through the sundoors that connect our star system to four others.

I kid you not, I could have walked from the Shacheng sundoor to the fourth planet—the only one supporting an Earth-like environment—by stepping from stern to bow of all the cargo vessels and passenger starships cramming space. Six-braces, navastels, feluccas, galleons, liners, ore haulers. *Marconi*'s Nav system had splattered more pips throughout the gorgeous spherical display screen encasing the bridge than I could handle. Made me think it's a pirate's dream come true.

Except the Tiaozhanese Navy took no chances. All four sundoors are patrolled by trireme gunboats, three -engined in-system craft built to chase down most mis-behaving interlopers. What they can't catch, they leave to six flotillas of seahawks. Tangle with one of those Raszewski drive-equipped destroyers, fast and heavily armed, and you'll wish you never made the tract shift, because they'll hunt you clear into the main trade route linking the Realm of Five.

That route isn't called the Tiaozhan Path for nothing.

Given how crowded this star system is, I forgive people for wondering why a solitary guy like me chose now to come back. I've missed a few Hong Quans since I left home, and I'm not a fan of large gatherings of people.

For one thing, I didn't have a choice. Today is my eval-uation appointment with my district supervisor. MarkTel has questions about the way in which I've spent my, err, extracurricular hours lately.

Also, I've discovered I need personal contact. No more ship full of bots. No more being the only person eating at a table stocked with two chairs.

Time to reconnect, the old-fashioned way.

For now, though, I'm content to let father guide me out of the chilly morning breeze into the sheltered sanctuary of the Chen family compound.

There could not be a starker difference in environment on the other side of the walls. One moment, I'm in a breezy, semi-arid hilly landscape. The next, I'm in a lush forest. It's the gardens Father manages, with flarebranch vines growing over a metal lattice. Their skin ripples from yellow to orange to red and back again as we walk a path of smoothed granite. Lilies bloom at the edge of a pond, the surface of which flutters with water skimmers. I kneel in pursuit of the aroma.

"Missed that, have you?" Father joins me. He digs into a small trench slashed across the grass, at the left side of the pond.

"The greenhouse aboard *Marconi* helps chase away the stale smells. But it's nothing like this." I finger the petals. "I've got some poinsettias in the skipjack. Grew them over the last month."

"Ah. For Christmas. I'm glad to hear you kept our tradition."

"I haven't forgotten everything, Father." In fact, I remember way too much.

"Well, if I can manage to coerce this pump into keeping the water properly cycled through the fountains, we'll talk about it more over breakfast. Hungry?"

"For something other than prepackaged meals and the sporadic vegetables I've grown in deep space? Yes please."

He twists something, grunts, and is rewarded for his labors with a double beep. A green light flickers across his hand. "There now. We'll let the system reboot and find the new parts. Come." He wipes his hands on his pants.

The entry path from the garden forks here, with the left way leading past hovercraft parked next to a pre-fab hangar. The right continues around the main house, toward a pair of guest cottages with pearly white walls, outlined in red.

I squint against the sun shimmering off the house. It's eight-sided, like the walls surrounding the compound, though it's a story taller. Same color scheme as the cottages, but with more flarebranch vines creeping up to protruding rafters. A quartet of sail-like nets extend skyward, diaphanous as the dragonfly wings I imagine Copper should have. A faint dripping is audible; they're collecting the scant airborne moisture for the gardens.

The house hasn't changed, not outwardly. More importantly, the tantalizing scent of raisin bread beckons from the long, open section of wall that exposes the entire kitchen and dining area. I may be drooling.

"The recharging slab has a few openings," Father says. "You know the rules."

I smirk. "Of course, Father." I send Copper the command [Dock] and he whizzes ahead, rotors gently humming. He plunks himself onto a long, black counter lined with silver traceries. A pair of brassjackets, of a larger and more robust design than his frail frame, are already dormant atop the recharging slab. Copper joins them, lights dimming, his systems falling into standby.

"Is he here already?" Mother hurries from the dining area. "I told you he'd be here before breakfast, Walter. You should have woken me up sooner."

"If I had, it'd be left to you to bake." Father winks as he bypasses her for the ovens.

Mother swats at his retreating backside with a glowing delver. For me, she reserves a sly smile. "It's good to have you back, Vincent."

"Likewise, Mother." It's a short, but warm hug, and then she's off to the table, her delver spewing complex diagrams in 3-D. Fortunately, I recognize most of them. Annabeth Chen handles telecoms for Yun Medical, meaning she has six facilities in four cities which she's got to keep linked and updated. I'll bet I learned more from leaning over her shoulder than from the MarkTel Institutes. She's not showing as much gray as Father—not yet—and her hair's a rich mahogany shade, the same as her eyes. Eyes which don't stray from her data as she says, "How was your traffic inbound?"

For my return after a decade's absence, the reception is… subdued. I roll my eyes. What did I expect? Lanterns and fireworks? "No hassle. A couple of private yachts were running on manual control when they shouldn't have been, causing headaches for traffic control, but the navy got them towed off before they were too much trouble."

Father hands me a plate. Two slices of raisin bread, still steaming, the butter rapidly melting, threaten to reduce my capacity for coherent speech to zip. "Sit. Eat."

"Yes, sir." I plunk down across from Mother and let the duffel bag hit the floor.

"Your commnotes home were shorter and less frequent," Mother says. "We were worried for you. Even more so when MarkTel contacted us to mention the incidents."

Ah. There it was. The questions. But she's not kidding about the concern. She's got the delver shut down—and turned over, so she's not tempted to reactivate. She's watching me as if I'll vanish mid-chew of the bread.

I touch her hand. "No need for worries. I'm fine. See? Hearty and hale and ready to enjoy real gravity underfoot for a while. Though, I gotta say, it's nice to have a roof overhead. Waiting outside under open sky was—disorienting."

"That's because you're canned inside that starship," Father says. "It's not healthy."

"We wouldn't want Vince to do anything unhealthy, would we?"

You've got to be kidding me. The words are micrometeorites stabbing through the hull. They set off alarms in my head.

"Well, well, well." The young man walking into the kitchen from the garden paths is as tall as me, lankier, arms ropy with muscle. The right sleeve's cut off at the shoulder; the rest of his blazing chartreuse shirt covers every inch of skin from his neck down to his left arm and waist, ending at a formal fold.

He stops his approach a half meter away, waiting for me to rise. Which I do. Like a blasted fool. This guy's got shaggy black hair cascading in front of his eyes, eyes as dark as mother's.

"The space vagrant comes home," he says, maintaining a cordial smile but using his speech like a pulsed particle cannon. He's aiming for a reactor explosion, I just know it. "Hey there, Vince."

The memory barges into the present:

I'm screaming and crying, until my throat is raw. My brother whimpers next to me, like a pet who's been kicked one too many times.

The Kesek constables drag Uncle Ethan to his feet. "Ethan Chen, you are under arrest..."

Martin Chen.

My brother.

I punch him in the face.

Chapter Two

Probably that was a bad idea.

Everybody starts talking at once. Or, I should say, shouting at once.

"Vincent! That's no way to act in this household!" Classic Mother, recitation of the law. This isn't going well. I've been here ten minutes and I've already been scolded.

It makes me wish I'd never escaped from the enslaved colony planet.

"Help him up!" Father's command carries the weight of my district supervisor's, though disobedience here won't lead to my losing my job. He's standing at my side, arms folded, the heavenly raisin bread abandoned on the stove. "Now, Vincent."

My fists are still clenched. One of them throbs. I glare at Martin, who's leaning on the backside of a chair a few paces. Help him up? He's not even *down*.

Martin rubs his jaw, the bruise already blossoming. The steely gaze that matches mine promises retribution, but his speech is anything but antagonistic. "Father, it's okay. I'm fine. Could be better, but considering how long it's been and everything that's passed..."

"You reported my friends to Kesek." I couldn't have put more venom behind the words if I'd spit them onto the tile floor. I wish I could.

"Those were dark times for everyone," Mother says. "Your brother regrets his decisions, but they were in-fluenced by fear. Many of us did the wrong things out of a desire to protect our loved ones."

"Not you."

"No? I didn't inform, true, but I deleted Kesek orders, introduced program errors, anything I could in a subtle fashion to ruin their foul work." Mother taps her delver. "This was their weapon. I learned how to use it against them."

"But you never got anyone hurt." I jab a finger towards Martin's face. "He called them out, got them locked up. Jeong and Mack and Grant."

"And that horrifies me to this day." Martin's tone is somber. He takes a deep breath. "You'll remember the friends I lost, won't you? Deon and Serra? What about them?"

I shake my head. "Don't turn this around on me. My actions didn't get people dragged into Kesek holding cells. Interrogated. Memory-sifted. All for having the Nicene Creed on their delvers." And since Kesek could read any device connected to the Reach network—and it was *mandatory* to be so connected—there was no hiding what they'd done. Not for long.

"I fully recognize what I did was wrong. But, Vincent, we were children. I was thirteen! They had gray delvers and I was fascinated by that illegal technology. When Kesek came asking at school, there wasn't a way to resist. I didn't know a thing about what the correct way was to act in this galaxy!"

"You knew the way," I snap. "Father taught us."

"That is *enough*." Father slaps the table between us with that last word. The sound echoes through seconds of silence in which I plot my escape. "Your brother has been pardoned by the king himself. Everyone who informed for Kesek has been so."

"Yeah, I know that. Believe me."

"Then believe me when I say those who are cleared of charges suffer as much as those who did not inform. You know nothing of the counseling Martin has had to undergo, or the mockery he's endured in public. It has only lessened in the past few years. Those first months, after Kesek's coup failed, when Congress and the throne were restored, were harsh as our worst winters."

I immediately remember slogging through two feet of snow and bracing against blizzard conditions after my first hovercraft broke down three klicks from the compound. Those walls never seemed so embracing when I stumbled inside. "I understand that."

"How can you, when you've been gone so long?" Mother holds up a hand, forestalling the argument she must have guessed I was about to make. "Don't protest. We all know you had your reasons. That's behind us. What's important is that our family is reunited. This rot-tenness between you must come to an end."

"It's not easy." Martin's back on his feet. He offers his hand. "For what it's worth, Vince, I get why you're upset. Angry. All those things. I don't blame you for that. And if you need to blame me, well, that's fine. I'll work around it." He manages a lopsided smile. "But it is good to see you."

I sigh. "Yeah, it is." Even though I still want to smack him. Again. But haven't I given up this baggage? Carrying around bitterness like an extra duffel bag of useless parts? I thought after my experiences on Sylvanak with a settlement full of ex-Kesek agents and their families that I'd have learned better. Yet, as soon as I saw Martin's face, I walloped him.

"Sorry about that." I shake his hand.

Martin claps his other hand atop ours. No hug. Not yet. Possibly more punching, later. Roughhousing was always our way.

Father nods. "Good. If you're both done with this nonsense, I'll be back at the pumps. Join me this evening with Scripture, won't you? After the dinner guests leave."

"Dinner guests?" I glance at Mother.

She's reactivated her delver and is nose-first in comms data. "Just a small gathering. A few friends. Token family. Perhaps a neighbor or two."

I roll my eyes.

Martin chuckles. "You know what that means."

"Yeah. My graduation all over again."

"Precisely."

"That was not a large gathering!" Mother says. "I invited only those closest to us."

"Mother, I wanted ten people, max. You had the com-pound full of a hundred of our nearest and dearest, including the tech who helped clear up a comms line break at your office."

"I'd met Rei several times before."

"He lives on our third moon!"

Mother waves her hand. It's our family signal that means, Transmission ended. Argument over. Parents 1, Children 0.

"I have an appointment this morning. 1100 hours, in Yinse Haian. It's a job evaluation."

"I did read your last commnote. That's why the dinner doesn't start until 1800."

That's her, always planning.

"Go tend to your sister. And give me a kiss, first."

I peck her on the cheek, unable to avoid the grin, and snag the raisin bread from my plate. Father had better preserve some of this for my voyage later. I'm not leaving without it.

Martin walks beside me, maintaining an arm's length distance as we tread the path to the machine shop. "So, you've been busy."

"Not sure I'm ready for small talk."

"Look, that was the only apology you'll receive. If you want to sulk, that's fine, but I choose to be happy my brother's home."

I chew on the last of the bread. "It's not like I hadn't prayed for that to go smoothly, Martin. Emotions over-rule the best of intentions, sometimes."

Martin nods. "Try always. But I'm glad you're okay. Unhurt."

"Oh yeah? How much did you hear?"

"Come on, Vince." He grins. "Sylvanak hit the Reach network in a big way. Rescue Ops sending that frig-ate in, rounding up those crazy Restorationists, plus the talk about your collaboration with the ex-Kesek—"

I stop glower at him.

"Hey! Easy." Martin's face is flush. "Poor choice of words."

"Blazes." I rub a hand through my hair, then belatedly remember it's covered in crumbs. Great. "Just shut your hatch, okay? Let me absorb all this."

"Sure thing. I'll walk with you."

Ten steps later, he says, "Lily's missed you."

I sigh.

"She has! I'm preparing you, is all." He winks. "In more ways than one."

Martin speeds around the corner of the pre-fab structure that houses all the compounds tools. There's a long line of robot parts and cables stuck on the far wall. Light flashes from a plasma torch, as a slender figure leans over the metal bench in the corner.

But I'm struck by the object by the entrance.

There's room in the shop for two vehicles, end to end. Anything that doesn't fit there goes on the parking tarmac. Today, only one craft is nestled inside.

My old hovercraft.

It's a sleek body with chunky hoverjets suspend-ed underneath. Iridescent blue-green, like a hook-eye beetle's carapace. The long scratch on the left side has been laser-etched from existence. There's no jagged crack through the right half of the windscreen, the one that used to blur a quarter of the navigation warnings displayed by the computer. Digital readouts now scroll across the projected surface without a hiccup.

"Ready to take it for a spin?" Martin asks.

I run my hand along the frame. Same odd undulation it developed when the parts were printed. "Only if the resident mechanic gives me green status lights."

The same slender figure preoccupied with her torch glances up at the last comment. This girl—she was one, a decade ago, but now she's a young woman. Any guy in the whole Western Province would trip over himself to invite her to the Hong Quan Median Dance, if she's wearing a traditional silk dress. They might overlook her in the current attire—lubricant-stained overalls, a blazing red work shirt singed in four places, and goggles reducing her eyes to buggy exaggerations.

"Vincent!" Lily Chen shoves the goggles up, and tears well up around those gleaming emeralds that are sharper, bolder versions of Father's eyes. She drops the deactivated torch and does a running slide across the hovercraft's front sensor nodes. Boots hit the perma-crete slab underfoot and skid into mine. She flings her arms around my neck and smashes her lips against my cheek in a big, adoring kiss. "Vincent! It's about time! Oh, I've been waiting and waiting! You know, I was going to sell this piece of rust if you didn't come back like you said you would."

"Pretty lousy way to greet a guy. I've missed you, too."

She tweaks my nose. It's an easier feat, now that she's nearly my height instead of the spindly 10-year-old I left behind. "Judging by the drool on your chin, it's the only way. It's so good to see you in the flesh and blood and bones! Come here, let me show you how I've been treating her."

"You kids have fun playing with your specs." Martin jerks a thumb toward the house. I hadn't noticed the glowing text rippling along his bare arm. "Father's got something in mind for me. You and I will catch up later, okay, Vince?"

"Of course." I should be able to speak with him in some way other than this, with my insides frozen like a vacuum-flashed corpse. Lily's appearance thawed bits. Not enough.

"Right. Remember, the offer to talk stands, okay?" Martin mock salutes and disappears around the side of the hose.

Great. Now I'm left with a headache pounding be-hind my eyes. I don't think it's outwardly apparent how irritated I am until Lily shakes my arm.

"That wasn't painful interaction between you two. Oh, no, not at all." She rolls her eyes, just like I do. One of my many habits she must have picked up. Like the sarcasm. When you have a sister eight years younger, often times you're a combination of babysitter and role model. "Did he greet you as soon as you landed? Smile and wave and beg your forgiveness?"

"He was the third person I saw. And I punched him."

Lily giggles, the musical sound ending in a snort. It takes her a microsec to smooth the expression into one of mock seriousness. "Oh, of course. A sound decision. Not that the vac-head didn't have it coming. Let me guess: Mother and Father chastised you soundly for your rash action."

"It's like you had a bot scanning our every move."

"That's my brother." She wipes her hands on a rag. "Oh, also, tune up your port ion drive. It's at least five percent out of sync with the starboard unit. Sounded terrible when you flew overhead. Now, get in the seat and let me show you how I improved her."

For one thing, she didn't replace the seat upholstery. Cleaned it better than I ever managed, but my body fits the contours as well as it does *Marconi*'s command chair. I flex my fingers around the control sticks. An ownership greeting springs to life, followed by the Nav screen. "Download it for me, Sis."

Father meets me at the cottage set aside for my stay. He smiles. "I couldn't very well convert your mother's expanded office back into your bedroom. But as cramped quarters as you're used to living in, I imagine this is still an upgrade.

My brain's still aching from everything Lily told me about the hovercraft. Still my ride, yes, but with so many modifications I'm glad they've been transferred from the vehicle's onboard computer and, via wrist-comm, into the delver unit tucked in my pocket. But breathing in the sweet-scented air from the nearby nectars in the garden, drifting through the open wall into the cottage, dulls the pain. The living area is bigger than my cabin, greenhouse, and galley on *Marconi* combined, and there's a bedroom beyond a short passageway, as well as a bathroom. No kitchen. Meals at the Chen compound involve all guests and family.

"It's the best." I collapse onto a long couch. "I didn't think I needed something like this."

"Like what?"

I wave my arms, as if I can pluck the words from the air. "Time. And home."

"Good. If we can deprogram you from your comms ferry replacement schedule for a while, it will be time well spent." He turns around. Footsteps approach.

Martin's there, with a basket of plums. "All picked. The bot's cleaning up the limbs. I'd be of more help if I had six limbs like him." He chuckles.

"Well done, Martin." Father takes the basket from him. "There's another errand I have in mind. Will you go down to the spaceport and pick up a replacement strand of illumination cable for the living space? I need a new roll. The old one burnt out last night."

"Of course. Is it on your account there?"

"No but charge it." Father plucks his delver from his pocket.

Martin holds his palm over the surface. The name "Walter Chen" prints along Martin's arm, followed by an amount of money, then a transaction code. "Will do." Martin glances at me. "So, Vince, what say we take your ride out for a test run? See how well Lily's work has paid off?"

I was looking forward to the re-inaugural ride by myself. Of course, that's not the reason for coming home.

Come on, Vincent. You haven't seen each other in a decade. Are you really gonna spend your entire leave time wallowing in bitterness?

It's not just Martin. There's been the heartache of seeing fellow believers acting as cruelly as the people who persecuted them.

And then, there's Izzy.

That stab in the gut makes me rise from the couch. Better keep moving if I'm not going to think about her. "Okay, sure. Probably a good idea."

Father nods. "Good. It's best for you two. Spend a long time, if you must. I transferred extra to Martin in case you boys opt for lunch. See what the morning's catch contains."

A few minutes later, after I retrieve Copper from his dock, Lily punches the control to the vehicle gate. It slides up, revealing the shallow hillside, and the slope of aspens to the right.

She leans in. "Be careful."

"Don't worry." Martin winks. "I don't think Vince will hit me again."

"Oh, a girl can hope." Lily mutters. "I meant Vincent needs to be careful he doesn't scrape *my* work against a tree."

I nurse power to the hoverjets and the hovercraft hops forward, kicking up dust outside the compound. She swoops down broad lane blown by years of vehicle traffic, engines thrumming, wind whipping us.

Copper nestles into the center console, anchoring himself with tiny silver tentacles.

I laugh. Doesn't matter that we're only doing 120 kilometers per hour—a dying man's crawl compared to being thrust through deep space by *Marconi*'s anti-matter main drives. I haven't felt this alive since I was first licensed to operate solo. "Glad Father talked us into this!" I shout to Martin. "Look, about that stuff earlier—"

"Has your memory been completely wiped?" Martin sneers. "We're not going to get any illumination cable. I've got a delivery to pick up for some very impatient men. Head to these coordinates."

He presses his wrist to the windscreen. A new map interjects itself into my programmed route. The Yinse Haian waterfront, yes, but on the opposite end of the city. The end we were never allowed to stray into when we were growing up.

"And when we get there, shut your face and let me speak, so you don't get us both killed."

Martin pulls a compact AkTek Ballista pistol from his waistband.

Chapter Three

A gun?

I've barely arrived, and my brother's got a gun?

Tiaozhan's got some strict rules about firearms. Military and police aside, mercantile conglomerates and rural compound families can have them for self-defense. But numbers and firepower are limited if you're a civilian.

There's no way a concealed weapon like that is legal. It sure isn't a hunting rifle.

"What in blazes are you doing?" I goggle at him. "Put it away!"

"Relax. It's got no tracer. Even your dumb bot can't tell it's here." He waves it in front of the robot. No lights, no beeps, no emergency messages. "See? This thing's mag signature's been altered. Won't show up on most scanners. If it does, it looks like a delver with an overcharged core. So, quit worrying about it and drive."

"You can't take an illegal gun downtown! Why do you even have that? This isn't an Expatriate spaceport or some black-market station that pirates use."

"Vince, let me do you a favor. Let me assume you're a smart guy. You always were. Mother and Father raved over your grades, especially after you left." He scowls. "You think a subdermal delver is cheap? You think I earned money for it from the internship at the hydrology offices? If Father had his way I'd been slinging water conduits around for the rest of his life. Like you buried your head in comms ferries, just like Mother's got her nose stuck in signals every day."

"It's called an honest career, Martin."

"Whatever you say. I call it death." Martin slips the gun under his shirt. "This is an easy job. We go in, I take delivery, I give them the money, and then I transfer the goods for a second payment. Two parties get paid, and one party gets what they want. No mess."

"Perfect. No mess. That's what the gun's for."

"Don't be like that."

"Like what? Like reasonable? Rational?"

"Like our parents! Safe and boring. I'm not going to be a dirtsider forever. And I'm not going to spend my life enslaved to a corporation like you, either. Soon as I can, I'm taking my side job full-time and off-world. And you're gonna help me do it."

"I ought to turn you in."

"Turn your brother in?" Martin snickers. "That's good. I'll deny the gun's mine. Say I found it somewhere. I paid cash. A big old stack of currency for a gun that's got no name, number, or DNA attached to it. Besides, you think Mother or Father will believe you?"

My hands tighten on the control sticks. We fly past the local compounds. Yinse Haian's agro-towers and the residential blocks at the city's fringe shine like glassy cubes beyond them. "You were the one who informed."

"Yeah, and I've turned that new leaf all the way over. Shut up. Your role is driver, not analyst." Martin shakes his head. "I need your help. How about it?"

"Are you serious? What about the big show you put on for our parents? Your contrition, my forgiveness that you supposedly want so bad—"

"Oh, I do want it. Eventually. Right now, I've got bus-iness to conduct. And the better Mother and Father think of me, the easier it is for the transactions to take place, because I'm above suspicion. The good kid. The one who's there for all the Bible study and church services and helping around the compound." He presses his hands together and looks at the sky, putting on the blandest expression. I suppose he's playing at being pious.

He's right, though. I turn him in, it will tear our family apart. Bad enough Uncle Ethan vanished years ago. What would be left of us if Martin were grabbed for a weapons charge? And what sounds suspiciously like smuggling?

This is my brother. Even though he made bad choices long ago, he needs my help. My love for him should override everything else.

Almost everything. He's breaking the law.

But I'm not.

Not yet.

I grind my teeth. "I'll drive you down there. But I'm not waiting around for you. I've got my review appointment—"

"Yeah, 1100. I remember." Martin smiles. "What better reason for you to stay in the city until then, and when you're done, you can drive me back to the com-pound? I'll be done well before that."

"Fine. Perfect." And as soon as we get back, as he put it, Father will be the first one to whom I'll report. Mother next.

No wonder Lily made faces at Martin.

The glassy cubes at the city's edge give way to massive inverted pyramids. It looks like someone dropped a bag of jewels onto the ground from a great height, and they've all become embedded in the savannahs along this shore of the Inland Sea. The closer to the sea the city spreads, the less exotic the shapes become. Spindly gantries and sprawling docks replace elaborate structures. I'm hard pressed to find a building that isn't a huge dome or a row of boxy warehouses.

Long Haul Road takes us deeper into this commercial heart on the south end of the city. Overhead, skipjacks and lumbering barges and flitting gigs fill the air like a flock of birds startled into flight. We should be going the other way—north, to Bright Sky Spaceport, where all the aerial traffic's headed. Instead I'm chauffeuring my brother to some clandestine courier job in the docks.

We pass tiny storefronts and bustling markets. I lose track of the number of artisans we pass, lost as they are among the booths operated by family compounds. Anyone who's got a couple agro-towers is selling produce. There's seven varieties of *ning* alone, all grown on the same arid hillsides where home is, being readied for export throughout the Realm of Five. I dare anyone to find a better coffee.

Martin's coordinates lead me from the busier routes under the shadows cast by the gantries. Looming hydrofoil freighters block even more light, until what should be a warm summer's day becomes as cool as local autumn. The darkened piers stink of saltwater and decomposing kelp. When we emerge from the shadows of the freighters, we're amidst the unloading of seafood from much smaller fishing vessels. Most dump bushels' worth of pinceen, big, surly crustaceans prone to sever a limb if they get loose. One of the old comms jockey vets, Captain Carl Passarella, likes to rave about Ches-apeake Bay blue claw crabs you can hold in your hand. They sound cute compared to these two-meter monsters.

"Up here," Martin finally says.

Random Plans. That's the name of the trawler. It's a rust-lined, orange-hulled fishing vessel that doesn't look like it would last a day on the Sian Reefs, let alone in the Inland Sea's deep waters. Eight women are scattered about its deck and the docks, some tying off mooring cables, others wrestling new power cells aboard, still others off-loading pinceen. Claws crash against flexible but impenetrable nets that warp to match the creatures' efforts at freedom.

I'm ready to climb out of the hovercraft. Martin puts a hand on my arm. "Stay here, right? No need to cause trouble."

I glare at him. "You've got the gun and crazed ideas about being courier. You won't even tell me what you're couriering. Who's trouble?"

He winks and hops from the hovercraft.

I drum my fingers on the controls. Hard to make out a word anyone's saying with all the clanging racket. Hefter robots lumber about, great metal golems aiding in the cargo shuffle transpiring around us. *Random Plans*' all-female crew shouts orders and arguments. The pinceen aren't quiet, either. Their claws rake against metal.

Hefters take the lead in lashing those offensive weapons down. Then they start filing a shimmering, rainbow-hued coating off the tips. Cytori. That's the name Tiaozhan's settlers gave to the gleanings. You can find some in coastal waters, shed by pinceen when they molt every couple of years, or you can scrape miniscule amounts from live ones if you're lucky. I've never seen one happen like this. Few people do.

Whoever the captain is, she's going to make her people rich today.

Speaking of captain… the woman Martin's gabbing with is half a meter taller, hair bleached by constant sun to a golden sheen. She has the musculature of a person who, unlike me, doesn't spend all her time fiddling with data systems and comms relays. She hauls traps and wrestles pinceen. Scars up and down her arms testify. At least she has all her limbs.

That's why it's surprising Martin's arguing with her. She shakes her head, hands on the hips of a padded, leather-armored worksuit, but Martin stands his ground. He points a finger in accusatory fashion.

Her hand shifts, coming to rest on a hip holster.

This is why I didn't want to come down here. I keep expecting patrol craft to hiss along the road, bring-ing security robots or worse, a contingent of Crown Marshals. You're not supposed to transact business down here, directly. And nobody's supposed to be armed with personal weapons.

Except scramblers. Mine was back aboard the skipjack.

I clamber from the hovercraft, activating Copper as I move. He ejects, rotors humming. I slap [Observe and record] into my wrist comm.

Words resolve through the noise as I close the distance. "…you think? That I'm going to walk out of here with half the package?" Martin's snarling with the ferocity of a mountain panther. "I bring that and they'll come back here for the rest, after they dump me in a reclamation chute."

"Sounds like your problem." The captain's smile is way too predatory for my liking. "You tell them I want to renegotiate the price, or I'm hanging on to the other half."

"Martin!" I pull up beside him. "Got a problem?"

The woman draws her gun and levels it at my gut. "Who's this one?"

"Driver," Martin snaps. "Ignore him."

"Probably better if I don't."

I shake my head. Time was, being held at gunpoint with give me a severe case of panic. Not anymore. "Look, *captain*. You're not blind, so I assume you can read the logo on my outfit. It's not for show. Shoot me, and MarkTel won't take it kindly. Especially not with my bot transmitting everything skyward to my starship."

Her gaze flicks to Copper. Wondering, no doubt, if she can knock the bot out of the air and then blast me. "This rusts, Chen."

I don't know how to answer, until Martin speaks and I realize she's talking to him. "What was that phrase, Rilla?" he sneers. "Sounds like your problem."

She seems to consider this but holsters the gun *way* too slowly. "Fine. Fine." Captain Rilla-Whatever pulls a small blue box from her pocket. It carries a faint aroma of vinegar. "The rest of my payment better get transferred."

"You already got the third. Next third when I deliver. Final third when the product makes it off-world." Martin snatches the box from her hand. "Insurance, you'll recall, in case you try to turn on anyone. Enjoy your morning."

He grabs my arm and steers me back toward the car. "Why didn't you stay put? I had this!"

"If 'this' stands for 'magnetically-accelerated proj-ectile in your gut,' then yeah, I'd agree." I yank my arm free. "Are you insane? What's in that box?"

"Expensive stuff. Nothing you'd find on an approved trade list."

I rub the bridge of my nose as the hovercraft's engine hums to life. I steer us out of there as fast as possible, heading back for the main roads. "I don't want to know. We'd better get back to the compound."

"Whoa, whoa, we can't just drive out of here."

"That was my plan."

"No. Listen, you've got your appointment. I'll catch a tram north to the spaceport and get the illumination cable for Father. By the time I run a few more errands, you should be done with your review-thing and you can come pick me up."

"Letting you roam Yinse Haian for hours on end un-supervised seems like a terrible idea. Especially because that Captain Rilla seems like she wants to shoot you in the face."

Martin waves off the suggestion like he's swatting a pest. "Rilla? Nah. She doesn't hate me. I've helped her earn tremendous cash. She needs me. She just doesn't realize how badly."

Lord above, grant me patience. Because my gauge reads empty. I check the hovercraft's sensors and notification screen. No indication law enforcement is clamoring for our attention. No police or Crown Marshals leaping out of side streets, aiming scramblers at us and disablers at the hovercraft's engines. So that's an answer to prayer.

Except, shouldn't I be praying for us to get caught? I mean, I don't want to help my brother break the law.

But I don't want him locked up forever. Or killed.

Family churns my stomach. "Father's going to deal with this, Martin. Whatever 'deal' you're involved in, I'm getting you clear of it once we get out of town."

"Is your brain that blank? As soon as we hit the city's perimeter sensors, they'll pick us both up! Get onto Long Haul and pull over."

I park us in the nearest slot, between a pair of heavy delivery groundcars, hulking six-wheeled vehicles that smell of vegetables. I grab the box. "Give me that."

"Hey, wait—!"

The contents shine like a field of stars. I suck in a breath. Cytori. Cupped in my hands. I could get arrested right now.

"You happy?" Martin folds his arm. He sulks in his seat, like he's that 10-year-old from whom I got my stolen power cores back. "I was thinking about cutting you in on the deal. But sure, let's drive right out through the sensors. That's a much better idea!"

"*Hun dan*!" I grab his collar. "This stuff is on the controlled list! No one without a House Jiangxi can sell it, much less transport it *off-planet!* We're talking a world-class felony. Not to mention, the eternal anger of the biggest trade consortium on Tiaozhan!"

"Yeah, no kidding." Martin breaks free and vaults out of the car. He swipes the container back and shoves it into a pocket. "That's why I'm not getting caught."

Next thing I know, he's disappeared into the teeming crowds swarming the markets.

Chapter Four

Perfect. He's gone.

No sign of Martin. And I've been looking for a half hour, with Copper flying overhead. Three times, he reports back with possible sightings based on facial and gait recognition of my brother. Three times, I end a long walk with a negative result.

Vac-head isn't answering his comm, either.

So, he's run off from me, in a city I haven't traversed in a decade, with an illegal firearm and an even more illegal commodity.

I wasn't being hyperbolic when I warned him. There are certain spices and other products over which Tiaozhan's trade consortiums hold very profitable and fiercely territorial monopolies. Cytori is one of them. You'll find the pinceen claw gleanings in polished form as jewelry among the king's court at New Cyrene on Earth, and in the dining halls of the great shipbuilding docks in orbit around Muhterem. If that didn't make it a hot trade item enough, extra effort can be taken to powder the material and serve it in drinks. It's got a mildly narcotic effect, one that lasts only a few seconds.

Since House Jiangxi regulates its possession and shipment, local fishing captains have to report its acquisition. It's enshrined in planetary law. Not saying I'm a fan of monopolies, but given I'm a MarkTel employee, I really have no room to talk.

I glance about the crowds. They've decreased, which helps me, but within a couple hours the lunch rush will bring them back in force.

The sun's out in earnest, this late in the morning. Humidity helps superheat the air, this near to the west shore of the Inland Sea. Sweat makes my shirt cling to my chest. I was gonna have to ditch the MarkTel jumpsuit when I got back to the Chen compound.

Part of me wants to keep up the search. That's the heart instructing. But the brain? It's reminding me of my impending review appointment. The one vital to continued employment.

Blazes, Martin.

Okay, reconsider: whatever my idiot brother is doing, he seems like he's been at it for a while. Probably knows his way around the city better than I. It occurs to me then, this is where Martin's gotten the money for his implanted delver technology. That sort of messaging doesn't come cheap. It isn't just the memory and processors that have to be implanted. No, the skin has to be altered at the genetic level. Specialists have to induce bio-luminescence. Then you've got to get it all programmed, after cross-wiring it with the processor.

That kind of enhancement is cost prohibitive. So, Martin would need extra cash.

As for his courier work, I seriously doubt Mother and Father are aware—especially Father. Martin would be herded off to the nearest kelp processing facility on the South Shore, tending the vats while underwater robots harvested their crop for hungry customers.

What's the alternative? Alert the police, again, my parents come into play. No way I'm instigating heartbreak. Plus, they'll probably think I'm unfairly targeting Martin, since it's obvious I hold a grudge.

This was way easier with the ex-Kesek colonists. I could forgive them. Didn't know them from Adam, as the saying went, but then again, they're not family.

So, I opt for a compromise.

I recall Copper and issue new commands: [Continue search and report findings, non-urgent.] That last bit means he won't interrupt my meeting with a noisy alert or a distracting hologram.

Copper flits off, joining the intermittent swarms of personal brassjackets and law enforcement bots skimming between the buildings.

Once he's gone, I log in with my MarkTel access codes. There's a nice one for emergencies. It lets me tap into any local law enforcement channel—for monitoring purposes only, of course. I can't tamper with what they send and receive, which is for the best.

A couple of swipes, and I've got my very own condensed version of the Yinse Haian Constabulatory's incident feed scrolling along the lower half of my wrist comm's tiny screen. The contents are compressed onto my delver's memory, in case I miss something real-time and need to retrieve it for review. I make certain I program the algorithm with all the variables of this name:

Martin Impatiens Chen.

I snicker, despite the seriousness of my predicament. The only thing redeeming this mess is Martin's middle name is more cringe-worthy than mine. Such was my parents' resolution of their disagreement. Thankfully Father won when it came to our given names.

I'll bet they were relieved when Child Number Three was a girl. Lily has it easy.

My possible avenues of investigation covered, I jump back in the hovercraft and leave the markets behind. Nothing shows up on the incident report. Not yet.

I swear, if that fool gets himself arrested for possession of contraband goods, I will be first to testify against him at his trail.

Right after my parents stop hollering at me.

The MarkTel Communications Headquarters, Region Six, is downtown. Calling it the heart of the city is both geographically and psychologically accurate. It's the tallest building in town, forty stories, of which the top half is a transmission spike. The bottom half is polarized green, reflecting an emerald version of the city around us, while the transmission spike is a pearly bronze. Rumors abounded that the thing could punch a signal anywhere in the system, while simultaneously sucking up every bit of data seeping from every linked computer in the same space.

Two slender robots on treads greet me outside the front door. Sentry-shade series, Model IX. Programmed to subdue intruders with the scrambler stun weapons mounted on their shoulders.

Their human counterparts, clad in lightweight full-body armor and gray fatigues, carry Tegest automatic rifles and are under no such compunctions.

My wrist comm and delver chirp in unison as the HQ security system marks me as not only an authorized employee, but a comms ferry captain. A guard nods in deferential fashion. I salute back. Seems the thing to do.

The climate system keeps the air blessedly cool and drier, like in the tops of the foothills west of the family compound. Here's hoping it's enough to dry the sweat before I stand in judgment before the director.

A lift whisks me to the twentieth floor, and deposits me in a white box of a waiting room. No one else around. Just a pair of red couches, and two vines creeping across the walls. Flarebranch again. These are an anemic mustard color, with only dull pulses of orange. That's what happens when you try to keep them growing indoors.

Speaking of doors, the pair opposite the lift open onto a gorgeous view of the region west of Yinse Haian. I'm sure one of myriad compounds sprawling over those hills is my family's. Clumps of aspens crown the vista.

But it's the guy sitting in the middle who occupies the focus of my attention. I'd be less alarmed if an asteroid fragmented in the middle of *Marconi*'s high-velocity course.

"Captain Chen. Come in." Director Solomon Margate clears a pair of holographic display rectangles from between us—which is good, because he's got so many barricading his desk they might as well be a physical fence. Each one carries schematics for a comms ferry, with diagnostic reports and 3-D models. It takes me a microsecond to realize they're all *mine*—units I've repaired or replaced over the past year.

There's an image of me, too, though I'm looking at the hazy version from the backside.

Margate waits for me to stand in front of his desk. He's a tall guy, lanky, with gaunt cheeks. His suit is a soft gray, with silver highlights on the black shirt worn underneath. Sandy brown hair is cut with as much perfection as a laser-carved tunnel on an asteroid habitat. Powder blue eyes track my every move. "Thank you for coming in person."

"Sir. I didn't think it was a choice." I've never served a day in anyone's version of the military, but I do my best to stand at pseudo-attention.

"True, it wasn't an invitation, but your promptness is appreciated." Margate's desk is made of marble lined in metal. He sits on a corner, then orients a screen so I can see it. "Your response rating, from last year. Read it for me."

"Eight point five."

"Putting you among the top five percent of comms ferry jockeys in terms of response time, accuracy of reports, and efficiency of repairs. I'm talking galaxy-wide. You're one of the best in Region Six. I'd only rate Captain Passarella more highly."

I studiously avoid rolling my eyes. If Carl were here, the veteran would elbow me and remind "Vinnie" of his ability and superiority. Keeping my face neutral takes every ounce of energy I'm not spending on giving good and true answers. "Thank you."

"You're welcome." His smile slips, and there's a mask as solid as a spacesuit's faceplate in its place. "While there's no denying you are efficient at your job—and MarkTel thanks you for that—you've shown increasing lapses in judgment."

Here it comes. First up? Planetary scans of Sylvanak, followed by the text of a Rescue Ops report and news footage from the Reach of people being herded onto a barge landing craft painted white with blue edging. People in dark green jumpsuits.

"Your actions led to the arrest of dozens of Restorat-ionist colonists."

"Sir, in my defense, they'd enslaved a planetary population."

"I wasn't asking for you to defend yourself, Captain. I certainly understand the situation. This is me laying out the facts." The reports and imagery fade. The profile of a woman replaces them.

"Izzara Neoh," Margate says. "Formerly in the employ of the

Intelligence Service of the Realm. Incarcerated by ISR following your rescue of her from Comms Ferry 550 two months ago."

Better I keep my mouth shut on this one. It's bad enough I can't control my heart's crazy pace. There's a sickening feeling deep in my guts. That face. How many times had it smiled at me over a 48-hour period? Right up until she admitted the truth.

She wasn't a spy, but an ex-spy, turned industrial saboteur and thief.

Bigger problem? ISR claimed this was classified data—my involvement, Izzy's true name, the whole packet. Yet here was my boss, laying out the information for my perusal.

If I ever wondered how much pull my MarkTel supervisors have when it comes to galactic politics, I know the answer.

Margate stands in front of his desk, hands clasped behind his back. His face is even with Izzy's. Too easy to imagine she's in the room with us. "This, Captain Chen, is when I'd appreciate some explanation."

"Sir. I've filed all the proper reports."

"Yes, and all very detailed, too. What I want is your assurance MarkTel property is safe."

"You have it, sir."

"Stop with the 'sir.'" Margate shakes his head. "This isn't a Lancer division. Did Neoh get something from us?"

"No…Mr. Margate."

"Solomon."

Okay, this level of offered familiarity doesn't set me at ease, if that's the purpose. "Look, I don't know what else you want me to say. I helped people out. Was it the wrong decision? Maybe in Izzy—Izzara Neoh's case. But I wouldn't change my actions. In the end, both situations turned out for the best."

"For you. And for the individuals involved. What about MarkTel?"

"Sorry?"

"What about our corporation? Our public image? Our shareholders?" Margate raised a single finger. "Don't forget the king himself. His Royal Highness maintains control over the Realm of Five through MarkIntech, which in turn supplies and owns MarkTel."

"I think we're probably okay, considering we're the only way people have to communicate with each other through the sundoors." I shrug. "No one wants to wait years to get messages from loved ones and business partners."

"We are considerably more than 'okay,' but my job is, in part, to make certain MarkTel's image is polished to a shine. These reports, Captain, don't paint our corporation as a reliable, unintrusive provider of interstellar comm-unications. At best, they show us to be meddlers in affairs that don't concern us."

"I'd say the safety and security of public data concerns us."

"This is true. But take into account these." Margate bends his wrist. A spray of holographic text erupts from behind his knuckles. So, he's paid up for the implanted delver, too. His is far subtler for than Martin's garish display. "A statement from one Captain Brian Gaudette about the 'godly' actions you portrayed on Sylvanak. And a recording from your bridge's security system…"

There's me, discussing Scripture with Izzy, Bible in plain view.

So much for "unintrusive." Forget the submissive pose. I fold my arms. "Spying on me. That's classy."

"Don't act offended. Your ship, and all its hardware, belong to MarkTel."

Blue letters slide by on my wrist comm, at the periphery of my vision. The police incidents? My heart skips.

No. It's Copper. [Martin Impatiens Chen located. 17000 Block, north of Tabernash Street. Coordinates noted. Action?]

There's my brother. Lingering in a park, at the edge of Yinse Haian's sensors. The scan seems fuzzy—and then it makes perfect sense. Flarebranch. The vines, in great concentration, muddle sensors.

"Captain Chen?"

"Hmm?" I snap back to attention.

Margate's staring at me. "Do you agree?"

"Ah…"

"I said, your personal beliefs have no bearing on your employment. This is the post-Kesek era. Freedom of religion is the law of the land." Margate's eyes narrow. "However, if your faith interferes with your work, I will terminate your employment."

"I understand."

"I wonder if you do. The *Koninklijke Stabiliteitskracht* may be gone, but its consequences linger. Consequences that include generations trained to view unsanctioned religion with suspicion. That includes directors of our corporation, and despite the king's personal endorsement, members of the royal house." Margate steps close. He prods my chest with a finger. "Do not mistake free-dom from persecution for insulation from consequences."

I whip north on Tabernash to the spaceport. Don't want to forget Father's illumination cable.

I ignore the relentless aerial traffic, and the mass of people swarming the giant, lumpy domes of the terminal so I can purchase the cable. My head's a blur of emotion and thought. MarkTel is fully aware of my faith. And they aren't happy. At least, Director Margate isn't.

But he's also head of Region Six, and good luck to anyone trying to find similar work in another region if he personally dismissed me. The thought of losing my ship and my crew appalls me. It isn't just transport, or a job.

It's home.

Speaking of which, as soon as I leave the city borders and bank north again, the last place I want to go is home. Especially when I spot Martin lurking in the shadow of a tall, gnarled bole tree dripping with flarebranch vines.

There's so much traffic about that it's easy to wind my way through the groundcars and hovercraft toward the city boundary. Hong Quan's brought hordes of people, so many that there's hundreds on foot exploring not only the park but the gardens scattered all along the city's edge, mingling with the agro-towers.

Like I suspected, Martin's got a plan.

"About time!" Martin slips into the seat next to me. He flashes a brilliant grin. "Go!"

I turn the hovercraft toward the compound—home, again—and pray I wasn't making a mistake the size of a red giant star.

Chapter Five

I successfully avoid human contact for the rest of the afternoon. Martin stays busy tending plants in the garden. Mother's ensconced in her work, speaking with representatives from her office. Father's scrambling about prepping dinner, solo, until Mother breaks free to help. They've got an army of local caterers incoming to lend a hand.

Lily finds me fiddling with the skipjack's engines.

"You were right," I say. "Five percent out of sync."

She sits on the lower wing, kicking her feet like we used to at the Endless Beach. I'd scrounge for shells, while Martin rode a waveboard. Lily liked to hang about on the rocks, bare toes swinging above me, the sun winking out and blazing on with each stroke. "What's wrong?"

"Um, it's out of sync. Like you said."

"Not the engine, vac-head. You."

"I'm fine."

"No, you're not. Something bothering you. Something you don't want to talk about." She squints.

Great. She's still got that way of boring into my soul. Getting me to talk. Especially when I don't want to. "It's, ah, personal."

"Then it's better I found out." She tips her head. "It's the girl, right? The one you mentioned in your commnote."

Oh. "Yes. Yeah, it's her." The more we avoid talking about Martin's shady dealings and his general being a pain, the better.

"I know you can't say what she was up to, but I know she must have hurt you. I'm sorry."

I shrug. Doesn't make it less uncomfortable. "Thanks. You don't have to be. I learned my lesson."

"Really? Like the long-distance comm relationship you had with the tech at Alcova's research station? That ended badly."

"We got along all right. Visited each other a few times. Melinda Qin. She was nice, and a believer, but we just did-n't sync. I know that sounds stupid, but when we were together, things were just okay."

"And you've got exacting standards."

"Doesn't everyone?"

Lily smiles. "Don't ask me. I'm seeing Dan Gillard."

"Danny? Danny the chemistry major?"

"Chemist, now. Apprenticing under Dr. Yun."

I nod. Never thought Dan was particularly bright, but he must be, if Yun took him on. Yun didn't suffer incompetence. "Good for him. And you, too."

"He's nice. And funny. Handy with hoverjets, too." She winks at me. "I wish you'd find someone nice like that."

I don't have the heart to tell her I'd probably jet from the tarmac if Izzy appeared in the flesh and never look back. That, or turn her in to the Crown Marshals for escaping incarceration. "Why'd this have to be complex? I could have stayed home, taken up hydrology, and married local. That was the plan."

"I know. Until Uncle Ethan." She reaches for my shoulder.

I touch her hand. "Glad you weren't there."

"Of all the nights to visit a friend..." She sniffs. "Father said Martin cried for days. You, though, went quiet."

"I was mad. Angry at everyone. Spent the last year home that way." I cycle through diagnostics. Engine's back in sync. Wish the same were true for me. I slam home the access panel and make sure the magnetic seals are secure. "Mother broke me free of that. She pushed me to make a decision. When I did, Father blessed it. Told me to find my life but remember never to trade away my soul."

"What good would it do if you did?" Lily smiles. "But I'm glad you came back."

"Me, too." I return her smile. "For the most part."

"Vincent! Lily!" Father's at the kitchen. "Guests in one hour!"

I moan.

Lily hops from the wing and nudges my leg with her boot. "No more sulking, Captain. This isn't robot updates or a comms ferry's reboot. You've got to put on your formals. Time to be sociable!"

I hate being sociable.

One time, I almost died of hypoxia when I drifted free of my ship and had to ride a jury-rigged comms ferry back to safety. Even then, only the attentiveness of my robot crew saved me from death.

This is worse.

Two hundred people, in and around our compound. Thirty of those are relatives. I remember maybe another twenty by name and face. The rest? I wasn't kidding about Rei the tech. He shakes my hand and says something hurried about, "Thank you for your service," before attacking a tray piled with spiced kelp and roast duck.

"Service? You're in the military now?" Martin leans against a doorjamb, sipping on a cider.

"I think he means working for MarkTel. Commun-ications kept clear for the Realm and all of that."

Martin snorts. "Yeah? Communications monitoring is more like it."

"That was under Kesek. There's a different set of management on top."

"I'm sure they have better things to do than snoop in our private messages, right?"

I want to say yes, and on the whole, I believe it's true, yet I recall the ease with which ISR operatives were able to access MarkTel equipment and even my personnel files. Sure, MarkTel and the Realm of Five's govern-ment are tied closely together. The king's family name is Markham, for crying out loud. That's where the company comes from.

But arresting people because of what they read? Those days are gone.

As far as I know.

"Vincent! Vincent, it's lovely to see you!" The woman who hugs me around the waist could be half my height, even though her voice is twice as loud as mine. She's got white hair and what looks like a vision stabilization implant in her right eye. "I thought for sure you'd be in uniform."

"Not tonight. Mother insisted." She didn't want me standing about like an awkward tech in my rumpled black jumpsuit. Instead I'm in tan pants and a lightweight peach-colored shirt. The day's heat is on the wane, but it's still swampy in the dining area, living space, and kitchen, all of which have their walls open to the garden.

"Well, how have you been? I think it's been ten years since I saw you!"

And possibly longer, since I have no clue who this lady is. I glance at Martin, desperate for a hint, but he's already got his arm around a lovely young woman with blond hair who may or may not have been one of my classmates. He winks and raises his glass in salute as they walk away.

Traitor. "Yes, work's been like that. Long voyages. Deep space. It's, ah, far away."

"Oh, it must be wonderful!" The lady's hanging on my arm. She drags me around the room. "Kei-shan! Come here! You remember Vincent, don't you!"

Kei-shan… as in, Lun? Mother's cousin. A widow for two decades now. And if the tall, spindly Kei-shan was responding to this woman's call, the one wrapped around my arm must be Victoria Yun. Wife of Dr. Yun the chemist. Mother's supervisor and one of the partners in Yun Medical. The practitioner of all manner of healing and programmer of the finest surgical robots on this side of Tiaozhan.

I think. She could be a garden hand, for all I know.

"Hi, Victoria!" Lily sweeps in, as welcome as a cool breeze off the hills. She's transformed herself from mechanic to that young woman I mentioned earlier, the one all the guys would like at their sides. I spot four young faces that turn her way, in fact. She's let her hair down long and flowing, secured by a bronze barrette. Her dress is white with blue flowers, and as everyone watches, golden stylized streaks of wind gust across the print, making those flowers shudder and scattering petals. Then the imagery resets and replays. It's a seamless display of programmable fabrics.

"Lily, darling, you've cleaned up nicely." Victoria and my sister exchange friendly hugs. How Lily manages to not drop twin glasses of wine I have no idea. "Tell your brother he really must work on his manners."

"That's why I come back home, Dr. Yun." I smile. "For training."

The women laugh, and thankfully, Lily hands me a glass. The bold scent of Xeng wine hits me right as she pulls me into another crowd of people talking so loudly in four languages, they don't notice us. "You're welcome."

"Thank you and *xiexie*." I sip the contents. There's a reason '88 Xeng is the best on the interstellar market. "That was as bad as—"

"Pirate raid? Asteroid collision? Some other space-related comparison?" Lily giggles. "You really do need to get off that ship more than once every Hong Quan, Vincent."

"I won't argue it."

"How'd your review go?"

"As well as I could expect. You know, the basic 'you're doing a good job, now don't mess it up' speech."

"Basic."

"Yeah, well, other than the special aspect for me. Keeping my faith out of it."

"Your faith that drives you to help people? I'd think they'd be happy with that. Good public relations for the company."

"Good, in the sense people see the logo related to compassion. Less than good, in that my actions have the label 'Christian' attached to them. Nobody's calling the secret police, but the habit's hardly been broken."

"The habit of blame." Lily shrugs. "I don't worry about it. Whether or not the hovercraft are operating, whether or not Father needs new parts for the garden pumps, whether or not Mother's comm systems are on the fritz—that's what I worry about. Even then, it's not worry, really, but vigilance. You know why?"

I smile. "Because we're not supposed to worry."

"Aced." Lily kisses me on the cheek. "You do your readings, from time to time. I'm glad you didn't forget everything when you raced off into space!"

"You're a pain, sometimes."

"Only sometimes? I must be slipping. I'm gonna go find Dan. You good?"

"Good enough for now."

"Stay out of trouble. I won't be back for a second rescue!"

She's gone deeper into the crowds and I slip out by the gardens. There's Mother and Father, laughing along with the jokes made by the Fullers, long-time neighbors. Childless.

Ronnie Fuller was held in a Kesek cell until he committed suicide.

I rub my forehead. This is what home is: fond mem-ories, boundless love, both mingled with tragedy and heart-break. This is why I don't come home. Space is better, right? Only the memories follow me there.

Until I make new mistakes and create my own memories. Ones which, shockingly, don't stay in orbit.

"Vince."

If Martin sneaks up again, I'll recommend him to ISR. There's a woman I know there in need of talent. "You're not borrowing my hovercraft."

"I wasn't—how'd you know?" He shakes his head. "Never mind. No, spacebrain, I was going to suggest you drive me out. To Cratered."

I stare at him. "You're serious? You want to me to eject from the dinner party our parents threw for *me* so I can drop you at your favorite club?"

"Something like that. Actually, I was gonna say you should stay there with me. Loosen up." He rolls his eyes. "You're not enjoying this, are you? This walk down memory lane. I'd rather be run over by a groundcar convoy hauling kelp."

Huh. So, he does understand. I glance at my wrist-comm. 2030 hours. It's really dragged on *this* long?

"This isn't you," he murmurs, hand on my shoulder. "Forced mingling with people who don't really remember you, just like you don't really remember them. You don't belong in a part. You're the lone pilot, the fearless captain. You solve problems, solo, when no one else can. Ditch this and let's go have some fun."

Probably he's planning an outing to Cratered as a cover for delivering the cytori. At this point, that's fine by me. The sooner he gets rid of this, the better. "Okay." I prod his chest with a finger, and suddenly I'm Margate's clone. "But after this, you're done. No more of these jobs. If you need money, I can transfer some. Not a bunch, but enough you shouldn't have to skirt the contraband laws anymore. Deal?"

"Absolutely." Martin shakes my hand. "Let's get the blazes out of here."

Cratered is a couple klicks north of Bright Sky Spaceport, out of reach of Yinse Haian's sensor grid. It's a flashing swath of neon and glow-crete, walls that shine as glaringly as if they're reflecting the midday sun. You get all kinds of advertisements across the outside panels—drinks, food, Inland Sea tours, cliff-soaring, even behemoth-worm tube surfing. Never tried the last one. Mostly because I don't like the idea of coming face to gaping maw with a tunneling worm as big as *Marconi*. They eat dirt, yeah, but…

As surprised as I am that Cratered looks the same as when I left, the sensation pales compared to the shock that the scanners let Martin and I waltz through like we're members. Which, admittedly, Martin must be.

"I helped the owner out a year and a half ago!" Martin has to shout over the thumping music. I can barely keep track of him in the pulsing lights and mass of bodies packed in the double-door entryway. "Cytori! Only a tiny portion, but it was enough we both earned serious cash!"

I nod, glad I understand but dismayed he's blasting his mouth off like a particle cannon. "Where's the meet up?"

"Table Twenty-One, in the back corner. Come on!"

Martin leads me deeper into the club. There's an actual live band tonight, come all the way from Oportunidad performing *vibrante*. Wailing brass and frenetic strings make for an infectious dance.

There's all kinds of people around. Tiaozhan's initial stock were Han Chinese, yes, but over the centuries, there's been a sizable influx of all ethnicities and races. Most of that minority is from African bloodlines—and they themselves hailing from most corners of good old Earth—not to mention extended family of the royal clans. There's a goodly chunk of Muhteremi-slash-Arabic, plus the mixed Caucasians of Starkweather.

Tonight, they're all dancing under the lights.

Ten minutes there, and some old classmates rope me into their crowd. I've never had so much laughter, so many old jokes, and it's as if all the dark memories get shoved right of out of my head, as surely as if I've wiped a comms ferry's databank clean. Martin's off talking to someone, a couple someones, at a table in the back, and for the first time I could care less. I let myself soak in the moment, enjoying the laudations from the guys I used to know in secondary school and relishing the dance I share with one of the women.

Right up until Martin crashes through a tray of spring rolls and slides into our midst with a *thump*.

There's not even a skip in the music as everyone around us erupts in shouts. I stand there, arms at the woman's waist, and the two of us stare at Martin, whose face is upside down.

"Hey," he croaks.

Hey, indeed. I look up.

Nine men shove their way from the back of the club, all grimaces and bodies stacked with muscle.

And they're armed.

Chapter Six

I help Martin to his feet. He brushes spring roll off his shirt. "That's gonna stain."

"You've got worse problems," I mutter. "Those the guys who shoved you?"

"Don't worry." He draws his gun. "I've got this."

"You most certainly do not 'got this,' Martin." I clamp a hand around the barrel and push it toward the floor. "Are you blind and unable to count? They're *all* armed."

"Back off and let me handle this!"

Doesn't matter what I do, because two of the men advance on us without any fear of Martin's meager defense. Both guys look like their buddies—short, stocky, athletic. Their heads bristle with buzzcut hair of varying lengths, some pink, some yellow, all shifting hues as they move. The left sides of their faces are covered with tattoos, stylized images of behemoth-worms curving from their brows to their necks. Their clothing is a motley mix of colors and styles, all bright.

The pink-haired one pulls Martin's gun from our grasp. He sweeps my legs out from underneath me and the next microsecond, I'm on my back, trying to get up, except there's a handgun much bigger than Martin's illegal, compact model glaring at me. Red streaks flash through Pink Hair's buzzcut.

The second guy, this one with gold spikes, puts Martin into a bear hug. Martin gasps, color draining from his face. It's hard to hear with the band still jamming, but something mechanical *whirrs* in the background. I really hope it isn't coming from Gold Spike.

"Marty." The leader's voice is rough, like he's guzzled a bottle of the cleaner they use to polish starship drive nozzles and survived. He's bald, with a thick, sharp goatee and moustache. His eyes are brown, but they spark with illuminated circuitry. Red shirt, with the stylized behemoth-worm image his boys have on their faces, and black pants. He could be a nightclub owner, right down to the rings on his right hand—one each colored black, white, gold, silver, and bronze. "How's Captain Rilla?"

"Rilla? She's great. Yeah, great. I'm finishing a transaction for her." Martin's answer comes out in wheezes. Gold Spike doesn't seem like he's willing to let go.

"I know why you're here. I also know what you've got." He grabs the front of Martin's shirt. "I also know who's the top smuggler of said goods—and, hint, it isn't you or Captain Rilla."

"Hold on." I push to my feet, slowly, because I don't want Pink Hair shooting me. The leader looks at me as if I've barged into the wrong restroom. "Let's take this outside and see if we can't figure out our problem."

"Our problem?" He sounds ready to inflict violence, and I'm bracing myself for an incoming punch, when his scowl all of a sudden disappears. "Great steaming drive nozzles. Vincent?"

"Yes. Captain Vincent Chen." My hands are on my hips, posture as straight as it's ever going to get—enough to gain Father's nod. All I need is triumphant brass and I imagine I can use my MarkTel authority to counter violence with reason.

"It's Grant. Grant Liu."

He could have stunned me with a scrambler and I'd be less astonished. "Grant? You're still here? I thought you left years ago."

Grant snorts. "Where else would I be? Unlike you. Word was you ran off-planet, chasing comms ferries."

"Good way to do honest work, helping other people." I fold my arms. "I take it your career path went differently."

"Let's say I'm carving out a niche market, and I don't appreciate others trying to elbow in." He stares at Martin.

Grant Liu. Childhood pal. Smartest kid in our class. Graduated earlier than the rest, right before he got picked up by Kesek—courtesy of my brother's rash decision. I'd have put money on him becoming a Raszewski sphere physicist or a medical tech.

Instead, he's got a gang of eight armed goons at his back and is threatening my brother.

"Let Martin go," I say. "No one's been hurt. We can all walk out of this."

"Sorry. Not possible. Your *bái chī* brother has been dipping his toes in our end of the pool. Unfortunately, there's piranhas."

Odd way to put it. The left side of Grant's face twitches. He rubs at his eyes. They seem bleary, unfocused, until something flickers around their edges. He's got a vision stabilizer implant, keeping his sight from degenerating. I've seen specs of those come through Mother's delver when she's routing Yun Medical commnotes. "Okay, so, Martin isn't known for his impulse control, or his common sense—"

"Hey!"

"Shut up," I snap. "Listen, Grant, take the cytori and we'll go."

"No way!" Martin wriggles free of Gold Spike, and for a moment I assume I've underestimated the guy who's got cybernetic limbs. Except Gold Spike is staring directly into Grant's eyes. He's got a similar implant.

Huh. So, it's doing something other than stabilizing Grant's eyesight. Covert communication?

Grant puts a pistol to Martin's chest, a big, black AkTek model. Martin's wide-eyed, pale. Grant doesn't blink, or respond in any way other than a cold, hard glare. "Not happening, Vincent." There's that twitch again, an odd rictus. "I've got customers to please. Money to make. Your brother's impacting that. Rilla needs to learn a lesson. A couple holos of Martin suffering as the object of that lesson should send the right signal to her, don't you think? You're the comms expert."

I don't think it's possible for Martin to look any more terrified. "Are you serious?" he stammers. "I'm not going anywhere with you! I've got a delivery to make! You know what happens if Rilla finds out I lost the cytori?"

But a quick glance confirms that there's no one left at the table Martin had been visiting. The people with whom he'd been making a deal must have bolted as soon as Grant's crew threw their potential delivery man across the floor.

"Take him," Grant says.

Pink Hair and two more men encircle Martin. Grant pushes me aside so Gold Spike can join them. That leaves four more of Grant's people forming a loose perimeter around our—negotiation?

It doesn't matter much, because the dance floor has cleared out. No one offers a rescue, even though the crowds vastly outnumber Grant and his eight men. Blazes, most of the patrons are laughing and enjoying drinks at the edge of our scene like it's a high-resolution hologram.

Even the girl I was dancing with and our fellow classmates have vanished.

"You're not taking Martin out of here," I tell Grant. "He's leaving with me."

"Really? I don't see a squad of police with you." He snaps his fingers. "Oh, right, that's because I paid them to steer clear of Cratered for a few hours. Like I do everywhere I need to transact business in the Western Province."

Grant shoves me again, harder, and this time I swing back, since he's got no one stationed between us.

The punch catches him by surprise, because it catches him in the jaw. He staggers, hand to his face—the twitchy left side.

Pink Hair and Gold Spike are on my arms as securely as docking clamps. They pull until I feel like I'm about to become a double amputee. Pink Hair drives his fist deep in my gut.

I lose all breath. Never been hit that hard. I sag in their grip, gasping for air. I'm gonna pass out. Can't do that. Martin needs me.

Speaking of Martin…

"Get your hands off Vince!" His spit sprays across the face of the nearest thug. "You want me? Let him go! He doesn't have anything to do with this."

"Sure he does," Grant mutters. "Because he rose to your defense. Really. The spineless informer, begging for his brother's safety. I was irritated when I got word some amateur was sneaking cytori of Yinse Haian's docks. Bad enough for the stupidest *èr bai wŭ* this side of the Tiaozhan Path to show up thinking he'll sell contraband under *my* scans, sneaking cytori off-planet with the Hong Quan traffic as cover. Then I hear it's Marty, the sneak who got me thrown in a Kesek cell for thirty-nine days."

Martin's studying his shoes, that spark of bravado snuffed.

Grant grabs him by the hair, and shouts in his face, "Thirty! Nine! Days! No food. No water. The barest nutr-ients delivered to keep me alive. Light when they felt like it. Deafening sound when they felt like it. Nerve torture. So, excuse me if I take this one personally. This is payback."

Grant glares at me. "You know what he did. And you still defend him."

"Not what he's done. But…" I cough. Close to throwing up. "I'll lay down my life for his, if I have to." It galls me to make the admission, but there it is. I'm unable to deny.

"Right. Greater love and all that trash." Grant spits on my shirt. "I've had my fill. All the prayer in the galaxy didn't save me from that cell. No miracles. No friends protesting my release. And if God wanted me to go through that, if it was all part of his plan, then you Chens are welcome to him, blind and brainless as you are."

Grant's men drag Martin toward the back of Cratered, as he screams and thrashes in their grasp. He's putting up a supernova of a fight, but it isn't enough, not again-st these musclebound opponents who've got cybernetic enhancements.

"Martin!" I pull against my captors, even try for a kick, but nothing works. I can't even reach my wrist-comm to call for help.

A gunshot brings the odd combination of shouting and revelry to a standstill. Even Grant and his men stop what they're doing, perplexed. No doubt they figure they should be the ones shooting. My captors release me.

An old man parts the crowd. He's taller than everyone else in the room, skin as dark and rich as the soil Father gardens with. It's highlighted by the snowy white moustache that droops down either side of his moth. The man's dressed in black trousers and wears a brown leather vest over a formal white shirt so crisp it could be fresh out of its wrapper.

Of greater note is the gun he holds. You can't get a Hunsaker Sentinel with a civilian permit. I'm not even sure you could find one on the black market. I've certainly never seen one. It's not your standard self-defense firearm. The silvery-blue barrel reflects the dizzying dance floor lights.

Whoever this guy is, though, he doesn't dress like military.

And then I see the badge—golden bear, rampant on a silver shield.

"Mr. Liu." His voice is deep, resonant, and commands everyone in the room to shut up and pay attention. Yet, there's also a warm, grandfatherly quality to it. "Reckon you and your boys didn't get the commnote."

"And what message was I expecting?" Grant's bravado is gone. The words sound like he's pushing back but there's no mistaking the tension in his body language. He wants to get out of there.

"Told you plenty of times. Police won't show, mind, 'cause you've paid them off. Can't say the same trick will help you now." The man waves his gun. "Let the kid go."

"This doesn't concern you, Tyler." Grant tries a smile. "A simple disagreement between businessmen."

"It's Marshal Tyler, and you'd best not forget." Tyler gestures again. "Let the kid go."

Great flashing nova. This old guy's a Crown Marshal. A member of the only law enforcement agency whose jurisdiction extends throughout the Realm of Five. They track criminals across every world, to every star system. Kesek made sure they were disbanded a long time ago, but for the past eleven years, they've been pressed back into service.

And this Tyler must have been one of the first recruits.

"Don't make it a third request, Grant. You and your boys disperse. Turn over your transport for inspection."

"We won't be doing that. We're leaving." Grant clasps Martin's shoulders. The thugs already released him, and have spread out into a loose semi-circle, something I missed. "Our associate is coming along for the ride. Right, Martin?"

Okay. Tell Tyler the deal went wrong, own up to your mistake, and we can all walk away. Let him know Grant's after you because you and Captain Rilla are upstart competitors.

"Sure, yeah," Martin stammers. "Overdue visit. Grant's a school friend of my brother's. We've—got some things to work out."

"Martin!" I snap. "Don't do it!"

Pink Hair swings for me again, on the offensive, and I take the hit, but I roll with it, and it glances off my shoulder. Painful as anything, but it leaves me able to strike back.

Our fight is cut short when Tyler presses his Hunsaker to Pink Hair's temple. "Nope."

Grant and four of his men herd Martin toward the backside of the club. There must be an exit. I have to intercept, but there's so many people stampeding, and so many emergency drones ushering people out the doors, that I'm stuck between the crowds and the remainder of Grant's guys.

Pink Hair sweeps his hand up, faster than I thought possible, to knock Tyler's gun from his grasp.

But Tyler's apparently familiar with this maneuver, because he sidesteps, letting Pink Hair's palm slice through bare air. Tyler smashes the butt of his gun down on Pink Hair's face, right between his eyes. There's a thick *crack* and a spray of blood from one very broken nose.

Another guy pushes into our midst, but I hook my shoe around his ankle. He dives face first for the floor. I land atop him, wrestling his arms behind his back, and crank one limb so far up to his neck that he cries out.

Then there's Gold Spike. He appears among the last panicking dregs of the club's crowd. He aims Martin's contraband pistol.

"Look out!" I'm still trying to restrain the squirming guy pressed under my knees.

Tyler's faster. One shot thunders in the confined space.

Gold Spike collapses, like a felled tree. He clutches his side, moaning.

Something gray and tangled spirals through the air. I catch the binders. They wrap around my prisoner's wrists, self-sealing, and extending miniscule barbs into the back of his shirt. The guy's hands are essentially bonded to his lower back.

Meanwhile Tyler turns his attention to the last of Grant's men. This one challenges Tyler's height, slim, pale-skinned, but just as crazy-haired and tattooed as the rest. He barrels into Tyler, driving the Crown Marshal against the wall. He backs up, unleashes a flurry of strikes at Tyler's face and upper body.

They're mostly blocked. Tyler's no martial arts expert, but he's passable, and when the attacker makes the unfortunate mistake of letting his opponent get a grip on his shirt, Tall Slim gets slammed onto the stage. He knocks over chairs. Good thing the band has long fled, taking their instruments with them.

"Get on up." Tyler hauls him to his feet, spins him around, and presses him against the same wall that he got introduced to with all the gentleness of a hand slapping a spider. "You are under arrest by order of the Crown Marshals Service, under authority of His Majesty King Andrew II of the Realm of Five. You may remain silent if you so choose. What statements you do choose to make will be used as evidence of your collusion in the crime for which you stand accused."

I elbow the backside of the guy I'm seated upon. "Likewise."

With two prisoners secured and Pink Hair still out cold from the impact to his face, Tyler attends to Gold Spike's wound. The adhesive bandage he applies hisses as it injects a quick-clotting foam. Judging by the way Gold Spike unclenches his teeth, I'll bet it's laced with a painkiller.

Alarms are blaring around us. Patrol drones swoop into the room. There's no way they got here this fast from Yinse Haian after the first shots were reported. Probably they were lurking nearby, held at bay by corrupt local police.

"Much obliged." Tyler offers a hand. "Horatio Henry Tyler."

"Vincent Chen, Tyler. Thanks."

"Call me Hank."

I meet his handshake. But he clamps a binder around the wrist and puts me in custody just like the guys we team-ed up to defeat. "Best we find a private place to confer, Captain. Got to get to the bottom of our case."

"Our case?" I shake my head. "I'm not involved in your investigation."

Tyler shrugs. "And yet, here you are."

Chapter Seven

Punching Martin in front of Father and Mother was bad enough.

Telling them he's been abducted is worse.

"This is preposterous." Father's pacing the length of the kitchen, not slowing or stopping as he interrogates me and the crown marshal. "Martin's no criminal."

"Afraid we have to disagree," Hank Tyler says. "Kid was smuggling cytori shell. Taking payments for delivery. Dealing with unsavory folk."

"Smuggling?" Mother laughs, but it's not a happy sound. It's one of those caustic, derisive sounds, the laugh she'd always make when I was trying to pull a fast one and she wasn't buying. "He doesn't need the money. He has a job, right here."

"Come on," I say. "You didn't think he would stay in the family gardens forever, did you? He saw his deliveries as a path to freedom."

"He could have left whenever he wanted."

I roll my eyes. "We all know *that's* not true."

"You certainly left when you were ready."

Ah, there it is. "Because my options were limited, Mother. You even urged me to acknowledge the very fact. And, sorry, but memories of secret police opp-ression didn't make this a place I wanted to hang around one microsecond longer."

Father clears his throat. "Marshal, pardon, but are those restraints necessary?"

Hank's leaning against the open door to the kitchen. The air's cooler now, in the dead of night, filled with the gentle rustle of aspen leaves and the chirp of insects. The party's long since over. Hamster robots, slender machines the size of my shoe, scurry about the house, picking up the detritus of the celebration. "Captain here's a witness, and an accomplice."

"I am *not* an accomplice."

"Helped your brother get out of town with cytori, right? Provided transport to and from his pick-up and delivery?" Tyler's moustache twitches. "Accomplice."

"You are not arresting our son, not when our other child is in the hands of—" Father sputters out, like a skip-jack low on fuel. "I'm sorry, but did you say Grant Liu abducted him?"

"Mm-hmm."

Mother's swiping through her delver. "But Grant was always a good student. Well-respected. He never gave us any trouble."

"I did hear he'd hit a rough bit of turbulence in his life," Father says. "Local infractions. Vandalism. But now you're telling us he's not only a smuggler but a kidnapper."

"Boy's got a database of charges as long as my arm," Hank says. "Won't be but a matter of time before the Crown catches up with him. Brings us to the matter of your son. If we can get him back, his testimony about local smuggling operations will help."

"You don't even have proof," Mother says, chiding Hank as if he's a recalcitrant child.

"Sure they do." Lily's come downstairs, in a T-shirt and flowing sweatpants. Her approach went unnoticed, I assume because she's barefoot. She sinks into a chair, crossing her legs. "Father, Mother, a crown marshal wouldn't show up at our door with Vincent in binders if there wasn't proof. Right, Vincent?"

Everyone's looking at me. It's worse than facing angry settlers with a bunch of scramblers and guns pointed at your nose. "Yes. About that. Martin did have cytori. I saw the container."

Father throws up his hands and stalks to the other end of the room.

"Blast it, Vincent!" Mother snaps. "You have a responsibility to the truth! Your brother was in trouble—*is* still! You should have come to us."

"Are you kidding? You don't even believe he's capable of the crime, and you want me to turn him in? You would have laughed in my face." I glare at her. "I bet you're teetering between belief and disbelief right now."

"It is convenient timing, with your recent spat—"

"Annabeth!" Father snaps. "Vincent would not invent his brother's criminal activity to settle an old score."

"People will do all manner of awful things when they're upset, or when they feel betrayed. You know it's true. We've seen plenty of it. How many neighbors turned against each other? One family calls Kesek down upon a household of Muslims. Then their relatives point their fingers at a Christian couple, and once the wife disappears, the husband is brokenhearted and bitter enough to reveal the Jewish clan down the street is reading from the Torah. It cycles and cycles and cycles until our homes are full of empty chairs and scarred souls!"

No one's got a reply to Mother's tirade. Mad as I am that she thinks I'm trying to frame Martin, she's got a point. And those aren't hypothetical situation she rattled off. The El-Zeins, the O'Shaunesseys, the Aaronoviches… Mother wasn't kidding about scars.

"That's stupid," Lily mutters. "Of course Vincent's mad at Martin. But he's not going to fabricate a story about how he's a smuggler, any more than he'd turn him in to the police. You don't do that to your family."

"You don't let them break the law, either," Father says. "This isn't an issue of conscience, Lily. Martin wasn't protesting a corrupt government or defying a repressive edict."

"I know that."

"I wanted him to turn himself in," I say, since all this talk is orbiting me without my input. "But there was no way he was going to do that. Why would he, when he could make money independent of the family?"

"He could have told us," Father says. "He could have—"

"Hate to break this up." Hank strides to the center of the room. It's like watching a panther stalk, if a panther were a tall man who seems unhurried by events around him. "Got a limited window in which to pursue. Grant and his boys are gone. No sign of his transport, so wherever he's at, gonna be awhile before he surfaces. Now, that's bad for your boy. Grant's got no reason to keep him alive, other than to send a message to Captain Rilla 'bout how no one but Grant is going to rule cytori smuggling on Tiaozhan."

"You can't just let them kill our son!" Mother balks.

"Reckon that's not our plan," Hank says dryly. "Am going to need Martin's comm codes, his vehicle, anything that'll help us track him down."

"Whatever you need." Father's right there. "You can search the entire compound."

Hank does exactly that.

Over the next few hours, he has a trio of young deputies and a squadron of brassjackets scan every square centimeter. His resources must be considerable, because there's more of the same back at Cratered. Between the two scenes, streams of data pour forth from Tyler's delver.

"Hmm." He strokes the moustache as if it were a favored pet. That's why I stay clean-shaven. Too distracting. And trust me, my attempt at facial hair quickly turned into a shaggy mess the one and only time I tried. "Got to hand it to Liu—he doesn't leave much behind when he vanishes."

"You've got to have something." I prod his shoulder. "And, seriously, if I'm gonna help with your investigation—"

"Right." Hank presses a tab on his delver.

My restraints fall into his outstretched hand. I rub the wrists. "Thanks."

"Mm-hmm."

"What about ion drive trails? You can trace a course from those."

"Trickier in atmosphere, Captain. All manner of particles get in the way."

"Okay, but local scanners?"

"Don't show much but blips. Whatever Liu and his people fly these days."

I frowned. "Fly? There weren't any aircraft at Cratered. Not even after."

"Nope. Reckon they drove to wherever they had it stashed, then flew out." He takes me aside, away from the family and the deputies. "Got wind Liu likes to make his home at the Endless Beach, or thereabouts. Can't pin-point, yet, but we're keeping a close eye."

"So, you can track from orbit, right? We can tap into *Marconi*'s sensors—"

"Already got a fine set of satellites doing the scan work."

I spread my arms. "Then what in blazes do you need me for?"

"Comms." Hank turns the delver so I can read it. "What do you make of this mess?"

What I make is that he's right—it's a mess. I've never seen a signal quite like it. Hidden behind local comms traffic, piggybacking on comm note frequencies, but so fragmented, and encoded, that it resembles the low-level messages sent between bots to guide their nav-igation. "Offhand, I'd say it was two brassjackets pinging coordinates off each other. Except it's way too heavily encrypted for that."

"Yep. Reckon so."

I wave my hands over the delver, as if I can, I don't know, pull a creature out like a classic magician. "Did they have bots with them?"

"Not that anyone saw. Nothing on scans, either."

I push the data aside. Results from Martin's comms aren't good. The marshals can't find any trace of his devices, his profile, nothing. It's like he's vanished. Not even the implanted delver in his arm is putting out any kind of signal.

"See now why it's important," Hank muses. "Got no sort of trail to track. What we do have is a hovercraft path to a secluded gulch near Bright Sky Spaceport. But no hovercraft. And no aircraft. Like they leapt off the ground and disappeared." He reaches past, returns the screen to the strange, coded transmission. "This here's our clue."

And it isn't a single clue. It's many. There's a pile of these brief bursts of communication. I scowl at the screen. "Okay, let me uplink to *Marconi*'s computer. I can plow through…"

Oh. Right.

"Problem?"

"My supervisor. Director Margate, MarkTel for Region Six. He's, ah, made it clear I need to stay out of this kind of—outside consulting."

"Chen." Hank nods. "Knew I heard the name. Didn't believe it until I ran a check. Seems you're the fella who's been busy with things not within a comms jockey's purview."

"Yeah. Something like that."

"Okay, then. Best find a way to keep you off MarkTel's scans." Hank smiles, the corners of his moustache arcing. "Good thing we got someone who knows a thing or two about that."

Mother stares at me. "You want me to *what*?"

I sigh. "It's simple enough for me to disconnect. The problem is the *why*. MarkTel's gonna know it's not a malfunction, but a deliberate disconnection from their systems. My wrist-comm, its link to my deliver, their links to *Marconi*'s onboard computer, even the pings I send to Copper—it's all recorded. Which means MarkTel knows I was using my override to see if the police were after Martin back in Yinse Haian. Hence my warning from Director Margate. Which is why I need you to use your connections to make it seem like I'm staying put at the house."

"And then you can track down Martin."

"Possibly." I show her the odd signals.

"Those are peculiar," she murmurs. "Brassjacket talk?"

"That's what I thought. Too complex. And far too secure."

"They certainly are." Mother taps a finger on her delver, and slowly, like the sun that's peeking over the horizon, a smile dawns. "I'm sure there's a way I can manage to misguide your comms, Vincent. Assuming the crown marshal is okay with something that is, technically, a crime."

"Won't hear a fuss from me," Tyler says. "Gets filed under the purview of my investigation."

"And if MarkTel finds out? They could lodge a protest."

"Let 'em."

"Um, the goal is for them to *not* find out," I remind them.

Mother pulls up transparent holographic displays, and begins issuing commands. "I'll need half an hour to make certain you can't be recorded. Then you're free.

I kiss her on the cheek. "You're the best, Mother."

"I know," she says, that smile brightening.

We're on the tarmac, loading supplies into my hovercraft.

"Better to take your ride than one of mine," Hank says. "Got too many folk familiar with what the crown marshals drive around these parts."

I don't know if "these parts" include all of Tiaozhan, but he's the trained investigator. I hand him an oblong case with a significant heft to it. "Sensor equipment?"

"Nope. Firepower."

Really wishing I had that scrambler, or the gun that's stashed near it, but again, they're both in orbit. And we can't take the skipjack, because even with Mother concealing my personal activity from MarkTel, there's no fiddling with the hardwired transponder.

Unless Izzy were here. She could do it in a flash.

Try not to think about that.

"Vincent." Father intercepts us. He has a leather case and belt in his hands. "Take this."

It's his handgun. Delete that. Grandfather's handgun. A mag-accelerated Hunsaker Wasp. Registered to our family for self-defense use. I strap the belt on.

"We put this together, as well." He gives me a sleeve made of green plastic.

I undo the heat seal. Wow. I haven't seen that much money in one place since Father and I took my savings into Yinse Haian to buy the hovercraft when I was still in school. There have to be fifty Gagarins, the taciturn face of the ancient cosmonaut staring up at me as I flip through the red bills edged with silver. "Five thousand?"

"If Grant Liu has become what you say he has become, this may help recover your brother. Appeal to his greed. It seems to be all he respects." Father clasps my hands. "The Lord guide you and keep you."

"Make His face to shine upon you," I answer.

"Amen," Hank murmurs.

Then Father disappears into the gardens, replaced by Lily, who's frowning at me. "I should come with you."

"You'd be great, but Father and Mother need you here." I don't tell her the idea of having all three Chen offspring in danger makes me sick to my stomach. "Think of Uncle Ethan."

She sighs. "I know. 'Strategy, not sentimentality.'"

I chuckle. "Said the guy who got choked up when we listened to the Christmas choirs on the gray delver hidden in the basement."

Lily puts her arms around me. "Be careful. We'll all be praying for you.'"

"Thanks, Sis."

"Bring Martin back, the little snot."

Considering she's the youngest, the comment makes me snicker. "I can't promise I won't punch him again, but I'll wait until after he's rescued, okay?"

"Fair. And make sure you read this—" She holds her wrist comm to mine. A file flashes over.

Upgrades, 2.0. Acceleration, Countermeasures, etc.

Et cetera?

I glance over my shoulder at Hank, who's got his back to us as he loads his gear. "Hovercraft legal?"

Lily grins. "Legal-ish. Outside city limits, probably more so."

Tyler clears his throat. "Chen."

Lily and I look at him at the same time.

He's waggling a tiny container in front of us. "Might this belong to the wayward brother?" The lid pops open.

Cytori.

Martin hid the contraband in *my* hovercraft, rather than turn it over to the police or let it get stolen by either the people to whom he was supposed to deliver—or Grant Liu and these thugs.

"Vac-head," I mutter.

Chapter Eight

We can't take the skipjack. And Hank shies away from using one of the Crown Marshal Service's private barges. Getting a ticket on planetary flights that can accommodate my hovercraft is next to impossible. There's a week-long wait.

That leaves the hyperfoil.

It's a massive wedge, sleek on all sides, sitting on the outskirts of Yinse Haian's harbor. A hundred groundcars and hovercraft slide aboard, secured in their moorings by a flexible mesh. The people, too, are strapped into their seats on the upper decks, surrounded by yawning viewports that give us a majestic view of the Inland Sea's coastline and a cobalt sky.

Acceleration presses us into our seats, until the ship's compensators kick in, low-powered versions of the ones that protect starship travelers from being mashed into biological goo. A public information graphic shows the hyperfoil slowly lifting from the water, until it's skimming along 20 meters above the sea surface at speeds in excess of 600 kilometers per hour. Spindly wings barely touch the water, whipping up huge, feathery sprays. How the hoverjets keep the thing balanced, I don't know, but the relevant data is that we'll reach the Endless Beach in about six hours. It's a decent trip from the Western Province to the Eastern Province, with this portion of the Inland Sea the boundary between the two.

As soon as our course stabilizes, we get the green light to walk about. Hank and I head to the upper observation deck, which is full of a couple hundred passengers milling about. There's a full bar in on corner, lounge chairs and couches scattered around, and tropical plants growing from boxes embedded in the floor. I'm sure Father would be jealous of the exotic varieties crammed together.

The best part is, there's plenty of places in which we can stand partly concealed, and all the constant rumble of conversation atop the thrum of the hyperfoil's fusion engines makes covert discussion simpler.

"Got a signal to Captain Rilla," Hank says. "Mighty glad to hear from us. Deputies are with her at all times."

"Did she get any word from Grant?"

"Nope. Mind, we'll know when she does."

"Hopefully we can triangulate the incoming communications and track Grant that way." It sounds good, but I'm not hopeful. Grant's skill at evading auth-orities—or flat out paying for their silence—means hiding the origin of a signal is probably child's play for him.

"Mm-hmm. Got ourselves satellites waiting to help. A ship, too. Rescue Ops."

"I thought you guys would have your own starships by now."

"Crown Marshals need to be mobile, but don't need a fleet. Starkweather Navy, Tiaozhan's patrols, Rescue Operations—mighty nice of them to share and provide us a lift when need be. Got our presence on every Rescue Ops vessel in the Realm."

Mighty nice? Rescue Operations used to be Rescue Corps, more like the seagoing coast guards of Earth. Somehow, I doubt their captains cheered when they were transformed into a more militaristic branch.

"How's about that bot signal?"

I'm frowning over my delver, perusing that weird communications for the umpteenth time. "Whatever encryption they're using isn't tied to any algorithm I recognize. That's why Copper's lending a hand—or a processor."

My brassjacket's hovering by the viewport, his tiny jets hissing. White lights sparkle in a loop on his left flank. Copper's cycling the communications Hank intercepted through the same system he uses to talk with nearby bots. They're constantly trading impersonal data—weather, environmental factors, location coordinates. Anything useful for the bots to know both how they're doing and what the status is of nearby mechanical and electrical systems. They keep data about their human companions private, unless there's a medical emergency, and depending upon the parameters set by their owners.

Right now, Copper's not actively talking to any other bots on the observation deck, but he is observing them, while sifting this signal through his databanks.

Meanwhile I'm shifting lines of code and puzzling over some of the indicators.

"Problem?" Hank leans against the viewport.

"Other than frustration at my inability to crack this? Yeah. For one thing, this signal's been repurposed. It doesn't use the same frequencies as bot-to-bot, yet it's not a commnote link or even a delver-to-delver message. The worst part is, I feel like I've seen it somewhere, and yet…"

"Aboard your ship?"

"No such luck." I pull up a small holo from my wrist-comm. "*Marconi*'s computer checked it against recent communications we've monitored. Zero."

"Reckon you took a risk talking to your ship's computer."

I run a hand through my hair. The delver screen blurs for a second. I should probably grab a few hours of sleep. "Sort of. I've got enough skill to bounce a signal off a public satellite and send a query to the computer without MarkTel figuring out it's me. You'd be surprised how many merchantmen ask us questions—they know we soak up a bunch of navigational data from the comms ferries stored aboard. Besides, Mother's got my tracks well concealed, so I—"

Mother. That's it. That's where I've seen this.

"Captain?"

I flick frantically through the screens of data from Hank's scans.

A big, dark hand waves in front of my face.

"Quit!" I snap. There. Pull up that line of code. Run a comparison…

"This mean you've found something?"

"Yes, it does." I route the new info through the wrist-comm and project the holo against a viewport stanchion. There's a couple lines of blood red amongst the yellow digits. "See it?"

Hank nods. "Red."

I sigh. When you spend weeks as the only human aboard a comms ferry tender crewed by computers, analyzing nothing but signals and their attendant data, you forget that the meat and bones of interstellar communications look like gibberish to the average person. Or even veteran crown marshals. "It's an update link, meant to relay information about a device to a network, so that the manufacturer can find and fix glitches."

"What sort of device?"

"Medical prosthetics." I tap the screen. A schematic appears. If this were a casino, I'd be cashing in on a jackpot this very second. "Specifically, ocular."

Hank's moustache twitches. "Fake eyeball."

"No, stabilizer implanted onto a biological eye. Grant has one. If I had to bet, its purpose—at least, it's *original* purpose—was to prevent further damage to his sight. Probably a medical procedure he underwent after he was freed from Kesek custody."

"Nerve torture. Their favorite."

My imagination supplies a sensation that makes me dizzy. It doesn't help that I haven't eaten breakfast yet, either. "It keeps the eye's cellular structure from degenerating. But, this signal you found? The stabilizer wasn't sending an update to anyone. It was pinging another nearby implant."

Hank blinks.

"Covert communications!" I tap my eye socket and then point at Hank's. "Unidirectional. Grant sends messages, encoded, via the stabilizer's update signal—"

"To implants in the eyes of his boys," Hank says slow-ly. "Mighty clever."

"Yes!" I slap his arm, meaning it as a gesture of cam-araderie and celebration.

But since Hank's hand seizes my wrist in a blink, stopping the palm a centimeter from his sleeve, the slap never connects.

"Sorry." I withdraw.

"Training." Hank shrugs. "'Bout that signal, now…"

"Yes. Right. If I can tap into the networks used to monitor the updates, I can find him."

"How close?"

"How close… to what?"

Hank rubs his chin. "Hundred kilometers? Ten? One? Couple meters? How close can you get?"

"Oh. Um…" I shrug. "I don't know."

Hank snorts. "Well, it's something."

"Hey! I've never tracked down a smuggler using encoded eyeball communications through an ocular im-plant, so I think I'm doing pretty well," I mutter. "You're gonna have to take what you can get. Especially since the crown marshals can't seem to do it on their own."

For a moment, I wonder if my rebuttal's going to earn me arrest—or possibly a punch. But Hank cracks a toothy grin. "All right. Glad you found your spark. Find a spot for rest." He walks off.

So, we're done, I suppose. "Where are you going?"

"Get some grub." He pats his belly.

Grub? My stomach rumbles in response. But as I watch the sea race by, a wave of exhaustion smothers me. There's a couch nearby. I could sit for a bit, let the software continue its decoding. Maybe Copper will come up with something helpful…

I manage to cobble together a tracing program and get it running. Then I toss off a curt commnote to Mother: *Ocular stabilizer network. Passcode? Can track Grant via implant.*

Her reply is swift: *Genius! Passcode attached. Here's a possible interception point.*

And, man, is it ever—one of the most common nodes used by ocular stabilizers for updates. I hook my trace program into it and lean my head against the back of the couch.

Big mistake. My eyelids droop, and there's no fighting it.

Hang in there, Martin. We're coming for you.

The vibration of the deck rises through the cushions and is as soothing as hanging from a hammock in the Chen compound gardens.

I swear I smell syrup as I drift off to sleep.

When I snap awake, it's to the sound of chewing.

Hank's in a chair opposite mine. The last remnant of a pancake disappears into his mouth. "'Morning. Again."

"Morning?" I rub the last bits of sleep from my eyes and the drool off my cheek. That was syrup. "Of all the food they've stocked aboard, you're eating flapjacks?"

"Second stack." Hank brushes crumbs from his moustache and sets his plate aside. "There now. Back to work."

"How long was I out?" My vision's bleary, but the time's clear enough on my wrist-comm. "1200 hours?"

"Breakfast, lunch." Hank shrugs. "Won't quibble about which meal. Come on, now, we're due to arrive."

He's right. The hyperfoil's slowed its insane rush across the Inland Sea, cruising at 200 kph. The forward observation viewports reveal a long, glorious stretch of pearly sand, disappearing at both ends of the horizon. The Endless Beach takes up more than 2,000 kilometers of gentle coastline. Even from this distance, it's easy to make out clusters of people, their skin hues and swimming outfits mingling in a colorful mishmash more exotic than the plants here in the lounge.

I check the delver. The trace is still running, but there's no results. Not yet. Neither has Captain Rilla forwarded any communications from Grant—which is good, in a way. He hasn't demanded a trade, nor has he sent her a ghastly vid of Martin's torture.

I push that possibility into the deepest corners of my mind and concentrate on retrieving the hovercraft from its tie-down slot.

An hour later, we disembark onto a searing hot permacrete ramp that empties vehicle traffic into Báishā, the primary resort town and home to ten massive piers set up for visiting ships. There's also a sprawling spaceport in the hills farther east, and from here there's seemingly no end to the stream of barges and gigs rising and landing. Expansive walled compounds of gleaming glass topped with traditional tiles mingle with massive apartment complexes. Individual family dwellings adorned with *duogong* cap and block are sprinkled throughout, some of them no doubt dating back to the earliest settlement of Tiaozhan, judging by their wear. Everything's painted white and soft pastels, with ochre and crimson edging around the gables and windows.

The streets are full of people from across our planet and the Realm of Five. Police and patrol drones stick to the outskirts, and merchants sell every kind of food and clothing and artwork you can imagine.

This is the kind of place I want Izzy to see, if she and I had a different life. Kind of difficult, seeing as she's imprisoned by ISR and I'm beholden to traveling the stars for the majority of my days.

I shake off the daydream because Copper's chirping for my attention. He's sandwiched between the gear Hank stuffed into the hovercraft's back seat.

"Little fella's got some good news?" Hank asks.

"Maybe." I route Copper's prompt through the hover-craft's control panel. [Confirm?]

[Analysis complete. Results as follows.] He transmits a flood of data, hundreds of messages in plain speech, every one decoded. Most of it is irrelevant—Grant telling his men where to go, what to do, who to punch—but the excitement at having cracked the code and getting to peer over Grant's shoulder, electronically speaking, makes up for that.

[Narrow search. Terms to include: Martin. Base. Home. Also include coordinates, if any.]

Copper's lights whirl. Numbers spray across the console.

Hank leans forward.

"That's it. Here." I feed the numbers into the hover-craft's navigational system. Next thing you know, we've got a lovely 3-D map of the Endless Beach's north section, which is where the smooth sands give way to giant boulders, gaping ravines, and rocky cliffs.

Unfortunately, the best Copper can get me is a rough circle 40 klicks in diameter.

"Lot of ground to cover," Hank muses. "Best get started."

He doesn't have to tell me again. I weave the hovercraft onto side roads, aiming for the open countryside. Here, the crowded houses and apartments give way to scattered family compounds and the occasional resort complex. Other than that, the road is a broad, flat stretch of plasma-baked earth that's as smooth as any permacrete tarmac.

I goose the hovercraft's engines and we blaze ahead, joining dozens of other craft on the drive north.

Keep him safe. I figure a quick prayer doesn't hurt. Then I ponder the situation, and tack on, *Don't let Martin do anything stupid.*

Chapter Nine

The road breaks up not long after we pass the final beach turn-off, a long, gentle ramp leading onto the sand. Umbrellas and canopies dot the white sands.

I'm more interested in the jagged orange rocks jutting up farther ahead.

The shortest is twice as tall as me. The largest, according to the hovercraft's sensors, have peaks 20 meters off the sand and are three times that length. There's all manner of them—skinny and sharp angled, stout and crumbling, undulating and smoothed. The nearer the water they are, the more likely they are to be worn by centuries of tidal erosion.

I guide the hovercraft between the boulders, mindful of occasional beachgoers even this far north. They tend to be couples out for romantic picnics, with their vehicles parked nearby, or groups of families on camping excursions. Roomy, flimsy versions of survival tents are pitched behind and among the stones, for shelter from the wind.

The farther I drive, with the 40-kilometer circle as our destination, the fewer people we see. Soon, no one's left. I'm reduced to scaring off crustaceans. Hank even points out a lone pinceen, albeit a female, laden with eggs and lacking the shimmering claw growths harvested for cytori.

As soon as we cross into the imaginary circle, I wave my hands in front of us. "Here we are. About the same as everywhere else we passed."

"'Cept this ain't it."

"Um, I think we can take longer than five seconds to determine that."

"Who's the expert tracker?" Hank's face is stony as our surroundings; still, it sounds like he's cracking a joke. Or attempting one.

"My guess is… you?"

He points over the hovercraft's nose. "See any groundcar ruts? Hoverjet blast marks?"

"I've been watching the scanners. They haven't war-ned of extra traffic or power sources."

Hank snorts. "Machine's only going to take you so far. *You* have to look. With the eyes, Captain. Mind, your surroundings won't always be obliging. Got to ignore ev-erything but what you need."

Sage advice, I'm sure. "So, they didn't come this way, is that it?"

"Nope."

"Do you want to drive, then, or sit there being cryptic while I navigate in circles?"

"Rather you drive on until they stop following us."

"What? Who?" I crane my neck behind us. No sign of another vehicle. Only the dark spots in the sky. Distant avians.

Oh. Avians. Or…

"Better send that bot of yours out for recon," Hank mused. "There's two of theirs. South, southeast of us by a couple klicks. Undercarriage painted to match the sky. Clever. Still catch glints off their hoverjet exhaust. Might tune your sensors for that."

"Right. I've got it." I recalibrate the hoverjet's nav system to keep an eye on small aerial craft. It's not terribly accurate, but it will give me a rough location for any following robots. Meanwhile, I send Copper the command, [Fol-low coastline until further orders. Maintain watch for au-tonomous vehicles.]

He hops from his perch between us and zips toward the water, staying low to the ground until he reaches the shore.

"That's the opposite of the best course," Hank mutters.

"Relax. I'm not going to fly Copper right up into their faces." Well, not directly. Copper stays low to the water, paralleling our drive. I feed him a set of commands that I've been playing with in my copious amounts of free time aboard *Marconi*, when I'm travelling between star systems with nothing better to do.

The nav system catches up with my initial pro-gramming. Hank isn't kidding: two brassjackets, larger versions of Copper, are flying a couple klicks southeast of us. They're maintaining a discreet profile, staying as high up as they can without losing us from whatever miniature scanners are packed aboard.

I grin. Won't do them any good in a microsecond.

As soon as I give Copper the order to initiate my new commands, the nav system blinks, then turns to static. So does the comms board. I'm left with the hovercraft's basic controls. Since I'm already driving manual, I don't lose control and let us smash into the side of a looming boulder.

"Seems like that was a malfunction," Hank observes.

"It was—for them as well as us. Copper's broadcasting a signal that's basically a sensor jammer. It's brute force, at first. Mucks up everything. But give it a few minutes and our nav will clear up.

"What about your bot? Got to be more than a minor inconvenience."

"It doesn't affect Copper. My brassjackets are shielded against that kind of interference and coded to resist unauthorized tampering."

"Sounds like someone's paranoid."

"I like to think of it as being better prepared." And since someone's already used all twenty-four of *Marconi*'s hamsters and brassjackets to mutiny, I don't think it's unreasonable.

There's a few tense minutes in which I doubt the effectiveness of Copper's interference. But soon the brassjackets shadowing us veer off. I can't tell from the hovercraft's sensors—because they're still fouled up—but Hank assures me they're gone with a quick glance skyward.

I exhale. "That'll help."

Hank's apparently not listening. He's staring off to our right, where the rocks are more tangled. I catch flashes of open sand and clumps of tall, lilac colored reeds waving in the shore breezes. "Turn here."

"Where?"

"Right there." Hank points at a gap between boulders, less than fifty meters ahead.

I crank the steering controls. The hovercraft whips up sand, banking hard to the right, tilting us at a… well, at a fun angle. I can't resist goosing the engines just a bit more, accelerating us out of the turn.

Even Hank's got a smirk growing beneath that mou-stache.

I level us out and, after taking a better look at our new surroundings, slow to a more cautious speed. The sand is full of reeds, even more so ahead, and the lanes narrower between the boulders. Those boulders, too, are more jagged, taller.

"Stop."

I reverse thrust and kill the hoverjets. We drop the last half meter with a soft bump, the undercarriage using the sand as a cushion. Hank's already clambering from his seat with an agility I didn't think Father could manage, let alone this guy.

"What've we got?"

Hank kneels. His gaze starts at his feet and slowly pans up and ahead, deeper into the rock field. "Hovercraft tracks."

I lean over the windscreen. I suppose one could infer that we're looking at hovercraft tracks, sure, but they could also be furrows dug by the wind or leftovers from behemoth-worm young. "Any chance we're looking at something made by nature?"

"Nope. Pattern's too regular. Can see the distortion from hoverjets." He points. "Here. And here."

"So, you've got a new course for me to follow."

Hank returns to his seat. "Ahead and to the right, through that crevasse. Mind the tracks, so we don't erase 'em."

"Oh, sure." I ease the hovercraft forward. "Whatever you say, sleuth."

A few hours later, we're out of luck, and room.

We've been heading the right direction, according to Hank. But the rocks are too tight here. The hovercraft has to park.

We've got to proceed on foot.

No sign of the Inland Sea from where I stand, but if I hold my breath, I can hear the constant rumble of breakers. I crane my neck.

Hummingbirds zing overhead, and swallows blast between the boulders, sharply banking from turn to turn in maneuvers that make the pilot in me jealous of their reflexes. I slap at the itching bite from a sandgnat. They're only going to get worse.

Hank's muttering to himself, so I only catch inter-mittent words like "vantage" and "range" and "wind speed." Not of much use to me. Instead I tally my inventory.

One Hunsaker Wasp pistol, with two magazines of projectiles.

One envelope stuffed with five thousand in crisp currency.

One tiny container of contraband cytori.

Any or all of these things could be handy.

"Gonna have to hand over the cytori when this is all said and done." Hank hefts the oblong case's strap over his shoulders, like he's fitting a pack for a long hike. "Ain't got to tell you possession is illegal."

"And yet you're not slapping me in binders. I'm bet-ting capturing Grant's gang—or at least gathering more intel on their base of operations—is worth more than the penalties you'd levy against someone like me or Martin."

"Might be. Might not. Best decide if you think it's worth the risk." He sets off over the sand, his stride quite a bit longer than mine.

I'll have to hustle to keep up.

We're on foot for a while, trudging through sand that slows our progress considerably. Every step is a chore. Sweat trickles down my face. Man. I'll have to program the bots with reminders for me to up my exercise time. There's only so many laps I can make of my starship's deck before I get bored, though.

I've completely lost track of where we are. All the rocks look the same to me.

Hank walks along in front of me. His pace isn't much better than mine, until the sand gives way to clay baked by the sun. He never stops, never doubles back. If he's made an error, I can't see it.

Of course, he could be long out of practice with this thing and covering for his lack of skill.

I nearly slam into him when he finally does stop. His hand's upraised.

"What is it?" I look around, but don't see anything other than the rising hills and rough cliffs to our im-mediate east.

Hank nods. He sets his pack on the ground. "Time to set up camp."

"Are you serious? This isn't a holiday." I shake my head. "Is this where Grant's holed up?"

"Close enough." Hank hands me a drink tube. "Here."

I toss my backpack against a rock and slump along the side. Then I yelp, pulling away, because the rock surface is as hot as a main drive's reactor.

"Mind the temperature." Hank drains his water tube, eyes watchful of the horizon.

"I'd rather we push forward."

"Rather we did, too. But it's Liu's game now. He knows we're here. Those bots have to have reported back by now. Best rest up for when they show."

I guzzle the water tube. I'm exhausted. Sweating. Don't know why I didn't drink anything sooner. My backpack forms a passable cushion to lean against. "Well, whatever plan you have, you'd better download it for me, because I don't want to sit around while Martin's in danger."

Hank taps the delver stored in a pouch on his belt. "No updates. Rilla's quiet. So's Grant. Means they're waiting on something."

"Like what?"

"Us." Hank watches the cliffs. "Reckon he'd like to clear us off the board before he makes his next move. Time to wait."

As much as I want to argue, I'm too tired. Way too tired. My eyelids droop. A rest is probably a good idea. Hank's standing guard. Just a few minutes…

I jolt awake.

Sunset isn't that far off. Already part of the horizon's turning gold. The rest of the sky remains blue.

It's the second time I nodded off, but man, it was sorely needed. Between that and the sleep I managed on the hyperfoil, I feel close to rested. "Okay, that was a good idea. When do we..."

Hank's gone.

I scramble upright. First instinct? Draw Grandfather's gun.

There's no one else around. I check the ground, like Hank would, but I can't make out footprints. Blazes, I don't even know if you *can* leave footprints on the clay.

Think, Vincent.

I send him a signal on my wrist-comm. Nothing. Again? Still nothing.

By now I've accelerated from drowsy and almost awake to full alert. If I'd been strapped into the command chair on the bridge, with *Marconi*'s main drives burning as we tried to escape incoming missiles, I'd have been calmer.

He can't have just *left*.

But all his gear's gone. It doesn't make any sense.

My mouth is dry with fear. I lick my lips. Dry, yes, but funny-tasting, too. There's a bitter tinge.

Hank filled those water tubes on the hyperfoil. I drank from the same source. It was anything but bitter.

I retrieve my tube. There's a residue inside the rim.

It's got a vague medicinal scent. Like a sedative.

Like the same compound my med-scanner's robot arm injected Izzy with when she was first a guest aboard my ship, and I had to keep her sedated.

"Blast it!" I fling the tube aside.

He drugged me! What was he thinking? Why would a crown marshal, of all people, abandon me this close to getting my brother back?

"Where are you?" I shout, not caring one bit whether Grant's goons discover me. And then my thoughts go darker. To God. As in, *Where were You? I'm trying to do the right thing here! And I keep getting stepped on!*

Izzy. ISR. Margate. Martin.

I'm sick of people and things I care about pushing back.

"Keep your voice down. You don't want to attract att-ention."

Grant steps out from behind a copse of rocks, from the same direction as the cliffs.

I lift the gun, but movement to either side tells me that's a bad idea. Two of his thugs are there, with compact rifles aimed.

Two more emerge beside Grant, dragging Martin. His face is bruised, and one eye is swollen shut. His shirt's torn. There's bloody streaks along his bare arm, where the implanted delver lives.

"I have to admit," Grant says. "I didn't really think you'd show up."

Chapter Ten

I didn't really know where to look first.

There's the gun-toting guys to my left and right. And the other two, similarly armed, on either side of Grant and Martin. Speaking of Grant, he hadn't been exaggerating his smuggling supremacy. There's no way he could have acquired four Tegest automatic rifles for his gang without some serious cash and a great deal of black market contacts.

"Where is he?"

"Who?"

"Don't do that. I'm tired, and ready for dinner. Where's Marshal Tyler?"

"Good question. I woke up and he was gone. I was gonna ask you guys if you'd seen him."

Grant seems to weigh this, but eventually he nods. "True. We spotted him leaving a few hours ago, while you were dozing. Don't worry. Our brassjackets will track him down—now that we've fixed the glitch you introduced."

I shrug. "It's just a little something I do." Sounds a lot braver than I feel. This time, I've got no one by my side, no allies either biological or electronic in nature. I've got no idea where Hank's gone off to. I can't check my wrist-comm for Copper's update.

It'd be nice to have Izzy here in a gunfight, given her spy training. Blazes, I'd take my fellow comms ferry jockeys, strange as they are.

But I'm on my own. Well. Almost.

Whatever's going on, God, I hope You've got it.

"Are you going to make me ask?" Grant gestures at my hands.

The men flank me, their boots shuffling across the clay. I glance at one, and he looks anything but friendly. He makes the guys I tussled with at Cratered seem like happy concierges at a summer resort on the Endless Beach. I hold my hands up, trigger finger standing free, so they know I'm not entertaining thoughts of firing.

The guy on my left grabs the gun away. It gets tucked in his belt. You'd think with as big a rifle he has and the insane blend of reds and greens rippling through his wild fringe of hair, he'd be happy. Not even a hint of a smile.

"Search him," Grant says.

Before Smiley can touch me, I indicate for them to wait. "I didn't come here to shoot you and take my brother. Let's be clear about that. I came to deal."

Grant laughs. It's a grown man's chuckle, but its cadence is that of the kid I knew in school. "You want to deal? With me? I already told you what I want: Martin's hide, and Rilla off my turf. I've got the first part. Rilla can wait while I prep this package for delivery."

Grant elbows Martin, eliciting a sharp cry. Martin falls to his knees.

"Hey!" I start forward, forgetting there's four guys with guns aimed at me. "Enough. Just let him be. Here."

I draw the envelope from my backpack.

That earns me a rifle's muzzle jammed in my ribcage.

"Relax!" Grant snaps. "That's not a gun."

I glare at Smiley and extend the envelope to Grant.

He steps closer, leaving Martin under guard. The familiar twitch ripples across his face. He halts, grimaces, and waits as whatever the optical stabilizer does to complete its work. Finally, he sighs. "It's bad enough those things send a wave of fire through my nerves. But to have people see it?"

"I'm sorry for what happened to you. But it's not like you're alone in that."

"Oh, I'm alone." Grant snatches the envelope and rips it open. "Mother and Father are gone. Living off-world. The rest of the family can't bear the shame of their twitchy black sheep. Especially since it's his irrational faith that got him in that mess."

His expression brightens a bit when gets a good look at the envelope's contents. "Hello there, Cosmonaut Gagarin. That's a pretty pile. Well-paid at MarkTel, are you?"

"The cytori's in there, too."

"What? No!" Martin staggers upright. "That's Captain Rilla's! She's got a buyer!"

"Martin, for the love of all that's good and holy, *shut up!*" I snap. "We're going home. Money and stupid cytori don't matter at this point. Don't say another word and let me get you out of this mess!"

Grant shakes his head. "This is sweet. Brotherly love. Where'd you get the money?"

"Not your concern."

"Ah. So, not yours. Your parents, I presume. Nice to know they still stand by their sons." Grant sneers. "Even though you're all a bunch of superstitious fools."

"Are you done with that?" I roll my eyes. "I'll be honest—this kind of talk doesn't bother me anymore. I've had these conversations a thousand times. If you want to think God's not real and my faith's a sham, fine, go ahead. But you're taking the money and cytori, and I'm taking Martin. Everybody goes home."

Grant's face goes cold and solid. "No. I don't think so. We don't all get to go home, Vincent. It was nice of you to drop by. But I'm keeping the gifts you brought right here with your brother. Oh, he'll go free soon enough—when I drop him on Rilla's deck with the cytori shoved down his throat."

I move then. It's stupid, I know, but I'm hoping they won't expect a comms jockey to attack them.

For a microsecond, I'm right. Smiley might have a military-grade weapon, but he's no soldier. I grab the gun and shove its stock into his face. A great swing of the rifle smashes across his shoulder, and I bring the weapon upright, ready to fire. Not that I've ever used a gun like this. A hunting rifle in the Western Province's hilly forests is one thing. This is another.

The other guy must have moved while I was attacking Smiley, because the next thing I know, I've been tripped, and I face-plant on the clay. Only by using the gun as a brace do I avoid smearing my face across the rough terrain. But it gives the other guy the chance to bash his gun into my side, sending me tumbling. Then the muzzle's pressed to my neck.

"Stop! Stop." Grant leans over. He picks up my discarded weapon—Smiley's rifle—and hands it back to its owner. "Hold onto this, idiot."

Smiley takes back his rifle, glaring at me the whole time.

"This is new," Grant says. "Since when does Vincent Chen, the guy with his nose in a delver all his life, try to smack one of my guys? The armed ones, nonetheless. Guess the rumors traveling the Reach network had some byte of truth to them."

The pain in my side won't subside. I grin up at Grant, regardless. "Come closer. I'll demonstrate."

"Excuse me if I don't." He straightens, then pulls Grandfather's gun from Smiley's belt. "I hate to do this. Really. But, you know, I've actually shot people before. I doubt you have. The first time is ghastly. You throw up. You don't sleep for days. It haunts. After a few more, it gets easier."

Whether or not he's messing with me, employing that dry wit of his, I'd rather not know. Yet, as I wait, staring at the gun's muzzle, I know there's no reason to despair. Mother and Father will miss me. Lily, too. Maybe even Martin. What would happen to my ship? My bots?

Would anyone get notice to Izzy? I wish I could send a message through her jailers at ISR.

"Sorry, Vincent." He pulls the trigger.

Nothing.

"What the blasted—?"

A gunshot echoes off the rocks. Something red sprays across me. The guy with the gun pressed to my neck falls by my side, screaming. There's a hole in his right shoulder. Tears stream from his eyes. Eyes fitted with those same implants.

"Hide! Move!" Grant tosses the gun aside. He reaches for Martin…

But I'm already moving. I tackle Grant. We slide in the clay, kicking up dust.

Martin yelps and staggers back.

Another gunshot.

Smiley's down, now, clutching his knee. The clay's stained the color of wine.

Grant slugs me in the gut, but I've got adrenaline pushing me to do stupid things. I scoop up Grandfather's gun and bash him across the head. Now I've got a limp body on my hands.

More gunfire, but this time, it's not a booming echo. It's the staccato of the Tegest rifles, shooting on full auto-matic. The remaining thugs are blasting away at the upper levels of the rocks, sending shards spraying like rain. The magnetic accelerators of the guns whine as they fling projectiles with eye-searing white flashes.

"Come on!" I grab Martin's arm and run.

"But the money! The cytori!"

I drag him along, until we're sprinting outright. "Keep moving!"

Behind us, Smiley's getting to his feet. Not possible. That gunshot blew open his knees! How could he…?

No, it wasn't his knee. Nearby. The wound, however, fills with a thick, gooey gray-white substance that's rapidly turning pink.

Great. These guys come with their own sealant.

"Aren't those kinds of cybernetics illegal?" Martin's panting, and limping. Not really running.

"Of course they are! But I don't think Grant cares!"

This time, bullets *spang* off the rocks around us. Apparently, our pursuers are more worried about their prey disappearing. I can hear Grant hollering.

I push Martin around a corner, hoping I can make him move faster. As I do, Smiley bursts into view. Still armed.

This time, I don't think I'm blessed enough for *his* gun to be unloaded.

Another gunshot. This one's near enough I'm sure I'll be struck deaf and the breeze of its passage brushes my hair.

Smiley's head snaps back. He topples. There's no way he's getting up from that.

Martin doubles over and vomits.

"Get up." Hank's voice is laden with contempt as he seizes a handful of Martin's shirt and pulls him up right. "Ain't no time to mourn his ilk."

"Where have you been?" I storm after Hank, who's herding Martin along like he's his prisoner. And Hank, I notice now, is bereft of his giant gray case. Instead, he's got a rifle, a compact model with a long, slender barrel.

"Might say, 'You're welcome,' instead of fussing."

"Reckon I would," I snap, "If you'd let me in on your plan instead of vanishing!"

"Had to backtrack."

"For…"

My hovercraft sits around another bend. Hank shoves Martin in. "Let's go."

"How'd you drive that here? It's not safe, according to the nav system."

"Very carefully."

"And the ownership codes—"

"Perk of being a crown marshal. Universal override." Hank pats his rifle. "And Master Sniper citation. His Majesty's commendation."

"That's wonderful. Just great." Shouts ring out behind us. I jump aboard. Hank's already in the passenger seat.

"Suggest you drive. Fast."

"Suggest you seal your hatch while I keep us all from getting killed." I spin the hovercraft around and send it hurtling into the rock maze.

There's a reason the nav system didn't want me to come deeper among the boulders, and why we continued on foot. I have to use a full manual override to get the computer to quit complaining about safety hazards.

"Watch out!" Martin ducks in the back seat.

The left side of the hovercraft scrapes a jagged overhang. Hank and I have to duck to avoid it taking our heads off.

"Mind the road," Hank says.

"Yes, I'm doing that!" The wind whips by. Sunset's glare blasts from our right, making the shadows deep. Moving at this speed is bad enough. Not being able to see enough of what's around the corner makes it all the more difficult.

But we're near the end of the maze. That's not the problem.

The problem is the new sound rising over the hovercraft's engines.

"Grant's got cycles!" Martin yells. "Three of them!"

I hit the rear-view screen. Yes, yes, he does. The jet-cycles weave between the rocks with practiced ease. Obviously, Grant and his crew have done this before. They cling to short, spindly vehicles that look like hovercraft that have been squished on the sides, then elongated on either end. Hoverjets whine and throw up dust behind them. They're wearing goggles to guard against the grit and the glare.

"Soon as you get in the open, this thing had better prove to be fast." Hank twists in his seat. He rests against the seat's back and puts the rifle clear across Martin, who yelps and wedges deeper against the cushions. Hank's squinting down a scope at our pursuers. "Do a fella a favor and keep her steady."

"No promises."

The boulders finally space themselves out enough for me to really accelerate without fear of battering us to pieces, as if they're keen to help us escape. Of course, such a blessing is also handy for Grant.

Then I notice the flashing reminder. Lily's file, down-loaded to the hovercraft's onboard computer.

Upgrades, 2.0. Acceleration, Countermeasures, etc.

I can't help grinning, even with the constant anxiety roiling my guts and screaming through my brain. I tap the command.

Install.

Chapter Eleven

First thing? The hovercraft jolts with a sudden burst of acceleration. The new program politely informs me of a component attached to the engines. I'm not familiar with the specifications. But I know from reading the summary Lily attached to the file that it has one purpose—increased engine performance.

And man, can I tell it.

We pull far ahead of the jetcycles. I'm expecting the engine readouts to redline any second, but they stay com-fortably in the orange range. There's strain on the system, yes, but nothing to worry about at this juncture.

Martin whoops. He slaps the back of my seat. "Vince! I didn't remember this thing blasting off like it could make orbit."

"I guess Lily's been tinkering a bit more than I imagined!" I elbow Hank, not daring to take my hands from the controls at this speed. "Hey! Where are we headed?"

"Far away from here as we can make it." He lays across the seats like he's sunning himself, except that he's fully clothed and staring down his rifle's scope.

"I meant, do you have people waiting for us back in town? Or on the hyperfoil?"

"Nope."

"Well, maybe you should call them!"

"Would. 'Cept we're being jammed."

I hadn't noticed the quiet yellow indicator flashing on control panel's right side. Communications signal interference. Either Grant's jetcycles had a way of jam-ming comms in a broad radius, or his brassjackets were back at it.

Speaking of which.

Something whizzed overhead. Then there was a sharp *crack* against the hovercraft's backside.

"Shooting!" Martin hollered. "They're shooting at us!"

"Much obliged for the observation." Hank sights, ex-hales.

BLAM.

One of the jetcycles swerves, sparks jettisoning from its left side. It stays upright, but it drops back.

"Shame." Hank reloads.

I'm more worried about what's ahead than what's behind. We zip past a family camping in prefabricated shells, and then kick dust toward a cluster of off-road groundcars encircling a sprawling picnic. That has to be a whiff of pork, of all things.

There's an increasing number of people. That number's only going to climb the nearer we draw to the beach town and hyperfoil port of Báishā.

None of that will matter if we can't call for help.

I punch the control console for communications. Specifically, with Copper. At first, there's no response to my prompt. Which puts a glitch in my plans. If he's holding station, somewhere out of range…

[Standing by.]

Atta boy. I wasn't certain the signal I use to talk with my bots would be able to punch through the jamming, but it seems whatever hardware Grant's using isn't up to the task of stopping more sophisticated MarkTel gear. More's the better for me. [Find and interdict sources of jamming frequencies. Use tracking profiles for previous tasks.]

Wherever Copper is, his swift acknowledgment is good enough for me. It's just as well.

The beach is filling up in earnest.

I veer as much away from the edge of the water as I can, because the herds of beachgoers are thickening. But that efforts hindered by the sloping rocks to our left. If I could find one of the ramps leading down onto the beach—

Another flurry of gunshots cracks the air, these sou-nding much nearer. Yes, they are. A quick glance reveals Grant and the other jetcycles closing on us.

"Seems you're not the only one who likes to tinker." Hank fires again.

This time, a jetcycle veers wildly of course, hits sand, and tumbles end over end. The driver—if he's not already dead—gets rapidly encased in a cushioning foam. It'll disintegrate as soon as the crash ends.

"That still leaves three of them," Martin notes. "Can we go faster?"

"Speed's not really the problem. It's space." I whip us by a huge stretch of vacationers. Even at this velocity, with the hoverjets whining and the wind roaring, their screams and shouts carry through.

I cringe at the idea of getting away from people trying to kill us, only to run over innocent bystanders.

Times like this I miss deep space.

"Steady," Hank says.

A gunshot scores a crease along our left flank. Blue shards of the hovercraft's exterior cut through the air. Once of them slices my cheek—not a deep cut, I hope, but enough a jolt of pain I swerve. When you swerve a couple hundred kph, your vehicle covers a lot of ground in those very brief seconds.

"Tent!" Martin warns.

Someone's set up the perfect sun shield for a family of sixteen people—elderly great-grandparents all the way down to toddlers. It's a billowing, pyramidal canopy draped in flowers, their colors changing with the shifting sun.

And they're right in my way.

"Hold on!" I crank the controls sharp right, ignoring the irrepressible safety system that blares a stability caution—as in, the hovercraft's in imminent peril of tipping over.

It's a second too late. The right side clips the tent, snapping a support, and tearing it the canopy free of the frame. The latter is bent and twisted. I glimpse people tossed aside, and others running for shelter. There's no turning around to check on their safety. All I can do is fire off a prayer for their well-being and hope they forgive me.

A blip appears on the comms panel, and just as quickly disappears. "Blast!"

"No luck?" Hank fires off another round. I don't hear a crash behind us; he must have missed.

"No. Copper's working to breach the jamming but it's taking longer than I expected. If their algorithms are more sophisticated—"

"Mm-hmm." Hank lines up another shot. Fires. Then a third. Fires again.

This time there's an explosion.

The rear-view screen shows off a flare of yellow and orange, accompanied by a rolling thunder that shakes my insides.

"That'll do," Hank says.

"You think so?"

"Can you get this bucket to go faster?" Martin leans between us, reaching for the control panel.

"Hey! Get off!" I smack his hand away. "Whatever else has been programmed in, I haven't touched yet."

But it's a valid question. Speed's not going to solve our problems, because Grant and his remaining rider are right on top of us. Colors flash by on either side, and my heart clenches when I realize those colors belong to people.

Nav blinks. There's the first ramp for the road.

If we can make it onto that stretch, no more worries about running over beachgoers.

Suddenly, a speck drops from the sky. Something boxy gouges a crater to our right, and as we whip by, I spot a spray of plastics and wires. Copper? Or one of Grant's bots?

I hazard a skyward glance. It is Copper. He's bearing down on the other, larger robot that Grant's using to jam our comms. Before I can send a warning, Copper rams it broadside, snapping a hoverjet clean off. They tumble together, throwing up a shower of sand where they hit the beach.

"Copper!" I can't turn back for him. But the comms console lights up, and the emergency signal that's been begging to be sent finally transmits. I hope Hank's got his people standing by somewhere. We could use backup. Any kind.

Hank swivels. His rifle's pressed against my back—the barrel, with the muzzle protruding from the hovercraft.

I reach for Grandfather's gun, then smack it against Hank's side. "Reload this for me! With an actual magazine this time!"

"Didn't want you taking undue risk." With one hand he inserts a fresh magazine and hands it back over.

Grant, meanwhile, has pulled even with us. His last goon is on the other side.

Martin squeezes as low in the back seat as he can manage.

Everyone shoots at the same moment.

Hank's rifle cracks just beyond my left shoulder. I fire, aiming opposite, but who knows if I can hit anything because I'm reluctant to take my eyes off the terrain. Bullets zing across us. The hovercraft's body shudders with each impact. Hank grunts. Blood begins to soak the front seat cushions. The coppery scent mingles with the sea salt air.

We're only a klick or two from the ramp leading off the beach.

But the crowd—blazes, there have to be a hundred people in our way.

"Hang on!" I hit the override and pop on the emer-gency airbrakes.

The hovercraft's engines cut out, and there's a moment of no sound save for rushing air and the jetcycles' whines. Then the hoverjet pylons catch on the sand. They drag long gouges, bucking the vehicle so thoroughly we'd all be tossed out if the restraints failed to tighten their grasp until every breath is labored. Collision foam seeps between us, fills the seats, and cocoons the front end. It finally shudders to a halt, the front end buried in shimmering sand. Pain lances up my right forearms.

Our pursuers can't compensate for the sudden maneuver. The guy on the right—who I'd apparently missed, even after firing five shots his direction—veered off so hard away from the crowds that he plowed a furrow right into the surf. Vacationers splash through the waves, intent on retrieving his limp form.

Grant? He manages better, racing up the ramp to the main road. His jetcycle catches a lip of permacrete, tips on its side, and drags along until it slams against a rock. How he walks away, I've got no idea, but teeters as he crosses the road, gun in hand.

And we're all still stuck in foam. It's dissolving, yes, but not fast enough for us to beat a retreat. I can't find Grandfather's gun. Hank's rifle is gummed up. He gets an arm free as Grant gets near enough I can discern the sneer on his lips, the angry set of his eyes. That's a man ready to kill. A guy who's full of hate.

I strain until my hand breaks through the foam. Finger-tips brush the hovercraft's floor. And something else—Grandfather's gun. It skitters away. Just a little far-ther—

Wait. My wrist-comm. Copper's sent another mess-age, this one recent. [Orders?]

He's survived his crash! But how badly damaged is he? Only one way to find out. All MarkTel robots are programmed with human preservation protocols, in case of pirate boarding. How he'll interpret it is beyond me, but if it's anything like his solution for the jamming drones… [Hostile presence. Threat to captain. Interdict.]

"Vincent!" Grant's voice is raw. Nothing's stopping his facial twitch. It's rampant. Maybe the stabilizer eye was damaged in the crash—he certainly looks bloodshot.

Hank grunts. He tears free of the foam, drawing a handgun as he pulls up out of the hovercraft.

"Don't!" I force Hank's gun back into the sticky foam.

Hank scowls. "'Bout to get us killed."

I hope not.

Grant fires.

But the shot goes wide—as in, a couple meters to our right—because Copper bashes into Grant's forearm. Grant cries out, at the same time I hear a meaty impact and a sickening crunch. The gun flies from his grip. He clutches his wrist, shaking.

Copper nosedives into the sand, again. There's a soft hum as his miniature engines die out.

I rip myself out of the foam, Hank a step ahead of me. He grabs Grant's arms and bends them behind his back. Grant yells again, but Hank forces him to the ground, applying his knee to Grant's back. The shout is immediately muffled by sand.

"Reckon you've caused enough of a mess. Grant Liu, you are under arrest by order of the Crown Marshals Service, under authority of His Majesty King Andrew II of the Realm of Five…"

Hank's reading of the rights fades under the onrushing roar from a bright orange Rescue Ops barge, a broad-hulled, wide-winged aircraft. It's accompanied by a sleek black skipjack, armed and deadly in its appearance. Slate gray hovercraft round a bend in the road, their emergency sirens joining the howl surrounding us.

Martin grabs my shoulder. His eyes are tear-filled. "Thanks. Thanks for saving my life."

I smile, hands still shaking. We hug each other, and I'm glad for this moment with him, amidst the chaos. "I'm always there for you. No matter what or when."

It doesn't make it any easier when Hank takes him aside and puts him in binders, just like Grant.

Yeah, I can save my brother. But his mistakes are his.

I can't fix everything.

Chapter Twelve

Margate pages through Hank's report. It's so quiet in his office that every flick of his finger across the holographic text could be a cyclone. He hasn't asked any questions. Which is good, because I don't have many answers.

My right forearm aches, so I reposition it. The slender white splint pulses with a soft light. An orange indicator flashes on my wrist-comm, but I'm not interested in the healing update. My priority is the fate of my job.

To his credit, Hank kept my name and actions out of the news grids. As far as the general public is concerned, Crown Marshal Horatio Henry Tyler and his deputies foiled a gang of notorious smugglers and kidnappers. Thankfully, there were only a few minor injuries among the public.

But two men are dead. Two more are hospitalized, clinging to consciousness as nano-surgeons worked their frantic medical magic.

None of that's relevant to MarkTel, because they found out about my involvement. The culprit? Copper.

I'd forgotten that when I had him try to break thro-ugh the jamming employed by Grant Liu's robots, the al-gorithm I set triggered a MarkTel systems alert as soon as it was out in the wild, so to speak.

Fast forward to the next day, and that's why I'm back in the regional office in Yinse Haian.

I sag into the chair. All I wanted to do was keep my brother safe. No one should have been hurt, let alone dead.

Apparently, that's not Hank's philosophy.

"Well." Margate sets his delver on the desk with a *clink* that could have been an ancient judge's gavel. His face is as unreadable as if he were wearing a spacesuit helmet. "There's no denying your penchant for meddling, is there?"

"Look, sir, before you get—"

"I didn't ask for your input." His voice is even, and soft, but there's no denying the authority.

"All right, but if it's an apology you want, there isn't one forthcoming."

"Nor do I expect one. I understand the pull of family. You'd be better off trying to resist a planet's gravity well. It can override all imperatives—including the survival of one's position and security of one's economic status."

There it is. My future. I've never given any thought as to what I'd do if I weren't a comms ferry jockey. There has to be other maintenance work that doesn't require a massive amount of retraining. Time to start that calculus.

"Be that as it may, there's elements of this situation that are beyond my grasp. Fortunately for you."

He waits for such a long time I takes me a while to realize he's waiting for *me*. I shift in my chair. "Okay."

Margate sighs. "What I'm hinting at, Captain Chen, in my too subtle way, it seems, is that you still have a job with MarkTel."

He sits back, reclining against the chair's cushion, fingers interlaced. "Do you have any questions?"

I blink. "Do you mean, other than why you haven't revoked all my access codes and had me escorted from the building by the security guys in the lobby? Yes, a few."

"They will have to wait. Your leave is over. You're to report back to orbit and transit for your next assignment within the next 48 hours. I've forwarded the agenda to your wrist-comm. Standard comms ferry replacement track."

My wrist-comm beeps. He's telling the truth—there's the notification from the scheduling system. If this is a prank, it's one of the most elaborate I've ever encountered. "I don't understand. This mess, it's almost specifically what you told me *not* to do. And you're not only letting me keep my job, you're sending me out on another assignment."

"As I said, elements are beyond my grasp."

"What elements?" I snort. "You're MarkTel. You can find out anything you want from anywhere in the galaxy."

Margate raises an eyebrow. "And yet, I still have to answer to those above me. Those far above me. It seems, Captain Chen, you have developed admirers in that upper echelon. That will serve you well. For now."

He rises. I match his move, standing stock still as he approaches from around the desk. Margate offers his hand. "I don't approve of the way you disregard personal safety and that of others, but there's no denying you get results," he murmurs. "Let's make certain those results have our organization's benefit in mind."

Then I'm walking out the headquarters' front door, into the swampy morning of Yinse Haian's downtown, wondering if my boss letting me off the hook is a good thing.

Hank meets me at the Chen compound. Martin's in the back seat.

I avoid meeting his eyes. "So, thanks for all you did."

"Call of duty," Hank says. "Might've had a troubling time cornering my quarry, had you not stepped up."

"It wasn't much of a choice."

"Mm-hmm. Family determines the choice. You look a might unsettled."

"Not surprising. We left dead people out there." I can still see the one guy's body, his expression empty, his face covered in blood, as he topples onto the hard-packed clay. What was his name? I never knew. Yet, his life's over. Whatever the status of his soul was before that moment, it's too late for adjustments.

"That's the hazard. Sin comes for a man when he least expects it."

"Sin didn't kill him. We did."

"Not you." Hank taps his chest, the motion apparently free of doubt. "Got the burden right here. Nothing left to do but take it to the Lord, call on Him for forgiveness."

I shake my head. "I can't get used to it."

Hank smiles. "Reminds me of a fella from years ago. Good man. Brave. Faithful. Couldn't stomach the need to end a life when a man's 'bout to take yours. That didn't make him weak. Far from it." He puts a hand on my shoulder. "If that's you, hold onto that strength. God will provide it."

Then he opens the door. Martin clambers out. He squints into the sun. Give him a few days and his injuries, such as the bruises clouding his face, will have faded. "I thought I was gonna be locked up forever."

"Nope," Hank says. "Dropping the charges."

I stare at them. "Are you serious? What about the smuggling?"

"Going to recommend for community services. Got to be consequences, sure as gravity pulls us home, but your brother's providing good evidence. Solid stuff."

Martin shuffles his feet. "Captain Rilla," he blurts. "I'm… telling the crown marshals everything I know about her operation. You were right, Vince—I can't keep doing this stuff. Never mind what I can get away with. And beyond it being dangerous." He chews his lip.

"What is it?"

"I can't face Father," he mutters. "Or Mother. Or Lily. Especially Lily. I know you all hate me for what I did. And keeping that mask up while I ran around behind their backs, betraying the principles they taught us… I'm sick of it."

My heart clenches, a docking clamp squeezing so hard I'm afraid it will burst. He's right. Father and Mother won't take it well. But it has to be done. Has to be *said.* "If you want, I'll stand with you."

Martin nods. "Thanks."

Hank slides back into his hovercraft. "Safe travels, Captain."

"Likewise, Marshal."

He leaves us in a cloud of dust, waiting outside the compound entrance. We enter through the visitor's hatch, which is already yawning open because my poor hovercraft is inside. It rests on a tow cradle Hank used to bring it back.

Lily's boots protrude from underneath it. She shimmies out, her hair askew, face streaked with grime. She shoves a diagnostic scanner into a belt pouch and shoves her goggles onto her forehead. Her finger stabs toward the hovercraft. "Vincent! You trashed her!"

"Sorry, Sis. But it was worth the damage. She per-formed like a champion." We embrace. Her tears soak my shirt. Mine are about to follow, as hard as I push back against them.

"Don't do it again." Her voice is hoarse. Fingers dig into my back. "I didn't know… I thought you weren't coming home."

"I'll always come home, understand? I won't abandon you."

She nods. Her eyes are red around the rims. She sniffles and smiles at me. "What a pain."

"Vincent."

Father and Mother are there, waiting beside the wrecked hovercraft. Father's pulling at his fingers, his expression pinched. Mother looks like she's been ill. She grasps father's arm with one hand and clutches her delver with another as if it's her escape pod.

"Father. Mother." I hug them together, squishing us into a mass of love and tears. It's all I've ever wanted. It's what I left behind. Knowing I have to leave again hurts like getting shot. Or at least, worse than my aching arm.

"You—you did it." Father breaks free, heads straight for Martin.

My brother shies away, his arms folded. "Father—look, I failed you. Both of you. What the marshal said? It's true. But I… made a choice. The right one. I'm fixing what I did wrong. So, whatever you need to do, whatever penalties you've got, I'm prepared. I'll pull extra shifts in the gardens, take over the fabricator so we can get replacement parts made faster—"

Father embraces him in the middle of his confession. He's openly weeping. Martin can't resist. He breaks down, too, and when the two of them part, they're smiling at each other. "Forget all of that. We're going into the city to celebrate tonight. All of us."

My elation falters. Is he serious? Martin gets off, again? An ugly feeling cuts through the warmth of reunion. This is happening. Martin gets a reward. I have to leave everyone behind, and Father's letting everything that he did—the way he endangered our family name—just slide?

"Come on. Let's get you checked up." Mother pulls Martin along. "I have a med-scanner ready. My son." She cups his cheek.

They disappear into the house. Even Lily's fawning over our wayward brother.

Father joins me. "Vincent? What's wrong?"

"Nothing." Tell that to my jaw. It's sore from grinding my teeth—which I didn't realize I was doing.

"Hardly. You can't be the teen sulking in your room. Out with it."

"You just—took him back!" I throw out my arms. "I mean, that's great—we're all happy now. But…"

"But?" Father squints. "He made a grave mistake. In-jured our reputation. Put himself and others at risk."

"Yes. Exactly."

"There will be consequences. Most won't be levied by me. He'll have to deal with more stares, more sidelong whispers." Father sighs. "Your brother does not have the restraint you do."

I chuckle, despite the bitterness in the back of my throat. "You wouldn't have said that if you'd see us on the Endless Beach."

"That's why I'm proud of you. The things you've done, the work you've accomplished—the lives you've changed. Every action you take is for a reason, Vincent. The paths we're on are set before us with a purpose in mind. Mine. Yours. Your brother's." He holds me by the shoulders, face to face. "Before this time slips away, I'm rejoicing that my boys are home. I thought I had lost one son and faced losing the other. No parent should have stand at the edge of that pit. Rejoice with us."

He's right, of course. I can't believe my own arrogance. I rub my face. "You're right."

"As I tend to be." Father winks. "Come. Let's be a family again. This moment will end all too soon."

Twenty-four hours later, I ease back on the skipjack's controls and boost to orbit. There's fresh raisin bread sealed in a pouch, tucked into my duffel bag.

Father, Mother, Lily, and Martin wave to me from the compound's edge, tiny figures caught up in the dust scattered by the engine exhaust. Huh. The ion drives have a slightly different hum to them. I check the readouts. They're running with less than a half percent variance. I grin. Leave it to Lily to steer me right.

As I clear orbital traffic and enter the queue circling Tiaozhan, I sight *Marconi*. As much as leaving home fills me with a terrible longing, the familiar starship draws me near. She's awkward, with four spherical comms ferries hitched to the bow spar, and the bulging engineering section dangling from the aft, but with sweeping cooling vanes lending her a rakish look, I can almost feel the power of the main drives.

Soon, I'll be back among the stars.

Soon, I'll be home, even as I leave it behind.

I check on the box strapped to the passenger seat. Copper's in there. Mending. I'll have to get the primary hamsters aboard ship, Blue and Scarlet, to do a full repair. They'll get him good as new.

As soon as I sync with *Marconi*'s main computer, a flurry of messages stream onto the skipjack's console. Father. Mother. Lily. Martin. Even Director Margate and Marshal Tyler. Well wishes and instructions. Love and respect. Same things I'll help others communicate across the light-years.

Except there's one I don't expect.

Melinda Qin.

Well. I haven't spoken to her in forever. I hesitate, finger over the panel, wondering what I fear. But it's time to put aside these artificial distances. There's no reason, no rationale I can employ to stay apart from people. I'm the one who makes communication possible through the void, for star's sake.

I open the message, grinning like a big dope as the text unfolds. It's a friendly intro from a person who I haven't visited with in a long—

I'm sorry for the deceit, but I needed to know you'd open the message. If it had come addressed from me, well, that couldn't be guaranteed, could it? Send me the coordinates for your second stop on your new schedule. We'll rendezvous with you there.

Izzara Neoh needs your help.

--Juliana Ward-Verge

Operative, Intelligence Service of the Realm

The message spits a series of comms codes into my databanks. Then it deletes itself. Somehow, the trans-mission log gets scrubbed, too. It's as if I imagined it.

But the codes remain.

I sink into the command chair, stunned. Izzy's in trouble. And the spies with whom I worked to capture her want me to lend assistance?

Are they insane?

My hand's poised over the main drives.

Come on, Vincent. You know the answer.

Full acceleration.

Book 4

Mixed Messages

Everything on the line...

Vincent Chen is loyal to a fault.
That's why the Intelligence Service of the Realm
has tasked him with finding a lost operative—
Izzara Neoh, the woman who broke his heart.

He stopped her from stealing secrets from the Realm of
Five, but ISR had different plans for their wayward spy.

Vincent's not the only one searching for her.
An old adversary is one step ahead, determined to
claim the same storied treasure from
a legendary starship the spies are tracking.

It could be filled with unfathomable riches.

It could hold terrible dangers.

And when all else fails, it will cost Vincent
everything he thought was valuable to
stand against unyielding greed...

The Realm of Five

circa 2614

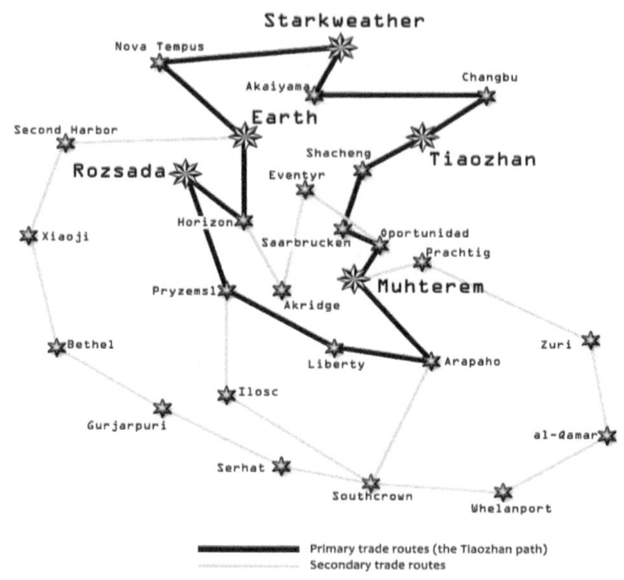

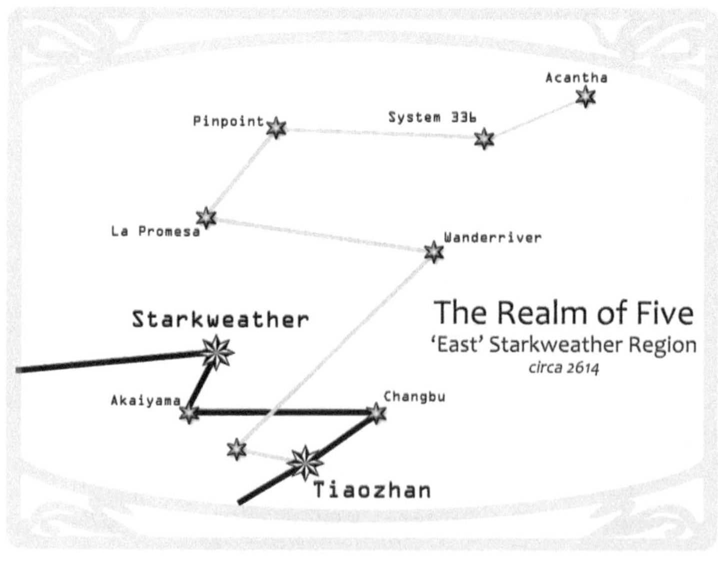

Primary trade routes (the Tiaozhan path)
Secondary trade routes

Chapter One

16 January 2614
Wanderriver Star System

The warship is waiting for me when I exit the long jump between stars.

Maybe warship isn't the right word. *Havoc* is technically property of the Intelligence Service of the Realm, making her a spy vessel. Since her midnight hull makes her all but invisible against deep space, and that same hull's armor prevents all but the galaxy's best scanners from divining her secrets, I won't begrudge that designation. But she's also crammed with weapons where she doesn't have engines, fuel, and tight living quarters, so she performs well in a combat capacity. Her crew fought off criminals who would have killed me and my colleagues a few months back.

Which is why I'm both relieved and anxious when *RMS Marconi*'s sensors pick up *Havoc*'s engine exhaust. She's headed my way.

I pick at the worn leather cover of the Bible tucked next to the command chair's seat cushion. This is crazy. Not part of my job. Nowhere in MarkTel regs does it say Interstellar Communications Ferry Deployment and Maintenance Specialists like me are authorized to lend assistance to the primary intelligence agency of the Realm of Five. Much less fake logs that show my ship, *Marconi*, should be a star system away, replacing a malfunctioning comms ferry.

And still, I'm a willing participant.

Havoc hails me. I ignore the signal, my brain ravaged by contradictory thoughts. "Took them a few days to make the rendezvous," I mutter. "A couple of minutes won't kill them. Except their message was urgent. Izzy's in danger. You have to move."

Sigh. Talking to myself. Again. Not out of the ordinary, to be sure, when the rest of my crew is composed of two dozen maintenance bots. It's an easy habit to fall into. I try not to indulge.

My fingers won't leave the Bible cover alone. Pick. Pick.

Havoc hails again.

Pick.

I toggle the comms console, acknowledging the transmission and preparing a reply. "This is *RMS Marconi*, Captain Vincent Chen commanding."

There's a handful of seconds lag time as the signal zips across a few million kilometers, gets listened to by my visitors, and earns a reply. The voice that filters through the comms speakers is clipped, stern, with an edge that reeks of impatience—Ray Ward, ISR operative. "*Marconi*, this is *HMS Havoc*. Stay at your current speed and maintain your present trajectory. Prepare for intercept and docking."

That's it? That's all the explanation I get after accepting their summons? Again, this is *not* typical of my job. Then again, little has been during the past few months. "Not like I have any questions."

Ack. There I go again, with the talking to myself.

A blue indicator lights up on the main monitor. The navigation computer paints a glowing green arc for *Havoc*'s course, one that wraps around the inside of *Marconi*'s spherical bridge. It's just my command chair and the attendant consoles perched at the center of this big, flashy nav display—more a work of art than basic tech. Numbers appear next to the blue indicator, dwindling as it moves. *Havoc* will meet me in 12 minutes.

Time enough for me to speculate why ISR wants my help to find

Izzara Neoh, former spy and current criminal.

The woman I rescued and then helped these guys arrest.

Thankfully, it's Ray's partner, Julianna Verge-Ward, who meets me at the airlock. She smiles, her eyes blue-gray stars, and nods. "Captain Chen."

"Operative Verge-Ward." My irritation allows only a civil greeting.

"Enough chit-chat, I guess. Show me to your bridge." Julianna smirks, reminding me of my sister Lily when she's feeling mischievous. Julianna's a bit younger than me, I think, with auburn hair curling at the collar of a navy blue shirt. The white jacket ISR favors is as bold as a deep space beacon in the corridor's dim lighting.

I gesture, and she steps out of the airlock. The hatch seals. I give her two steps down the corridor in mutual silence before I blurt, "Where's Izzy? What's this all about? What happened to her?"

She raises an eyebrow. "I'm fine, how are you?"

"I'm not in the mood to play games."

"Good. They're a waste of time. Thanks for your patience, by the way."

"You guys didn't give me much choice."

"My orders are to communicate as much as possible face-to-face. Less chance of this being… scrutinized. But I knew you'd be a good fit for this assignment."

"No, don't call it that. You asked, I'm here. It's a polite response."

"Nine light-years out of your way."

I sigh. "Give or take. I almost lost my job because of the actions I've taken beyond, well, work. This can't be an assignment, not if I want to keep getting paid and, more importantly, hold on to my ship."

"Don't worry about it." She plucks a tiny delver from her sleeve. It's a quarter the size of the handheld device I've got tucked into my belt, not much bigger than a couple fingers pressed together. It lacks a screen, at least until she pulls it apart and a transparent sheet expands. I recognize the MarkTel logo and the somber countenance of my immediate supervisor, Director Solomon Margate, next to a raft of glowing text. "A memorandum of understanding between MarkTel Region Six and ISR. You are hereby seconded to me and Operative Ward for the duration of this assignment, however long that may be. All MarkTel equipment aboard and including this vessel is available for our use."

She lets me hold the micro-delver, so I can read it as we continue to the bridge. If it's a fake document, it's a good one. And if anyone was going to falsify MarkTel orders, it would be ISR. "Am I supposed to sign, or did you already fill in that blank?"

She chuckles.

"Seriously, Julianna. What happened?" I lead her inside and gesture for her to take a seat in the command chair. Manners shouldn't be forgotten, even in a situation such as this. Mother taught me as much. "When I left *von Arco*, Izzy was in your custody. Don't tell me she escaped, because if she's a fugitive, this is a job for the Crown Marshals, and I know one on Tiaozhan who'd be happy to oblige."

"If she had escaped, I would gladly contact the marshals." She picks up the Bible. An undefinable emotion crosses her face. I'm used to getting reactions from people when they touch the book that up until twelve years ago was banned, and still not that many have encountered printed materials. Whatever she's feeling, her features tighten. "Except she didn't escape."

"Then why—oh, blast." I rub my forehead. "You let her go. She's working for you."

"You are astute, no matter what Ray says."

"So glad your husband came along for the ride."

"He's my partner and one of Izzara Neoh's handlers. It's not optional. What he lacks in interpersonal skills he more than makes up for in starship combat tactics and weapons proficiency." Julianna smiles. "Plus, he's cute."

I roll my eyes.

"You're right: we let Izzy go. That isn't to say she's free and clear. She has to pay for her crimes, but as we both know, locking up someone of her considerable talents is a waste. ISR is nothing if not conservation-minded."

"So, what's she doing?"

"We needed her to help us track a starship, one of great value to the Realm, and as such, to its enemies."

"You mean the Martian Tiu."

Julianna reclaims the micro-delver from my grip. "Don't assume the descendants of the original Mars settlers are the only threat since they're the only other military power in this part the galaxy. There's always internal discontents that could destabilize the Realm. And if this ship were to enter anyone's possession, well…"

She streams data through the command chair and onto a huge swath of the monitor. If any organization prides systems security, it's MarkTel, the company with a monopoly on interstellar communications. You can't get a message from one star system to the next without dumping them into a comms ferry they own, the same kind of which *Marconi* carries four. That's why my adrenaline spikes when Julianna bypasses every byte of vaunted security in a couple seconds.

But all that worry about tampering blows out of my mind like the atmosphere from a vented airlock when a ship's schematics materialize on the screen.

The basic design is familiar to anyone who's traveled between star systems—blazes, to any child born in the Realm, really. There's a Raszewski sphere in the center, without which the ship couldn't jump between the sundoor regions found around most stars. The fore and aft sections are equal in length, each one about twice the dimensions of the sphere, but they're ragged, blocky, lacking the smooth lines of hull plating common on modern vessels. It means this is an older model. How old, I don't realize until I count just two bulky cooling vanes branching off the dorsal and ventral hull, ahead of anti-matter drive nozzles that seem half-constructed. Those, too, are obsolete.

"She's a ten-brace," I say. "About the same tonnage as the swift frigates Rescue Ops sails. Smaller than a cargo felucca, far bigger than a navastel. Why anyone's using one nowadays is beyond me."

"No one is. The ten-brace went out of style two centuries ago." Julianna points. "This one was sighted among the Starkweather worlds a month ago. Sensor records are incomplete, because the ship that took them was destroyed. The man piloting was captured—one of our assets."

"You sent Izzy out to find him and the ship."

"That's correct. The vessel in question disappeared in the star system in which it was found." Julianna lifts a trio of tiny stars from the micro-delver's holographic display. A flick transfers the relevant data onto the main monitor. "It's a trinary, called Acantha, with suns orbiting in close proximity. Nothing of interest besides proto-planetary discs, which means the system is full of swarming debris. There's ample cover for losing or hiding objects."

I shake my head. One man lost. Izzy missing. An ISR ship destroyed. "This ship must be stocked with big secrets if you're resorting to covert tactics to get it back."

"It isn't ours. It's legal salvage. But that doesn't diminish its value." She opens another file. The contents pour alongside the ship.

My brain freezes like a hamster bot's operating system stuck in a diagnostic loop. I had to be reading the designation incorrectly. "That's—the *Coronado*."

"The very same."

"Not possible." She might as well have told me she found the Dragon's Gate, the one my grandfather spun tales about. If a carp swam up a special waterfall and leapt over the gate, it would have been transformed into a mystical dragon. "It's a myth. A treasure hunter's tract fever dream."

"I'm convinced it's fact."

"Then you're as spaced as your sources." I fling my arms wide. "There isn't a captain who's punched through a sundoor at some point in his life who didn't expect to find *Coronado* waiting on the other side of the touch tract. Jewels, spices, rare art, exotic metals—you name it, someone's said it's aboard."

"No one has a manifest, that's true. But our man spent the past few years reconstructing *Coronado*'s route. It was something of an obsession for him." Julianna turned aside, her arms folded, waiting as the data finished streaming out of the micro-delver. "The ship vanished from shipping records for decades, reappearing only at the height of Kesek's power."

Kesek. The king's secret police, who later turned on him, but not before they had spread the fear of the Royal Stability Force—their formal title—through the Realm of Five. They kept every religion in check. Some, especially Christians and Muslims, bore the brunt of their oppression. Holy books were banned. Families were sundered. Loved ones were killed.

I lost Uncle Ethan. The Chens never fully recovered.

The micro-delver beeped. Download complete. Julianna crossed the bridge, treading cautiously across the curved deck-slash-immersive screen, and highlighted a star system on a new chart. "*Coronado*'s last known port of call was made almost twelve years ago, at a planet no one knew was accessible via sundoor—Alexandria."

"The repository? There was rumor some group stashed Christian relics there to hide them from Kesek. Relics and writings and…" I stop and stare anew at the ship glowing on my monitor. "And art."

"We have sources who confirm *Coronado* was loaded with a portion of the contraband items. The cultural significance is huge. That doesn't even take into account the wealth involved. Those items never made it to the museum on Bethel, which of course remains under royal sanction and protection and funded by private donations." Julianna shrinks *Coronado* until it's a gold diamond inside the trinary stars, which in turn diminishes among other stars outlined in green.

Bethel. The safe-world of the Christian faith and home to the greatest museum of such relics in the galaxy. They never would have gotten there if Baden Haczyk hadn't found the last known printed Bible floating in space and heeded the call that led to not only its revival, but the downfall of Kesek and restoration of religious freedoms for everyone in the Realm.

He'd taken everything from Alexandria.

Yet, here Julianna is, telling me Haczyk had missed something.

"Vincent, ISR still hasn't completely regained its strength since we were re-chartered after Kesek's dominion. We can't be everywhere at once. Add to that the political instability in the region, I need you to help me find Izzy and our asset she went in search of. We can't lose people. Two gone in short succession means someone is interfering with us."

"I understand, but… why me?"

"Let me be blunt: You're inconsequential." Julianna shrugs, perhaps to soften the cold, hard edges of the word she let escape. "If a MarkTel comms jockey goes missing, no one will bat an eyelash. But if more ISR personnel are lost…"

"Stop there before you continue your terrible job of complimenting me," I mutter. "Surely you can get the military. Like Starkweather, right? This is their turf."

"And I'll direct you back to my earlier comments about political instability."

"You're talking about the incident of 2612." No wonder the name of Starkweather, one of the Five and perhaps the Realm's greatest independent military power, stuck in my mind. "There's still word filtering through the Reach about two Starkweather Navy ships that blew each other up. Rumors, really."

"Not rumors. Fact. One rogue captain's aims, stopped by the sacrifice of a loyal commander." Julianna sighs. "Keeping that sort of thing quiet is difficult at best, considering how many civilians were involved. And we're still dealing with the fallout from that mess. Let's just say we're not sure who in Starkweather's military hierarchy we can trust. Commodore Drivakis had many supporters, so many that official inquiries from Earth and the Congress of Worlds have been stymied."

"So, I'd better not call them for help."

"I'd rather you didn't."

"Speaking of you…" I point at her. "This sounds less and less like you'll be my immediate, on-site supervisor for a rescue mission."

"It isn't wise for me to leave *Havoc*."

"Why not? I'm sure your android frames can keep an eye on things."

Her lips twist, like she's eaten something sour. Probably remembering the last time she deployed ISR androids was when she was chasing down Izzy and used them to attack *RMS von Arco*, the place I'd fled to for safety. That was before we got our differences sorted out, and she revealed to me I was harboring a criminal instead of rescuing a spy.

Which I hope she no longer holds against me.

"Can I trust you to handle this?" Julianna clasps her hands in front of her belt. They're reddened around the palms, as if she's been picking at them. It doesn't escape my notice that she leaves my question unanswered. Her prerogative, I suppose. "I'm out of options."

I grimace. "This because of the *von Arco* incident, isn't it?"

"That, and the Sylvanak colony, and your handling of a smuggler ring on Tiaozhan a few weeks ago."

The real question, of course, wasn't whether she could trust me but whether I could trust ISR—and when it came time for a full burn at maximum thrust, would I put this life of mine in jeopardy for a woman who befriended me, betrayed me, and begged my forgiveness, all in the space of a couple of days.

Not that long ago I'd turned my back on her and pretty much everyone else. I liked my solitude.

Now, though, I recognize a higher calling at play. Father's voice breaks into my thoughts, from our last time together before I departed Tiaozhan: *"Every action you take is for a reason, Vincent. The paths we're on are set before us with a purpose in mind."*

He's right. I can't deny it.

I'm not a soldier. I'm not a cop. I'm not a hero. But I won't let the Keseks of the galaxy step on others anymore.

"Okay." I plant my hands on my hips and pray this isn't an asteroid-sized mistake. "Tell me where I can find her."

Chapter Two

La Promesa Star System

Going through a sundoor takes forever, and yet the tract shift happens in barely the blink of an eye.

Blue Alert douses the bridge in azure. *Keep my transit safe and my soul in Your hands.* You could say it's rote prayer, but I mean every word of it every time it flits through my mind.

I throw the lever. The artificial singularity at the core of the Raszewski sphere unleashes its energies. They course out along four tendrils, the braces that have extruded from the miniature hologram of *Marconi*. I glimpse a row of green and blue lines—everything's working fine.

When your ship is stretching itself between two points in space separated by thirteen light-years, it had better be fine.

Sights and sounds swirl. The scent of oil paints comes from nowhere. How'd that get in the ventilation?

Mother sits in among the lilac trees in the Chen family compound. The warm, damp air of a Western Province spring on Tiaozhan carries the caw of shinhawks. "Like this, Lily." Her brush sweeps red across a pearl canvas.

My little sister sits cross-legged. She's torn open a brassjacket robot's access panel. Wires and links are strewn on the grass. Lily's fingers are stained with lubricant. Spots mar her blouse. "In a microsec. I've almost got it rebooted."

"Hardly. Concentrate on your lessons."

Lily mouths the words back, rolling her eyes for emphasis.

"Look at how well Vincent's doing."

I'm there. I remember. The brush glides across the canvas, leaving a serpent's curves. It takes on a sinister form as I add blazing eyes and rows of fangs.

"Oh," Mother murmurs. "I didn't anticipate that."

Back on the bridge. I see the world around me in double. It takes a dozen blinks before I can clear away the disorientation. I kill Blue Alert, returning my surroundings to their usual hues.

The shift went off without error. I, the ship, and all our attendant molecules made it through the sundoor.

Nav wipes the main monitor of the Wanderriver star system's details and replaces it with the La Promesa system. There's a habitat a quarter of an astronomical unit away, about 38 million kilometers. Three comms ferries ping me, each one stationed at the sundoors leading into and out of La Promesa. And there's traffic. Even as *Marconi*'s tremors subside and I retract the Exform braces into the hull, two navastels blink into reality a third of the way around the star.

Forty minutes later I light the main drives and burn at 20 gravities acceleration toward the habitat. The sentry vessel hails me a minute after that.

"*RMS Marconi,* this is Sentry Eight Six Bravo." The voice is female, as stern as Ray's. Those Starkweather accents lean heavily on the consonants and they talk, well, rapid fire. "We have you flagged as entering the La Promesa system at 1337 hours Galactic Time. State your business and prepare your shipboard logs for inspection."

That's a first. I'd heard Starkweather was cracking down but… "Sentry Eight Six Bravo, this is Captain Vincent Chen, *RMS Marconi*. Shipboard logs are open for your inspection. I'm transmitting the code now. Bear in mind corporate data is restricted and will not be available."

"Roger that, *Marconi*. Submit your delver for query, too."

I frown. "Sorry, must have gotten a garbled transmission, Sentry Eight Six Bravo. Did you say delver?"

"Affirmative. Standard EF protocols."

And there it is. EF. Enrolled Faiths. Starkweather's answer to the king's edict that repealed the Charter of Tolerance—which, ironically, was anything but. His decree restored freedom of worship to everyone. But the Bethel Laws passed afterward gave the Five worlds the option to restrict that freedom in the name of internal security. Some, like Tiaozhan, didn't bother.

Starkweather, though, took a more paranoid stance.

"Sentry Eight Six Bravo, take a second look at my registry. This is a MarkTel vessel."

"Confirmed, *Marconi*, but EF status applies to all travelers."

"I think you'll find it's only relevant to Starkweather citizens." Because I haven't been sitting here patiently waiting. I've run the search through the Reach, twice, and come up with the specific clauses as written in the Bethel Laws. Plus, MarkTel keeps a handy primer ready for its employees who are of a religious bent, because my employers don't want government regulations causing too much trouble for business. "Your request to access my delver is denied."

Sentry Eight Six Bravo sits there on the edge of communications range, well-with the light-second required for instantaneous ship-to-ship talk. It's a short, stubby patrol trireme, not much more than a trio of upgraded anti-matter drives and weaponry that could easily take a big chunk out of my hull. If they wanted to cause a problem, I'd have to submit.

"Not the best start to a spy mission," I murmur.

"*Marconi*, you're cleared to proceed. We won't be needing your delver." The tone loses some of its officialness but none of its bite when she continues with, "Just watch your step, cross-hugger."

The transmission cuts out. The trireme moves off toward the next ship coming by.

I shake my head. Yes, Kesek is long gone. But the fear that infects the Realm remains.

Puerto Hueco is a world under construction.

The famed asteroid clans, those *los pastores de montañas*, the mountain shepherds who made their communities on huge rocks they shepherded throughout the solar systems, are a determined people. How else could they take a 20-kilometer body of carbonaceous material and bore a tunnel 6 kilometers wide from one end to the other? The resulting shelter teems with myriad tiny craft—barges, skipjacks, shuttles of all shapes and sizes—and is home to sixteen starships at the moment. They're slender six-braces and bulky feluccas, a school of languid interstellar fish, their cooling vanes folded down as they traverse the interior.

A pair of Starkweather Navy battle corvettes circle the bustling habitat at 300,000 kilometers, keeping themselves in constant comms distance—and striking range for their pulse particle cannons.

I watch them on the main monitor as Puerto Hueco's dockmaster takes over the helm. The remote nav program pilots *Marconi* inside the gaping maw of the tunnel, ion engines at their lowest thrust, maneuvering us past a navastel that's offloading hundreds of silvery containers into a chute. A long, spindly grappling gantry lunges for the hull. *Marconi*'s deck shudders.

A green light appears on my control panel: Airlock secure.

Right. My uniform is crisp and clean as it will ever be. Besides my delver, which links me to all the data I'll ever need, I take only three more things with me: the weary Bible; a stubby gray scrambler which hangs in a prominent holster slung from my belt; and Copper, a brassjacket robot who bobs on tiny hoverjets, following my every move like a loyal pet. A loyal, electronic pet who's managing pretty well, considering I had to patch him together after a smuggler's bullet blasted him from the air.

The port swarms with people from all walks of life. I feel I'm back on Tiaozhan, where the Magnificent Return had just finished, except this isn't a uniform collection of Tiaozhanese, who are majority Asian stock. Merchants from the big shipping houses walk in tight clusters, their bright, clean uniforms a warning to pirates and the independent Expatriates that they're not to be trifled with. Meanwhile, the Expatriates bounce around in ragtag bunches, boisterous in their greetings and free with their money as they pinball from tavern to restaurant to stores to machine shops.

The few quiet, murmuring men and women hunkered in the corners. Pirates. They don't want attention. Not here. They stay far from the merchant companies because of those bright jumpsuits and give Expatriates the same wide berth because everyone knows they're not afraid to defend their family shipping interests—and because the Expatriates are just as well-armed.

It helps that I count fifty men and woman in Starkweather Navy tans scattered throughout the boulevard, in their own cliques. Nobody wants trouble with military, even off-duty personnel, not with those warships circling. I don't see any marines but they're doubtless on leave of their own, or else standing by to launch to Puerto Hueco if things get dangerous.

Everyone has one of two goals here—spend money or make it.

There's plenty of cash in my pockets. I figure I'll need it to gain me access to places my credentials won't. But for now…

I board a crowded magtram bound for the interior offices. It whisks a couple hundred of us three klicks farther along the boulevard that follows this side of the tunnel.

Takes me right to the local MarkTel comms office.

It's a three-story wall of glass spread along the upper promenade, above endless rows of shops. Everything's reflected in shades of pale violet. My MarkTel ID gets me past the security bots posted at the door. They hunker in recessed alcoves, silver and spindly like mechanical versions of the mantises that buzz the summertime fields outside the Chen family compound, except these ersatz insects are as tall as children.

Nobody stops me or even attempts small talk. The black jumpsuit of a comms jockey lets me walk wherever I want among executive offices, programming stations, and processing centers.

I don't need any of those rooms to help in my search for Izzy. I just head for Signals Extrapolation.

Sig-extra is on the top floor. Delete that—it *is* the top floor. Row after row of ebony columns stand like bare trunks in a dead forest, but the breath of ventilation systems, mingled with the hum of cooling lines and the pulse of processors, override that image to give the impression of a massive, living organism. Blue lights flicker and stream across fifty-six processing towers this is where every comms signal in and around Puerto Hueco winds up—routed here from the comms ferries sitting back at the sundoors, then out into the thousands of personal, home, and business communications networks. I'd bet even the Starkweather Navy's secure transmissions wind up sneaking through.

I can't help but think it's the kind of place Izzy would have loved to rob.

"Something I can help you with?" The kid at the entry cubicle looms overhead. I'm lucky if the tip of my hair reaches the peach fuzz sprouting from his chin. He's pale-skinned, except where swirling orange tattoos lined in silver coat his skin, and light shines off a bald head so perfectly smooth it could be *Marconi*'s Raszewski sphere.

"Captain Chen, ICFDMS." A quick flash of credentials off my delver is all it takes for the tiny domed scanner on his desk to blink from yellow to green. "I'm slated to run a full refresh on my ship's transmission logs and get the ferries aboard purged."

The kid—Specialist Graves, according to the white lettering on his badge—stares at me like I've sprouted dragon wings while leaping out of an airlock. "Oh. Right. Sure, Captain. You've filed a request?"

My heart triphammers as I scroll through the contents of my delver. There's a formal request, all right, stored in the memory of the handheld device, but it's a falsified one. This time I don't have to wonder, because Julianna's the one who sent it to me. "It's already been approved by the Region Six director, through Region Five."

And that's what Graves reads off the holographic projection—a commnote from Director Margate to his Region Five counterpart. A full refresh and the accompanying purge will take gobs of processing power. I'll tie up a lot of the office's capacity running it.

Which will give me plenty of time to achieve my actual goal.

Graves lets me have at a private console deep in the computing forest as he dashes off message after message to his bosses. A quartet of towers emit a higher-pitched hum, their lights shifting to amber and synchronizing their pulses. An image of *Marconi*, its four comms ferries docked along the forward hull like berries on a vine, and the accompanying registry numbers of all five appear. An endless strand of numbers and letters races along the bottom in a blur that makes my stomach churn if I stare at it for too long. This will take hours.

I access the signal logs—not for my ship, but for all of Puerto Hueco. A comms jockey has clearance for this. Specialists like Graves are more glorified clerks. We're independent captains, given much higher access so we can affect repairs, make split-second decisions that deal with hardware valued in the millions, and safeguard the communications traffic of the Realm of Five.

A perk of that? Being able to track individual comms codes.

The refresh and purge is my cover, sucking up so much processing power that I can initiate the search for Izzy's ISR comms code without drawing suspicion. Thankfully Julianna had the code. I wonder if they let Izzy have her ID ring back. Of course, that jogs the memory of finding it in her spacesuit.

And memories of time spent talking in the comforting silence of *Marconi*'s bridge.

I grimace and push through the search. If Izzy's used her code anywhere within a light-second of Puerto Hueco, I'll know where, when, and how often. The ISR code mimics a typical civilian strand, except that it can shift its identification into another one at random, to prevent tracking.

This isn't new for me. Digging out illicit programming and finding rogue signals designed to steal data from comms ferries is part of the job, requiring a skill I don't get to use often. But one in which I've had lots of training.

So, I'm not surprised when the first sweep turns up nothing. "Okay, then, let's try something else," I murmur.

I call up a second search algorithm to watch for abrupt changes in personal comms codes. I've heard that pirates have the same kind of signal shift, but those are choppy. Easily spotted. They're meant as emergency channels pirates use to slip past law enforcement, not as dedicated covert lines.

Give me five more minutes.

Four minutes and thirty seconds later, Graves come by to check on me. “Everything’s proceeding, sir. Looking aced.”

“Thanks.” I’ve got multiple contacts downloaded onto my delver. I leave him frowning over the active display screens and their dizzying array of data. They’re his problem now.

Izzy’s last call was a pre-programmed emergency signal sent to Julianna via ISR’s network. All the rest were local. And none were to the same person. Most of them don’t have names listed, either—they’re identified by alpha-numerical code only. Lots of need for privacy when doing business in this place, I guess. My delver has the contacts sorted by proximity, the nearest one being at a cluster of food stands a few sections from here.

But the one I’m most interested in is the one made right before her emergency signal. It used up far more bandwidth than any of the other calls, indicating she was transferring information. A lot of it.

Copper floats alongside me, the exhaust from his miniature hoverjets brushing my skin. Text dribbles across my wrist comm’s screen. [Two individuals following, 20 meters behind.]

Well. I’m kind of surprised no one had shown up before now. After the run-ins with smugglers I had on Tiaozhan on what was supposed to be a family reunion, I spent some of the long hours between tract shifts in deep space setting up a new program for Copper. He’d already proven adept at watching for my wayward brother; why not modify his parameters to include people who were tracing my steps?

Call me paranoid, I guess, but you have to admit, there’s been precedent.

I decide I want a look at these guys. I turn sharply through a gap in the crowd, so I’m heading toward the nearest store. The move—which is pretty clever, I must say—lets me catch a glimpse of a man and woman. Shorter than me, Indian or Pakistani descent, bronze skin, jet black hair. Their clothes are a typical civilian mix, and if I hadn’t been looking for tails, I wouldn’t have noticed them. Those clothes, though, are grungy. Dirt-stained.

Not merchant spacers, then.

But they don’t have that lean, predatory look of the pirates. In fact, the man makes eye contact and gawks. He nudges the woman. They bump into a family of six as they hurry away, leaving an irate mother and two crying children in their wake.

So much for me thinking they were spies. Talk about the worst practitioners of espionage ever.

A warning from Copper flashes across my wrist comm. [Inappropriate destination.]

What the blazes does *that* mean?

Pale neon light floods my face. I look up into the bold holographic lettering that informs me I've crossed the threshold into a store that carries women's, um, fancy undergarments. The kind of attire that's not seen anywhere outside a bedroom.

The heat in my cheeks has nothing to do with the press of the crowds. I pivot, reverse course, and wind up face to face with three ladies old enough to be my mother.

"*Zepsuty*." One of them rolls her eyes as they brush by me.

Some spy I am.

Chapter Three

Whoever those two are, I don't catch sight of them over the next half hour it takes me to reach Level Thirty-Three. The crowds thin up here, nearer to the asteroid's surface. Not surprising, given that most of the level is home to fabrication shops. Huge lifts carry custom parts for starships deep into Puerto Hueco and the docking tunnel. It's a long, narrow corridor with a ceiling so far out of reach I get only glimpses of skeletal rafters hiding in the sickly glow of orange beacons.

The clientele is… less diverse. Lots more pirates skirting the edges of Expatriate crews. Hefter robots abound, too, trundling along with heavy loads of parts and cargo strapped to their backs and lifted in their thick arms. The stink of solvents and reactants permeates the air, until my nostrils burn.

So, what had Izzy been doing up here?

Whoever was her contact, that person met up with her nearby. All I have to do is find out where and maybe I can figure out who the individual is. And, hopefully, find Izzy. Not to mention *Coronado* and the missing ISR agent.

I blow out a breath. “Sure, no problem.”

Of course, there’s the complication of me not being law enforcement. I can’t just wander up to security officers and ask to see their vids or holos. They’ll want to know why, and I seriously doubt Julianna’s letter of understanding with MarkTel extends to me acting like a crown marshal.

Not for the first time, I can’t help but wonder why she isn’t out here trawling the corridors in search of her missing agent.

Because she knew you’d drop everything to go find Izzy.

What was the deal with that, anyway? We haven’t even reconciled. As far as I was concerned, she’d betrayed me. Never asked to be forgiven. Or had she? It was—unclear.

And that’s why you want to find her. Because if she’s looking for forgiveness, you have a responsibility to grant it, as she repents from the choices that led her to that moment.

I push the internal argument aside and focus on flashing Izzy’s image among the lounging Expatriate spacers, clumps of whom are gathered at taverns at hundred-meter intervals. Waiting for their manufactured orders, I figure. Few claim to have seen her. No one offers specifics. Why should they, for one missing woman? They’re not exactly beating down the security office’s hatch to identify pirates hanging out nearby.

Their interest piques when I offer cash with the image.

“She might have been here.” This from a tall, thin woman with blond tufts that resemble a bird’s plumage. She’s got a silver star with a black circle at the center—the universal badge of an interstellar ship’s captain—pinned to a towering red collar that brushes her chin. I make sure she can see the same badge affixed to my jumpsuit. “There’s a lotta folks come this way. No one stays long. Get your deliveries, then boost.”

“Sure, but if you saw her, you might remember where she went.” I twist the delver so she can get a better look at the wad of four orange bills. The smiling ancient astronaut could almost be encouraging my success. “As in, specifics.”

“How about that,” the woman murmurs. “Aldrins do reboot the memory banks, don’t they?”

She ups her volume as she adds, “This guy’s asking where the best place to eat is!" She winks at her shipmates, a cluster of men and woman bearing crossed lightning bolts on the sleeves of their jackets and jumpsuits. That earns me her raucous laughter, and in those seconds, the money vanishes from my hand. She moves in close and prods my chest with a finger like a dagger, as a flash of orange bills slides into her pocket. Her expression's gone stony, the anger visible to anyone who happens to walk by behind me, but instead of a threat, she mutters, "Papa Alberto's. Three units away. Smells like garlic and pesto."

I back off and circumvent their gathering in a faked hurry, their insults bouncing off my jumpsuit. Then a shout draws attention back down the opposite direction, and hopefully, no one else is paying close attention to either of us.

My wrist comm pings. It's linked to my delver, which has been monitoring local comms traffic and tracking the activity from Izzy's signal. A pleasant green indicator tells me that she was there, at this pseudo-Italian restaurant. For a moment, I assume it's one of the knock-off storefronts that offers vac-flashed "fresh" vegetables and pasta that's drier than the surface of Mars, but the placard outside the smoky glass windows and silver frames says it's run by an Earth family.

The bot hovering outside the front door is a squat, hexagonal big brother to Copper. In fact, the older model brassjacket exchanges data with my companion.

First thing I get out of the meeting is a menu download. I swipe it away. [Looking for the following individual.] Izzy's image follows the return message.

[MarkTel business?] The bot's reply acts as a query for my credentials, which automatically flash cross the wrist comm's screen and into the bot's memory.

[Yes. Answer.]

[Individual was a patron of this establishment. Dinner reservation for two. Further information restricted to owner's database.]

"Fine." I have to admit, I should have eaten hours ago. "I'll take a seat, if you're serving."

But first thing's first—I send the server bot a command that wipes from its memory our text and data exchange. No record of my credentials.

No memory of anything but me asking for a seat.

Handy.

The bot triggers the door release. Copper whisks inside, as the tantalizing aroma of sausage and marinara provides a welcome replacement for the industrial stench I've been breathing.

"*Buona sera, signor.*" The owner smiles up at me, a thick moustache and beard shrouding all but a hint of his lips. His right eye whirrs—a cybernetic implant, silver with black lines and a gentle blue glow. No doubt he's scanned every square centimeter of my official jumpsuit. "Alberto Detti. Forgive me for my bot. It's malfunctioned. Can I get you a seat?"

There's a few open. The dining room must have been just another prefabricated industrial module, complete with dingy, bare bulkheads and support beams, but Detti's done a great job making it into a comfortable space. Faux wood boards and stucco panels hide most of the bulkhead. Reproduction paintings of bucolic landscapes dot the new walls, lending splashes of bright color in the subdued yellows and browns. A few couples and scattered handfuls of young men are already seated, their murmur of conversations blending with violin tunes squeaking through concealed speakers.

"I'm actually looking for a friend." I let him get a good look at Izzy's image. My stomach's rumbling makes it difficult to concentrate. "She was here a bit ago. Maybe you can tell me when."

Detti's smile vanishes. His beard might as well be a sealed hatch. "If you're with her, I'm gonna ask you to leave."

"I just have to find her. Not looking for any trouble." Of course, that presupposes *she* didn't come here to cause trouble—or didn't manage to, even if it wasn't her original plan. But two large, dark-haired men—boys, really—get up from their seats on either side of the restaurant. I'd ignored them with the rest of the diners. "She was with someone. I've got his comms code, but it's secured. All I need is a name and a face."

"Is this an official request?"

I'm starting to think I should have donned civilian togs before I left *Marconi*, but I'm so used to work attire it never occurred to me. And, well, in truth I'd hoped it would open more doors. Which it is. But now people are wondering about the MarkTel guy who won't stop asking questions. "Will it matter either way?"

The two young guys have me hemmed in. Closer up, they seem familiar. Huh. That's because they're taller, broad-shouldered, clean-shaven versions of Alberto Detti. Twin sons?

Both armed.

Really, who isn't in this place?

"She and her friend caused a scene," Detti says. "Both left without paying."

"Her friend?"

"A skinny youth. Looked a lot like you—Tiaozhanese, Akaiyaman, I can't tell them apart."

I roll my eyes and bite back commentary.

"Kid could have used a lesson in manners. Talking too loud, in that annoying accent. He sounded like he came off a Liberty lunar ranch. And his hair? A supernova would have been dimmer! No wonder she smacked him."

Wait a microsec. "They had a fight? Are you telling me we could have skipped this, and I can find them both resting in the security office's brig?"

"Security doesn't bother with much up here. Not enough money. We take care of things. Anyway, she ran into a bunch of his friends." Detti shrugs. "I don't know where they took her."

"Then I'm going to need access to your register," I say. "So I can figure out who he is and where he went. Security vids, too."

"You're not a crown marshal, last I checked." He lifts his chin. "Carlo? Lorenzo?"

Which is which? I suppose it doesn't matter. That must be the signal for his boys to transition into bodyguard mode, because they reach for their guns.

"Like I said, we take care of things without security," Detti says.

Fine. Me too. I brush my wrist comm against my belt.

Copper sweeps in from where he's been floating by the door and thumps Carlo—I think, to my left—on the back of his head. His startled yelp gets everyone's attention.

It's enough of a distraction for me to unlimber my scrambler. One hot white burst later Lorenzo is sprawled on the tile floor, limbs smacking like appendages of an out-of-control bot. That's you get when a scrambler disrupts your voluntary nervous system.

Sinfully satisfying to have someone else get stunned for once.

I angle the barrel up at Carlo, who's rubbing the back of his head with one hand and trying to aim for Copper with his pistol. "Listen." My voice sounds distorted through the keening that lingers in my ears, courtesy of the scrambler pulse's high-pitched squeal. "I'm going to find this lady. There doesn't have to be trouble. Unless you want. Believe me, after everything I've had to deal with lately, stunning the rest of you will be trainee-level. Blazes, I was ready to bribe you vac-heads. One more time: the guy's name, the guy's face, and the guy's everything else you gathered when he ate here, so *I* don't have to call security. Because I'm sure they'll love to hear you roughed up a MarkTel comms jockey. It'll make it easy for my bosses to triple your transmission rates next time you go to call up the family back on Earth."

My pulse pounds against the sides of my head. I don't want this. Would I really use company influence to restrict this guy's family contact? No. Not at all.

I have to keep telling myself that. I can pray for this sin later.

I'm short of options, and patience.

Detti's face is pale, as bad as poor stunned Lorenzo. "All right. Fine. *Stronzo*. Carlo, put it away."

Carlo holsters his gun and stands there, fists ready. Detti retrieves a delver from a nearby counter, stepping over Lorenzo, who's thankfully stopped twitching. His breathing's steady.

Speaking of breathing, all of ours thunders in the sudden silence. The rest of the diners stare.

Great. And me in uniform.

My delver syncs with Detti's. There we go. Restaurant records—who paid, when, and how much. Even if you used physical currency, the comp for the restaurant still marked a comm ID...

Hold on.

Tatsuo Nakano?

No mistaking his face when I pull up the restaurant vids. He's got that same smirk, that same awful white hair tinged with orange. His tattoos are hidden under long sleeves of a green jacket. He slaps aside a drink glass and hurries for the exit.

Izzy follows him.

I pause the recording. Izzara Neoh, safe and sound—at least, she was, three days ago. No mistaking that stride, equal parts graceful and athletic. She's wearing a form-fitting black blouse, gray trousers, boots. The brass-colored belt is laden with pouches and a long strap for a holster with a giant Hunsaker Black Bull pistol. She's got her hair pinned tight, except for long strands framing her face. Dusty blue eyes flecked with green are locked onto the imager that took the footage.

"If that's all you need, get out."

Right. Detti and his unfriendly sons.

What I really need is a plate of linguini, not a confrontation with a business owner who has to defend his turf.

I hurry outside, Copper buzzing along beside me.

This blasted *Coronado* had better be worth the headache.

Tatsuo's comms code leads me down to Level Twenty-One, and a full klick back the way I came. This section is full of agricultural modules—sprawling enclosures of hydroponic vegetables, interspersed with huge orchards. My eyes can't absorb the unending walls of green. Don't get me wrong, I love the tiny greenhouse cabin on *Marconi*, the one and only space that reminds me of home—even when I don't want to be reminded of anything to do with it. It's almost enough to make me forget I'm in the lonely depths of space.

Funny. Up until a few months ago, I tolerated the greenhouse. Now I can't wait to get back.

Storage cubicles are nestled between the modules, long, gray panels with white doors that break up the transparent barriers on either side. The signal went through Router 21-019, just beyond Cubicle ST21-F.

If there were fewer people on Level Thirty-Three, Twenty-One is almost deserted. Hefters and automated anti-grav sleds comprise the bulk of the traffic. But there's enough rumble from their passing that I don't hear the sounds from behind the cubicle hatch until I'm a couple meters out.

That is, the banging and shouting.

Blast it. No way I've come all this distance to let Izzy down at the last second. The hatch is sealed. There's no lock, however—or maybe it's disabled.

I toggle the release. The panel sparks, drops to one side, and spews wires and a loose circuit. Well, that explains the lack of security.

The hatch snaps open with a bang louder than a gunshot.

First thing I notice is Tatsuo, tied to a chair, with a black eye and blood encrusted on his lower lip. A man is sprawled on the floor—the same guy, I realize, who followed me earlier in the day.

The second thing I see is Izzy swinging a chair at his female companion.

It catches her in the jaw, spins her head, and slams her against a stack of containers. The whole mess tumbles into a corner. The gun that woman was holding spins into a shadowy corner.

A third man fires at Izzy.

I'm already in motion, springing through the hatch, my boots squeaking on the rippled metal of the deck plates. Our shoulders collide—or rather, I collide with his shoulders like a discarded spacesuit helmet rebounding off a starship's hull. This guy is big, burly, with a thick gray jacket sporting a tall collar.

My action's rash enough to throw off his aim. The bullet caroms off a rafter over Izzy's head, sparks, and ricochets twice more. Someone shouts.

Izzy spins around, hair askew, and grants me the biggest grin I've ever received. "Vincent! What in nova are you doing here?"

"Vincent Chen?" That's when the fourth person in the room steps out of the darkened corridor on the other side of the cubicle.

Governor Ray Nakano.

Same immaculate hair, somehow unruffled by the tussling in this compartment. He's forgone the fancier togs he wore when he ruled the colony on Sylvanak, in favor of a slim black sweater with gray stripes at the waist, and workman's trousers.

"This won't do." He sighs and shakes his head, as if a favorite pupil has missed the easiest answer on the final exam. "Another unnecessary complication.

I can't believe it. He should be locked up. Him and all the other Restorationists. I was the one who found out the colonists were ex-Kesek officers and their families who had relocated to Sylvanak, thanks to a pardon from the king, so they could start anew in this post-oppression era. But the Restorationists didn't think much of redemption and had no qualms about making indentured servants—slaves, really—of the colonists, under threat of financial ruin and death.

At least, until I led an uprising, commandeered their ship, stole back *my* ship, and called in the proverbial cavalry.

Wait a microsec. That's why the Hindi couple looks familiar. They were Restorationists, too.

And the big one who tried to shoot Izzy? Red beard, red buzz cut, hazel eyes. He sneers at me and takes a step, legs whirring in a mechanical way the average human's should not.

"Keegan?" I blurt.

Nakano's chief enforcer. The one who liked to give beatings to people who slowed production on the varmo root terraces.

People like yours truly, and like George Cotes, the former Kesek constable who did his best to take some of those blows for me.

Keegan's appearance is like finding out your airlock seal failed while you're transiting between your ship and a space station.

Last thing I see is the backside of his gun before a thunderbolt of pain makes me black out.

Chapter Four

Wake up.

Seriously, Vincent. Get up.

"Hey." Warm, soft hands cradle my face. Lips brush mine. A kiss? "Come on, I need you on your feet. This isn't the time for rest."

I blink until my vision stabilizes, like a glitchy monitor the comp can't get to focus. Izzy. Two of her. I blink harder. Good, she's down to one of her.

Izzy smiles. "Thank God. I thought they'd badly hurt you."

"The back of my head agrees with that assessment." I prop myself up on my elbows. The room spins, until I slap a hand against a support beam.

Izzy clutches my shoulder. "Steady. You're fortunate if you don't have a concussion."

"And you're both fortunate you're not dead." I stand. Better. Everything sways. Or maybe it's me. Either way, I'm regaining my footing one step at a time. The lights are too bright, though. I squint. Nothing lessens the ferocity of the headache that squeezes my skull.

I'd better assess the situation.

Tatsuo's picking at the access panel for this side of the cubicle's hatch. The chair Izzy swung is crumpled against the collapsed stack of crates.

There are legs protruding from underneath. "What happened?"

"The red-beard's shot—it ricocheted and hit one of their people." Izzy kneels beside the body and pushes a box aside.

Stars. It's the man who followed me. He stares, lifeless, at the ceiling. His chest is soaked a garish crimson.

I gag and dry heave. Thankfully, I haven't eaten. But I know why the man's dead—I slammed into Keegan and threw his shot off course. "He's—what did I do?"

"Hey." Izzy stands and turns my chin. Her grip is firm and the gaze she offers me is as steadying as anything I could take from a medkit. "You saved my life, again. Red-beard would have killed me."

"Keegan. His name is Keegan. He's one of the Restorationists I helped get arrested at Sylvanak colony."

"Keegan." Izzy's frown sharpened. "It's nice to have a name to go with the target's face. I was going to switch to Mech-Legs if he kicked me one more time."

"They caught you?"

"I was pursuing my lead to find a missing starship and the confidential informant who brought us the intelligence."

"The *Coronado*. I know."

Izzy's mouth snaps shut. Her eyebrows raise. "Julianna?"

"Operative Verge-Ward sent me a signal, and, well, it turns out I couldn't say no." I can't look at the dead body but screaming inside my head won't let it go. It's not that I haven't seen death before—blazes, after Crown Marshal Hank Tyler shot the smugglers who tried to kill me and my brother, you'd think I'd be numb. But this man was dead by my actions, even if it was Keegan's bullet.

"Are you serious?" Tatsuo glances over his shoulder. "You're after the *Coronado*, too?"

"No, I'm here to find Izzy and get her back to ISR." I touch her arm. "And I'm doing that right now."

"Uh, yeah, only if and when we get through this door." Tatsuo points a finger at the ceiling. "And if those shut down."

I crane my neck. Pain lances to the top of my head. What shuts down? I catch a keening wail on a repetitive loop, somewhere outside the cubicle's confines.

"Security alert." Izzy scoops up my scrambler and hands it over. There's no other weapons in the room. "Keegan wiped the stock of his gun with your hand."

"Trying to pin the killing on me?" I shook my head. Ow. I'd have to stop that. "Then we'd better wipe it off."

"Great plan," Tatsuo mutters. "Except it's on the other side of the hatch."

"Then let's get out of here!"

"I'd love to, Vincent, but we're kinda locked in," he snaps. "And since I'm clean out of communications gear—because they don't let you near a major comms array when your dad is charged with human trafficking and slavery—I can't really call for help!"

I join him at the hatch. With my wrist comm I can—

It's gone.

I sigh. Really? They took that and my delver. No use for the Bible, though, because it's still tucked in a jumpsuit pocket.

Okay, focus, Vincent. This is an obstacle.

Get over it.

I ram the scrambler's stock on the hatch. "Copper! Access and open."

Nothing but the nearby hum of tiny hoverjets.

"How hard did you get hit on the head?" Tatsuo sucks in a breath. "Ah. Aha! I think I have it. If I cross-connect…"

The hatch zips open. Copper bobs in midair, lights rippling around his scanners.

"Nice work." I snatch him and open an access panel on his dorsal surface. "We're going to have to stay vocal for a while, okay? At least until I can get replacement tech back on *Marconi*."

"Your ship is here?" Izzy eases out of the hatch, scanning the traffic. No sign of security. Not that many people, either, though a few handfuls are murmuring to each other and pointing at us. "What about *Havoc*?"

"Not around. Well, okay, Julianna said she'd stay nearby but without an immediate way to contact her we'd better get to the tunnel first."

We look at each other. The obvious stays unspoken.

"I'm sorry," Izzy blurts. "Again."

"It's, ah, okay." I scratch the back of my neck. "I think I already said that."

"Yes, you did, but I was hoping you could forgive me."

"Well, you didn't actually ask."

She puts her hands on her hips and smirks.

Admittedly, I'm having a hard time communicating. Ironic, right? That's not to say I haven't wondered about this moment—my heroic save, her swept up in my arms. Turns out being gracious and confident in the moment is a lot harder than it is in your imagination.

Especially with Tatsuo rolling his eyes between us. "If you're done, somebody'd better pick that up."

The gun? What a vac-head I am. It's right there, between our boots. I kneel.

"Security! Drop your weapons and submit."

Oh, perfect—three men and two women, clad in black jackets and blue trousers, all wearing gray caps emblazoned with triple gold concentric rings. Four brassjackets light up the air around them with flashing blue and red lights.

"Everyone stay calm." Izzy's voice raises but is as steady as a hefter's stance. "Officers, there's been a mistake…"

She yanks the scrambler free of my belt and sends pulses shrieking down the corridor.

Tatsuo grabs my sleeve. "Move it!"

The three of us run, as scrambler bursts from the security team howl past us. I thought there'd be more. A glance back supplies answers—apparently Izzy's a fan of that old adage, "spray and pray," because one officer is down, twitching, and a pair of scramblers are clumps of dead circuitry on the deck. The rest pursue us, using the automated cargo sleds as cover, because Izzy's slinging more pulses their direction.

"This would be a better rescue if you knew where we were going!" she shouts.

"Away from them is my first choice!" I snap. I'm trying to read directional signs. Ramps to different levels. Lifts. Where's the one for the magtram? There!

I veer for an open hatchway. Before I can reach it, though, the frame glows red. Letters drop from the ceiling, a holographic warning:

SECURITY ALERT. ACCESS DENIED.

"Hey! Wait!" I pull Tatsuo back from the threshold.

The hatch slams shut. Clanks echo from its edges. If I'd been a second slower, it would have crushed Tatsuo.

More clanks. The ramp to our left seals.

"Security protocol." How is Izzy not out of breath? "They're locking this level down."

"That's a problem."

"I agree."

We keep running, though I have no idea to what end, because I don't have my delver's downloaded map of Puerto Hueco and the increasing crowds are making it more difficult to see exits.

Something catches my eye, though—a broad screen with a familiar schematic. "There!"

We veer of as more scrambler bursts whine. The crowds scatter, with parents shouting for their children to get down, captains commanding their crews to shelter, and spacers as a whole yelling their outrage. Delvers and comms everywhere echo miniature versions of the security alert klaxon that's just as annoying as the one blaring overhead.

I skid behind the schematic board. I was right—a station map. "There's a straight shot down to Level Ten, tunnel side, which will put us pretty close to *Marconi*."

Tatsuo scowls at the display and, specifically, the long, slanted portion of the diagram. "What in space is that?"

"Transect Arboretum." A smile plays at Izzy's lips. "It's lovely. I spent an afternoon walking one of the trails up from the lower levels. They offer reduced gravity excursions in its core."

"So?" I duck as a scrambler pulse dissipates against the top of the board.

Izzy fires around the corner. Two people yelp. Hopefully they're security. "So, it's our way down. Good plan, comms jockey—we shall make an operative out of you yet, or at the very least, a fine criminal. Come on."

The entrance to the top end of Transect is a couple hundred meters ahead. The glowing gateway has a steady stream of visitors. Watching their faces brighten—literally—as they entered the 20-meter-tall gateway is heartwarming, at least to the small part of my mind that isn't worried about getting stunned by station security officers. Also, it occurs to me they'll make an excellent barrier between us and our pursuers.

Except the rest of the crowds have thinned out, leaving those couple hundred meters wide open between us and the gate, except where people are hunkered along the sides of the broad corridor.

"We're out of cover!" I shout at Izzy, as a scrambler pulse dissipates on the deck plates just beside my boots.

"Well aware of that, thank you." She banks right, heading straight for one particularly disgruntled-looking gang of men.

Pirates.

They reach for weapons as she continues her headlong flight, takes aim, and kicks the nearest man in the face, without hardly slowing her step.

Another dives at her, but misses, because Izzy grabs his collar, spins him around, and launches off his chest with both feet. She launches into the next one and punches him in the nose.

Their brawl spills into the middle of the corridor and brings another band of spacers running. More pirates?

"She's insane!" Tatsuo tries to get me to stop. "Those guys have the kind of weapons that kill people!"

"I noticed!" I drag him through the fracas. Someone's gun goes off. Another follows. Next thing I know, the groups separate, leaving three men unconscious on the deck. I force Tatsuo to duck and we speed through the morass.

"Come on, you two!" Izzy's at the line, waving a gun. An AkTek pistol. She tosses the scrambler.

I catch it, drop to a knee—and promptly rip a hole in my jumpsuit. That's great. I fire indiscriminately into the mix of pirates, hoping to hit the security personnel behind them. All I manage is to clip a single brassjacket.

Copper spirals down from the ceiling and sideswipes the last remaining bot.

Our wayward gang bursts through the line, which parts like Biblical sea when Izzy waves her weapon around. "We have two ways to the bottom, gentlemen."

I gawk.

Transect Arboretum is full of trees, projecting from every side of the octagonal corridor—top, bottom, all surfaces between. Gnarled oaks, stately pines, somber willows—there's no end to the variety. Gray and white and brown trunks mimic the overhead rafters I saw up on Level Thirty-Three. I've never experienced so many shades of green. It's like being spun around a leafy color wheel.

And drifting lazily down the center of this massive enclosure, marveling at the branches reaching for them, are a hundred tourists.

"A microgravity nexus?" I can't stop staring.

"Hang on." Tatsuo swallows. "We're—going to follow that thing?"

"Follow nothing. We're going to have to outfly the crowd." Izzy tucks the gun into her belt. She takes the steps onto the launching platform two at a time. "Isn't that right, Vincent?"

She's insane, but she's right. A quick glance confirms the security officers have the pirate brawl quelled, and they've brought back up personnel. I shove Tatsuo. "You heard the lady."

"Yeah, I did, but … I'm a dirtsider! This isn't the kind of thing I'm experienced with."

We're atop the platform. I center my hands on his back. "Do much swimming?"

"Some, I guess…"

"It's just like that. Only, not wet." I send him shouting and tumbling down the invisible corridor.

Izzy snorts a laugh, then recovers into a giggle. "That was awful."

I can't help but grin. "But fun. Ready?"

She takes my hand.

We leap into the center, our bodies buffeted by directed waves of gravity, until we settle into the long glide. A warning indicator flashes as we leave the platform—INADVISABLE VELOCITY. INJURY MAY OCCUR.

True. But we'll go a lot faster than everyone else.

I release Izzy's hand and tuck my legs together. Despite the microgravity environment, there is enough of a pull to keep people moving toward the bottom level. I zip past the tourists, twisting around them with centimeters to spare. Izzy soars behind me, just as agile.

It's tough business maneuvering in this way. Four times, I have to hook around a branch, spin, and push off. My muscles ache. Sweat brushes my forehead and soaks my underarms.

Halfway down I catch up with Tatsuo, who's stopped flailing and is actually enjoying his sojourn—at least, until I bash into him. He becomes a wobbly missile, until we push off another branch.

"This is terrible." He, too, has gone sweaty, but the clamminess of his skin hints he's going to vomit, rather than just being tired like I am. "What happens when they catch us at the bottom?"

I slap the scrambler on my belt.

"That doesn't reassure me."

"I hate to tell you, but it's not making me feel better, either," I mutter.

But our mutual worries dissipate when we land on the broad, cushioned pad on Level Eleven. Not a security officer or bot in sight. No alarms, even.

Izzy alights beside me. She brushes back her hair, which has flown wild and free of its clip. "That was wonderful! I'd love another go."

"Some other time, when we can sightsee without getting arrested." I point a thumb. "*Marconi*'s docked this way."

"They probably know where your ship is," Tatsuo grumbles.

"Hey, relax." I try a smile, now that we're out of imminent danger. "ISR has our backs."

I hope.

Our departure can't be any smoother.

Marconi is just as I left it. No one's bothered with the airlock. Even the customs officials are busy elsewhere.

I fully expect one of those Starkweather battle corvettes to burn straight for us, or pulsed particle blasts to end our voyage once we clear the end of *Puerto Hueco*'s tunnel, but as soon as I get the high sign from the dockmaster to engage the anti-matter drive in a full burn, I gasp for breath.

Nothing.

I'll be dumped in a black hole.

Izzy sighs and rests her forehead on my shoulder. She's standing behind the command chair. "Here I thought Julianna would have left us to be confined and disavowed. It wouldn't be the first time for me."

"I'd count it as a new experience." I make sure our course for the sundoors is set and then shift in my seat. Her head lifts, and here we are, watching ourselves. "Thanks for not leaving me behind."

"Oh, Vincent. You know I wouldn't do that."

"Actually, I don't know. Most of what I knew about you was a lie."

She sits cross-legged on a clump of stars, since the monitor doesn't leave a lot of room for visitors on the bridge. "Not all of it. Your—peculiar background gave me a lot to think about. Could I borrow that Bible again?"

I'm reluctant to part with it, especially since she mocked me when we faced off back on the *von Arco*. When she was a clever thief and ex-spy. Now she's a spy again, and, what, a failed thief? "I just wish I could have gotten to you fast enough so you could have avoided capture."

"Nonsense. Capture is what I wanted."

Tatsuo walks through the open hatch. He slugs on a water tube. "Nice galley you've got back there. I'm sorry, what do you mean, 'wanted'? I took you to Father so you could negotiate. He knows I'm not about to help him on his crazy quest, and he sure knows I'm not about to purposely turn anyone over to him as a prisoner."

"Either way you look at it, you got me into the room with ex-Governor Nakano for extended contact." Izzy extends her hand with a flourish. There's that ID ring.

I point and smirk. "That would have been great as a surprise weapon, you know."

"Of course. But the scrambler functionality has been removed, to make room for massive memory. Everything I snuck from Nakano's delver is right here. I can take us to *Coronado*, and with your help, we'll recover the ship before he can."

I'm impressed. How can I not be? "Julianna will be pleased enough when we get back her missing man. Your contact."

Izzy cocks her head. "Contact. Is that what she's calling him? Quite the demotion."

I fold my arms. "I'm not in a mood for vague, Izzy."

"Old habits, Vincent. Here. I downloaded vids of the interrogation

Nakano conducted. If you don't mind…"

I gesture at my console.

Izzy presses the ring against it. Data streams onto the monitor, bypassing MarkTel restrictions as easily as Julianna managed with her micro-delver. A fuzzy image coalesces. Nakano leans over a man whose arms are bound high above his head. Tatsuo makes a noise like he's disgusted. I'm paying too close attention to see if he just spat on my deck.

No, I'm more stunned by the ISR contact being slapped around by Keegan while Nakano barrages him with questions: "Where is it? Do you have the coordinates?"

Ray. Operative Ray Ward. Julianna's partner and husband.

He's the one who was captured after tracking *Coronado*'s last known coordinates.

"Sorry, Captain." Izzy must sense my frustration, because her tone's gone soft. "I thought she told you."

"Apparently I didn't get that commnote," I murmur. "But it's time I pay another call to *Havoc*."

Chapter Five

Pinpoint Star System

My second visit with Julianna introduces me to a spy who's far less subdued than the one with whom I met early on.

Havoc docks with *Marconi* thirty-six hours later, on the edge of the sundoor. An android greets us at her hatch. It's eerie as all get out having a lifeless, rigid automaton lead us into the spy ship's innards, without so much as a greeting.

"Since when does the Realm have humanoid AI?" Tatsuo whispers the question. Somehow, I doubt the android cares.

"They're simple remote frames," Izzy says. "They can move like a person, but there's no advanced intelligence. I doubt a hefter or a brassjacket is much smarter."

"They make good shock troops," I note.

"Only in confined spaces, and especially when ISR has the element of surprise." Izzy winks. "But we've seen them in action enough to know they serve a good purpose, haven't we?"

Right. I ignore the jibe and try to figure out which of these unlabeled hatches conceals Julianna. When they held me in the interrogation room,

ISR didn't exactly grant a guided tour. I do recognize the white hatch outlined in red that opens into a tiny sickbay, but otherwise the sterile, slate gray environment sports identical doorways in yellow and black.

Our silent escort stops by a black hatch with a silver slash across its middle. I halt, Tatsuo at my side. He glances at me. "I'm not knocking."

Izzy rolls her eyes and keys entry with her ring,

The bridge. Has to be. It's a flattened sphere, with an encircling display that makes *Marconi*'s seem quaint and poorly designed. Our view of space is a breathtaking real-time image reproduction, one that renders the stars so convincingly I wonder if I can scoop up a handful. I turn to port, knowing my ship is docked by a ten-meter extendable tube to that side of *Havoc*, and get to see *Marconi* laid out in flawless 3-D. I can even make out micrometeorite impacts along her hull plating, and a patch where the sealed paint of her registry number has chipped away.

There's two seats at the center, identical in appearance, sporting what look like the same console layouts. A star map floats in front of the left-hand chair. Julianna stands before it, arms wrapped around her midsection. She bites at a nail.

I haven't seen anyone do that since Lily stepped into a fight between Mother and Father.

"I should have told you," Julianna says. "I know it. Can you blame me? This hasn't gone anywhere up the chain of command in ISR. We keep our missions compartmentalized. Small teams of operatives, acting independently."

I wait, arms folded, until she starts making sense.

"He's my husband."

"I know that. You could have told me from the start."

"Again, compartmentalization. Telling you could have led to a greater breach in security."

"Right. Because Izzy wouldn't have told me anyway." I roll my eyes. "Come on, Julianna. It wouldn't have matter who the missing man was. You know that about me."

She nods. "Yes, well, this is a difficult business. Trust is in short supply."

I glance at Izzy. "I'm aware of that. So, let's recap."

"Where should I start?"

I spread my arms, as if to encompass the entire bridge and the galaxy pictured in the expansive monitor. "Take your pick. How about, what did Ray find out about *Coronado*? How did Governor Nakano capture him? And probably most important, what in blazes are Ray Nakano and that vac-head Keegan doing wandering around Puerto Hueco when they should be locked up!"

"I'd better answer the last one." Tatsuo blows out a breath. His hair's aglow from the recreated starlight. "I testified against Father at his hearing. It was—rough. Contentious. But the crown marshals and Rescue Ops argued for reduced charges in my case, since I helped end the Restorationist efforts."

"Don't tell me they threw out the case against your dad."

"No, not at all. He and the bulk of the settlers were being transferred from the Charter Office near Sylvanak to Earth itself when the ship suffered a malfunction."

"What kind of malfunction?"

Izzy drops into Ray's vacant seat and spins it twice. "The kind that results in the prisoners breaking free and commandeering the vessel, and said vessel disappearing in a region well-known for being frequented by pirates who can strip a hulk of registry and transponder faster than pushing a man out an airlock."

I rub my forehead. None of this does any good to lessen my headache. Fitful sleep and a couple visits to sickbay over the past day and a half haven't helped, either. "I'm betting you don't think it was a true accident."

"They had inside help. Or, someone *outside* with the funding, personnel, and access to free Nakano and his people."

Julianna clears her throat. She gestures with her thumb, as if the digit could eject Izzy from Ray's chair.

Izzy slows her spin, but instead of doing as ordered, she props both boots on the console, never breaking eye contact with Julianna. "They brought me out of confinement to look into the matter. My assessment stands. I picked up the Restorationists' trail when they wound up in the Acantha System."

"Our trinary system. The one where Ray found *Coronado*." Funny that Nakano would stumble onto the same place. "Do we know if they were looking for it, too?"

Izzy opens her mouth, but Julianna answers first. "It's unconfirmed, but likely. We all know the odds of stumbling onto something so remote in a star system, especially one as crowded as Acantha."

"I was pursuing and observing." Izzy shrugs. "They had Ray's outrider disabled and captured before I could react. Not that I could affect a rescue, not against the thirty people they had."

Thirty Restorationists. How many were Keegan's goons, the men and women who kept the Sylvanak colonists slaving on the varmo root terraces? I glance at Tatsuo. "Let me guess: You were looking for them, too."

His cheeks darken. No way he's going to meet our inquisitive gazes. "I wasn't going to let Father get into more trouble or hurt someone else. We'd stayed in touch, so I knew when he'd arrived at Puerto Hueco. I tried talking to him, to get him to turn himself and the others in, you know how he gets—absolutely convinced of his rightness. He wants *Coronado*'s wealth so he can get the Restorationists a new home."

"There's no way the Charter Office is going to approve them for a settlement, not after that fiasco," I say.

"I didn't mean a place. Father wants a ship big enough to maybe convert an asteroid into a habitat, something they can keep mobile. He sees it as a refuge from the galaxy's corruption of the Restorationists' souls."

Oh, wonderful. Julianna storms away from us, settling into a sharp pace back and forth at the edge of the bridge. Izzy stares off at the ruddy yellow sphere of the sun. Maybe she's wondering about how Tatsuo's statement fits into Scripture. She's got my Bible in a pouch on her belt. I haven't asked for it back; there's a copy on my delver for quick reading. What's she gleaned from the well-worn pages?

"Nakano's sense of what's right in God's eyes is warped," I say. "And he's convinced everyone else is on the wrong side. Including Tatsuo."

"And especially you." Tatsuo clears his throat. "It's probably for the best you weren't at the hearing."

"MarkTel wasn't about to allow it." Not that I would have given up my normal solitude for something as public as a criminal hearing. Could anything I'd added beyond my official report have done any good? I daydream Nakano livid, screaming at me in front of a judge and solicitors. "Okay. So, Izzy downloaded whatever your father found. Whatever he was able to glean from Ray."

"Which is nothing," Julianna snaps. "Because Ray would never break. He's been tortured by Martian Tiu and beaten by pirates. He'd never let anything slip to common amateurs and religious fanatics."

"But she has the vid of him being—interrogated."

"Lifted from a cam I planted," Izzy says. "After I found Tatsuo. His trail was easier to pick up because, well, he wasn't hiding, so I let him have the miniature sensor."

"Mini sensor?" Tatsuo scowls. "You put it on *me*?"

"Temporarily." Izzy smiles. "It hopped off and adhered to Nakano, then made a final leap onto whatever permanent artificial surface it could find. I received a decent 48 hours' worth of sensor recordings before it fried itself. You did well, Mr. Nakano."

"Don't call me that." He clenches his fist. "It's Tatsuo."

"You'd better register for an ID change, then."

"Hey." I stand between the two. "This doesn't help—and everyone being cagey about what we all know doesn't, either. Izzy, what data did you recover?"

"The scans from Ray's outrider." She rubs the jewelry. "Nakano's people have the wreckage. They pulled whatever wasn't ruined when the ship purged its comps—which is, of course, standard ISR practice when a vessel is captured. Ray was caught off guard, so the process was only partially complete. I have no doubt they'll get something off it."

She presses the ring against the console. The trinary star system, Acantha, springs to life in between the command seats and the forward curve of the bridge monitor.

Julianna steps into the midst of swirling debris that shrouds the three suns. "Did you get this off their devices?"

"It was simple enough, once they caught me and Tatsuo." Izzy stretches her arms. "The ring's snoopers sucked up whatever unsecured information was nearby. I'm sure Nakano thought what had was safe as safe could be. It's cute, really—he had some of the best private security settings you can buy through MarkTel."

Tatsuo snorts.

"I won't argue. I've seen what ISR can do to my so-called secure networks." I join Julianna in the system hologram. A red cube flashes. Ray's wreckage. "Is this it?"

"A part. Ray had managed to narrow down the search grid." Izzy brushes her palm over the console. A gold diamond appears. "This is *Coronado*'s last position, before the Restorationist's attack. No active propulsion, so tracking it should have been easy, but note how close it is to the trinary."

Too close. The ring's data highlights a circle between one twentieth and one tenth of an AU from the star. Seven and a half million to 15 million kilometers. And it's more than a circle—we're talking a spherical shell, a half shell, actually. "That's some serious gravity fluctuations."

"Hence the reason taking the tract shift into and out of the system isn't for the faint of heart. There's no imminent danger, but it's navigationally complex. The comp requires extra preparation."

Julianna pushes aside the holographic debris. "You're thinking those fluctuations obscure *Coronado*'s trajectory."

"Obscure and misdirect. Thankfully, Ray's scans narrow down a significant portion of the star system, or else you could spend decades searching every cubic kilometer of space with zero chance of finding the derelict." Izzy smirks. "With the sensors aboard *Havoc* and *Marconi*, we have a far better chance."

"Assuming you guys can beat Father there," Tatsuo says.

"That shouldn't be difficult." Julianna is at her console now. "The Puerto Hueco dockmaster reports a navastel registered as *Righteous Dawn* left 12 hours after *Marconi*—which, I'm told, encountered no difficulties on its own departure."

"Thanks for that, by the way." I nod.

"All part of the service." Julianna crosses her arms. "We can make the tract shift to System 336 soon. From there, it's six hours to the next tract shift that will take us into Acantha."

"Traffic looks decent." Izzy calls up a second hologram, this one a hologram of our current position in the Pinpoint System. The hazy white shape of the System 336 sundoor pulses at the end of a green arc. A handful of flashing indicators, none red, join ours. "Light cargo traffic. No visible patrols or anyone acting out of the ordinary."

"Well, if that's our plan, I'd better get this data into *Marconi*'s nav so I can calibrate sensors around the gravity fluctuations and debris before we hit Acantha." I stop at Julianna's chair. "I promised you we'd get your guy back. That doesn't change—even if it is Ray."

She takes my mild tease with a wry smile. "I appreciate that. It may have been poor planning on my part, keeping you in the dark at first."

"No one's perfect. Come on, Tatsuo. Two comms techs are better for this job than one."

"Sounds like a plan." He's already out the hatch, past the motionless android sentry.

Izzy joins me. "While we're doing that, I'll tell you what else I found of interest in my, ah, secondary data review."

What, the Bible? I watch her intently. How can I tell if she's using her knowledge of my faith to answer her own spiritual questions, or as a tool for manipulation? Isn't that corrupting the Gospel?

But if it's going to have an impact on her, I won't have anything to do with the outcome. That's the domain of the Holy Spirit. He works in hearts and minds. All I can do is reinforce.

And, Vincent, forgive.

"Let's see what we can do about that," I say.

An alarm rings throughout the bridge. A new icon blinks on the nav display—a starship accelerating from its passage out of the La Promesa sundoor, the one through which we entered a few hours ago. It's burning fast. They're only five light-seconds away. Forty-two gravities? I whistle. "Someone's in a hurry. Someone in a warship."

"Yes." Julianna frowns. "*Gauntlet* Class frigate. Starkweather Navy. Her ID comes back as *HMS Daring*. And she's hailing us."

The pounding inside my head returns. Another complication. But there would have been no way to know they were anything other than a standard civilian hauler until they exercised their far superior rate of acceleration. At least it was the military and not pirates. We could talk.

"I guess you'd better answer, Captain."

Julianna connected the signal.

"*Havoc,* this is *HMS Daring*. You will cut thrust and prepare for intercept. You are harboring two Enrolled Faiths fugitives. Detain them and ready both for transfer into our custody. They are wanted in connection with criminal acts aboard Puerto Hueco station."

Julianna sighs. "I don't suppose you want to send the reply yourself, Captain Chen?"

I don't have an answer, because I'm more baffled by the first half of the message than the second.

Two EF fugitives?

Me… and Izzy?

Chapter Six

The Starkweather officer whose head and shoulders fill the comms screen carries himself like he's In Charge.

Tall, broad-shouldered, with the thinnest outline of black moustache and beard turning his jaw about as square as humanly possible—he could have stepped out of Starkweather Navy's recruiting holo. There isn't a crease out of place on the tan uniform. The white shirt denoting his command reflects every bit of light from his bridge.

"Commander Kadir Gultasli, captain of *HMS Daring*." His voice has an operatic quality to it. Sounds like that of a singer from Akaiyama whose works are broadcast across twelve star systems. I know because I've listened to them through my suit intercom while repairing a ferry that was transmitting those recordings. There's no lag, either, since *Daring* has closed the distance to one-light second distance. "You're in command?"

"Operative Julianna Verge-Ward." She leans on the *Verge* part of the name.

"She's one of them?" Tatsuo leans inside the open hatch. "Did someone forget to mention that she's part of the most powerful family in the Realm?"

"Not the most powerful," Izzy says. "But one of. Let's say, in the top ten, shall we?"

Tatsuo's eyes can't get any wider.

"We're sorry to inconvenience you, Captain, but the two individuals I believe you're referencing are serving under ISR orders and, therefore, not subject to your jurisdiction." Julianna offers a flat, fake smile. "Any other questions?"

"Operative, I'm not interested in games about classified intel, and I have no directives regarding ISR's presence in this system." Gultasli held out his hand. A young female officer gave him a delver. "What I have is a crown marshal's arrest warrant for Vincent Chen and Izzara Neoh. They're marked EF."

"I'm not at liberty to comment on their personal beliefs."

"Don't play coy with me. This isn't about petty crimes. We all know what kind of people we're dealing with. Malcontents. Fanatics." Gultasli snaps off the words like he's opening fire. There's no inflection, though. His face is a mask that could have been carved from hull plating. "The EF registry exists for a reason. I have merchants clamoring about the disruption of commerce on what I'm told is the most lucrative trading post in the region, and I have a dead body in a storage cubicle."

Julianna's hands tighten on her armrest. "I'm aware of the situation. We can remedy it later. I'm dealing with a matter of the Realm's security. If you're through, we have a rendezvous to keep."

"That's not going to happen, Operative. The only thing I despise more than disorder is repeating myself, but here we go: Cut your thrust. Stand to and prepare for our rendezvous."

"Again, my apologies, Captain, but that won't be happening."

"Operative, I will open fire on your vessel if you fail to comply."

"Shooting at each other won't solve anything." Julianna stands, smooths the front of her jacket, and clasps her hands behind her back. "Surely that's something they've drummed into your fleet these past eighteen months or so."

I swear Gultasli can hear the *clank* of my jaw hitting the deck. Even the unflappable Izzy mutters something I can't translate under her breath.

Gultasli steps nearer to the comms' auditory and visual pickup. "You'd do best to not scrape the scab off that wound. Starkweather stays free because of the sacrifices of officers like Granza—not the treachery of a Drivakis. We've chosen our sides. I'm firmly on the correct one. Do likewise."

The transmission cuts off.

"All right." Julianna strides across the bridge. "That was a good start."

"To what?" I snap. "Making the captain of a warship furious? If so, then yes, you did great."

She scowls, seemingly surprised by my presence. "Why are you all still here? Get *Marconi* prepared to separate. We'll need both ships moving if this gambit of mine is going to work."

"What were you doing at your console? Besides talking."

"Sending over a digger that, by now, has settled into *Daring*'s arrays, both passive sensing and active scanning." Julianna pulls up a readout teeming with lines of code. "It's rerouting the information those pieces of equipment register before it arrives at the tactical computers. Once we get underway, we'll be able to slip through the sundoors."

My head's spinning, trying to catch up. "You're feeding Gultasli false data."

"It's a neat trick." Izzy leans on the hatch frame. "I've used it before. Not as simple as a module that falsifies a ship's transponder, but if it works, Gultasli will see too many ships for him to pick from. Fake drive signatures, electronic readouts, even bio-signs."

Tatsuo scratches the back of his head. "What about comms?"

"Same thing."

"Okay, I'm on board with that." Tatsuo looks eager for a problem to sink his mind and his hands into.

Julianna just scowls and flicks her hands toward the door.

Duly noted.

Marconi and *Havoc* part ways. I accelerate at full burn, which is only 20-something gravities, so I'm never going to outrun a warship like

Daring. She could catch up to me long before I can beat her speed.

Havoc alters her course, widening the gap between us.

"And here they come," Izzy murmurs.

The indicator for *Daring* continues its path, heading right for where we were. Gultasli's smart. He doesn't pick a target, yet, but if I had to guess—or at least try to think like a navy commander—he'll go for the spy ship before settling on the comms ferry tender.

"Got the signal." Tatsuo's stationed himself to my left, with an extra delver so he can access *Marconi*'s communications system. "We're ready."

I make the sign of the cross. "You might have been—now I am."

Tatsuo makes a face. "Father never put any confidence in those outward signs."

"His loss. I value the tradition." Which meant I had a physical link to my family, using the gesture my father's father would use. No, I don't need to do it. But I can. And I will. To remind myself whose side I'm on.

"There. The digger's active." Izzy reaches across my arm and taps a panel on my console.

Two blue blips—*Marconi* and *Havoc*—bend green course lines away from *Daring*. Four more blips appear, two from my ship, and two from Julianna's. They spread out, taking four different courses.

I'm in awe. So, frankly, is Nav, because the comp feeds me back transponders and drive signatures that exactly match both the real ships. Three of *Marconi*, three of *Havoc*, speeding away on six trajectories.

I'd give anything to see Gultasli's reaction. "At this rate, most of the six will wind up at the sundoors leading out of this system—the ones that don't make it look like they're heading deeper in the system. Won't that be a fun chase."

Izzy pokes my shoulder. "Sounds almost like you're enjoying the ancient art of cloak and dagger, Captain."

I smile. "Maybe. A little. If I'm forced to admit it."

Daring stays on its present course for interminable minutes. I have to loosen my grip on the arms of the command chair, because I'm leaving imprints in the upholstery. Come on. Pick one.

Fear jolts me. Wait a microsec. Gultasli doesn't have to choose. If he has disabler warheads loaded aboard his missiles, he can knock out all systems on whichever ship he shoots.

Izzy must be thinking the same thing, because she leans closer and whispers, "Point-defense laser and sandcaster canisters, correct?"

"Glad you remember the *Declaration*-class loadout," I murmur.

"I try to keep all manner of useful information stored up here." She taps the side of her head. "Keep your course."

"I'm doing exactly that."

Nav blinks out an alert: change in vector. One of the *Havoc*s has swung abruptly in-system, while a second burns at an acceleration rate that makes me want to reload the hologram so I'm sure I'm reading it right. Forty-nine gravities? With a ship that small? Its acceleration compensator must take up a third of the hull.

Daring does what I feared. It launches a spread of eight missiles which, a few seconds out of the ship's range, blast off on various courses.

"Uh, what are we going to do about that?" Tatsuo stares at the nav display, where the computer's busy tracing red lines to project the missiles' trajectories.

"Hang on. If this captain's as principled as he lets on, we may not have to do anything."

Izzy makes a face. "That's pretty naïve, even for you."

I point.

All eight missiles divide themselves among the three versions of *Havoc*. Gultasli's clever, all right. He's not taking any chances around civilian ships. Whether Julianna can dodge the missiles or not, however, could be for naught if just one of them clips her real ship.

Of course, I have no idea if the ghost ships concocted by the digger that she put into *Daring*'s sensor system will fake those phantoms getting zapped by disruption pulses.

I shoot off a prayer for her projection and—escape, I guess, because I'm unsure how God views an action that's similar to treason but for a good cause. I suppose He takes it on a case by case basis.

But I can play my part, too. "How's that transmission coming, Tatsuo?"

"It's nothing you can rush. One moment—there." He flicks the side of the delver and smiles. "It's ready to go, as long as you're sure about sending it."

"Not really, because I like having a job, but here's hoping being a temporary ISR contractor covers a multitude of sins. Transfer it."

The program Tatsuo's written shows up on my console, prepped for transmission. Thanks to the advanced communications gear aboard *Marconi*, it's getting a significant boost.

Namely, from four comms ferries.

I run through the protocols for an emergency eject, which I'd only use in case of catastrophic Raszewski sphere failure. The commands release the clamps holding all four spheres in place and focused thrusters send them hurtling away from *Marconi* in a man-made starburst. A copy of Tatsuo's program rides inside each one.

"Sorry about this, everyone." I send it.

Two seconds tick by. Then, one by one, the missiles cease accelerating. Their warheads are still active, but they're flying dumb as rocks, no longer homing on any of the *Havoc* ships, real or otherwise. Plus, bright streaks of gibberish fill up every communications screen on my bridge. The same thing's happening across the region around the sun, to civilian and military ships alike.

"Stars," Izzy breathes. "What did you do?"

"I used MarkTel's proprietary technology to scramble the comms on everything within range, not unlike a scrambler when it hits a body." I smirk. "The best part? It looks like all three images of our ship did it at the same time."

Here I am congratulating myself for interfering with the lawful pursuit conducted by a military vessel of the Realm of five. And to think, a couple weeks back, I thought I was going to lose my job for helping.

Well, I guess there's still time.

We make the tract shift smoothly, leaving Julianna and *Havoc* to escape via the second sundoor. System 336 is barren, devoid of habitable planets or even resource-heavy asteroids. The surveys show a handful of gas giants, their moons, and rocky worlds that are either cinders or ice balls.

"No sign of other vessels." Izzy's watching the sensor readouts, her eyes flicking to every new image nav throws onto the displays.

"Thanks." I glance over my shoulder. Tatsuo's down the corridor, examining one of the hand-woven rugs I keep on *Marconi*'s bulkheads. The splash of yellow and gold does wonders to buoy a soul on a long, dark voyage. Which leaves me and Izzy alone—as good a time as any to address the topic. "So, my book."

"It's not precisely *your* book." She nudges my shoulder.

I could get used to that. Her proximity does make it difficult to carry on a coherent conversation, especially with the sweet scent—like peaches—wafting from her hair. "You know what I mean. This isn't something I take lightly, Izzy."

"Except you described your people as 'chumps' before."

I wince. "That's true enough. Maybe you understand why."

"They're outrageous claims. Most commentaries dismiss them as fairy tales concocted by men who wanted a lot of power."

"Sure." I snort. "They wanted power so badly they preached things that got all but one of them executed, right? That sounds like a great way to rule over the galaxy—or the world, back then. Look, those guys wanted people's souls saved, nothing more. That's all it's ever been about—fixing the break between us and God."

"I understand that. Now." Izzy takes a seat on the deck, legs crossed beneath her. "That wasn't part of the act."

"You did mock my beliefs, when we faced off. When you tried to shoot me."

"That *was* part of the act. The act I perpetrated on myself." She seems puzzled by the admission. "Funny, really. I kept telling myself I listened to what you said about the Gospel solely to gain your trust, so I could use you as another ends to means. But it stuck. You made that happen."

"Not me. I can't save you. Not anyone. God does the work. Turn him down if you like, though I wouldn't recommend it."

"And yet even with people calling you cross-huggers and governments passing laws restricting what you do because of what you read, you stick with it."

Heat rises to my face. "I'm not a hero of the faith, Izzy. Men and women better than me already paid the ultimate price. I'm just surviving."

"Oh, Vincent. No 'survivor' constantly sticks his neck out for others." She touches my hand. "But either way, we can go a little more in depth this time around, because I'm on the Enrolled Faiths registry."

"I couldn't believe it."

She smiles. "I could."

There's so much more I want to tell her, but how do you condense decades of Father's readings and Mother's songs, the preaching and teaching of countless others, into the few hours we have?

I start with John's gospel and work from there, in between calibrating the scanners. Izzy sits with the Bible on her lap, paging through asking questions and challenging answers, as I'm neck deep in an access panel that lets me swap out hardware. Blue and Scarlet, two of my hamster robots, skitter back and forth between the scanner access with parts I need and to lend plasma torches. They're each the size of my foot, lumpen bots that look like mechanical beetles whose shiny carapaces are covered with spines and pincers.

One hundred eighty minutes later, we're lined up in the touch tract that links System 336 with Acantha.

I drag myself out of the access and slam the hatch shut. Izzy's watching me, a curious expression on her face. "I'm all out of answers if you've got questions—at least for now."

"No, that's not it. You seem different. Subdued."

"Well." I scratch the back of my neck. "Going home was more than I'd bargained for. Memory plays tricks on you. Just when I thought I understood my brother… That's not important, though. Thing is, I had to learn that it wasn't all about me. No matter how much my heart argued that it was."

"It's a difficult thing to reconcile. But I'm glad you're content. You're acting like it, anyway."

"Thanks. I think."

She stands up and holds out a hand, so she can pull me upright. We stay in each other's grasp longer than necessary. "I'm glad you came after me."

"And I'm glad you were, ah, okay."

Tatsuo clears his throat. "If you guys are ready, I think we can make the tract shift."

I strap in. Izzy and Tatsuo do likewise, at the two chairs bolted to the deck down in the tiny galley squashed at the end of the corridor. Once I'm certain they're secure, I trigger the blue alert and throw the lever.

I'm running through the aspens. Branches slap my face. Have to hide. Lily and Martin giggle. Their boots crunch on gravel. Five seconds until they find me. Four. Three. Two. One.

Ready or not...

I lurch into the real life at an insane speed. A second later, I realize it's the normal velocity of time, and I slow panicked breathing.

Nav beeps ceaselessly, the sensors on the verge of overloading due to the sheer volume of debris in the Acantha System. Scanners bounce back image after image of ice chunks and rocky fragments, more than I can count, but the comp sure tries to catalog them all.

I brush aside the technical readout, shrinking the data stream to a square meter, and toggle the image translators. They give me a picture like *Havoc*'s bridge monitors compiled, albeit one that's not as crisp.

But I've never seen anything so beautiful.

Dozens of rings, like those of a gas giant, fill the view screen, some truly massive, others slender and sinuous. They crisscross at myriad angles. The orange-yellow glow of three stars, one of which is five times bigger than the rest, suffuses the entire solar system, the color fading to a brilliant blue-white at the edges.

Izzy's footsteps jar me from my reverie. "They're gorgeous."

Tatsuo shakes his head. "And one of them is *Coronado.*"

"Right." I key up the main drives and set the sensors in a search pattern. Of all things, I remember that I set four comms ferries worth two million adrift a couple touch tracts back. "Let's get hunting.

Because the sooner we find *Coronado,* the sooner we can get Ray back.

And maybe some of that fabled treasure will keep MarkTel from docking huge expenses out of my much smaller paycheck.

Chapter Seven

Acantha Star System

Eight hours later, and we've found precisely nothing.

I shouldn't say nothing. Ice. There's a lot of ice orbiting in the accretion spheres that have gathered around the Acantha stars. If I wanted to start a refueling station and process good old H2O, I'd be a wealthy man, assuming this place wasn't off the trade routes.

But it is, and besides the water, no one else has a reason to visit.

One thing's for certain: Even with no sign of *Coronado*, I know we're not alone out here.

"Right there." I have the nav computer magnify a blip a half AU away. "See that movement? Nav tracked it as too regular to be an asteroid tumbling through the debris."

Izzy tucks a strand of hair behind her ear. "More treasure hunters. Do you think it's Nakano's ship?"

Tatsuo shrugs. "I have no idea. If it is, we don't have to worry about him running stealthily. He's not what you'd call a tactical genius. I mean, Keegan and some of the others have military experience, but it's more soldiering than deep space maneuvering."

I focus the sensors. At that distance, it's going to take a while to get results back, and I'm not about to ping them with active scanners. Of course, if they had half a brain between them, Nakano and Keegan would have noticed both our tract shift into the star system and the flare from running the main drives for the first hour or so underway.

Marconi eases through the debris field, plotting a pre-programmed course designed to avoid the bulk of the debris. Every so often, a tiny rock glances off the hull. I'm sure there'll be a lot of gouges to repair once this trip is over.

Hmm. Searching a debris field like this without probes or auxiliary craft is tedious, that's for sure. Even Nakano has to realize that. "Tatsuo, what kind of craft does *Righteous Dawn* carry?"

"Craft? Oh, a couple of barges, four skipjacks. That's it, I think."

Six small ships. I swipe through a series of commands on the communications console. There's the one. I feed it into Nav and let the sensors begin a new sweep. "If your father's deployed them to find *Coronado*, he's got to keep in touch with them, right? So, if I can listen for their intra-ship signals—"

"You can determine whether or not we're looking at a hunk of metallic ore versus a full-fledged vessel." Izzy thumps a fist off the back of my chair. "Brilliant."

"Well, pretty smart, yeah." My turn for a wink. "Not sure about brilliant…"

She sticks out her tongue.

"That's a great idea, but how are you guys gonna get this Ray person back?" Tatsuo gestures at the monitor. "No offense, Vincent, but this isn't a warship or a spy vessel."

"We trade." Izzy nods. "It's as simple as that. Nakano wants whatever's aboard *Coronado*. He's not going to kill Ray Ward, because he needs whatever knowledge Ray has so he can find the derelict—and Ray's not stupid enough to admit he doesn't know where it is now. If he's played along at all, Nakano's still behind us in terms of intel, unless he's cracked into the data from Ray's scans. When we find *Coronado*, we salvage as much as we can and contact Nakano for a parlay."

"You're not really going to give him what he wants, are you?" I'm appalled at the idea of a man like that gaining more power, the kind that obscene wealth brings.

Izzy's smile is a cold, stern version of her usual lovely expression. "We are, for at least a short while. Long enough for Julianna to arrive and hole their hull until they're forced to surrender, after we conduct the trade and give them the illusion of escape."

"Hey!" Tatsuo stalks around the front of my chair. "No one said anything about trying to kill Father. He might be a fugitive, but I'm not giving up on my family. He's all I have left. That's why I went after him in the first place!"

Izzy's hand rests lazily on the holster strapped to her hip. "Don't fret about it, Tatsuo. I have a mission. So do you. We can make sure our objectives overlap, can't we?"

I notice she doesn't give him any assurance Nakano won't die. "Cool your rockets, you two. First thing's first. We find out if that is *Righteous Dawn*, and we continue sweeping for *Coronado*. Tatsuo, how do you feel about taking my skipjack out for a spin? We could broaden our own range using Nakano's tactics and keep an eye on whoever else is out there at the same time."

Tatsuo's still glaring at Izzy, but he breaks his stance long enough for a curt nod. "Sure. I can do that. I've got some modifications in mind for the comms array that can help us avoid detection, if you like."

"Code them and let me take a look before you modify anything, but yeah, go get started."

Izzy chuckles as soon as his boot steps fade. "He'll be fine."

"As long as you don't assassinate his dad, yeah, he'll be great." I sigh.

"Can we trust him, though?"

"This is a weird time to ask that."

"Oh, don't get me wrong. I've been monitoring him. He hasn't made any outgoing transmissions. He hasn't signaled his father."

"I would have noticed if he did. Thanks for snooping about in my ship's comms system, though."

Izzy shakes her head. "Relax, Vincent. We're on the same team. Common goals and all that."

"Really? You do this for ISR, and you get your freedom, is that it?"

"Legal freedom, yes, among other things."

"Other things."

She sighs. "Do I have to download it for you? Monetary rewards, or at least, a share of whatever's aboard *Coronado.* That will bring me far more security than just the file saying I'm cleared of all charges, because data changes. Wealth doesn't. If anyone comes after me when this is finished, thinking of perhaps reneging on our arrangement, I'll have the resources with which to stay permanently off their scanners."

I had to figure the love of money would figure into her agreeing to take this assignment. Not that she wouldn't be thrilled at the chance to work off her sentence. I'd agree to the same deal. "What are the odds Julianna won't be overruled by someone higher up in ISR?"

"Not good. Hence, my need to keep my options open."

"Do you trust her?"

She shrugs. "Do you?"

"Not entirely."

"I trust you, if that makes a difference."

"It does." I shift in my seat. I really should get down to the hangar and check on Tatsuo, see how he's doing with the skipjack's comms system. "Which surprises me, because I'm the guy who turned you in."

"Once again—doing the right thing. It's possible that's attractive."

"Not much for the bad boy, are you?"

She's leaned in during our exchange, so close that I can feel her breath with each word. "I've had my fair share of the rule-breakers. Change is a good thing."

Okay then. "I'm going to make sure Tatsuo hasn't stolen our shuttle or tipped of his father."

I'm off the bridge before she can see how badly I've started sweating.

The skipjack is a tiny, four-seat shuttlecraft that's nestled into a small hangar on the lower deck. I squeeze down the corridor. Tatsuo's donning an extra-vehicular suit. "How's it coming?"

"Oh, I'm done." He waves a glove toward the cockpit. "I wanted to get your okay before I uploaded the changes."

I duck through the narrow hatch and peer at the instrumentation. Yeah, he's set up comms so he can blink at us in short, coded bursts. Nakano shouldn't be able to detect it. I drag his program onto my delver and duplicate it before dumping it directly into *Marconi*'s comms. "Looks good. Keep this up and I bet we could find you a decent job with MarkTel, if you're in the market."

"Really?" Tatsuo tucks the helmet under his arm and grins. "That'd be nice. I'm living off what our family had saved up, but I could only scrape so much out of the accounts before the Charter Office confiscated the rest. Restitution for the Sylvanak colonists—the victims, I mean."

"You know, you did good back then. I can't imagine what it was like to stand against your parent. That wasn't just disagreeing about politics."

"I… well." Tatsuo picks at the fabric of the EV suit, but he resists making eye contact. "I saw what you did. It meant… it became something I could do, too."

It strikes me that my actions have spilled over into more lives in more ways than I imagined. Sure, it was a thought I'd entertained when I was the one repairing comms ferries. Families and businesses and even governments relied on me doing my job well. But this level of personal influence? Not sure I'm ready for it.

"Your scanners are set with the same parameters *Marconi* has. Okay? so…" I offer my hand. "Good luck."

We shake. Tatsuo climbs into the skipjack. Its miniature powerplant hums to life.

I seal the airlock hatch to the hangar and watch as he launches into the icy void.

Deploying the skipjack helps broaden our search field. And Nav has good news for me when I get back to the bridge.

"We spotted them, all right." Izzy's lounging in my seat. "A navastel. It's running without registration. They have their transponder blanked."

"Not faked, but blanked?"

She nods. "And you were right about the support craft. There's two barges ahead of her, one heading above the ecliptic plane of the system and the other heading below. They're communicating quietly, but the transmissions are definitely there."

"Nice." I step out onto the monitor, sans boots. Izzy's replaced our tentative bogey's indicator with a red diamond and two smaller red pips. "Want to listen in on what they're saying?"

"As long as it's not encrypted. Then you'll need my help."

I jerk my thumb for her to exit the seat, which she does with a flourish and a bow. Let's see: The signals bouncing back and forth among the three ships are delayed by several minutes, thanks to the distance. Actually, so is the position of the ships themselves. Nav calculates where it thinks they should be, based on the last measure of course and speed, and then corrects its extrapolations when the real data bounces back.

Tapping into the signals bleeding from *Righteous Dawn* is easy. Doing it without alerting them to our presence…

Light flashes from one of the sundoors leading into the Acantha system. Then another. Nav brackets the new arrivals with white indicators for neutral intent.

"Unwelcome guests," Izzy murmurs.

"Think it's Julianna?"

"Not unless she rounded up more ISR assets in a very short time, and you heard how low-key she wanted to keep this operation. No, I'm afraid we've got competitors for the wreck.

Great. I pull up the coded channel for the skipjack and dash off a message to Tatsuo. *Incoming ships. Standby for details.*

"They got here a couple minutes ago," I tell Izzy. "We should know soon who they are."

I'm waiting for Nav to give me spurious IDs, for either cargo vessels or wayward private ships. But they don't tend to travel in groups, unless they're merchant convoys heading through dangerous territory. And this region? It's practically deserted. Not even pirates hang out here, because Acantha is on the way to, well, nowhere.

Nav automatically douses the two indicators in red and sounds an alert klaxon when the data streams in a few minutes later:

Tarasque-Class corvette, 150 meters.

Ghul-Class freighter, 250 meters.

My poor brain doesn't register those names with anything other than detached curiosity, until I pair them with the klaxon and the accompanying warning text.

"Martian Tiu." Izzy swipes across the display, enlarging the readout. Unfortunately, we're too far away for anything but the initial scans of the two ships' anti-matter drive signatures. As we watch, the drive flares dissipate.

"They've gone to their ion drives. Good chance they don't want to be seen, either." My guts twist around each other. These aren't greedy merchants. Or even scavenging pirates. These are warships of the fanatical human offshoot that's been in open conflict with the Realm for the past few centuries. Their attacks on Earth and other planets made it possible for the Kesek commissioner to orchestrate an overthrow of the king and Congress twelve years ago.

"You'd better call Tatsuo back." Izzy paces. "Blast it. Where's *Havoc*?"

"I don't think Julianna's firepower will make much difference if they get us on their sensors," I mutter. "Run a search in the database for *Ghul*-class. I've never heard of that one."

"I have. It's an armed freighter, with minimal crew and stores. Stripped down frame. It's meant for hauling large quantities, and that's about it."

"So, the corvette is an escort ship."

"Probably. I'm not anxious to ask them, are you?"

"No, definitely not." A fluctuation on the sensor reports catches my attention. "Weird."

"What's that? Nakano?"

"I don't think so. A beacon, more like—now it's gone." I play back the recording. "*Marconi* barely picked it out over all the background noise in the system. She's got more sensitive comms equipment than any other ship here, I'd put money on it."

"A beacon. Distress call?"

"It sure doesn't match the standard frequencies. And it's way too degraded. Might have been triggered by the Tiu arrival. Whatever it was, it came from nearby—maybe a couple of light-seconds." A thought flowers. I pull up the link to Tatsuo. "I'm sending the recording to the skipjack. Maybe he can pick up an echo between the debris."

"I'll take your word for it." She reaches under the main control panel. Something pops. A familiar but whiny little klaxon bleats. She gives me a look to say, without words, "Fix it, will you?"

I cancel the alarm. "Always nice to see you pack your fake transponders on every trip."

"Not just any trip, Vincent. Only the best for you."

I can't help a blush. "Who are we this time?"

"Nobody of consequence. Or a Martian Harmahkis mining scout, if you prefer."

"I'm impressed. Your fake transponders come with switching options now?"

Izzy smiles. "I tinker when I'm bored."

Me too. Copper's specialized tracking and vocal response tech are evidence of that. He's nowhere near as dumb as the average brassjacket. Which is why I'm not surprised when *Marconi*'s comms system alerts me to a recurrence of the strange beacon. I tap on my delver routes the results immediately to Tatsuo. There's a couple seconds' lag, and then a string of coordinates bounces back to me.

"He's got it." I slip into the seat and goose the ion drives. Just the barest acceleration, to alter our course and put us on an intercept with whatever's out there. We're moving at 500 kilometers per second, and I don't want to risk much faster than that, for fear of drawing attention from our new visitors.

Twenty minutes.

Twenty minutes that crawl by, as I stay glued to the command chair, tracking not just myriad possible courses for the Martian ships but the estimates on Nakano's search team. Nav's pretty sure he's withdrawn his barges—probably spotted the Martians, too. But he's not burning out of the system. The guy's as stubborn as I remember. Stubborn and stupid.

What's that make me? I suppress a smirk.

"Vincent." Izzy's eyes are wide. "I've got something. Big. The metal content is too refined to be an asteroid."

"You're sure?"

"Not yet. There's so much interference from the gravitational fluctuations…" She waves her hands at the monitor, as if she could clear away the solar system's incessant interference with her fingers. "Give me another half minute or so."

The comms console beeps. Text from Tatsuo scrolls in. *Locked on signal! You see it yet?*

There. The strange beacon, only much stronger, this close up. I slap the console—not out of frustration, though. Aced! I was right. "He's got it."

"The beacon? What is it?"

"A beacon, like we've been saying, but it's a ship-to-ship notice. A greeting between nav systems, announcing a safe path and docking procedures. Most of the data's corrupted, likely at the source, but that's fine, because Tatsuo can guide us in visually."

I tune the sensors in for a closer picture. We're just a handful of klicks out, so it's a simple matter to magnify the fuzzy gray blotch and run it through the comp for a resolution enhancement.

There she is.

The hull is beaten by innumerable impacts. There's tremendous gouges from for to aft, but the Raszewski sphere is intact. So are the drive nozzles. A yellow gleam races across the sphere, making frost streaks sparkle.

She's a ten-brace. Just as obsolete as the signal she'd been whispering for who knows how long.

Izzy puts her hand on my shoulder as the image expands to fill the breadth of the monitor, with our skipjack dangling in one corner as Tatsuo approaches the derelict. "That's her. Isn't it?"

"It is." The registry numbers confirm our discovery.

Coronado.

She's ours.

Chapter Eight

The airlock opens with a hiss as the last of its air bleeds out into *Coronado*'s abandoned corridors.

The three of us wear EV suits, because the ship's environmental controls are down. All we have is gravity. The light mounted on my suit's shoulder cuts a sharp arc through the darkness. There's no emergency illumination. No sign of life, except tattered bits of cloth and plastics strewn throughout the corridor.

"If this follows the standard layout of a ten-brace, the cargo hold should be fifty meters this way." I indicate the passageway to our left.

Izzy nods. She has her pistol at the ready. I should ask her if she's nervous about the possibility of ghosts, but given the smooth, purposeful gait with which she strides ahead of us, I doubt she's in the mood for teasing. This place is a tomb.

"What happened to the crew?" Tatsuo's voice is tinny in my suit comm. He wipes his palm through the air. It glows yellow, a built-in beacon that's not as strong as the one emanating from my shoulder but does boost the ambient lighting.

"Murder. Disease. Escape. Any of those could have emptied the ship." Izzy stops by an open hatch. She gestures for us to stop. "Anything?"

I aim the sensor rod on my left wrist toward the hatch. It feeds results back to a readout on my sleeve. "No power, no bio."

Izzy twists into the corner, gun first. Nothing leaps out and she doesn't shoot. She exits and continues down the corridor without a word spoken.

The lack of anything bothers me more than finding bodies or evidence of a fight. Stories of ghost starships circulate throughout the refuel depots and trading posts, but no one takes them seriously. Until official reports from Rescue Operations surface of an independent merchantman—usually with an Expatriate crew—stumbling onto a derelict in an odd location. Sometimes they're sent to sickbay for psych evaluations.

I'm not in a hurry to be one of them.

"Father wants the money," Tatsuo murmurs. "He's not interested in the ship itself—you know, historical value and all that. It's all about reestablishing the Restorationists. Restoring them, I guess. Which isn't good for anyone else, right? He's—"

"Tatsuo." I'm trying to keep the edge from my voice, because I'm as tense as he must be, and I'm not irritated with him. Not yet. "Focus."

"Okay. Sorry."

"Still no life-signs?"

"No. Nothing. Not even minor biologicals, like stowaway insects or other pests. There's barely any bacteriological readings."

I know already, because my sensors are feeding me the same results, but I've got to do something to keep Tatsuo occupied or his rambling is going to drive me nuts.

Izzy stops at another door. Here we go again. "Clear it."

A simple sweep with the sensor rod and… "Good."

She disappears inside. This time, the seconds flash by for what feels like an eternity.

"Izzy?" Tatsuo's question lingers in the comm channel. "Did you find something? Hey, Vincent, should we—"

"Quiet." I edge nearer to the hatch. Can't hear a thing. The deck vibrates through my boots, so that could be from her footsteps. My light strips the shadows away, but the rest of the cabin beyond the hatch is blacker than space itself. Izzy's life-sign is still the only one in there.

She materializes.

I yank the scrambler aside. Blazes. If I was the kind of guy who nursed an itchy trigger finger, I could have stunned her in the middle of this salvage operation. "I thought something happened to you."

Izzy hands over an oval of plastic and moves on down the corridor.

There's an image suspended inside—a dark-skinned man and woman, plus a handful of children, all teenaged. Their smiles gleam in my beacon's rays.

Where did they go?"

We plod along toward our destination, ignoring other signs of prior habitation. Maybe later I'll let myself wonder about the crew and their families. Sorrow and fear jostle for command, but I'm determined to get this done. Ray is still out there, as Nakano's prisoner. The sooner we find whatever *Coronado* was really hauling, the better for all involved.

I check my readouts again. The unit is also linked to *Marconi*'s sensors. I left my ship docked to *Coronado*, using its ion drives and thrusters to nudge the derelict free of most debris as we drift through the Acantha system. The Martian Tiu ships haven't made any sudden moves in our direction—their drive flares lit a few times, as they dove deeper in-system, getting closer to our position, but it seems they're conducting a search pattern of their own.

Nakano's ships are gone. Whether they're hiding from the Martians or off on another search vector, I can't tell not until we get back aboard *Marconi* and I can run more detailed scans. They're maintaining comms silence, though, which is bad for us, even if it keeps them safe from the Tiu's notice.

Tatsuo and I follow Izzy, shining our lights in passing open hatches and panels. He's gone mute. I hate to admit it, but this bothers me worse than his rambling. "Any ideas who broke your father out? Did he have a benefactor or two who supported your work on Sylvanak?"

"Father was always scouting for potential investors. He knew doing so quietly was the only way the colony could continue unnoticed. But I think the Charter Office hearing was too public. It would have scared off anyone with even an inkling of sympathy."

"You think it really was an accident that let him and the others escape?"

Tatsuo makes a face. "What? Oh, no, not at all. They had to have help. I'm sure of it. That was part of why I went to Puerto Hueco, to figure out who was crazy enough to support him. He wouldn't say anything, though. Which doesn't surprise me. He would barely speak in my presence, let alone give up major secrets. I don't suppose you have any theories."

"Someone who wanted this." I pan the light across broken conduits dangling from the ceiling like snapped branches. "Someone who wanted to find *Coronado*, too, and was willing to partner with your father."

"Use him, you mean."

"It's a lot easier to hire someone expendable than get your own hands dirty," I say. "The ex-governor knew that all too well, didn't he?"

Tatsuo shrugs, but that's all I can get from him for the time being.

"You two." Izzy's voice is shockingly loud, given how little she's said since we boarded. "Up here."

We face a hatch that fills the entire end of the corridor. It's locked.

"You have tools for refit and repair, don't you?" She runs her hand across the surface, searching, I assume, for a weakness.

"Some, yes, but if this hatch is armored, I'm not sure I can cut through it." I call up schematics from my readout. A gold hologram of a ten-brace springs into the air, filling a meter along the corridor. I have to swivel and step away from the others to give it room to expand. A green wave washes over it, removing some sections and adding others, in addition to denoting where the worst damage is. It takes a few seconds for the sensor rod, coupled with *Marconi*'s scanners, to update *Coronado* from old specs to existing condition. "Maybe there's another way in. Something we missed on our first review?"

"This is the only access hatch to the cargo bay from the interior." Izzy waves at the bulkhead. "So, if you think we should backtrack and go for a stroll along the hull..."

"No." Tatsuo's helmet shudders. "I'm *not* doing that."

"Take it easy. No one's walking outside. Not when we're this close." I check the access panel. It's shot, and I mean that literally. Someone's blasted it full of holes, with a large caliber weapon. I can see the ricochet marks around the edges. Talk about desperation. "There's always the possibility the panel's intact on the other side. What about ventilation?"

Izzy reaches into the hologram. She highlights two lines in red. "Good thinking. I see at least one duct that leads in there. It's a couple meters wide, too, which is perfect."

Now Tatsuo's staring at the ceiling. "You want us to climb down it?"

"Through it. It's not that small." Izzy pats my arm, making the whole holo vibrate. "Vincent can lead way. He has the most experience navigating tight repair spaces."

"You're not wrong." I douse the hologram and search for the nearest access panel that will get us into the duct. There we go. It's already loose. "Tatsuo? Lend me some muscle."

"Yes, sir." He mutters something in Japanese I'm pretty sure is an insult to not only my heritage but my hygiene. Whatever works for him.

The panel's stuck tighter than I first thought. I hand Izzy the plasma torch hanging from my belt. "The beam won't make it through the hatch, but it should cut through this junk fast enough. You'll have to steady your arm, though. The gyro's out and I haven't gotten it replaced."

"I promise I won't cut any of my appendages off, or yours." She winks. The torch pulses to life with a brilliant pink flare. Izzy slices expertly through the warped metal holding the panel in place.

Tatsuo grits his teeth and pulls. The panel snaps free. The sudden weight slams into my side. I shove it aside.

A hideous, grinning face with gaping sockets instead of eyes lunges for my throat.

"*Zhēn tǎo yàn!*" I shove the scrambler into its chest and light up the corridor with blue-white blasts.

Izzy cries out. She sweeps the torch at the interloper. There's a spark of flame and a spray of smoke.

A head rolls down the hallway.

"What is it? What is it?" Tatsuo flails at the access panel. I'm incredibly relieved we didn't give *him* a weapon.

"A prior occupant." It takes me a couple gasps to catch my breath. Probably won't be until the middle of next week before my heart returns to its normal rate. "Long since dead."

Izzy kneels beside the body, and I'm finally calm enough to get a better look. Male, I think, wearing a gray jumpsuit with green panels along the inside of the legs and under the armpits. The corpse itself was desiccated. Mummified, I guess. "I don't see any signs of violence."

"It could have been illness."

"A plague?"

"I don't know. Nothing shows up on the scans."

Tatsuo coughs, like he's got a tickle in his throat he can't get rid of. "Then it's a good thing life support's down, because I'm *not* taking off this helmet."

I step over the body. It seems cold, but my mind's not here. It's out beyond our ships, among the debris rings. All the variables spin at once. Time for the Martians to burn from the sundoors to this location. Time for Nakano and his crew to complete their scans and stumble onto *Coronado*. Time for *Havoc* to catch up with us. It's a mad jumble, hindered by the fact that I'm trying really hard to not panic. The only way out? Prayer. And action. "We're not going to recover the cargo by sitting around playing a guessing game, right?"

With that, I pull myself up into the top of the open compartment.

I unlatch a second panel and squirm into the duct. The scans were right—plenty of room to maneuver. I scuttle forward on elbows and knees. "Piece of cake, Vincent. Just like crawling inside a docked comms ferry to replace a transmitter. One way in, one way out."

Keep talking to myself like that and I might as well be back aboard *Marconi*. Alone.

I could have brought Copper, or even the other bots, but with all of us gone I needed every "hand," so to speak, back home. They can interface with the ship's controls enough to start the engines, send a distress call, and break away if need be. They're our getaway pilots.

Which is why I'm scooting through this dark duct that just dropped a dead body in my face.

Poor guy. I hoped his death was quick. It hurt to think of someone suffering alone, in the depth of space, on a dying starship. Of course, he'd likely been dead for decades before I was born, but in that moment, when I saw his withered body at Izzy's feet, he was just another guy.

It could have been me.

It still *can* be me.

Desperation makes me move faster. The desire to return to Tiaozhan and never again set foot aboard a starship overwhelms my senses. Izzy says something in the comms; Tatsuo's light glows past my shoulders. I can see a grate up ahead.

Move. Get it out of the way.

I put my helmet and the ceramic armor on my shoulder into the effort. Push it free. There's no latches on the inside. Plastic creaks on the other side.

Snap.

Well, blast.

I push too hard. Momentum carries me into a huge, dark expanse. The fall could very well kill me, which is exactly what I figure is going to happen until I land on my back on pile of what feels like loose gravel that somewhat cushions the impact. Loose gravel, covered with a thin membrane, like an emergency seal or something as simple as a tarp. I say somewhat because even though I haven't broken my back, there's gonna be a swath of bruises up and down my spine. My head spins, which leads to terrible pain, because I don't think I've fully recovered from the blow to my skull a few days ago.

"Vincent!" Izzy's voice crackles in my helmet. "Are you hurt?"

"Mildly." I groan. "Not dead, though, so I'm celebrating."

"You could have waited for an assist. This wasn't a race." There's a sharpness to her tone. A moment later, she lands on her feet in a graceful crouch, boots making a muffled crunch in the membrane. She kneels, her hands searching my suit. "Show me the readouts."

"See? Elevated heartrate. Extensive bruising."

"Minor concussion. Still." She sighs.

"Aren't you glad it wasn't worse?"

She presses her helmet to mine. "Always."

Tatsuo cries out. He flops onto the pile, rolls off the side, and lands on his rear end on the deck.

"The gang's all here." I wince as Izzy helps me up. The best part? I don't pass out. "If this is in fact the cargo bay, I'll be even happier."

She doesn't answer with a quip. Neither does Tatsuo. Seems unfair. No one else has much of a sense of humor, and maybe it's the battering my head took, but I'm fairly humorous, if I must say so myself.

"Vincent." Izzy's staring at her feet. "You've landed on it."

The gravel? Of course not. I don't know why I thought it was gravel. No starship would tract shift with such a worthless cargo when it could just as easily be mined by ore haulers in-system.

Our lights reveal the shine.

It's jewels. Rubies and sapphires and emeralds, the more prosaic among them. Those would fetch a high enough price. But starvapor? Tiu zikol? *Sio* from Ieri? They're about the only gemstones worth hoarding.

Coins are in the mix. My gloved fingers tremble as they brush atop the thin membrane. I was right—it is an emergency seal, the kind applied to a breach when there's no extra plating available to seal a gap. But I don't care much about that.

I'm starting at the pitted, gleaming gold doubloon that has to be a thousand years old.

Izzy sweeps a searchlight across the bay. Row after row of crates form long avenues. Some of the containers aren't the standard shipping variety at all, but simple frames with clear sides, reinforced for fragility during transport.

"I'm… I'm gonna see if I can find the power panel." Tatsuo backs toward a wall, his thumb over his shoulder. "We can use the backup powerplants we brought…"

I nod, slowly.

My shoulder beacon sets the contents of a clear-sided container alight with glittering gold. It's a book. Maybe bound manuscript is a better word. It's been locked in a special bracket, propped it open to huge pages full of flowing script I can't read. Ancient lettering, surrounded by bold, colorful illustrations.

I swear I can smell the age.

The deck plates tremble. Lights blink on overhead, one after the other.

Izzy gasps into the suit comm.

There's hundreds of containers in the cargo bay. Ours is the one of a dozen sealed with membranes instead of lids. Each sports clear panels that give tantalizing views of rare manuscripts, sculptures, ancient pottery, framed artwork, and heaps of riches.

I can't fathom the wealth in here. No wonder Nakano wants it. No wonder the Tiu are hunting for it.

So why don't I feel any better that we found the motherlode first?

Chapter Nine

How in space are we going to get all of this out of here?

"I can restart the engines. I think." Tatsuo's bouncing on his heels so much he'd better take care before he creases his forehead on one of the support beams 40 meters overhead.

Izzy rolls her eyes. "That's not part of the plan. Not yet. Piloting *Coronado* out of here under her own power is a last resort. Besides, Vincent and I have far more experience with main drives. You're best put to use cataloging the inventory.

I'm staring at the manuscript when she uses the word. "Inventory." Hoard is more accurate. A hoard of treasure. *Actual* treasure. "Besides, if we light off the mains, the Tiu will come running. There'll be no hiding us, we know we can't outrun them."

"Okay." Tatsuo paces. He tugs at the membrane. It goes taut before springing back into place. "We'll need something to cut through this or break the lock. That plasma torch, maybe. But you're right. We do need an inventory, so we can call Father in and negotiate."

"For Ray's release." Funny how stumbling onto a compartment of unimaginable wealth can make a man forget about another man's life. "I bet we can use the same covert signal I bounced off the skipjack for our communications and send him a private message without tipping off the Tiu."

"Agreed." Izzy, too, seems like she's having trouble keeping her gaze off the treasure, though she keeps glancing down the aisles at the unopened containers. Probably daydreaming about what they hold and whether she can use the contents to secure her personal freedom if ISR backs out of their deal to let her work off her sentence. "But if Nakano has too many people, we're not going to be able to hold them off if the deal collapses."

"Right. Thirty Restorationists." I give Tatsuo a look. His nod is confirmation. "You and Julianna had a plan for dealing with this, I take it?"

Izzy unseals a pocket on her EV suit and removes a long, slender brick. It has a device attached to one side. Four rounded cylinders nestle at the opposite end. "TCE. Thermal concussion explosive."

Tatsuo and I stare at her for what seems like an hour before I finally blurt, "A bomb? You brought a bomb aboard?"

"How else are we to deny them the contents of this ship? If we can't reclaim it for the Realm—"

"Hang on. Reclaim? For all we know this is a vast box full of private property." I point at the manuscript. "That sure isn't property of His Royal Highness or the Congress of Worlds."

"It's free salvage. Since ISR found it, that confirms our ownership."

Tatsuo snorts. "If you're gonna split atoms like that, it's only one-third spy treasure. The other third is private citizen find—me—and the other is, I don't know, MarkTel, I guess. Unless Vincent's really working off the clock."

"It's a gray area," I mutter. "Seriously, Izzy. How were you and Julianna figuring on getting this stuff out?"

"Piloting the ship, as Tatsuo suggested, but that was before the Martians showed up." She waves her hand, as if she can pinpoint their location outside the hull. "I would slowly sneak the ship free of the debris cloud and Julianna would cover me, using *Havoc*, in case the

Restorationists or any other salvagers were on the prowl. If that wasn't an option, she was authorized to find alternative solutions."

"Like what, commandeering a cargo hauler from some unsuspecting Expatriate?" I ask.

Izzy smiles and tucks the TCE back into her pocket.

I shake my head. "I'm not a fan of either of those possibilities."

"As you said, the Martians—"

"This is stupid." Tatsuo kicks the container. The sides shiver, sending a tremor through the jewels. "We can't even get those doors open. So, we have to get the ship moving."

"No, no, the Tiu are still out there. We have to eliminate that threat, first."

I hold up my hands between them. "Or, we get as much of the treasure back to the airlock and aboard *Marconi*."

Izzy smirks. "Now you're thinking."

"That won't be enough to make Father happy," Tatsuo says. "He wants everything."

"I meant for us."

"What do you mean?" Light glints off the manuscript case.

"Come on, Vincent. Look at all this! There's so much, ISR or Nakano or even the Martians would hardly miss a crate or two—which would be more than enough to make each of us rich."

"But the mission—to keep it out of everyone else's hands—"

"Do you really think that's what ISR wants? What sob story did Julianna feed you? One about lack of resources?" She snorts. "Please. I've seen their forward operating base. There's eight more ships like *Havoc* and dozens of personnel. Trusting her isn't your brightest move. After all, she let you believe someone other than her own husband was captured."

I don't like where she's going with this. Not at all.

There's a great metallic rumble, one that shivers through my boots and suit. Tatsuo's opened the cargo bay hatch into the corridor. "I'm going back to *Marconi* for a plasma torch. You two want to keep arguing ethics? Fine. But I'm getting rich. *Then* we call Father."

He's gone into the shadows before I can think of an excuse to stop him.

Izzy rests a hand on my shoulder. "Go with him. Send that message to Nakano."

"You'd better be right about him being willing to negotiate." I tap a finger on the faceplate of her helmet. "Or Ray's a dead man."

She smiles. "Of course he'll negotiate, because you'll make it clear that if he doesn't turn Ray over, we'll blow every bit of the priceless goods aboard *Coronado* to useless slag."

It only takes a few minutes to upload the code, compose a brief message, and send it along to Nakano.

I have no idea if he'll get it, or if he'll respond. The idea of meeting him face to face again sickens me worse than thinking about his people getting ahold of the treasure.

Of course, I'm not comforted with the notion of ISR coming into a windfall, either. Izzy and Tatsuo are going through the treasure right now, no doubt picking out what they want for their own personal gain.

I sit in the greenhouse at the back of *Marconi*'s main corridor. I've got plums growing. Not quite ripe. But the scent of their leaves and burgeoning fruit, mingled with damp air from the hydroponics, are a welcome change from the stink of, well, me in my EV suit and the constant artificial stink that even my ship accumulates.

I haven't touched any of the treasure. But I want to. Lord knows, I could use extra funds stashed away. Don't get me wrong, MarkTel pays a good salary and affords me a higher than average health rank, which means medical care isn't a worry.

It's the rest of the family that's on my mind. Father and Mother are well-off, however, they'll both stop working at some point. Lily? She's great with machines; not so much with finances. Not that she's ever in trouble but she does have a tendency to overspend, especially when it comes to semi-legitimate upgrades to whatever hovercraft or ground-car project she has running.

Then there's Martin.

I sigh. My wayward young brother, only just recently delivered from a smuggling ring's grip. Avoiding major charges from the crown marshals was a minor miracle. Him staying out of danger longer than a few months? That will take serious divine intervention.

So, what, then? Am I expecting a sudden huge influx of money to solve all those problems? I guess. There's nothing wrong with wealth, not in and of itself. But look at what it's made people do.

Still… Why shouldn't I get my fair share? Haven't I given enough of myself to others? When could I go back to the way things were? The way things were before … what, exactly?

The thought clenches my heart. Before I cared so much about too many things and people.

I snip dead branches and wipe sweat from my brow. I've got the temperature turned up to something comfortable for the vegetation, which means I'm in a blue T-shirt and black MarkTel drawstring pants better suited for warmer climate. Take a few leaves off here, the wilted ones. Simple motions. They help clear my mind, which then reorients me to the important stuff.

Let me find the right path through this. I can see the wealth consuming others. I don't want that to happen to me.

Setting my mind on things that are above, not the things that are on earth—or in this case, on the *Coronado*.

Izzy knocks on the door frame. "Hey. I thought you might be in here."

"I needed a moment away."

"I understand that. Any word back from Nakano?"

My replacement wrist comm is silent. "Nothing. Give him time, though. He's probably wondering if we're bluffing."

"About the treasure or the explosive?"

"Both." I indicate a nearby stool with the trimmers.

Izzy sits, fingers interlaced as she leans forward. "What's bothering you?"

"This whole mess. The consequences of turning the hoard over to people who can't be trusted."

"Don't you trust me?"

"You haven't betrayed me yet, so, yes, for now."

She recoils, a temporary break in the pleasant façade. I cringe inwardly at the pain I glimpse. I touch her hands. "Sorry. I didn't mean that."

"I think you did." Oh. She hasn't reapplied the mask. But she doesn't break contact, either. "I suppose I can't blame you. But I'd hope that talking about your faith—my belief, too—would mend the damage."

I blow out a breath and set the trimmers aside. "I'd be lying if I didn't think there was a slim chance you were putting on another act."

"I'm not. I don't know how else to prove it to you, any more than I can make you prove your faith is real." She intertwines her fingers in mine and presses them to her chest, at the collarbone. Heat bleeds through her jumpsuit. And my internal temperature spikes to match. "Do you know the real reason I was so glad you were the one who burst through that door on Puerto Hueco? Because I just wanted to see you again, in person, and when I did, I was happier than I'd been since—since I was found, instead of being lost for so long."

My pulse pounds, and for once, it has nothing to do with my headache. "I'm trying to believe you. I really am. I need time to get used to it."

"Time isn't always a luxury we have." She releases my hand and turns away.

But I slide my hand to her back and draw her near. There's no need to announce my intentions, because she's already leaned into me, head pressing against my chin. I duck my face as she raises hers, for what's only our second true kiss.

I hope she really has found God. I pray for it, badly. Selfish? You bet. But if the Holy Spirit's move, not mine, so I can't dwell on—

Who am I kidding? That's not what I'm thinking.

I'm thinking about how I want to spend every minute of the minutes that follow with her, and her alone. And if she's willing to step away from the spy life, even better.

The question is, what would I be able to step away from for her?

That's how it works, after all. Two flesh become one.

An alert beeps through my wrist comm. It's followed by the ping I'd been awaiting, the one indicating Nakano's response.

Izzy breaks our kiss. Her cheeks are flush. "I … That's him, is it?"

"Yeah. It is." I check the message—and it's the other alert that stops my heart. "He's, ah, agreed to meet. He's on his way."

"That's good." Izzy frowns, having correctly read the consternation on my face. "What's the problem?"

"The problem is, I underestimated how impatient our pal the ex-governor is." I let her see the readout transferred to my wrist-comm from the nav computer. "*Righteous Dawn* is on its way, burning at full thrust to get to our coordinates, which means we'd better prepare for the Martians—because there's no way they can't see that flare."

Righteous Dawn docks on the opposite side of *Coronado*'s hull. I've got the airlock to *Marconi* sealed, with orders to only open for me or Izzy. Tatsuo and I find the controls for life support and tweak them enough to get fresh air circulating. It will last a couple days, running off the auxiliary batteries, until someone can restart the main reactor.

The ship smells faintly of rot and dust, but otherwise, is sterile. I wonder how long maintenance bots kept things tidy before they shut down. Plus side, the haz scans come back negative for contaminants, biological or otherwise.

We wait in the cargo bay, the three of us, for Nakano and his goons to arrive.

I glance at Tatsuo. "Where's your haul?"

"I didn't get the container open yet." He makes a face. "Blasted box sprayed foam into the torch's aperture. Probably better to wait until we let Father have a look."

"Probably." Disabling foam, triggered by an attempt to open the container? Not an easy withdrawal, then.

The Restorationists appear at the cargo bay hatch, prodding Ray Ward ahead of them.

Ray's face is a mass of bruises. One eye's welded shut by the swelling. His lips are chapped. The bottom one's bloodied. Speaking of blood, his gray shirt is stained with it, blotches smeared together.

Keegan's behind him, with a Tegest rifle aimed at his spine. "Keep walking."

"I'll maintain a shuffle." Ray nods at us. "Captain Chen. Ms. Neoh.

Nice work."

You'd think he'd be more agog at the three of us poised with endless crates packed with riches, but I'd be disappointed if Ray were anything but unflappable. "Sorry your wife couldn't be here."

He smirks, but then grimaces, because the gesture reopens a partially-healed scab on his lips. "I'm sure she's made arrangements. She'd never leave me to die."

Nakano steps from behind the other six people he's brought. Hmm. Eight total. How many more are back on *Righteous Dawn*? If it's thirty like Tatsuo thinks, there's still more than twenty people who could make our lives miserable.

"Vincent Chen." Nakano stops two steps from me. How he's managed to stay perfectly groomed while the authorities are hunting him is beyond me, but there's no denying the clean press to his outfit or the slickness to his hairstyle. Looks like he's lost weight, though. "I can't believe you found the bounty for us. I'm grateful you changed your mind."

"Changed my mind? No, I don't think so." I pat a stack of crates beside me. "This is for Ray. You take these back to your ship, and he stays here."

"That's a bad idea," Ray grumbles.

"You shut your hatch," I snap. "And in case you're planning to shoot us full of holes, Nakano, Izzy has that covered."

She waves a tiny device at him. "TCE detonator."

Keegan scowls. "That's legit, sir. I've seen them used, but never in civilian hands. They're supposed to be restricted for military activity."

"I suppose that makes me special," Izzy says.

Nakano folds his hands and takes in the voluminous cargo hold. He walks slowly around us, pointedly avoiding eye contact with Tatsuo. "I'll want to check the contents, of course. I'm not about to take this on trust, Vincent, given our history and your need to associate with people who openly oppose me and the truth of my crusade."

"Father, enough!" Tatsuo grabs his arm. "You're insane! Turn yourself in to the marshals and they might go easy on you. Blazes, do you think this is what Mother would have—?"

Nakano slaps him with a backhand so hard the *crack* echoes like a gunshot across the cargo bay. Keegan sweeps in, his rifle raised, ready to—I assume—blow Tatsuo's brains all over the containers.

Izzy swings her pistol to the center of Keegan's forehead. "Stand down, or I trigger the explosives." No bravado. No anger. Just a cold, hard promise.

I have my scrambler trained on the Restorationist bunch, ready to immobilize as many as I can, but the idea's hampered by the fact that they're all armed too. "Everybody stay calm. Nobody do anything stupid, okay? Because even though collapsing on the deck will hurt, Izzy shooting your guy in the face will hurt him a lot more."

"You are a traitor to your family and your people." Nakano sneers at his son who, as far as I knew, is his only surviving relative. "I should have known you would never see the error of your ways."

Tatsuo glares back, ignoring the deepening red mark on his cheek. "I did what was right. You'll know it, even if you don't understand now."

"It doesn't matter. We'll take what's ours and Captain Chen is welcome to you." Nakano examines the clear panel of a crate. His expression brightens, as if the blow he delivered to Tatsuo never happened. "This is… magnificent. A true treasure. Not of the heavenly kind, but it will do us a great deal of good in this mortal plane. I accede to your terms."

He doesn't sound any less crazy. If I could have locked him up again, I'd gladly do so, but with seconds ticking by, I'll settle for escorting him *quickly* back to his ship. "That's great. Now hand over Ray and get your stuff out of here before our visitors show up."

"Visitors? You mean the Martian Tiu ships."

"Yeah, and thanks for nothing, by the way. We did our best to keep our heads low, from an electronic standpoint, but you had to rush on over with your engines at full burn so they could see you from millions of klicks away."

"I wouldn't let it concern you."

"See?" Tatsuo points at Nakano. I hope he doesn't touch him again, because he'll get slapped once more and I don't know if Izzy can restrain herself from shooting Keegan if the guard-slash-mercenary takes action to protect his boss. "He's insane. Wiped his own hard drive."

"I've done no such thing. When the Martians arrive, you three—and Ray Ward, operative of the Intelligence Service of the Realm—will make valuable additions to the deal."

Izzy lowers her gun.

"You have to be kidding me," I mutter.

"How do you think the Restorationists went free?" Ray says. "The Tiu are funding his treasure hunt, and they've come to collect."

Chapter Ten

I haven't even processed the lunacy of Nakano's statement when Keegan shifts his stance and bashes Izzy's gun from her hand.

She's knocked against the crate. The impact sends the TCE remote clattering onto the deck. Give her credit, she lashes out at Keegan with a blow that was meant for his neck, but he twists so that her hand strikes his shoulder blade.

His boot crushes the detonator.

"There, now. Nothing more to worry about." Nakano nudges the bits. "Remove the explosives."

He's talking to Izzy. Keegan has the rifle's barrel aimed at her chest, and he's backed up far enough she can't reorient the weapon or try to take it. She seethes, shoulders rising and falling as a bruise blossoms across her wrist.

"Do it." Keegan's finger shifts to the trigger.

"Hey! Put it down." I aim the scrambler at him.

"Stun me and I'll still take her out." Keegan's gaze doesn't leave Izzy's face. "You're not dumb enough to try it."

I'm not, but I'm desperate for options. Something other than us losing our only leverage, especially with Martian Tiu on the way. But he's right. And I hate it.

"Lower it, Captain." That's Ray, who doesn't seem fazed by any of the proceedings. He could be watching a recap on Puerto Hueco's imports and exports for the month. "You'll get her killed."

I grimace, but catch Izzy nodding out of the corner of my eye. She retrieves the TCE. Blazes. Fine.

I set the scrambler on the deck. A Restorationist picks it up. Great. Now we're all unarmed, and our explosive is disabled.

"Good." Nakano brushes his hands across the clear side of the container. There's a golden chalice underneath. "Garris, return to the ship and get our cargo sleds. We'll begin loading as soon as the *Impeditus* arrives. The captain assures me a *Ghul*-class freighter can handle the volume of whatever we found. I'll be happy to see him proven correct. Then send our people to Engineering. See what can be done about restarting the reactor."

Garris, a tall, spindly man, trots into the corridor. Nakano replaces the chalice, then circles back to me. "Keegan, put our guests to one side. I don't want them interfering."

Keegan motions with his rifle. Izzy and Tatsuo gather Ray, each providing an arm for him to lean on, so he can limp to the bulkhead where the treasure pile accumulated. Meanwhile, Nakano cocks his head, examining me as if I'm another interesting piece of the bounty. "Once we return power to *Coronado*, and we've taken what's ours, you'll be allowed to leave—with Mr. Ward, of course."

"Of course." I scratch the back of my neck. "I guess I should thank you for keeping your end of the deal, but I'd prefer to see you imprisoned again."

"Vincent. I don't know why you're surprised. I don't have any desire to hurt anyone."

Ray coughs. "I take exception to that."

"Shut your face," Keegan snaps.

Nakano shakes his head and waves at Keegan as if he's dismissing a surly child. "There's no need for any of that. I've made my peace with the past. This wealth is our future—a future in which the Restorationists can rebuild the stability of the Realm. But I need your help to do it."

I chuckle. Yes, an actual laugh.

"Don't be so dismissive. We have the lists. You can help us trace comms codes with your MarkTel clearance so we can start finding the people who should pay—the Kesek officers and their informants."

That wipes the smile from my face. "Everyone's been pardoned. The officers, the clerks, the people who informed—stars, there wasn't a settlement where someone didn't turn a neighbor in to Kesek out of fear for their own lives." My brother included.

"Pardoned." Nakano spits the word. "The king abdicated his duty. We'll take it up and finish the job. Our friends the Tiu have promised us the resources to do so."

Tatsuo makes a choking sound. "They're giving you—weapons?"

"Weapons and technology." Nakano raps his knuckles on the crate. "What did you think this was all for?"

"You—you said you wanted a new home!"

"I do. And we'll have one. But I'm fiscally responsible. There will be plenty left with which to arm ourselves."

My God. He means to wipe them out—former Kesek officers and their families. "Holding one colony's worth on Sylvanak wasn't enough for you? Murder's the best thing?"

"It's a cleansing, Captain. One based on faith."

I grab his collar and yank him toward me, his shoes thumping against my boots. I hear Keegan coming, probably to bash my brains in with the rifle, and spot a flurry of motion from the Restorationists. If I'm dead, then let it be for the right reasons. "This has nothing to do with faith. We're commanded to love even our enemies, and I'm no expert on Scripture, but I know He didn't mean we should cut them down in cold blood."

Nakano lazily raises a hand. Keegan halts. I can hear his breath rasping. Nakano frowns at me. "I'm not satisfied with how God works," he whispers. "Not at the moment. If I'm mired in sin, let me take full advantage of that and commit myself before I repent. You can argue semantics, if you wish, but this is going to happen, and if I'm to be cast into hell for it, then so be it. It's worth the price to save the galaxy."

I release him, too taken aback to form a retort. Which is just as well, because Keegan plants the rifle's barrel into my gut. I double over, air expelling from my lungs, and land on my hands and knees. The rifle smashes into my back, putting me prone on the deck.

"Stop it!" Tatsuo and Ray try to hold Izzy back, which works for a moment, until their boots slide and squeak on the deck.

"No, I think Vincent needs this lesson." Nakano's shoes move around me. "He's been too long without discipline, correct, Mr. Keegan?"

Another blow. Pain lances clear through to my chest. "Just like old times," Keegan snarls.

But I've had enough.

I wait for the barrel to descend once more, and as soon as the blow fades, I roll into those shoes. Nakano flops onto his back, an outraged cry my reward. I straddle him, hands about his neck, and squeeze.

BOOM.

I can only pray that vac-head Keegan didn't puncture the hull with his shot. The magnetically-accelerated projectile blasts through several crates. My head rings like a struck bell.

"Next one splatters your brains, cross-hugger," Keegan snaps. "Get off him—"

I pull a gun from my pouch and jam the barrel to Nakano's head. "You back away. Do it now. Now!"

My last shout reverberates around the bay. Even Keegan looks startled. He doesn't drop his gun, but he doesn't shoot either.

And here I am, one hand clutching Nakano's neck, the other shoving Grandfather's Hunsaker Wasp into his skull. I kept it hidden this whole time. I didn't even tell Izzy. Trust, after all, is in short supply.

"You'd do it, then?" Nakano gasps. "Shoot an unarmed man, or strangle him? For which will you seek forgiveness when this is all over? A sin's a sin, Vincent."

My breathing is fast and light. I could do it. Shoot him. Maybe Izzy could move fast enough, and we could stop the rest of these lunatics, and get out of here before the Tiu arrive.

Then what?

There's still Starkweather ships in other nearby systems, looking for *Marconi* and us, because of the man Keegan killed on Puerto Hueco. Going on the run would only worsen the situation. And if we turn ourselves in...

The rage dissipates. I can't believe this is me. With Grandfather's gun. Father gave it to me, as a sign of trust, to defend our family and save my brother. Is this how I'm going to repay him? No matter how disgusting Nakano's become, there's still a right way to do this, and a law to which he's got to answer.

I'm not going to play games of chance with forgiveness.

My hand trembles. I switch on the safety and put the gun in its pouch. Then I lean back, allowing Nakano to stagger upright.

Keegan helps him, the rifle never leaving my sight. I can hear its charge humming down the black pit of the muzzle. "Back away, sir. I'll disarm him."

"Let him keep it." Nakano straightens his hair. "He won't use it. Not on me. His misguided faith made him weak—no conviction, only platitudes."

"You're wrong," I say. "Someone will stop you. Me, or the crown marshals, or ISR—it doesn't matter who. And even if it doesn't happen in this lifetime, God's judgment's waiting for you. There's still time to turn aside from this insanity."

"Said the fool to the visionary." Nakano shakes his head. "I pity you. All of you."

Footsteps. It's Garris, returning with three grav-sleds stacked atop each other. The Restorationists separate them and set out among the containers. Garris goes for the open one first.

"Clear some from the hatch, first," Nakano says. "We'll need room on that end for when *Impeditus* docks."

"Yes, sir." Garris waves for a couple others to follow him deeper into the stack of containers.

Keegan shoves me toward our cluster. I'm numb to further prodding, though the pain sure isn't going to fade from the blows he inflicted. "I don't care what the boss says," he growls. "Reach for that pistol again and I'll shoot *her* first, let her bleed out, and then you."

Izzy takes me into our group. "Are you okay?"

"No. Definitely not." I stare at her. "Did I do the right thing?"

"Yes. You did. You're not a killer." She touches my face. "I'm glad he didn't make you into one. We'll find a way out."

"Probably not," Ray says, "You should have shot him. Taken your chances. Sort things out with your limp deity later. That's something to think about when they jettison all of us out the nearest airlock."

"What?" Tatsuo backs away.

"You're as big a fool as he says you are if you think anything else." Ray's arm shakes. "And if you think we—"

A hum rises, filling the air. The *shush* of the ventilation system grows louder, steadier, and even the lights brighten. Access panels glow. A couple of old-style monitors blink to life, showing interior views of Engineering, the bridge, the docking bay's interior and the outside image of its main doors, even *Marconi* and *Righteous Dawn* docked to their respective airlocks.

Nakano's eyes flit from side to side. "What's going on?"

Garris trots to the nearest monitor. He taps in commands. The screen fills with graphs and charts, alongside a diagram of *Coronado*. The aft end of the ship glows with a green hue. "The main reactor's come online. Not at full capacity, but that's to be expected after being dormant for so long."

"Well done. I didn't expect our people to get it up and running so fast."

"Sir, there's no way they could have finished." Garris checks his delver. "I've got a message from Ryu—he says they're getting started on rerouting one of the connectors."

"So... the ship restarted itself?" Tatsuo makes a face. "How likely is that?"

"Not at all, unless it's got a timer running, which I've never heard of." I lean against the cold bulkhead. Doesn't alleviate all the stabbing pain in my side, but it helps. "More likely it was activated by something you did—maybe your guys messing around in Engineering. Do you even have anyone who knows a drive nozzle from a fuel line?"

"Call our people back." Nakano ignores my jibe and instead zeroes in on Garris. He grabs him by the arm and points toward the containers at the head of the cargo bay, near the main doors. "Those containers. Which ones did you move?"

I can see a few are dislodged. One's sitting cockeyed on a grav-sled. Garris nudges it with his boot. "Only managed to get the first one up, then the power back on—"

"That's because there's an open circuit from there into the ship's main computer." Tatsuo has commandeered the console Garris had consulted. "It's embedded in the power conduits running under the deck. Moving the crate activated a dormant subroutine."

"Yeah it did." I peer over his shoulder. "It's a command signal to bring the ship's primary systems on line, prioritizing the reactor and fuel management, though I can't tell why it's starting up like that. The amount of power it's putting out, you'd think someone on the bridge was preparing to get underway, but I don't see any evidence of the codes needed to fire up the main drives."

"The two of you had better figure it out then, if you'd like us to maintain our end of the arrangement," Nakano says. "Garris, continue the loading. Make sure—"

A klaxon, its tones grating and missing a few notes, blares throughout the cargo bay. Everyone has to hold their hands to their ears, as Tatsuo and I scour the screen for a way to kill it. I finally locate the right panel. The sudden silence is as bad as the abrupt noise before.

"That's a proximity alert." Izzy joins us. "Incoming ship."

I parse the data until I find what I need—a navigation feed. It's a basic map, grainy, of three-dimensional space with *Coronado* as a white circle at the center. A red blip is decelerating hard toward us. *Coronado*'s antiquated sensors don't know what to make of it, except to balk at its high rate of speed and accompanying rate of deceleration, something it wouldn't have encountered back in its day.

It has to be one of the Martian ships. My guess is the freighter, judging by the mass readings the computer spits at us.

"There, you see?" Nakano nods. "Our sponsors would never turn their backs on us. They recognize—"

A flash of light blinds the external camera that shows *Righteous*

Dawn. The ship lists away from *Coronado*'s hull, spewing white feathers of atmosphere. Fragments of the airlock tube splinter and disintegrate. The force of the decompression rattles the hull, right down to the deck plates. Far above us and out of our sight, an emergency bulkhead sweeps into place.

"What…? No." Nakano's face drains of color. "Our ship."

One of the male Restorationists cries out. A woman falls to her knees, tears streaming down her face, as another man grasps her hand. But their horror doesn't stop the attack. More flashes lance across the screen, even as Ryu and the others return from Engineering. *Coronado*'s sensor readouts inform us that multiple strikes from a laser turret are tearing into *Righteous Dawn*'s hull, while a second ship approaches *Coronado*'s bow. The blasts slice off plating, until there's whole decks open to space. The repeated explosive decompressions propel the freighter farther away, subjecting it to increased collisions from fragments of ice and rock. Eventually it starts a tumble deeper into the debris clouds, plowing through with seeming reckless abandon.

The view from the main hatch, also external, reveals a long, boxy starship painted a deep, brick red with tan and gray armored plating as it slides slowly into position. A flexible cofferdam extends over the hatch. *Coronado*'s hull rings with the impact of its anchors.

I can't look away from *Righteous Dawn*, drifting from us without power or hope, flickers of light dying deep in the yawning gaps opened to the vacuum. Broken metal, plastic, and bodies mingle with the asteroids, becoming part of Acantha's sprawling clouds.

"They're—they're gone." You know it's a terrible circumstance when I feel sorry for Keegan. My insides ache at the sheer innocence on his face as he fails to comprehend what the Tiu have done to his comrades—his friends, most likely. The hurt matches the pain from the injuries he inflicted on me.

"Why?" Nakano steadies himself against a crate. "Why would they do this to us?"

Ray takes a step. He collapses, but Izzy's the one who holds him upright. "Because you're of no use to them," he wheezes. "Once the Tiu have no use for an object, they discard it. Especially if that object is an

Earth-type human. If you don't thrive in one-third standard gravity and yearn for an independent Mars, you're of no value."

A clang echoes through the main hatch leading into the cargo bay. Green lights ring the frame. White letters read ATMOSPHERE STABILIZED. AIRLOCK SEAL HOLDING.

A harsh, guttural set of commands filters faintly through.

"This is what you get for making your deal with the devil." Ray shakes his head. "He comes to get what's his, regardless of how much you think it should cost."

Izzy eases up behind the Restorationists who are nearest, the ones in tears and shock over the sudden and horrific loss of their ship. She glances at me. Pats her suit's pouch.

Grandfather's gun is in the same pouch on my suit.

My scrambler's on the deck, discarded by the Restorationists. I nudge Tatsuo, who's closer than I am. His eyes widen.

A new alarm sounds. The hatch splits open. Air hisses as the two volumes pressurize.

Another sharp, mechanical command snaps through.

Nakano holds up his hands. "Greetings! I am Governor Raymond Nakano, the keeper of the Restoration. I have what was promised—the riches of the lost freighter *Coronado*. You'll find more than enough to take as our payment for the arms you promised. In response, you will provide all—"

There's a *BLAM* and the whip-crack of a mag-accelerated projectile. A red burst flowers on Nakano's crisp tan shirt, as if he's gained a boutonniere, but it's a fatal wound despite my mind trying to erase the sickening sight.

"Father!" Tatsuo lunges but Ray trips him, bringing them both to the deck.

Which is a saving grace for both when Martian Tiu warriors barge through the yawning hatch and open fire into our midst.

Chapter Eleven

There are just six Martian Tiu soldiers. But there might as well be a hundred, as ferocious as they are.

Gangly. That's my first impression. And sickly skin. I wonder if I should subject them to a med-scanner. They're variations of gray, with the palest eyes I've ever seen. Stylized tattoos in crimson and violet slash their cheeks.

My brain tells me they look strange because they're humans who have spent generations in gravity that's one-third as strong as Earth's and that of most of the Realm's worlds. If not for armored exoskeletons—thick frames of artificial muscles and whirring supports partially covered by armor plating that's the color of rusty soil—they'd be incapacitated by the gravity inside *Coronado*'s cargo bay.

All that fades out when I have to duck for cover.

"Vincent!" Izzy holds out her hand.

I toss Grandfather's pistol to her. She snaps off a handful of shots before diving behind a container.

Keegan, for all his faults, protects his people. He barks orders at the

Restorationists, urging them to shelter even as they defend themselves. The woman who was crying falls, shot through the chest. So does the man with her. But the rest duck behind crates.

A few score hits on the Tiu, but their armor plating makes it difficult to stop them. I scoop up my scrambler and let fly a few bursts. One of the Tiu snaps something harsh as sparks skittered up his left arm and throughout his chest. He topples into a container, part of his exoskeleton inoperable.

One of his comrades spots me, crouched with Ray and Tatsuo. His rifle pivots our way.

A single gunshot hits him dead center in the forehead, slamming him onto the deck.

"*Gelditu filmatzea*!" This comes from the soldier with the most tattoos on his face, the swirls of red streaked with gold that encircle his eyes and forehead, making his gaze eerily phantomlike. "All shooting—stop."

The voice chews on Mixed words like it has little practice. But the gunfire cuts off like someone's flipped a switch.

Keegan thrusts his hand into the air. "Cease fire!"

No one else shoots from the Restorationist side.

Izzy crouch walks to our position. She helps me drag Ray behind a container. His face is covered in a cold sweat and he's grinding his teeth. "Hang on. We'll get you out of this."

"Unless you plan to snag one of those grav-sleds from behind enemy lines, I'm not about to skip down the corridor to your ship," he grumbles.

Our ship. I spare a glance at the screens. Yes, *Marconi*'s still docked there. The Tiu didn't carve her off the side of *Coronado*'s hull.

"Relinquish all weapons," the Tiu commander says, "And no more harm will happen."

"Tell you what!" Keegan snaps. "Do the same and we won't shoot you through your Martie faces!"

I wince. Probably not the best idea from negotiation standpoints.

"You killed our leader!" Emotion cracks Keegan's voice. "He had what you wanted."

Cooling metal on the recently fired weapons *clicks* for a few seconds, as the commander withholds an answer. "Stand down and disarm. We are taking all. No more have to die."

Another Tiu soldier has taken care to drag their slain comrade back through the hatch. Two more warriors take their place, returning their force to six strong. Eight so far, and who knows how many more aboard the *Ghul*-class freighter.

"That corvette is still out there," Izzy whispers. "It must have hung back toward the sundoors, waiting."

"For our backup to arrive?"

"Ours or theirs."

Ray grimaces as Tatsuo helps him sit up. "Julianna will be here. Trust me."

Working on that. It occurs to me that if I sit here, letting Keegan do all the talking, we're all going to die anyway.

Tatsuo's on his knees, sobbing. Tears leak from between his fingers.

I can't help staring at Nakano's body. Unseeing eyes gaze at the ceiling. His mouth is part open, slack—surprised, maybe.

"I'm sorry he's lost to you." Izzy holds Tatsuo's shoulders.

Tatsuo sniffs. He rubs furiously with his sleeves. His eyes are red-rimmed. "He did it to himself. The course he took—it ruined him. I'm only glad Mother's long since gone. She would have been sick."

Nakano didn't have to die. No one did. Maybe I could put my skills at communications to use in an entirely different way. I raise my hands and, praying feverishly that this isn't the stupidest thing I've ever done—which is saying a lot at this point in my life—I stand from concealment.

Every Martian weapon swings in my direction.

"Vincent!" Izzy grabs my belt.

"Hey!" I wave my hands. "I'm unarmed. I want to speak with your commander."

I wonder what it'll feel like when six rifles shoot me simultaneously. But the commander rises, his weapon's aim shifting to the floor. He's taking an awful risk walking toward me, because I can see Keegan ready to open fire.

At least, until Izzy whistles. Keegan peeks sidelong. She has Grandfather's pistol pointed at him. He lowers his rifle, perhaps remembering how Izzy shot the Tiu soldier off me a moment ago.

The commander considers my uniform, ghostly eyes searching every square centimeter. "MarkTel."

"Yes. Most of the time." My palms sweat. I've never stood face to face with a Martian before. Never seen one in real life, outside of news footage on the Reach. If Kesek were the boogeymen of my childhood, Martian Tiu were catastrophic weather events—something that would show up once in a while, wreak havoc indiscriminately, then fade from memory until the next terrible incident. After the couple years' campaign against them following the coup of 2602, they'd been reduced to sporadic raiding.

And, apparently, that extended to financing treasure hunts. The commander leans his rifle against his shoulder. "What is your legend?"

"Legend? I'm here because I promised to rescue a friend and save another man's life." I indicate Izzy and Ray. "This ship isn't my goal."

"You stake no claim to the treasure?"

"Well..." The gilded manuscript draws my attention. How beautiful would that be sitting in the Bethel museum? How happy would my fellow believers be when they see it? They'd be so grateful that another Christian saved a remnant of their past. I'd be a hero of a different sort. Worthy of even greater fame. A name to be remembered, forever.

What? Where in blazes did that come from? I shake my head. "No. I stake no claim."

The commander looks at my trio of companions, then targets Keegan and the Restorationists with his stare. "You are not their allies."

"Not even close."

"But you are Terrans."

"Sort of. But we're not on the same side." Sorry, Nakano, even though you're not here to hear this. "They're criminals. I only want them brought to justice."

He nods. Then he touches my chest with his rifle. "*Utzi hau.*" He waves a hand toward Izzy, Tatsuo, and Ray. "*Utzi hiru horiek. Gainerakoa hiltzea.*"

With that, the Tiu soldiers take aim once again at the Restorationists.

"No, wait!" I stalk away from the commander, into the midst of the raised weapons. What am I, spaced? "Nobody else has to die on either side. Just take what you want from the treasure and leave."

"Not gonna happen!" Keegan's hands twitch on his weapon.

Izzy takes a step closer. "Do it and you'll never pull the trigger."

The commander shakes his head. "Mad. All of you. We are taking the cargo. Any interferers will be shot."

There's nothing to do but hang back as four more soldiers exit the docked ship and wrestle with the abandoned Restorationist grav-sled. Two men heave another crate off the floor, next to where the second one had triggered the engine restart.

Lights dim and change color. The cargo bay's bathed in red. A new klaxon sounds.

"*Zer gutatu zen*?" The commander spins around. "What did you do?"

"Nothing! The ship… it must have an anti-tamper mechanism." I point at the monitor. "Let me check."

He nods.

Tatsuo and I peruse the screen. The reactor levels are skyrocketing. It's pumping out so much power I expect the main drives to roar to life any second, but the second indicator freezes my blood. No fuel for the engines. No coolant for the reactor. *Coronado*'s run completely dry. What's the reactor powering, then?

"It's self-destruct." Ray watches over our shoulders. "The ship's rigged to blow."

Tatsuo yelps. "We're—we're all still docked to it!"

"Shut it down." I swipe through menus, searching indexes for a way to tell the ship's computer to cancel the command. No luck.

"I can't find an access point."

"We can re-task the code."

"No way. See?" Tatsuo taps the screen. "Locked out. If we could get to the bridge, maybe, or Engineering—"

A tremendous impact shakes *Coronado* so hard we're all thrown to the deck, Realm citizens and Martian Tiu alike. I'm at a loss, assuming we're all about to be blown to atoms, when a message grates from the commander's communications device. I can't make out what he said, but the look of shock on the commander's face translates across any language. "Fall back! Fall back!"

They swarm through the cargo hatch. It rumbles closed, sealing us into the bay once more.

Tatsuo slaps the screen. "Those look like mag-clamps. Please tell me I'm wrong."

I can't make sense of what he's seeing, but it looks to me like a pair of spikes buried deep in *Marconi*'s ventral hull. The same spikes must have shot from the opposite side of *Coronado,* aiming for where *Righteous Dawn* was, but now trail long, thick cables into space.

"They snared the Marties, too," Ray says.

He's right. I can see the spikes jabbing deep into *Impeditus.* No wonder the Tiu fled back to their ship. A quartet of spacesuited crew, assisted by skittering bots with eight legs, attack the cables, plasma torches blazing against the darkness. One of those spikes is embedded deep in the aft hull, where a huge spray of water is crystalizing as it hits vacuum—their fuel supply. I tap my wrist-comm, panic-stricken about the state of affairs aboard *Marconi.* [Status.]

The response from Blue is swift and perfunctory. [Hull breach repairs underway. Life support stable. Main drives primed and ready.]

Good work, crew.

"One thing's for certain," I say. "We need to move now if we're going to survive. Keegan? I'm not going to make you do anything but if you don't want to die when this thing goes nova, you'd better follow me. Tatsuo? Help me with Ray."

We loop our arms under his and hustle him into the corridor, not waiting for the Restorationists to debate their options.

"Wait!" Izzy is by the crate safeguarding the heaps of coins and jewels. "Shouldn't we…?"

I pause long enough to answer, "Trust me."

She doesn't hesitate.

Keegan is apparently a practical guy, because by the time we hit *Marconi*'s airlock, I have the five surviving Restorationists with me.

Five. Out of thirty. "I'm sorry for your losses, Keegan."

He blinks, as if I've awoken him too soon. "There were six aboard, plus us. Fourteen, before the shooting started. The rest—everyone else is under arrest. I could, maybe, get to see them again."

"Only if we don't get vaporized," Tatsuo snaps.

Have to separate those two. "Take Ray to the infirmary and get the med-scanner going. Izzy? Bridge."

We're finally alone for a second, which is great, because I don't want anyone else to see me shaking. I punch in calculations. None are reassuring.

Izzy pulls up a vid that shows the bots out on *Marconi*'s hull, slicing away at the cables with their torches. "How long until they cut us free?"

"Twenty minutes."

"And we have—"

"Sixteen before the reactor goes critical."

She expels a shaky breath. "All right. Burn the drives. It will traumatize the hull, but we should be able to accelerate—"

"Izzy." I pull up a diagram. The red lines have stabbed almost through the other side of our hull and have bent. "They're in deep. It's only the bots' quick repairs that prevented us from venting all our atmosphere."

A proximity alert beeps. The Martian ship has broken free, but it's trailing debris and air. Pulsing blue ion drives flicker as it shoves itself away from *Coronado*.

I feed more data into Nav. No happy results. "They won't make it, either."

"You have to have technical wizardry that can help us out."

I shake my head. Of course, I have two programs perfect for such an emergency, and they're both digging away at *Coronado*'s mainframe, but the time estimates on cracking through the treasure ship's protective software aren't in our favor. Not enough solutions, and not enough time.

"You're not inspiring hope, Vincent." Izzy touches my shoulder. "I'm not ready for this to be the end."

"I know. I've got an idea."

A new sound—incoming transmission, from near the sundoors to the Acantha System. The sensors deliver the welcome sight of *Havoc*, along with another ship. A bigger one.

I let the message play out, delayed as it is by several minutes. "*RMS Marconi*, this is *Havoc*. Please advise of your situation. I have *HMS Daring* standing by with the Tiu warship under her guns. They're playing it cool, for now, after receiving a transmission from their other vessel near your position." Julianna's voice, a welcome sound after wondering where in the galaxy she's been, breaks, and for a moment, I wonder if the signal's lost. "The intercepted message spoke of casualties. Please advise—if *Coronado*'s reactor really is building to critical levels, there's nothing we can do from here."

She's trying anyway, because *Havoc* is racing at an eye-watering 51 gravities. How a ship that small can maintain that acceleration, I can't figure, but I have to send a reply. "*Havoc*, this is *Marconi*. We're impaled on a self-defense system. The Tiu ship has broken away, but none of us will be out of blast range when the reactor breaches. Tatsuo's tried cracking into the control system but it's more hard-wired than programmed. I've got an option." Sorry, MarkTel Region Six. "I'm directing *Marconi* to run its mains at full thrust and push *Coronado* as far away from us as it can get before the reactor blows. There's enough of a chance for the debris to shield us from the shockwave that we have a shot at survival. All of us—Izzy, Tatsuo, Ray, and five surviving Restorationists—have to leave aboard the skipjack. Do what you can but know that I wasn't willing to let anyone else die, not even the Martians. *Marconi* out."

Izzy's staring at me as I send the message and turn away from the console. "You're sure about this."

"No."

She sighs and kisses me on the forehead. "Yes, you are. Let's get everyone moving."

It's a blur of stunned expressions and milling bodies as she herds everyone below to the hangar bay. I hunch over the console, inputting directions to Nav, sentencing the comp to death. I rig up one final transmission to *Havoc*, hoping that she's got deep enough memory banks to absorb everything important left aboard my ship. The course is set. *Marconi* groans as thrusters reorient her and *Coronado* along a vector that will arc them both away from the slowly fleeing Martian ship.

I tuck my Bible into my pocket and pause at the bridge hatch. How many days have I spent working in here? How many nights were spent alone in my cabin? How many years of my life did I devote to making this Declaration-class comms ferry tender something other than a metal can churned out of the Muhteremi shipyards?

This is home.

I pat the frame. Tears burn my eyes. "Sorry I have to go," I murmur. "But it'll be worth it."

Then I'm squeezing past shoulders, slipping into the pilot's seat of the skipjack. Izzy's my co-pilot. Tatsuo, seated behind me, straps Ray into the fourth chair. The Restorationists are crammed in the back, braced against the bulkheads, crouched under the sloping ceiling.

It doesn't help that all two dozen of my robot crew are packed into every available nook. Copper alights on the corner of the viewport by my left arm.

There's a *clang* from the back. A green light blinks on my console. "Hatch secure!" Keegan announces.

"Hold on!" I crank the emergency launch release.

The mag-clamps holding the skipjack reverse polarity well beyond their rated speed. The force makes the compensator hiccup, as acceleration presses me into my seat. The darkness around my vision tells me I'm about to black out.

Just wait. A few seconds…

We're clear of the ships. I fire up the ion drives, then slap the controls for two chemical rockets the skipjack sports for moments—well, like this.

The skipjack boosts away from the ships, as *Marconi*'s main drives light up in a shining corona on the nav display. She can't accelerate much beyond the upper 20s, but I instructed Nav to run at the highest possible rating, 32 gravities. *Marconi* can only manage that for an hour or so.

We don't have nearly that long.

The skipjack races off, my course bending us around huge chunks of ice and rock, toward the Martian freighter. It's taking impacts as it goes, though the stream of air trailing it has subsided to the barest trickle. I wonder what the Tiu captain makes of this situation. If there was time, I'd explain.

All I can do is pray.

Minutes fall away far too quickly. The skipjack vibrates under the strain of the acceleration. Sixty seconds remain. Forty. Twenty.

I made the calculations. Nav confirmed them.

What if I'm wrong?

What if I doomed us to a slow, agonizing death instead of a quick, painless one?

God in heaven, hold us.

Izzy grasps my hand. I squeeze back.

No more words.

One second.

Breach.

The explosion overwhelms the sensors with a flare of radiation, the shockwave so intense it obscures even *Marconi*'s drive flare. The chaos envelops kilometer after kilometer of the debris field, expanding out in a rushing, rippling wave that's even more terrifying because it's soundless.

Then it catches up.

My hovercraft in a windstorm never tossed like this. I fight with the controls, teeth grinding, arms shaking, as we're spun around an around. People cry, scream, pray. Alarms tell me the fuselage is developing microfractures. Those will get bigger if this keeps up.

If I die, I'll be okay. Really. But I can't let these people down…

Tremors slacken. The gravitational tempest settles. I can steer without effort.

It's passed us. We're alive.

"You did it!" Tatsuo slaps my shoulder. His hand's so clammy it about soaks through my jumpsuit.

I cut the rockets, which are more than three-quarters spent, and shut off the ions. A few bursts from the thrusters spins us so we're hurtling "backwards." There's a glittering cloud of the tiniest fragments—embers, really—where *Coronado* was.

Marconi's been reduced to seven tumbling, scorched fragments that are a quarter the size of my ship. My home.

"Yeah." My throat's raw with emotion. "We did it."

Chapter Twelve

We saved nothing from the *Coronado* except our lives.

I really don't want to face Julianna, since all I'd managed to do seemed like a failure compared to the magnitude of how big the haul aboard the lost freighter was. But it's got to happen.

We've all got to face the consequences for our actions.

Daring takes us into the yawning mouth of its hangar bay, which means I get to let the autopilot system park the skipjack—its fuselage pitted and streaked—next to a double stack of gigs and barges whose pale gray bodies gleam in the brilliant white lights.

After long, sullen hours packed aboard a small craft with five more breathing people than it was meant to carry, the hangar's air is sweeter smelling than the gardens at the Chen family compound on Tiaozhan. Which, of course, makes me think of my orchard aboard *Marconi.*

Perfect. Add that to my list of mistakes.

The hatch opens. Starkweather marines are there, body-armored and ready to take the Restorationists into custody.

"Take them to the brig." Commander Gultasli seems taller even than he was on the monitor. No less in charge. "Keep them in separate cells. We'll let the crown marshals sort this lot out when we return to Puerto Hueco."

"Captain?" Tatsuo squeezes past the marines and plants himself next to Keegan. "I'd like to put in a word on behalf of these people. They're—I guess they're all I have left, in a weird way. They were my people for a long time, but someone has to speak for them since Father—" His voice breaks. His mouth forms words but they're gone before he can say more.

Gultasli grants the Restorationists a look I can only classify as the ultimate disdain, but nods. "Go ahead. Accompany them and say whatever you need to when the duty officer takes their statements. Corporal?"

"Roger that, sir." The soldiers whisk Keegan and the others away, Tatsuo trotting behind.

Which leaves me and Izzy to help Ray out of the skipjack's hatch. A pair of white-jacketed medics are already incoming, with a stretcher that drips with sensors and med-kits.

Julianna leads them.

"Look." I scratch the back of my neck. "Sorry about the *Coronado*. I know you had destroying it as a backup plan but I—"

She sweeps past me as if I'm a phantom. Ray embraces her. I can't overhear their exchange, but his voice is choked with emotion. Julianna kisses him, making for an overly awkward moment. Well. Ahem. Izzy holds my hand and winks.

At least I can talk to Commander Gultasli.

"You'll be happy to know we recovered your comms ferries, the ones you dropped in your clever ruse that, I'm sorry to say, fooled one of the best tactical officers in the Starkweather Navy." He doesn't sound amused, but there's a tilt to the corners of his lips.

"I appreciate that. They're expensive pieces of hardware."

"So's a *Declaration*-Class tender."

I wince. "Yeah. That's not going to be a pleasant commnote."

"I took the liberty of contacting MarkTel in your absence. Operative Verge-Ward was successful at allaying their, ah, disappointment at the loss of *RMS Marconi*. I do understand you're to make for Tiaozhan at best speed for a discussion of said disappointment with Director Margate."

"Wonderful." I glance at Izzy. "I don't suppose ISR is hiring."

"Don't worry about any of that." Julianna's extricated herself from Ray's grip and finally allows the medics to treat his injuries. "I've already put the weight of ISR's authority behind your actions. The pursuit of *Coronado*'s wealth caused too much headache—and near disaster. It's for the best no one wound up with it."

It's reassuring to hear, but I can't help seeing an afterimage of the breathtaking illuminated manuscript. I feel nauseated at the thought of it lost forever, vaporized when the reactor went critical.

"You saved everyone aboard the ship," Julianna says.

"Not everyone."

"The ones who died did so because of their choices," Izzy says. "They let greed turn them onto the wrong course, and that killed them."

"It almost turned us the wrong way, too."

"That may be, but you're all here now, and you saved Ray from death—or interrogation by the Martians." Julianna shakes my hand. "For that, I'll be forever in your debt."

Ray brushes a med-scanner out of his face and props himself up on an elbow. "I'm pretty happy about it, too."

"Sir." One of the medics glares at all of us. "We need to get you to sickbay. Your internal injuries—"

"Really, really hurt." Ray sags onto the gurney. "Carry on, MacDuff."

Before he's left the hangar bay, Julianna slides through a string of text on her micro-delver. "You'll have an official after-action report ready well before we arrive to Tiaozhan, and yes, *Havoc* will transport you there."

I smile, grateful for the promise. "Any chance of finding me a replacement starship?"

She chuckles. "Not quite, I'm afraid. And you know they won't let you keep what you have left."

I assumed as much. Everything that's MarkTel property is, well, theirs. That includes the skipjack. And the bots. They'll wipe their programming and reset them to defaults. It'll be like the past five plus years never happened.

I glance through the hatch. They're all in standby mode, loyal to the end.

Which will leave me very much on my own. More than I've ever been.

I don't think I can do that.

"If you don't mind pushing against our deadline, I want to get to Tiaozhan a day or so before the meeting," I tell Julianna.

"Of course."

"Vincent." Izzy digs into her pocket. "Here."

It's a plum pit, sticky from the fruit's flesh. She presses its textured surface against my palm. "So you can restart," she says.

"We can restart." I close my hand around it and enfold hers. "If you're ready."

She kisses me.

Now it's Julianna's turn to feel awkward.

A week later, I'm back home. As in, home world.

The skipjack settles onto the plains outside the Chen compound. Permacrete and sandstone walls keep a lush garden and the pearly white walls of guest houses separated from the hilly grasslands over which stunted aspens are scattered. The familiar red outlines and flarebranch vines accenting not only the guest quarters but the two-story main house in the center force a smile from me.

Last time I was here, I couldn't make myself go through the front door until Father showed up.

"Are you ready?" Izzy's already at the hatch, a carryall case slung over her shoulder.

"Absolutely."

We set out across the burnt soil of the landing zone, boots crunching. A breeze from the distant coast sends a ripple through the flowery skirt she's wearing. My pale green jacket and the casual clothes beneath are as far from the black MarkTel jumpsuit as I can get.

Three days. That's when I've got my appointment with Director Margate. The stakes are higher than the last one. Before, I was causing minor headaches for my employers. This time, I've lost them a ship.

Copper flits over my shoulder. I smile, even though I know the bot can't read my expression. No matter what happens in three days, I won't lose him or Blue or Scarlet, because they're bought and paid for. No longer MarkTel property.

So, I could save some of my crew, for what it's worth. But whether or not anyone's going to call me Captain Vincent Chen any time soon, well, that's up to the company.

The gate opens. It's Father, Mother, Martin, and Lily.

Izzy blows out a breath. She edges nearer. The tension radiating from her is way worse than anything she let show when we were being shot at by Martian Tiu. "You'll be fine," I say.

"Says the man who's never brought a woman home to meet his parents," she murmurs. "I don't suppose you have your scrambler on you?"

I chuckle. "No, I—"

My wrist comm chirps. Incoming note. "Hang on."

"Take it. I'll go be charming. Nothing like getting past fear by jumping into the action headfirst." She shifts her carryall and strides toward my family.

I should hurry to make the introduction, but the message is from Julianna. [This was transmitted to *Havoc* not long after the Acantha incident, coded to you—or 'the MarkTel human.' I'll let you ponder it and remind you that you've proven your value to the Realm. I'd be happy to engage your services in the future, should the need arise.]

Ominous as that sounds, I tap the attached file. Audio transmission.

"Vincent Chen of MarkTel. I am Bikendigizon, optio of the 95th Cohort, Barritus Legion. You acquitted yourself honorably in our encounter. There was no need to rescue your enemies from death. That is why I could not rid your actions from my dreams. Had you not destroyed your own vessel and the ship of treasures, all of my comrades and I would have perished. The terror we faced was that our *Bahram lil hinn Bahram,* the Mars Beyond Mars which each of us carries, would be lost. Such a thing curses a slain Tiu soul, to be separated from the planetary soil in those emblems. You, Vincent Chen, of a people scorned by your own Realm, have earned the respect of mine. I shall tell your story to those who will listen and make it my quest to understand the why of your deeds. Our courses will cross again. I swear it by *Bahram*."

The audio cuts out, and I'm left staring at the blank screen.

First reaction? A prayer: *What in the galaxy am I going to do now?*

No response. Not yet, anyway.

I'm standing by, though.

Listening.

Visit

www.steverzasa.com

for more adventures in

The Face of the Deep universe

www.ingramcontent.com/pod-product-compliance
Lightning Source LLC
Chambersburg PA
CBHW030420310726
48979CB00009B/1541/J

* 9 7 8 1 7 3 3 5 8 5 1 9 4 *